App developer Mabel Skinner is about to discover something rotten on her late aunt's garlic farm—and it's not the compost heap . . .

Mabel doesn't know a stinkin' thing about garlic farming. She knows how to develop an app and how to code. But when her aunt, Peggy Skinner, dies suddenly, Mabel inherits her Stinkin' Stuff Farm in western Massachusetts. She arrives during peak harvest time—with three days to bring in the entire crop before rain can destroy it.

But Mabel has an even bigger problem: she suspects her aunt's "accidental death" was murder. As she digs for both garlic and clues, Mabel must contend with a mysterious crop thief, a rival garlic grower her aunt was suing, and a farmer who was after Aunt Peggy's green-thumb secret. It's up to Mabel to crack the code on a killer, before she joins the garlic bulbs six cloves under . . .

Also by Gin Jones

Helen Binney Mysteries
A Dose of Death
A Denial of Death
A Draw of Death
"A (Gingerbread) Diorama of Death" (short story in *Cozy Christmas Shorts*)
A Dawn of Death
A Darling of Death
A Display of Death

Danger Cove Quilting Mysteries
Four Patch of Trouble
Tree of Life and Death
Robbing Peter to Kill Paul
Deadly Thanksgiving Sampler
"Not-So-Bright Hopes" (short story in *Pushing Up Daisies*)

Danger Cove Farmers' Market Mysteries
"A Killing in the Market" (short story in *Killer Beach Reads*)
A Death in the Flower Garden
A Slaying in the Orchard
A Secret in the Pumpkin Patch
Two Sleuths Are Better Than One

Six Cloves Under

A Garlic Farm Mystery

Gin Jones

LYRICAL UNDERGROUND
Kensington Publishing Corp.
www.kensingtonbooks.com

To the extent that the image or images on the cover of this book depict a person or persons, such person or persons are merely models, and are not intended to portray any character or characters featured in the book.

This book is a work of fiction. Names, characters, places, and incidents either are products of the author's imagination or are used fictitiously. Any resemblance to actual events or locales or persons living or dead is entirely coincidental.

LYRICAL UNDERGROUND BOOKS are published by
Kensington Publishing Corp.
119 West 40th Street
New York, NY 10018

All Kensington titles, imprints, and distributed lines are available at special quantity discounts for bulk purchases for sales promotion, premiums, fund-raising, educational, or institutional use.

Special book excerpts or customized printings can also be created to fit specific needs. For details, write or phone the office of the Kensington Sales Manager: Kensington Publishing Corp., 119 West 40th Street, New York, NY 10018. Attn. Sales Department. Phone: 1-800-221-2647.

First Electronic Edition: April 2020
ISBN-13: 978-1-5161-0958-6 (ebook)
ISBN-10: 1-5161-0958-9 (ebook)

First Print Edition: April 2020
ISBN-13: 978-1-5161-0961-6
ISBN-10: 1-5161-0961-9

Printed in the United States of America

CHAPTER ONE

Mabel Skinner got out of her Mini Cooper at ten o'clock on a Sunday night, and peered through the pitch dark at the vague outlines of a two-story house and the gravel path that led to the front porch. Her GPS claimed she was at her aunt's farm, but the last time she'd visited, the sign next to the driveway's entrance had read "Stinking Rose Farm," not "Stinkin' Stuff Farm." The name was close, and it had been more than a decade since she'd been here, so she'd probably just remembered it wrong.

She took a moment to stretch after being cramped in the little car for so many hours. The small size was fine for the usual local errands she used it for back home, but not as great for a six-hour drive. It had left her feeling as creaky as the nights when she'd gotten caught up in some coding challenge and had stayed hunched over her laptop for too many hours without a break.

The moon was waning, and what little light it might have offered was obscured by clouds. She ducked back inside her car to turn on the headlights again to light her way to the front porch. She was used to the dark, living as she did in the wilds of Maine, and usually she found it comforting, like a barrier against unwanted visitors. But tonight it added to her uncertainty about whether she was where she belonged.

The building in front of her was white, like her memory of her aunt's place, with the wraparound porch and assorted gables that declared it to be a farmhouse, rather than some more specific architectural style. The house looked larger than she remembered it though. She distinctly recalled thinking it was too small for her and her aunt to share, even for a week's visit, and yet now she could see it was large enough for a family of four. Wasn't it more typical, when returning to a place after many years, to think that it looked smaller? Maybe her recollection was skewed by the fact that no home was large enough for her to share with another human being these days. Her three bedroom house in Maine felt like a perfect fit for her to occupy alone, and she seldom thought about how she'd once shared it with her grandparents.

Mabel also remembered her aunt's home as being square and symmetrical, but now there was an addition of some sort sticking out from the left rear corner. Either by design, in keeping with the history of old farmhouses getting additions as the family expanded, or possibly by indifference or lack of funds, the addition hadn't been particularly well integrated into the overall architecture. Its awkwardness was definitely something she would have remembered, so either her aunt had added it since the last time Mabel visited, or she was in the wrong place.

There was one way to know for sure: look for the key under the doormat, where Aunt Peggy's lawyer had arranged for it to be left for Mabel's arrival.

As she headed up the gravel path, a rustling sound came from her right, near where the barn was. She started, but then realized the noise had most likely been made by one of the barn cats. Aunt Peggy had always kept at least a dozen of them to deal with rodents and other critters that might threaten the crop.

Mabel jogged up the front steps and knelt to feel under the doormat. As promised, a door key was hidden beneath it. Of course, that didn't prove much. It wasn't exactly an inventive place to leave a spare key.

The Mini Cooper's headlights were at just the wrong angle to illuminate the front door, so Mabel had to feel for the deadbolt the estate's lawyer had arranged to be installed. She ran her hand over the wood panels, and bumped up against something affixed to the center of the door. It was metal and raised, but in the completely wrong place to be a lock. She felt along the edges of the metal, tracing an oval with a flattened base, which sparked a memory. It was the shape of a pineapple, she thought as she tested her theory by running her fingers over the center of the oval, finding the crosshatching she was expecting.

Mabel didn't have to see it to recognize the foot tall brass pineapple door knocker. She was definitely in the right place. Aunt Peggy had adopted the pineapple as her talisman when she'd made the life changes that had brought her here. If she could have grown pineapples in New England, this would have been an orchard instead of a garlic farm, but Aunt Peggy hadn't been willing to relocate to the tropics for her midlife crisis. In any event, it had never really been a matter of wanting to eat pineapples so much as believing in what they symbolized: hospitality. Almost to the exact same degree that Mabel preferred solitude, her aunt had craved companionship. The lack of frequent client interactions was about the only thing Aunt Peggy had missed from her career as an accountant.

Now that Mabel was confident she was in the right place, and wasn't about to break into a stranger's home, she quickly found the deadlock and opened the front door. Without conscious thought, she bent down to find the pineapple shaped doorstop right where it had always been, and used it to prop the door open. Her muscle memory was stronger than her conscious memory, so she let it guide her to the light switch. She flipped each of the three switches in turn, with no success.

The front porch lights had probably burned out after Aunt Peggy died, and no one had been here to replace them. Aunt Peggy had always left the porch lights on, so visitors would feel welcome. There were probably some spare bulbs around somewhere, although Mabel didn't particularly care if the exterior was lit. She didn't have her aunt's desire to encourage visitors, and she seldom went out after dark, since that was when she settled down to do her job, hunched over her laptop.

If she changed her mind and wanted exterior lights, she could always have the bulbs overnighted from an online merchant. For now, she just needed to get her laptop and duffel bag out of the car so she could get settled in. She could do that without porch lights.

Mabel pocketed the front door key and turned to go back to the car. She took the first step down from the porch and felt something move beneath her foot. She flailed and grabbed the railing, catching herself as a large and loudly irritated tuxedo cat raced across the corridor of light in front of the car, in the direction of the barn.

She kept her grip on the railing for a moment, waiting for her pulse to return to normal. She could have been killed, tripping over that animal. Cats were an important part of farm life, but shouldn't Aunt Peggy have found a way to keep them away from the house where they were a hazard to her beloved visitors?

Mabel continued down the steps, keeping one hand on the railing, prepared for another surprise underfoot. Aunt Peggy could have been hurt or even killed by the cats, just as easily as an unwary guest could have been. Mabel hadn't thought to ask how her aunt had died. The lawyer had said she'd been found on the farm, but he hadn't said anything about the cause of death. It was probably something too routine to mention, like dying in her sleep from an undiagnosed health problem. That was far more likely than a freak accident caused by a barn cat. Still, the cats needed to be rounded up, and a new home found for them before Mabel went back to

Maine. She already knew her attorney's opinion on pets—that they were a lawsuit waiting to happen—and she really didn't need to give anyone more excuses to try to get money from her.

Even moving cautiously in case the tuxedo cat returned, it only took Mabel fifteen minutes to carry everything she'd brought with her into the dark front hallway, just beyond the front door. She'd decided to travel light, taking only her laptop, dual widescreen monitors, printer, assorted cables and connectors, some spare hard drives, an extra mouse, and two speakers. Almost as an afterthought, she'd filled a duffel bag with a week's worth of underwear, a few pairs of jeans and a stack of t-shirts.

Mabel didn't trust her memory of the floor plan for navigating the farmhouse, so she used her phone as a flashlight while she hunted for more substantial lights. After trying the switches inside the doorways on either side of the hall, and the knobs on two table lamps in what she thought was the living room, all to no avail, she had to conclude that the problem wasn't limited to a few burned-out bulbs. The electricity was out, and she had no idea where the power came into the house or whether someone might have intentionally turned the electricity off when Aunt Peggy died. Or possibly even before then. Aunt Peggy had chosen a simpler life than the one she'd known in Boston, but had she continued simplifying since Mabel had last been here? Could she have gone so far as to give up electricity?

What about phones? Mabel's cell service had grown sketchy as she'd approached West Slocum. She turned her smartphone so she could see the screen, and found that she had no service at all here on the farm.

The last time she'd been here, there had been at least one landline operational, and she had to hope it was still working, so all she had to do was to get the electricity turned back on again. Mabel headed toward the kitchen, where she could picture a clunky old avocado green phone attached to the wall near the harvest gold refrigerator.

Mabel shone her light around the room. The phone was right where she remembered it being, on the wall to her right, just inside the kitchen. It was a relic of the 1960s that had barely been functional twelve years ago when she was last here. It couldn't possibly be the same phone, though. It had to be one of those nostalgia pieces, or even a real vintage phone retrofitted for pushbutton dialing, although she couldn't imagine anyone finding it attractive enough to want to replace it with an exact match.

She lifted the receiver and shone her smartphone's light on a dial that had definitely not been updated. She put the receiver to her ear. No dial tone. She tried clicking the plunger in case the circuit was stuck, but still no dial tone. That wasn't encouraging. Landlines were supposed to work, even when the electricity was out.

Mabel hung up the dead phone. Her aunt had probably replaced the landline with a cell phone, and just hadn't bothered to get rid of the phone. But if Aunt Peggy didn't have a landline, where did she get her internet service from? Mabel had planned to crack her aunt's internet account while she was here, and had been resigned to using dial-up service for the duration, figuring her Luddite aunt wouldn't have a faster service. Aunt Peggy didn't have a website for the farm, but surely she used email and other basic internet offerings for her business.

Mabel left the kitchen for the front parlor that Aunt Peggy had converted into a home office for the farm. From what little was visible in the light of her smartphone, nothing in the room had been upgraded since her last visit, including the twelve-year-old dinosaur of a desktop computer. The only difference was that the last time Mabel was here, the computer had been brand new, and now the beige plastic had a yellowish cast to it, beneath a solid half inch of dust.

The keyboard was missing, and where it should have been was a thick, leather bound journal. It was scarred and stained from daily use, but without any noticeable dust.

The light of the smartphone flickered, and Mabel checked her battery. It was running low, and there was no way to charge it. There was nothing she could do about the electricity or access to the internet tonight. It was only midnight, which left plenty of time to unpack and do a couple of hours' work on her laptop before bedtime. She could find a public internet connection tomorrow to send the work to her boss.

Expending the last of her phone charge to light the way, Mabel carried the absolute necessities—her laptop and the duffel bag—upstairs. She wasn't ready to face her aunt's empty bedroom, so she chose the door on the right, which opened into the bedroom where she'd stayed during her last visit. It was too dark, even with the smartphone's fading light, to see if the decor had been changed up here. The furniture was just as she remembered it, though, nothing more than a twin bed with the head against the wall just inside the door, a small dresser across from the foot of the bed, and a rocking chair in the corner next to the window. She tossed the duffel bag onto the rocking chair, and settled onto the bed with her laptop.

The alarm app on her laptop reminded her to get up and stretch after an hour, and as she did, she acknowledged the peace and quiet of the farm. She might not have any electricity, other than what was left of her laptop's battery, and she might have to wait until tomorrow to send the finished beta version of her current assignment to her boss, but those were minor nuisances that would soon be taken care of. The only noise she'd heard all evening had been the muffled sounds of barn cats squabbling. They wouldn't be a problem. She could work all night without any distractions and sleep until noon. After two more of the hourly reminders to stretch, Mabel decided to make an early night of it around three a.m. By going to bed early, she could be awake and on her way into town bright and early tomorrow, sometime around noon.

CHAPTER TWO

Mabel woke up to screeching sounds. It took a moment to realize she was hearing birds. Stupid, noisy birds. Even worse, she was fairly sure, from the gray light coming through the thin white curtains, that she was hearing the proverbial early birds. She checked her cell phone for the time, only to find that the battery was completely dead. She flipped open her laptop, still on the bed next to her pillow, and peered blearily at the corner where the time was posted. The first digit was a seven, and that was all she needed to know. It was still the middle of the night, when everyone, including noisy early birds, should still be sleeping. Quietly.

Where had the stupid birds come from, anyway? With all the cats roaming the farm, the bird infestation should have been taken care of.

She closed her laptop and pulled a pillow over her head to deaden the noise. Earplugs would have to top the list of things she needed to purchase later today, at a more civilized hour, when human beings were awake and stores were open. Of course, with her phone dead, she had no access to her to-do list app, so she was probably going to forget half of what she needed, and without internet access, she couldn't simply order things online as she remembered them.

Mabel concentrated on her mental list: light bulbs, earplugs, groceries, room darkening shades. She repeated the items to herself for several minutes until she thought she'd remember them, and was about to relax and go back to sleep when a pickup truck's engine joined the cacophony outside her window. The engine stopped, and voices took its place. They weren't as easy to ignore, but perhaps if she just pretended they didn't exist, they'd go away.

And then she heard a door open on the first floor, followed by the hushed sounds of someone moving stealthily around the kitchen. Cabinets were opened, hinges squeaked, and doors thudded shut, each sound followed by a prolonged pause. It brought back memories of Mabel's last visit here. Every morning, Aunt Peggy had done her best to cook breakfast without waking Mabel. Aunt Peggy had tried to be quiet, but it was impossible to cook anything without some little sounds escaping. Each little clink or thunk had been followed by a moment of frozen silence while Aunt Peggy waited to see if the latest noise had woken her niece. Mabel had always pretended to sleep through the noise, partly out of affection for her aunt, who was doing her best to cope with a lifestyle she just didn't understand any more than Mabel understood her aunt's, and partly because her aunt would have dragged her out into the piercing, early morning sunshine if she'd known Mabel was awake.

If only it were Aunt Peggy moving around the kitchen, Mabel would have been more than happy to forgive her for the early awakening. Unfortunately, it couldn't possibly be Aunt Peggy downstairs. She was dead.

Mabel sat up. What if someone had made a mistake, and Aunt Peggy had simply been gone for a couple weeks, and it was someone else's body that had been found? Mabel hadn't seen the body or even the death certificate for herself, after all.

She didn't take the time to change out of the t-shirt she'd slept in, but just pulled on a pair of jeans and bolted for the stairs. At the top, her sleep-deprived brain caught up with her, and she stumbled to a halt. Much as she'd like to believe the person in the kitchen was her aunt, it was more likely that the noises had been caused by a burglar, looking through the cabinets for valuables, rather than for cooking implements. It was a fairly common practice among thieves to target the homes of people whose obituaries had run in the local paper, especially if there weren't any local relatives listed as surviving them.

Mabel hesitated. Her best escape plan was to run straight down the stairs and out the front door, but then what? She still didn't have phone service to call for help. Could she get her car keys from the bedroom without alerting the burglar to her presence, and then get to her car before the burglar caught her? What if she was wrong, and there was another, less criminal explanation? For all she knew, Aunt Peggy had a housekeeper who came in once a week, and today was her scheduled day to stop by.

Mabel crouched against the wall, where she could see through the railing without being too visible herself. The sound of her heartbeat drowned out any noises the person in the kitchen might have been making, and anger started to replace the fear. She doubted her aunt had a housekeeper, which meant that some stupid criminal had decided to profit from a tragedy, and he didn't even have the human decency to commit his felony quietly. She might not have been so angry if he'd broken in at a more traditional hour, like midnight, when she'd have been awake enough to deal with him rationally, but no, he'd had to wake her up in the middle of prime sleeping time.

Mabel straightened, determined not to be chased from yet another home. Her aunt had never feared intruders, so it wasn't likely she kept any weapons handy. Farm implements, like hoes and pitchforks were excellent weapons, but taking the time to go to the barn and then returning to clobber the intruder with them would look a bit too much like premeditation, rather than self-defense.

Mabel crept back to the guest bedroom to search for some sort of weapon. In the light of day, she could tell that, like the kitchen, the bedroom's decor hadn't been changed since her last visit, except perhaps to fade a bit. The walls were papered in a pale blue floral print, with a scrappy blue and white quilt on the bed and with ruffled, pure white curtains on the one window. The top of the dresser held only a woven basket filled with soap and shampoo. Underneath her duffel bag on the rocking chair was a stack of white towels. Nothing that might be used as a weapon, unless she wanted to attack the burglar with one of the ruffle edged throw pillows she'd brushed off the bed and onto the floor last night.

Then she remembered the stack of electronics she'd brought inside. Most of it was downstairs, in the front hall, out of her immediate reach, but she'd stuffed a bag of spare cables into her duffel bag last night before carrying it upstairs. A cable wasn't as good as a pitchfork, but at least it wasn't soft and ruffled.

Mabel quickly retrieved a spare cable, removing the twist tie that kept it coiled, and wrapped one end of the cable around her hand to make it easier to grip. With a little luck, the burglar would be gone before she had to try to use it, anyway. She vaguely recalled a long ago lecture about scaring burglars away simply by letting them know the building was occupied. Apparently professional thieves knew that they were more likely to get a harsh sentence in court if they robbed an occupied home instead of a vacant one. All she needed to do was to make a lot of noise, and the burglar would leave on his own, without her having to cable-whip him.

Which was kind of too bad, she thought. Whipping him would work off a lot of her irritation at being awakened so early. Being in a state of sleep inertia might even qualify as a legal defense to assault charges.

Mabel stomped her way out of the bedroom and down the stairs. She felt a moment of triumph when she realized that she was making more noise than the stupid birds had earlier this morning. Maybe they'd hear her and think twice about waking her up the next time.

Mabel rounded the corner at the base of the stairs, her cable-whip trailing behind her, prepared to see the back door slamming shut behind the scared off burglar. Instead, a thin young woman covered almost head to toe in Aunt Peggy's frilly avocado-green apron was coming out of the kitchen and down the hallway toward her, arms spread in preparation for a hug.

Mabel didn't do hugs. She never had, that she could recall. Not with the grandparents who had raised her and definitely not with strangers. Most people knew better than to try, so she hadn't been prepared to ward off the impending assault. She froze for a moment, forgetting until too late that she had a cable for self-defense.

"You must be Peggy's niece." The woman wrapped her thin but surprisingly strong arms around Mabel. "I'm so glad you finally made it here. Peggy was always talking about you."

"I hope not." Mabel had been the subject of all sorts of gossip after her parents died, and it had made her extremely wary about sharing personal information with strangers, whether directly or indirectly. She finally managed to free herself and take a wary step back from her attacker.

"I'm Emily Colter." She waved in the direction of the barn. "I live over there."

"In the barn?"

"No, in the farm next door. On the other side of the trees."

Mabel liked trees. They kept people away from her. "Why are you on this side of the trees?"

"I was driving by and saw your car out front," she said. "You must have gotten in late last night."

"Not particularly."

Emily tugged Mabel in the direction of the kitchen. "Still, it was after I got home, and all the stores in town were closed by then. I thought you might be hungry, so I brought you some fresh eggs for breakfast, along with a few other basic supplies."

"There's no power for cooking. It was out when I got here."

"I already took care of that. These old circuits tend to overload pretty easily," Emily said as she deposited Mabel at the huge kitchen table that dominated half of the kitchen area. "Peggy kept meaning to update the circuit board, but there was always something more important. I'll show you where it is, in case the power goes out again."

Mabel had expected to know her way around the house, but the kitchen was a weird mix of familiar and new. The cooking half of the kitchen was the same as it had been before, from the wallpaper featuring little pineapples in a grid pattern, to the vintage phone and stove. The other half, where she stood beside the table, was new, with walls painted a lighter shade of the avocado green of the phone. The kitchen must have been expanded to include this huge dining area, big enough to feed more dinner guests than even her aunt could have expected on a regular basis. The expansion explained the change in the exterior of the house that Mabel had noticed last night.

Mabel coiled the cable and stuck it into her pocket where it would be easily accessible in case she needed to fend off another hug. Then she chose a chair where she could keep an eye on the exits and the woman returning to the avocado green stove. "Did Aunt Peggy's lawyer give you a key? I know I turned the deadbolt on the front door."

"Peggy would be turning over in her grave—if she had a grave, that is—knowing her front door was locked." Emily turned the stove on under a large cast iron pan. "At least no one touched the back door. The doorknob's been broken for years, probably since before your aunt moved here, but the door opens if you thump it in just the right spot. I thought everyone knew that, but I suppose it wasn't the sort of thing you'd discuss with your lawyer."

"Why not?"

Emily waved a spatula. "Oh, you know. Time is money, stick to the facts, no need for embellishment, that sort of thing."

"Seems like a strange way of working with an advisor. Withholding information, I mean."

"I'm sure Peggy told her lawyer everything he needed to know." Emily removed a dishcloth from the top of a handled basket sitting next to the stove. "How do you like your eggs?"

"Chocolate."

"Peggy always said you had an unusual sense of humor." Emily cracked an egg and held it above the skillet. "Fried or scrambled?"

"It's too early to eat. My stomach is still asleep."

"Early?" Emily released the egg into the crackling pan, and then dropped two more beside it in rapid succession. She looked at the wall at the other end of the room, past the huge table. "It's almost eight thirty."

Mabel groaned and laid her head on the table, cushioned from the solid wood planks by her forearms. "I can't do this. It's just too early."

"You'll feel better after breakfast." Emily slid a plate onto the table, next to Mabel's crossed arms. "I brought some bread for toast, and some of my goat cheese. Peggy's favorite variety. She might have mentioned me or my farm, Capricornucopia?"

"It's been a while since we talked," Mabel said, without lifting her head. If she'd had more than about three hours of unbroken sleep, she might have been tempted by the food. As it was, she just wanted to go back to bed. "If I eat, will you leave me alone?"

"If that's what you want," Emily said. "Otherwise, I thought you might want to see where Peggy died. I was the one who found her, you know."

"I didn't know." Mabel finally raised her head.

Emily had her back turned, so Mabel couldn't see her expression. Not that Mabel was much good at reading expressions, but there were some signs even she couldn't miss, and she'd taught herself to notice them. Was this Emily person crying? How close had she and Aunt Peggy been?

The guilt she'd felt when she'd first learned of Aunt Peggy's death threatened to settle permanently into Mabel's shoulders, tensing the muscles there. She'd tried to keep in touch with her aunt over the years. Mabel had set up a calendar app to remind her to send an email on major holidays and her birthday. The messages had definitely been sent and even received by her aunt's server, but there had never been a response. She'd always assumed her aunt wasn't big on correspondence, and didn't have the technical skills to set up an automated response. Now, she wished she'd made more of an effort to visit her aunt, or at least call her occasionally, even if something like Skype had been beyond Aunt Peggy's technical skills.

"I'm not ready to tour the farm, but I'd appreciate some information about the house itself. I was looking for a working phone last night and couldn't find one. My cell phone doesn't have service here."

"I'm not surprised." Emily delivered a second plate, this one containing a tower of toast spread with an herbed cheese to go with the existing plate of over easy eggs. "There's only one phone company that gets any service in West Slocum, and even that one doesn't always work out here on the farm."

"What about the landline?" Mabel glanced at the vintage avocado green phone on the wall.

"There isn't one. Peggy cancelled it a couple years ago when she got a cell phone."

"What about her internet service?"

"She didn't have any need for the internet out here." Emily removed the green frilly apron to reveal a white t-shirt and white painters' overalls with *Capricornucopia Farm* embroidered across the pocket of the bib.

"She set up an email account at the library, but I don't think she checked it more than once or twice a year."

"Once a year?" Mabel got twitchy if she went more than an hour without an email or text. "How can anyone live like that?"

"I forgot. You're a Virgo. Detail oriented, and love to have facts at your fingertips, so you thrive in a connected techie world. Still, you're also your aunt's niece, so I'm sure you're adaptable. You'll learn to cope with life here on the farm. Eat up now." Emily hovered the way Mabel's grandmother had done, especially the first few weeks after Mabel's parents had died, when her sixty-five-year-old grandparents had suddenly had the responsibility for the care and feeding of a ten-year-old again. Emily had the expression of motherly concern down pat, even though she was at least a couple years younger than Mabel.

Mabel had been awake long enough now that her stomach grumbled in anticipation of the eggs. Who knew it was possible to have the same sort of munchies she usually had at three a.m., except at—she glanced at the far wall, where there was a clock sporting a hand-painted pineapple in the center of its face—a quarter to nine. In the morning.

At least the birds had completely stopped their awful racket. It was probably pointless to try to get some more sleep now, but it was quiet enough to work. Or it would be, once her visitor left. Mabel could take advantage of the morning hours to go into town, get some supplies, and use the library's internet connection to get in touch with her employer. But first, she needed to eat breakfast. She picked up a fork and started to eat.

"I'm sure you have lots to do, now that you're finally here," Emily said, patting Mabel on the shoulder, "and I've got to get back to my chores. If there's anything else you need, stop on over next door."

"I'll be fine, thank you."

Emily collected her egg basket on the way to the back door. "I'm sure you will, but don't be afraid to ask if you need anything. Everyone here loved Peggy, and she'd want us to treat you the way we treated her."

Emily opened the door, letting in the sound of raised voices coming from the direction of the barn. "That sounds like Rory and Bettina. They're with the CSA group. You'll want to meet them."

"Why?"

Emily briefly looked taken aback, and then she smiled. "Sorry. I thought you were serious for a moment there."

"I am serious," Mabel said. "Is there some reason I should meet them?"

"Besides the fact that they were friends of your aunt?" Emily said. "Actually, yes. They're members of the CSA board, and they've volunteered to help with the distribution to the other members."

The only CSA Mabel had ever heard of was the Cloud Security Alliance, but it worked on security issues for cloud computing, not something that her internet-lacking aunt was likely to be involved with. "What's a CSA?"

"Community Supported Agriculture," Emily said. "It's a way to invest in local farms, except the investors get food instead of cash dividends. Your aunt teamed up with a few other West Slocum farms, including mine, as a sort of co-op. The investors pay in their money during the winter, the farmers use the subscription numbers and cash to plan the next year's crop and pay for supplies, and then during the summer, the investors get to pick up a weekly box filled with garlic products from here, goat cheese and eggs from my place, and all the usual summer vegetables from the other participating farms."

"Is it time for a delivery?" Mabel said. "Is that why the CSA people are here?"

Emily shook her head. "Part of the deal is that the investors will provide labor during the peak of the season. There's a board of directors to keep everything organized. Peggy was on the board, along with another farmer, Larry Rose, and one of the investors, Rory Hansen. Rory supervises the volunteers and makes sure the crops all end up at the pickup location."

"Are they all out there?"

"Just Rory, and, well, Bettina's one of the CSA's general membership, and she kind of tags along wherever Rory goes these days. I didn't see who the third person was."

The voices were getting louder and angrier. Especially the lone male voice.

Mabel pushed the now empty plate away and reluctantly stood up. She was going to have to go talk to the people outside if she wanted to get any work done today.

If the hordes of visitors to the farm didn't thin out soon, she could always go back home, and leave the garlic crop for the CSA members to do with as they pleased.

CHAPTER THREE

A behemoth of a shiny, black, luxury model SUV and a much smaller, older and more beat-up, green pickup truck were parked across from Mabel's Mini Cooper, next to the barn. Over in front of the barn doors stood two women and a man. The man and the taller of the two women were shouting at each other, while the shorter woman cowered to one side and a few feet behind the taller one.

The man had his back to Mabel, facing the barn and the tall woman. She had crossed her arms over her chest, and seemed determined to deny the man access to the barn, as if he were an underage teen trying to get into a nightclub.

The man held himself rigidly still, with none of the angry arm gestures that Mabel would have expected from someone that loud. It didn't fit what she knew about anger and the usual loss of self-control that came with it. Perhaps he was just so enraged he couldn't move.

She needed more data to understand what was going on. She started toward the barn, looking for more clues that would help her deal with the unwanted visitors. She couldn't see the man's face or even the back of his head, which was encased in a plaid flat cap style of hat. He was dressed for golfing in a light colored sport shirt and khakis, with a pair of white leather gloves hanging from the back pocket of his pants, but she couldn't tell whether he was on his way to or from the golf course. The women, on the other hand, were dressed for farm work, from their sun visors to their t-shirts, denim bottoms and rubber clogs. They even wore the same color shirts and visors, as if they'd coordinated their outfits with each other in advance. The only difference was that the taller woman's denim was in the form of jeans, and the shorter one's was in the form of a below-the-knee jumper.

Mabel hadn't even reached the far end of the back patio, where it joined the dirt driveway, when the man stalked off to the SUV. He'd left the engine running, so as soon as he'd climbed inside he backed up, gunning the engine, and then paused in place for a moment to spin the tires and dig a rut in the gravel driveway, before speeding off.

If Emily hadn't already called out a greeting to the two remaining visitors, Mabel would have turned around and gone back inside, but it was too late for that now. She might as well meet her aunt's stockholders—Mabel's stockholders now, she supposed—and get it over with. She was sure they were lovely people, but she hadn't come here to socialize.

"This is Rory Hansen." Emily pointed to the taller woman, who appeared to be about ten years older than Mabel, and solidly enough built that she could, in fact, have bounced the belligerent driver of the SUV off the property if he hadn't left voluntarily. She had the deep tan of someone who worked outside all summer, but the marbleized polish on her short fingernails suggested she also pampered herself. Her brilliant blue eyes were taking Mabel's measure and finding her wanting.

"It's about time you got here." Rory turned around and pushed one of the barn doors to the side.

Emily took care of the second door. "We came outside as soon as we realized there was a problem."

"Oh, that was nothing," Rory said. "We didn't need any help with him."

"In that case," Mabel said, "I'm not needed here, and I've got things to do. You can carry on without me."

"Wait." Rory turned to Mabel. "I'm sorry. I didn't mean to snap at you. It's just that I've been so worried about what was going to happen here, now that Peggy is gone. This farm meant everything to her. Now that you're here, I'm sure everything will be fine."

"Can we go now?" The other woman was a little older than her tall friend, maybe middle forties, and had the fussy sort of hairdo that required hours with a blow-dryer and a whole bottle of styling gel. Her clothing and accessories were equally perfect: both the denim jumper and the t-shirt underneath it looked freshly ironed, her gardening clogs were shiny, and her tiny gold apple-shaped earrings were just right for both her casual dress and her small build. She was barely five feet tall, but so perfectly proportioned that in a photograph, without something as a size reference, she could have been mistaken for a supermodel. In fact, if she'd been taller, she could have been a supermodel. She had the right facial structure for it, along with perfect skin and expressive green eyes. "Scott will be expecting me at the cemetery."

Over the petite woman's head, Emily and Rory exchanged a glance that spoke volumes to them, and nothing to Mabel, who was used to not understanding social interactions. Her usual strategy was to wait for someone to explain, and if no explanation was forthcoming, it probably wasn't important.

Emily nodded her agreement with whatever unspoken message Rory had transmitted. In a voice reeking of forced enthusiasm, she said, "I didn't get a chance to finish the introductions. Mabel, this is Bettina Parker. She's Rory's right-hand woman."

"Exactly," Rory said, with matching enthusiasm. "I can't do anything without Bettina these days."

Even Mabel could see that something was going on here that she shouldn't mess with. Bettina's expressive eyes held a distant sadness, and Emily and Rory were acting as if Bettina were an anxious five-year-old in need of encouragement on her first day of school.

In other circumstances, Mabel might have demanded an explanation, but she had a feeling it would take more time than she had to spare. She settled for simply saying, "It's good to have help."

"Exactly," Rory said. "Bettina's been particularly helpful this week, coming here with me to feed the barn cats."

That answered one of her questions, Mabel thought. Not about Bettina, but about the huge number of stupid birds living happily and noisily on the farm. The cats were too well-fed to do their jobs. It was time to cut their kibble rations and make them work for their dinner.

"Even with Bettina's help, there are some things we can't do," Rory added, her forced enthusiasm fading into a more natural, no-nonsense tone. "Everything is coming to a head this week, and there are things that have to be done by someone with legal authority. It's such a relief that you're finally here to take care of them."

"What sorts of things?" Mabel asked warily. She already had a full day's work on her to-do list, assuming she could remember everything without the app on her phone. "Do they have anything to do with that guy who just took his toys and went home?"

"Kyle Sherman? Don't worry about him," Rory said. "He's nobody."

His car screamed that he was somebody. It had to have cost four times what her own car had, and she'd considered the Mini Cooper a bit of an extravagance.

"He wanted to join the CSA," Emily explained, "but he didn't get his application in before the deadline, so we told him he'd have to wait until next year. Peggy, in fact, was the one who broke the news to him. She volunteered to do it, since she'd been the deciding vote against including him. She thought it would be unfair to the other members if we added him after the deadline, since the crops had already been planned, based on a smaller group. If he'd been allowed to join, then it would throw all the calculations off. The farms would have to produce more than they'd planned for, or each of the members would get a little less in their harvest boxes."

"I think Peggy was right to reject him." Bettina's voice was as small and timid as her appearance. "There are rules, and people have to follow them or the whole world falls apart. That's what Scott always tells me. Kyle didn't meet the deadline, so he couldn't join. That's all there is to it."

The cloud of dust and burned rubber from the departing SUV was still settling. The driver obviously didn't think the situation was even remotely fair, and Mabel could see some room for bending the rules if the missed deadline hadn't been his fault.

"Never mind about Kyle. We need to make plans for the harvest." Rory turned to her friend. "Bettina? Would you go on into the barn and check on the water bowls? I'll join you in a few minutes."

"Good idea," Bettina said. "The sooner we get started on the chores, the sooner we can leave. You know how Scott gets when I'm late."

Emily and Rory exchanged another meaningful glance, and seemed to hold their breaths while Bettina dashed into the barn. Once she was out of earshot, Emily said, "I can't stay to help this morning. You know how it is. Always something that needs doing on my farm." She took a step closer to Rory and gave her a hug. "You're doing a good thing with Bettina."

Rory shrugged. "Someone had to do it. I don't mind."

Emily turned to Mabel, preparing to repeat the farewell hug routine, but Mabel took a step back and raised her hands to ward it off. She'd been attacked by birdsong and sunshine at an ungodly hour, and she hadn't been able to prevent them. Invasion of her personal space was another matter.

"Right," Emily said as she dropped her arms. "Peggy said you were a bit of a loner. Just remember, if you need anything, I'm right next door. If you go around the barn, you'll see there's a path through the trees. It's quicker than taking the road. Stop by any time."

Mabel didn't have any neighbors within walking distance back in Maine, and she'd never missed having them. Her aunt, however, had loved visiting her neighbors regularly, and inviting them back here. Knowing she had such a good neighbor took away some of the guilt Mabel felt for not visiting her aunt more often. "Aunt Peggy was lucky to have you next door."

Rory didn't waste any time watching Emily leave. She took Mabel's arm and tugged her past the barn, down the extension of the dirt driveway. Just wide enough for a tractor or ATV, it looped around and between the fields of garlic, each about an acre in size. "Hurry up. Bettina will come looking for me in a few minutes, and I want to make sure you know what's critical before I have to leave."

Mabel reached for the phone in her pocket, so she could take some notes, only to realize that she'd left it—and its dead battery—in the farmhouse. "Perhaps you could email me later with a list."

"That won't be necessary," Rory said, stepping off the road and onto a path between the rows of garlic. "You just need to remember three things. Harvest, buyers, and market."

"Harvest, buyers, market," Mabel echoed. Presumably, the first one referred to the crop they were walking beside. From the research she'd done the night before last, the garlic should be ready to harvest sometime this month. She'd know it was time to harvest when the scapes—the loopy stalks sent up by the plants—uncurled into straight stalks topped with a flower-like head formed out of tiny bulbils of garlic.

The plants in the field in front of her didn't have any substantial stalks, loopy or straight. There were just little stubs, about a foot long, and the few remaining leaves were brown and dry along the edges. The east coast had experienced a dry spell for the last ten days or so, since shortly before her aunt's death. Had the garlic died from lack of watering? Was that what Rory was so worried about?

"It's okay," Mabel said. "I wasn't counting on the money from the crop. It won't be a problem if the farm loses money this year." In fact, it might be a bit of a relief. If the crop was already beyond saving, all Mabel had to do was refund the money to the CSA members, and then she could go home.

"What are you talking about?" Rory knelt to tug on the nearest brown-leaved stalk, and unearthed a dirt-crusted silvery-white head of garlic. "This year's crop is fantastic, like always."

"Then where are the scapes?"

"Peggy cut most of them to sell at the farmers' market and to include in the CSA boxes. They can be eaten like asparagus, but with a light garlicky flavor. Selling them extends the season a bit, since otherwise the entire crop is ready in a single week out of the summer."

"But the plants are all brown and dead looking."

Rory took Mabel's hand and pressed the head of garlic into it. "Does this feel dead?"

Mabel brushed more of the dirt away, and could see four plump cloves filling out the thin outer wrapper of the head. She broke it apart, and peeled one of the cloves, releasing a strong garlic scent. The clove itself was as moist and firm as the leaves were dry and crinkly.

"The best damned garlic on the entire east coast," Mabel said.

"You sound just like your aunt." Rory's voice was bittersweet. "She would have been so proud of you, taking care of her farm."

Mabel looked up from the garlic to take in the expanse of stubble around her, each dried stalk apparently marking a healthy garlic head below the surface. Beyond this field were four more of similar size. At least it was safe underground, where it could stay until she could figure out how to get it harvested.

"So, this is the harvest. What about the other two things on the list: market and…what was the other one?"

"We're not done with the harvest topic," Rory said. "I'm not as much of an expert on garlic as Peggy was, but I do know that it's best to harvest it after a dry spell, rather than after rain. The forecast is calling for rain later this week, probably starting Thursday night. If it's not in by then, you'll have to wait for another dry spell, and by then the garlic will be past its peak."

"Thursday?" Mabel looked around her, taking in the thousands of plants around her. And this was just one field. "I need to get all of the garlic out of the ground by this Thursday?"

"I can round up a few volunteers from the CSA, and Peggy usually hired a few kids from the local university. They're always looking for temporary work." Rory looked back at the barn, but seemed reassured that she wasn't needed there yet. "Now you can see why I was so relieved you finally got here. It's still possible to finish the harvest. The smaller fields of special heirloom varieties of garlic came in early, and Peggy pulled it before she died. It's just the main crop that needs to come in now."

Mabel knelt and tugged on one of the stalks, to see how it felt to harvest one of the plants. The stalk snapped off in her hand, leaving the garlic head buried.

"You'll get the hang of it." Rory dug in the soil with her fingers, apparently unconcerned about ruining her polished nails, and pulled up the missing head. She set it down, and then reached for the next stalk. "It has to be a smooth pull, no sudden or sharp movements. Slow and steady, and it'll slide right out." As she spoke, the bulb rose to the surface, still firmly attached to its stalk.

Mabel tried again, and this time she felt the roots release their grip on the soil, and the garlic head popped out of the ground.

"See?" Rory said. "It's easy."

The process was easy enough, but still, there were tens of thousands of plants to pull. When developing apps for clients, she'd always found that they underestimated just how many steps were actually necessary to complete the app's tasks. What seemed like a simple chore, like pulling up garlic, always turned into a much more complicated series of steps. "Do you really think we can get all this done in just three days?"

"We've got to try," Rory said in a bracing tone. "Anything that's not harvested by Thursday night is going to be ruined."

So much for getting some of her real work done this week, Mabel thought. When she got into town later, she'd let her boss know that she needed a couple days' personal time. Four days, actually. Maybe the whole week. It shouldn't be a big problem. She couldn't remember the last time she'd taken a vacation.

She just hoped a week would be enough to take care of the harvest. "What about the other things on the list?"

Rory must have realized just how overwhelmed Mabel felt. "They're not as big a deal as the harvest itself, but you'll need to talk to some people. You need to reassure them that you can fulfill the existing contracts."

"But I'm not sure I can." Talking to people wasn't her best skill, and she still wasn't convinced she could get the entire crop harvested before it was ruined.

"All you need to do right now is let them know you're working on it. Tell them they'll have a definite answer on Friday."

"What about the third thing I need to deal with?"

"The farmers' market," Rory said. "You need to talk to Darryl Santangelo. He's in charge of the local farmers' market, and he's been talking about assigning Peggy's space to another garlic grower. He's got an office in the Chamber of Commerce's suite. He's usually there on Monday, Wednesday and Friday. You should be able to catch him today, at least until lunchtime."

"That's easy enough." Bringing in Aunt Peggy's last crop for the CSA was one thing; hand selling it to strangers at the market was another. "I'll just tell him to go ahead and reassign the space."

Rory gasped. "You can't do that. Peggy counts…counted…on the income from the market sales. A good chunk of the farm's annual income is collected from there over the next few weeks. Plus, people here count on getting Peggy's garlic at the farmers' market. They all want Peggy's garlic, not the inferior stuff that someone else might grow."

"What if we just distributed the whole crop to the CSA members? They could sell any amounts they didn't want," Mabel said. "I don't really need the money."

"I'm sorry," Rory said. "This must be difficult for you, having to try to fill your aunt's boots. Peggy said that you're a very private person. But you've got to understand it's not just about the money. It's also about your aunt's memory. People will want to meet you, convey their sympathy, and show their respect for Peggy by buying some of her last crop. After this season's garlic is sold out, you can do whatever you think is best, and no one will be upset, but not this year. Everyone will expect to see you the first couple weekends after the crop is harvested. They'll *need* to see you. And I think it will be good for you too. Help you through the grieving process. Working the farmers' market will be like holding an unconventional memorial service for both the customers and you."

Mabel wasn't sure she needed help grieving. She was feeling more guilt than sadness. She hadn't known her aunt all that well, and they had been so different. Rory was right, though, that she owed it to her aunt to give her the send-off she deserved. It wouldn't completely make up for the neglect Mabel had shown her aunt over the years, but she could at least bring in the final crop and allow Aunt Peggy's friends to pay their pungent respects.

Mabel had been planning to go into town today anyway, for her earplugs and internet access, so it wouldn't be a major inconvenience to go talk with the market's manager. The internet access had to come first, since her boss was a bit high-maintenance. He tended to fret if his staff didn't check in with status updates at least twice a day—or, in her case, twice a night—and she was already one check-in behind. He didn't recognize weekends any more than she did, and she'd promised him he'd have the beta version of her current app by this morning. There were probably a dozen emails from him in her in-box already, demanding to know if she was dead or in the hospital.

"I'll talk to the market manager this morning," Mabel said.

"Good." Rory exhaled, as if she'd been holding her breath, waiting for confirmation that the market space wasn't going to be abandoned. "I'd better go see how Bettina's doing."

"Is something wrong with her?" Mabel said as they returned to the dirt roadway. She had to jog occasionally to keep up with Rory's long legs. How did the even shorter Bettina keep up with her friend? "I couldn't help noticing that you and Emily seem to be awfully protective of her."

"She's been through a lot recently. Lost her husband about six months ago, although in a sense she lost him a few years before that." Rory looked at the barn, where Bettina was standing in the doorway, looking toward them. "I'd better get moving. It's not good for her to be alone. It reminds her of what she's lost. She and her husband did everything together, except for their jobs. She took a leave of absence from teaching when he died, and when her leave period ran out, the kids were off for school vacation. I can't wait until the fall, when classes start up again and she goes back to work. It will be good for her, being surrounded by the kids she loves. Until then, I'm her designated companion."

"Don't you have your own work to do?"

"Not officially," Rory said. "I'm a stay-at-home mom, and my daughter's fifteen and pretty independent. I don't mind keeping an eye on Bettina for the summer. Someone needs to do it, and I have more free time than most people. Besides, I like bossing people around, and she mostly does what I ask her to do, so it's like having a minion. I might have exaggerated a bit about how much I've depended on her, but she's been more helpful here at the farm than just about anything else I've tried to get her to do. I never realized just how attached to the farm she was, until Peggy died, and we started coming over here."

"Aunt Peggy was lucky to have friends like you."

"No problem. Peggy was a lovely person, and she thought the world of both this farm and you. Helping you out is the least we could do for her. I'll keep stopping by until you're ready to fly solo." She dug in the pocket of her jeans for a piece of paper. "I'd been waiting for you to show up, so I could give this to you. It's a list of people you should know, and their contact information. I'm right at the top."

"Thank you." Mabel took the handwritten list and stuffed it into her own jeans pocket. She wasn't convinced anyone on the list could help her, but she could never have too much data.

Bettina had left the front of the barn, and was leaning against the green pickup truck, apparently talking to herself. "I think Bettina's done with the barn cats."

"I'd better run. Call me if there's anything you need. Otherwise, I'll be back later, after Bettina's had her daily visit to the cemetery." Rory jogged back to the parking lot.

Mabel, still caught in sleep inertia, followed more slowly. She watched Rory bundle Bettina into the battered pickup truck and leave more sedately and quietly than Kyle had done. Mabel waved at them, not sure if the women would notice, or if she was even doing it for their benefit or more to celebrate the fact that she was finally, comfortably alone again. She was tempted to barricade herself in her bedroom with her laptop, and if she hadn't seen what her aunt's friends had done for the farm in her absence, she might have given in to the call of her computer.

Not right now, though. She owed it to Aunt Peggy and her friends to make sure that their work hadn't been wasted. If that meant talking to the market manager to claim the space for this weekend, then that was what she would do.

There would be plenty of time to do her real job later. She always did her best work all alone in the dark, anyway.

CHAPTER FOUR

The West Slocum Free Library was part of the historic central district of the town, which ran from the massive stone Town Hall at one end of Liberty Street to about three acres of open fields at the other end. A ten-foot-tall sign listed a number of activities to be held in the commons, including the weekly farmers' market every Saturday from Memorial Day to Halloween.

Mabel was out of the house and on the road to town by ten in the morning. She had close to two hours before the market's manager would leave for the day, and her boss was probably foaming at the mouth over her missed check-ins. If she wanted to still have a job tonight, she needed to check in with him first. Assuming the library was open at such an early hour, and had something faster than dial-up internet access for transmitting her files.

The exterior of the library was old stone, at least a couple hundred years old. Even if it was open at this ridiculously early hour, Mabel worried that it wouldn't have much in the way of internet access. Dial-up was a distinct possibility, which meant that she could reassure her boss, but not transmit her work to him unless she wanted to be stuck at the library for hours.

The main door was unlocked, and, even better, she noticed that the interior had apparently been gutted and rebuilt entirely sometime within the last twenty years. Major renovations meant that there might be a dedicated computer room, possibly even outfitted with something better than dial-up access. On the other hand, the fact that they still had a row of public phone booths along the front wall of the lobby was a bad sign. She'd assumed that public phones were officially extinct, now that everyone had a cell phone. The booths might have been left as decoration, since they were actually quite lovely. They looked custom-built, like pieces of furniture, made out of solid oak with a dark, antique looking stain. Even the windows of the booths were real glass, not modern plexiglass.

Mabel headed for the checkout counter across from the entrance. Half hidden behind a reasonably modern flat-screen monitor was an elderly woman whose white hair had a jagged streak of hot pink on top, just off-center. Some of the strands matched the pink cardigan she was wearing.

The librarian looked up from her screen, blinked, and then zipped out from behind the counter. Mabel was still wondering how someone so old could move so fast when the woman tackled her, wrapping her in a baby powder scented hug. Despite the woman's unexpected speed, the weakness of her hug suggested that she was frail, and a glance at her deformed arthritic fingers confirmed it. Mabel was afraid to move, for fear of knocking the woman over, so she waited for the librarian to signal that she was done. It took several long moments, during which Mabel decided she definitely needed to arrange for the emergency installation of internet service at the farmhouse, so she could avoid this sort of attack in the future. People here in West Slocum were just a little too quick to invade her space.

Finally, the librarian stepped back. "You must be Peggy Skinner's niece Mabel. I'd recognize that Skinner chin anywhere."

"That's me." Mabel couldn't help reaching up to feel her chin, trying to figure out what was special about it, and whether her aunt had ever mentioned anyone who met this woman's description—a pixie in pink—and coming up empty on both counts. "You must be Aunt Peggy's favorite librarian."

"I'm everyone's favorite librarian, Josefina Marshall." The woman scooted back behind the check-out counter. "I'm so sorry for your loss. Your aunt was special, but I'm sure you don't need me to tell you that. So, what can I do for you today?"

"I was hoping to get a library card, so I can use the internet."

"We usually require proof of West Slocum residency." Josefina hunted and pecked on her keyboard, in what looked like a painful manner, given the arthritis in her hands, until Mabel was tempted to reach over the counter and enter the information herself.

Josefina looked up from her typing. "I think we can dispense with references in your case. You'll be settled into your aunt's house in no time, now that you're taking over the farm."

Mabel wasn't planning to be here long, but she had a lot of practice being careful about giving strangers information about her future plans, so she didn't correct the librarian's assumption that she was planning to stay in West Slocum. "I mostly just need internet access."

"You probably use an e-reader too," Josefina said without looking up from the keyboard. "We offer quite a few digital titles."

Between her regular work and the demands of her aunt's estate, Mabel wasn't going to have much time for pleasure reading. Still, there were times when she needed to do some off-line research to understand a client's business niche before designing an app for it. "That's good to know."

"I'll be right back with your card." The woman jumped up and speed walked around the corner. She returned a moment later, holding something that looked like a credit card, but with a picture of the library printed on it. She dropped into her chair, holding onto the card. "I just need to know one thing before I activate it."

"I promise I'll read the terms and conditions on internet use, I won't visit porn sites, and I won't send any spam."

The woman waved the card dismissively. "I wouldn't expect anything less from Peggy Skinner's niece. What I really want to know is when this year's garlic crop will be available. I'm a member of the Order of the Stinking Rose, you know."

Aunt Peggy had told Mabel about the nickname for garlic—the stinking rose. There was even an urban legend about an international secret society known as the Order of the Sinking Rose for serious garlic afficionados. Either it wasn't an urban legend, or Josefina and Peggy had started up their own, not-so-secret version locally. Mabel could see her aunt doing that, as yet another excuse to invite more friends to her home. If only Aunt Peggy had confided in her, Mabel would have developed an app for the members, and it might have lessened the guilt she felt over having neglected her aunt.

She couldn't undo her past neglect of her aunt, but she was prepared to do the right thing for her aunt's friends. "We're hoping to have this year's crop available at this weekend's market. I need to do my online work here first, and then I'll be checking in with the market's manager to make sure he'll hold Aunt Peggy's space for me."

"You tell him from me that he'd better," Josefina said as she finally handed over the library card. "Otherwise, he's going to have a lynch mob coming after him. People around here are serious about their garlic, and there's no garlic anywhere else on the east coast, maybe in the whole country, that's as serious as Peggy's."

"I'll make sure he knows." Mabel took the card and followed Josefina's directions to the computer room where, miracle of miracles, they had fiber-optic service.

As expected, about a dozen emails from her employer were waiting for her. Each one was a little more frantic than the previous one. In addition to routine status checks, he'd also sent her a change in the deadline for one of the apps she was working on. It had been due next week, but now the client needed it by this Friday, or he was cancelling the order.

Mabel sent a brief reply, explaining that she'd had a problem with internet access, and would only be checking in once a day for the next few weeks. She explained that everything was under control, she'd have some information he needed later today, and she'd have the completed app for him by the new Friday deadline. She attached the files she'd finished last night, and logged out of her session. The next time she was here, she planned to crack her aunt's email account, just to reassure herself that her aunt had indeed gotten Mabel's holiday and birthday greetings.

For now, though, she needed to get over to the farmers' market manager's office. Avoiding the risk of another hug from the librarian, she slipped out a back exit. Mabel left her car in the library's parking lot and walked across the street to the Chamber of Commerce's offices.

Like the library, the office building had an old stone exterior. Unlike the library, it hadn't been renovated inside. The wood paneling and intricately carved stair railings appeared to be original, and were nice features, unlike the dim lighting, which might not have been installed in the 1800s, but was at least fifty years old.

According to a sign that listed the tenants, the Chamber of Commerce was on the third floor. Not trusting the elevator, which looked to have been installed at the same time as the rusty old light fixtures, Mabel opted instead for the stairs.

The most gorgeous man she'd ever seen in person was leaning against the counter where the receptionist sat. He was tall and dark skinned, with the chiseled facial structure that was usually only seen in male models or the leading men in action-adventure movies. If she'd seen his picture online, she'd have assumed it had been airbrushed. His sport shirt and khakis were tight enough to show off his muscular physique, but with the necessary millimeter of breathing room to keep the outfit from looking tacky or X-rated.

The receptionist, a woman in her twenties, was intent on her computer monitor, radiating clear signals that she wanted the man to go away so she could do her work. He didn't seem to be picking up on them, continuing to describe a recent ball game.

The receptionist looked so grateful for Mabel's arrival that Mabel braced herself for yet another hug and reminiscences about her aunt. Fortunately, the receptionist settled for smiling genuinely and asking, "How can I help you?" in a tone that suggested she would gladly do just about anything, if it gave her a reason to send the gorgeous man away.

"I'm looking for Darryl Santangelo."

The receptionist's expression combined both relief and pity. She pointed to the gorgeous man. "You found him."

Darryl offered Mabel his hand and a broad smile. "And you are?"

Some men looked silly when they smiled that broadly, but not Darryl. If anything, he was even more stunning. Mabel had a feeling he knew it too.

She took his hand and shook it briefly. "I'm Mabel Skinner. Peggy Skinner's niece."

"I'm sorry for your loss," he said, but his voice lacked the depth of sorrow it had held when describing a missed play to the receptionist. At least his lack of any real attachment to Aunt Peggy meant that he wouldn't have any reason to offer a consoling hug. If he had, she wouldn't have been afraid to hurt him, as she'd been with Josefina, and kneeing him in the groin wouldn't have been a good start to their business relationship.

"Come into my office," he said.

Darryl's office was actually a barren conference room with nothing but a table and eight chairs. A couple legal pads, a handful of cheap pens and a stack of sticky notes littered the table's surface. Unlike the dim interiors of the building, this space was brightly lit from the oversized windows that overlooked the strip of public land across the street, which contained the town hall and library.

Darryl settled in the faux leather chair at the end of the table with his back to the door. The bright sunshine coming in from the windows across from him should have revealed any flaws in his appearance, but instead worked like a spotlight, drawing Mabel's gaze to his handsome face. He gestured for her to take the adjacent chair.

Mabel shook her head and leaned against the back of the chair. "I won't be here that long. I understand there's an issue with respect to my aunt's space at the market."

"It's not really an issue, so much as a clear violation of the rules," he said. "Anyone who misses three Saturdays in a row forfeits her right to participate in the market for the remainder of the season. Peggy missed the last two Saturdays, and this week will be the third."

"She was dead," Mabel said. "She couldn't be there. You can't blame her for something that wasn't her fault."

"That's what everyone says." He smiled again, as if aware of how distracting it could be. "Not that they're dead, of course, but that the absence wasn't their fault. I can't be making exceptions. Not this time of year.

Perhaps at the beginning or the end, when there aren't many vendors or buyers, but not right now. I've got a long waiting list to claim any vacancies. I can't leave any spaces empty, or we'd lose customers for everyone. Did you know that ninety percent of our farmers' income is collected in the next four weeks? For every space that's empty, we lose at least sixteen visitors to the market in subsequent weeks. That translates into about a three percent drop in sales each week, for each of the remaining farmers."

Mabel didn't want to hurt the other participants in the market. She just didn't want to have to participate herself, and it might take more than the few remaining days before the weekend to find someone who could oversee the sales on her behalf. She needed more time.

"I just got into town," Mabel said, "and I'm not sure I can be ready for the market by this weekend. From what I've heard, my aunt's garlic is a major draw for the farmers' market. Wouldn't you rather have it there for the rest of the season, even if it means skipping a week now? Give me this weekend off, and you'll have my aunt's garlic for the other two months of the season."

"It's not really up to me. I have to follow the rules. I've even got another garlic farmer who's interested in Peggy's space. That way, people would still be able to get some garlic, even if it's not their favorite variety." Darryl looked down at the gold championship ring on his right hand and twisted it back and forth. "I'm sorry, but I've got no choice here. I have to reassign your space if you don't show up this weekend. It would be better if we could work it out ahead of time, so the space wasn't empty even for one day. As long as I can say you cooperated with the transition, I'd be able to reinstate your space next year. If you leave me in the lurch, I wouldn't have that option. The other farmers would have my head if I played favorites."

Mabel wasn't particularly concerned about next year. She would be back in Maine, and someone else would be running the farm. Still, she wanted to give her aunt a proper send-off at the market, so she needed to keep her options open.

"Let me see what I can arrange," Mabel said. The garlic needed to be harvested by the end of Thursday, and if she didn't get that done, there was no point to reserving the space at the farmers' market, regardless of how upsetting its absence would be to her aunt's customers. "I'll let you know on Thursday afternoon."

"Okay, but I need to be able to get in touch with you, in case you don't call." He slid the cube of sticky notes over to her and handed her a pen.

Mabel jotted her email address on it. "You can reach me here any time."

He glanced at it. "I need a phone number," Darryl said. "I've got to update the information in the farm's records, unless you're using Peggy's cell phone."

That was the first really useful idea he'd had. She took back the sticky note pad and wrote on it. "Once I find her phone, I probably will use it. Until then, here's my cell phone number. But I'd rather you tried email first." Especially since her current cell phone didn't have service here. If she couldn't find her aunt's phone this afternoon she'd look into getting a temporary prepaid phone through the one provider for the area.

"Phones are easier for me," he said. "I'm not into technology all that much. I'm a simple, direct kind of guy."

Or else he'd found he wasn't as effective online, where no one knew what he looked like, and couldn't be impressed by his broad smiles.

"It doesn't really matter," she said on her way to the door, anxious to get back to the farm. "You won't need to call me. I'll contact you by the end of Thursday. I never miss a deadline."

Darryl stood to walk with her to the outer door. Or, more likely, to go back to the interrupted play-by-play account of the ball game for the benefit of the unappreciative receptionist. If that was his intent, he was out of luck. The receptionist was on the phone, and had someone else waiting for her to end the call.

The visitor was a wiry man, around Aunt Peggy's age, maybe a few years older, judging by the gray stubble of a not-too-recently shaved head sticking out from beneath a green and yellow baseball cap with the John Deere logo on the brim. The lower edges of his jeans were caked with dried mud, and his work boots left a trail wherever he walked. He must have been pacing before Mabel came out of the conference room; his muddy footsteps were visible even on the industrial carpeting that was designed to hide more casual amounts of dirt.

"Larry Rose," Darryl said, as he surged ahead of Mabel to offer the older man a hearty handshake and a thump on the upper back. "We were just talking about you. This is Peggy Skinner's niece, Mabel. She's going to let us know later this week if you can have her aunt's space for the rest of the season."

"I guess I got here at just the right time then," Larry shouted. It appeared to be his only volume, as if he'd hit the biological equivalent of the caps lock key for his vocal chords. "I've been thinking about it, and I think I've got a solution that would be good for everyone."

With Larry's voice bouncing around the room, the receptionist was struggling to hear the person on the other end of the phone line. Mabel would have suggested retiring to Darryl's office, but she was afraid they wouldn't go without her, and she didn't have the time to get dragged into a lengthy discussion. "I'm running late for an appointment, but I can listen on my way out."

She didn't wait for them to agree, just pushed the door open and stepped out into the hall. If Larry continued shouting, she'd hear him, even if he stayed behind.

"I could use a cup of coffee from the café downstairs," Darryl said.

The two men stopped at the elevator, with Larry shouting amiably at Darryl, while Mabel continued on to the stairwell. After a moment, there was total silence, and she imagined the two men looking around for her. Finally, two sets of footsteps approached the stairwell. She waited for them on the first landing where they would be unlikely to disrupt anyone else's workday, and where she could leave again if they became bogged down in the sorts of time wasters that made in person meetings so annoying.

"Here's the thing," Larry shouted. "I've got a crew, and nothing major to harvest for a couple weeks. Peggy's farm has her main harvest just waiting to happen, but no crew to do it. We can help each other out. I'll buy her crop from you and take over all the labor, along with the market space."

"That would work." Darryl said. "Win-win-win. The rules have an option for me to allocate abandoned space to the first farm that grows a comparable crop. That would definitely be you, Larry. Garlic isn't your main crop, but you do sell some, and no one else around here does."

The deal was tempting. Local residents would get their Aunt-Peggy-grown garlic, Mabel would be able to finish the app that needed to be done by Friday, and, best of all, she wouldn't have to attend the market herself.

"I'll think about it." There had to be a catch. Like when an app she was working on seemed to come together on her first try, with every feature the client wanted and none of the glitches that normally arose when some of the client's specifications conflicted with other specifications or with the various formats the app would need to work on. Whenever it all fell easily into place like that, she knew it was a bad omen, that there was something catastrophic she'd overlooked, and the app would blow up in her face during beta testing. "Send me an email to confirm your offer, with the price and any other terms, and I'll have my lawyer look it over."

"Email?" Larry managed to end his shout with a question mark.

"Lawyer?" Darryl asked, more quietly, but with an equal degree of shock.

"I don't do anything without my lawyer's approval." She started down the next flight of stairs and had passed the next landing before the shouting started up again. There was no ignoring Larry's side of the conversation, as he demanded that Darryl do something about the situation, but she couldn't hear the actual words of Darryl's soothing response.

She wasn't particularly interested in anything they had to say, at least not until one of them put it in an email that she could review with someone who knew more about the proposal than she did. Even though she'd threatened them with a lawyer, she actually thought Rory Hansen might be the right person to talk to about the offer. Rory would find the bug in the proposal, if there was one.

CHAPTER FIVE

Back at the farm, Mabel found the information her employer needed, and downloaded it to a flash drive to take back to the library. There was plenty of time to get him the information before the library closed, so she decided to look for her aunt's phone before heading back into town.

She didn't find the phone, but she found its service contract and instruction booklet in the home office. Aunt Peggy's records might have consisted of drawers full of paper, instead of bytes of data, but they were every bit as easy to retrieve as the information in a computerized system.

The phone's paperwork identified it as a surprisingly advanced model, with a camera and basic smartphone features, including internet access. Either Aunt Peggy had become considerably more tech-friendly over the years, or some salesperson had pushed her into buying something she didn't need. Mabel was inclined to believe it was the latter, but at least she could make full use of those features once she found the phone. Maybe the neighbor, Emily Colter, would have some idea of where it might be.

Temporarily abandoning her search for the phone, Mabel considered the laptop sized record book in the center of Aunt Peggy's desk. It had been well used, judging by the wear and tear on the leather cover. It held at least a couple hundred pages, and more than half of them appeared to have been written in the tiny but meticulously clear handwriting her aunt had perfected during her years as an accountant. Mabel couldn't quite imagine how her aunt could have filled so many pages with notes on growing garlic. According to everything she'd read online, garlic was a fairly easy crop to grow. Dig a trench, drop cloves in it, cover them up, mulch them for the winter, and come back nine months later to harvest them. Definitely nothing to write a novel's worth of words about. Just the right number of steps for a simple app, though.

Rory had said that the journal would contain contact information on the local restaurant owners who were getting anxious about the status of their orders. As long as Mabel was going into town to send her employer an email later, she could send the customers a reassuring message at the same time if she had their contact information.

Mabel opened the book from the back, looking for the most recent entry. The last used page looked like the notes from a science class, with dates, several weather parameters and then the harvest quantities. Flipping through the pages, she found some additional entries that were number based, with charts, budgets and schedules for plowing, planting, fertilizing and harvesting. Other entries were more like a diary, with general observations on how the current season was shaping up, or insights into past successes or failures.

So far this year, Aunt Peggy had been running a deficit, even with the investment of the CSA members. That loss didn't even include a living wage for Aunt Peggy. For all Mabel knew, it was normal for the farm to be that far in the red until the harvest came in, and the income from the farmers' market replenished the bank account.

Mabel flipped to the previous year's ledger page to see how the farm had been doing last July. It had been slightly in the red, but not as far down as this year. Mabel went back another year, thinking that it would have been so much simpler to understand the farm's finances if she'd had a computerized spreadsheet, which would extract the figures she wanted from all the past years, and put them into one clear spreadsheet or even a graph, showing the trajectory of the farm's income from year to year.

It took a while, studying the handwritten numbers and flipping back and forth among the various years, but Mabel could see a definite alarming pattern to the farm's profitability. It had broken even almost from the very beginning, although it had taken about three years before Aunt Peggy's reputation had taken hold, at which point her net income soared. The next several years, her income rose slowly but consistently each year. Then five years ago, there was a sudden dip in the net income.

Mabel knew that the profit from farming could be unpredictable, and there could have been some bad weather that affected the crop, so one year's drop wasn't surprising. But the income dropped a little bit more the next year and the next year and the next, on a slow but steady slide. That wasn't the effect of a single bad season. Whatever the cause, it was more long-term. It was also fairly small-scale, suggesting that Aunt Peggy hadn't lost an entire harvest, just an amount equal to somewhere between one and three percent of her profits each year.

The farm had provided Aunt Peggy with a reasonable income, but even a few percentage point drops in her income would have affected her living standard. Was that why she'd dropped the landline? Because she couldn't afford it, once she had the cell phone?

Why hadn't Aunt Peggy said something if she was struggling?

Because she hadn't wanted to make demands on her niece like too many others had done. Mabel's grandparents had controlled the life insurance and legal settlement monies from her parents' deaths until they too had died and passed along the remaining money, which was substantial, especially when added to their house and life savings. As soon as they were gone, everyone on the planet suddenly seemed to know she'd just been given access to hundreds of thousands of dollars, and she'd been inundated with requests for loans, gifts and donations from distant relatives, neighbors she'd never met, charities and outright scammers. She'd gone straight to a local lawyer, Jeff Wright, and hired him to deal with the requests, essentially by turning them all down without bothering her about them. He did give her a quarterly report, and she would have noticed if Aunt Peggy had ever asked for anything, but she never had.

What bothered Mabel now was that she hadn't ever thought to offer to help Aunt Peggy. Mabel could have made up Aunt Peggy's lost income several times over without doing any damage to her own finances. She had a well-paying job and hardly ever used any of the inherited monies, except when she'd bought her car and the occasional bit of irresistible tech hardware. Mabel would have been glad to help her closest relative, but it had never dawned on her that Aunt Peggy might have needed any financial help. Mabel had always envisioned Aunt Peggy living in a New Age fantasy, or an updated version of a 1960s hippie commune, not running a modern small business with all the work and risks that businesses entail.

Now that she had the facts, it was too late to help Aunt Peggy.

At least, Mabel thought, she couldn't help her aunt financially, but there were other things she could do. She could make sure her aunt's final crop was harvested, and uphold her reputation as the producer of the best garlic on the east coast.

* * * *

Mabel followed the shortcut to the neighboring farm, noticing how well the ten-foot-wide path had been maintained, with the undergrowth pruned back along the sides to allow easy passage. At the end of the path, just outside the reach of the outermost trees' branches, was a woven wire fence with a gate. Beyond the fence was a large, modern log cabin. Despite its size, it was dwarfed by three red barns. The farm seemed to be roughly the same size as Aunt Peggy's, but instead of open fields, here the pastures were enclosed with woven wire fencing to restrict the wandering of the dozens of goats nibbling on the grass.

In front of the house, the driveway split and formed a circle. Inside the circle was a neat garden of low-lying plants, which Mabel couldn't identify from this distance. It was divided into twelve wedges, with paths to the center, where there was a sundial, except that the gnomon rising from its face was a crescent moon. Each wedge of the garden contained an almost life-sized sculpture of one of the symbols of the horoscope.

Emily was working with a dozen or so goats inside one of the closer pastures. Mabel called out a greeting before turning her attention on the latch to figure out how it worked. She was reaching out to grab the top of the gate in preparation for releasing the latch when she heard Emily shout, "Stop! Don't touch the gate!"

Startled, Mabel stumbled backwards, tripping over a root and falling onto her rear end. By the time she'd stood up and brushed off the dirt, Emily was standing on the other side of the gate.

"I'm so sorry." Emily removed her leather gloves and tucked them into the back pocket of her white overalls. "I forgot you don't know as much about farming as your aunt did. The fence is electrified."

Mabel took another step backwards, managing not to trip this time. "I could have been electrocuted."

"The fence wouldn't have killed you," Emily said. "It's just aversion therapy for predators. It doesn't even kill the foxes and coyotes, but it does hurt, so they're inclined to look elsewhere for dinner."

"Next time, I'll call before I visit, so you can turn it off."

"That's not necessary." Emily grabbed the middle section of the gate and rattled it. "See? You can touch anything except the top wire and the bottom one. It was only when I saw you reach for the top that I realized you didn't know how it works."

As far as Mabel was concerned, electricity was supposed to be safely encased in cables, not left exposed. "I think I'll stay on my side of the fence, and not risk touching the wrong thing. I just wanted to ask you something, and I can do it from here."

"What do you need to know?"

"I was going to use my aunt's cell phone, since mine doesn't have service, but I can't find it. Have you seen it?"

"Not since she died," Emily said. "I assume she had it with her then. It's probably at the funeral home still. They usually end up with all of their clients' personal belongings."

"Why didn't they release them after the funeral?"

"There hasn't been a funeral yet. We've all been waiting for you to show up and make the arrangements."

"But it's been two weeks." No one had said anything about arranging a funeral, and she'd just assumed it had all been taken care of already. "I don't know what she wants. Shouldn't her attorney have taken care of it?"

"He thought you should decide. The funeral home was able to preserve the body, and you are her only relative, after all."

"Biologically, sure, but her attorney probably knew her better than I did. All I can do is ask you and Rory and her other friends to tell me what she wanted. He could have done the same thing."

"She always said she wanted to be buried on the farm," Emily said. "It's still up to you to decide, though, since apparently she didn't make any official arrangements. She had a will, but no directions for her final resting place. The farm is a big place—the better part of twenty acres, if you include the wetlands and the woods, so there are a lot of options, assuming you want to bury her here."

"I don't even know where the property lines are."

"I can help you with that." Emily came through the gate and then latched it behind her. She shook the gate to make sure it was securely locked, even though the goats all seemed to be safely contained behind yet another fence around each of the subdivided pastures. "Peggy would have killed me if I let my goats get into her fields at harvest time."

"Do they like garlic that much?"

"They like everything that much." As they walked back through the woods, Emily added, "Whenever Peggy had leftover garlic greens at the end of a market day, she'd give them to me for the goats, so they're used to eating them. Of course, they eat just about anything, but they're a lot like human beings in the way that they think the grass is always greener on the other side of the fence."

"Is the fence the boundary line between the two farms?"

"More or less," Emily said. "I own about twenty feet between the fence and the trees, but I doubt you'd be burying Peggy in the woods anyway.

You'll have to stay away from the wetlands too. Most of the front yard is wet, and if you follow the creek, you'll see some marshy areas near it."

"I'd forgotten about the creek," Mabel said as they emerged from the shade of the trees. "It's the rear property line, isn't it?"

"It used to mark the end of the cultivated fields, but not the end of the property." Emily set off down the dirt path that ran along the fields waiting to be harvested. "Come on, I'll show you where the property ends. You probably won't recognize the creek. It used to be an overgrown mess. About five years ago, Peggy cleared out the brambles and small trees on the other side of the creek to add another field. She'd planned to use it for a new garlic variety, but the first year she planted it the seed stock was bad, and it infected the field with white rot. That's about the only thing that will kill garlic, and once it's in the ground, the field is useless for ever growing garlic there again."

That might explain her aunt's declining profits, since they'd started about five years ago. At least now the unplanted field was a blessing, since it meant that Mabel had one less field to harvest this week. "If that field's useless for farming, it might be a good place to bury her."

"You'd have to dig up her lavender bed to do that," Emily said. "When Peggy couldn't grow garlic there any longer, she needed something that wouldn't be affected by the rot. She put in a whole field of lavender, since it has a completely different planting and harvesting schedule than the garlic does. She added a gazebo to the field last year, when she started to get requests from photographers to do wedding pictures out there. See it?"

Mabel looked at where Emily was pointing. A gazebo sat in the middle of a large field, surrounded by what looked like shrubs about eighteen inches tall. She assumed they were lavender plants, although they were too far away for the scent to be noticeable. "We wouldn't have to dig up the whole thing, Just a corner. Enough for a grave and a marker."

"I doubt the brides would appreciate having a tombstone in their pictures," Emily said. "Besides, Peggy hated the smell of lavender. When she put that field in, she even changed the farm's name from The Stinking Rose to Stinkin' Stuff Farm."

"We won't put her too close to the lavender then," Mabel said. "Somewhere near the creek would still be nice, though. The sound of running water is so soothing."

With a look that Mabel couldn't decipher, Emily said, "You don't know, do you?"

"Know what?"

"Peggy drowned. In the creek."

"But it's just a little creek. Not more than a foot of water in its deepest spots." Mabel peered in the direction of the little strip of water, no more than six feet across. She was too far away to judge its depth, but she'd splashed through it the last time she was here without getting wet above her ankles. "Unless she dredged it since the last time I was here."

"No, it's still just a few inches deep. Apparently Peggy fell, hit her head on one of the rocks in the creek, and passed out with her face in the water."

Poor Aunt Peggy. She'd given up her career and family ties in order to live a long, healthy life, and none of it had mattered. She'd died much too young, in a freak accident, just like her brother.

"I still don't understand what she was doing out there," Emily said in a pensive tone. "I found her in the creek, right across from the gazebo, like she'd been coming from there and was on her way back to the house when she fell. It took me forever to find her, because I double-checked everywhere else before I even thought to look in the lavender field. The flowers were gathered in June, and there isn't much that needs to be done with lavender plants this time of year, except some occasional weeding."

"Even I know that the middle of the night isn't the best time to weed," Mabel said.

"If there was work to do, she did it, regardless of the time of day," Emily said. "I was trying to get her to pay more attention to working in harmony with the moon cycles, but she was never interested. It's done wonders for my harvests, although my crops are pretty small, just a few herbs for the goat cheeses, and a kitchen garden for my own use. Peggy was a skeptic, and not just about moon cycles. She didn't think anything really made a difference, except for commitment and hard work."

Mabel vividly remembered that aspect of her aunt's personality. Aunt Peggy had definitely believed in hard work. It was something that the two of them had in common, although Aunt Peggy had never quite understood how her niece's staring at a computer screen throughout the middle of the night qualified as hard work. Somehow, anything done after dark was relegated to the category of "leisure." Still, Aunt Peggy had tried to understand her niece's work, which was, Mabel thought guiltily, more than she had ever done in return. She'd been much too quick to dismiss her aunt's work as simple, archaic and unnecessarily demanding physically.

It was too late to make up for her thoughtlessness, but she could at least make sure her aunt's burial wishes were carried out. It would be even better if she could complete the harvest and keep the farmers' market space, but those things might not be possible. If she could at least get her aunt buried properly, it would go a long way toward assuaging her guilt. "I'd better get to the funeral home, and make the arrangements."

As they headed back in the direction of the farmhouse, moving slowly in the summer heat, Emily said, "It's the Stevens Funeral Home on Main Street. The owner is a member of the CSA who knew Peggy, so Rory convinced Peggy's attorney to have the body sent there. I hope you don't mind."

"Not at all." It was one less decision for Mabel to get wrong. "I owe Rory a lot."

"Everyone in West Slocum does," Emily said. "She pretty much runs half the town from behind the scenes. If she weren't so good at it, we'd hate her for it. Instead, we're just grateful for everything she does."

"Like keeping Bettina on an even keel."

"Exactly," Emily said. "Rory's amazing. She was behind the formation of the CSA, and before that, she got the farmers' market going. She volunteers at the schools, organizes fundraising walks, helps out at the animal shelter. If you ever need something done for the town, and it seems impossible, she's the person to go to."

Another hard worker, Mabel thought. No wonder she and Aunt Peggy had been such good friends. "What does Rory get out of all this work?"

Emily shrugged as they approached the spot where the road connected with the path to her own farm. "It's just who she is. Her husband's pretty much the same, working as a cop. They're both civic minded, but not interested in politics. They want to make the town a good, safe place to live, and not only for themselves and their daughter, but for everyone."

"That sounds too good to be true," Mabel said. "Two paragons of virtue in the same family?"

"You'll see. Rory brings out the best in everyone." Emily glanced anxiously down the path to her farm. "I need to get back to the goats. They get a little restless during the mid-phase of the moon. Unless there's anything else you need?"

"No, I'm good." Or she would be, as soon as she got some earplugs, phone service and 24/7 high-speed internet access.

CHAPTER SIX

As Mabel headed for the farmhouse, she noticed that Rory's battered green pickup truck was parked next to the barn. A tuxedo cat was lounging on the hood, but Mabel couldn't tell if it was the same one that had startled her last night. There were five or six other cats rubbing against Bettina's ankles at the entrance to the barn, and none of them was black and white, but there could have been more inside the barn or out hunting.

Mabel *hoped* they were out hunting, and that they had a craving for bird meat.

She hurried over to Bettina. "I can take over the feeding, if you'll show me where the supplies are."

Rory emerged from the barn. "We don't mind doing the feeding while you take care of other things, do we, Bettina?"

"Of course not." Bettina bent to pick up the calico that was meowing the loudest for attention, so she didn't see the face Rory was making. Mabel didn't need to have the expression interpreted for once; Rory was threatening some sort of dire consequences if Bettina was replaced as the chief cat feeder. It was the same sort of look that Mabel's grandmother, who was usually the sweetest person on the planet, had assumed whenever Mabel had missed a social cue and was about to hurt someone's feelings.

"The cats all love Bettina," Rory added with a final glare, in case her expression hadn't been clear before.

"I wish I could have a cat or two." Bettina rubbed her face against the cat's fur. "Unfortunately, my husband is allergic to them."

Her husband was dead, and Mabel was on the verge of saying that his allergies no longer mattered, when Rory intervened, changing the subject. "The cats will have to wait. We've got people coming to start the harvest this afternoon. I rounded up a few CSA members to fulfill their labor pledges. It won't be much, but at least we can get things started. If you want the whole harvest done before the rain, you'll need to get some full-time workers here as soon as possible. I can post some flyers, but you'll have to make the final decisions."

"I can do that," Mabel said.

"Good," Rory said. "If we want to be ready for the workers, we need to get the drying racks set up in the barn."

"Drying racks? I thought the garlic was already dry, and that's why we need to harvest it before the rains."

"The harvest is just the beginning," Bettina said. "It needs to air-dry for a few days after it's pulled up."

"So even if we harvest it all before the rain, it won't be ready in time for the market this weekend?"

"It will be fine for the market sales to individuals," Bettina said, still cuddling the calico cat. "Small batches of garlic dry quickly on their own, as long as they're not put in an airtight container. The drying racks are only necessary for large, commercial quantities. Especially for the restaurant orders. The crop has to be thoroughly cured before it goes into the packing crates."

"Come on into the barn with us," Rory said. "We'll show you how it's done."

"I can't right now," Mabel said. "I've got to go make the funeral arrangements."

"Let us know when the service is," Rory said. "We'll be there."

"I was hoping you could tell me when and where it should be," Mabel said. "Emily mentioned that Aunt Peggy wanted to be buried on the farm, but that's all I know."

Rory nodded. "Peggy always said she never wanted to leave this place. It's the only thing that's reconciled me to losing her. Better that she die here than in a hospital or assisted living facility. It would be fitting if she could be buried here too."

"I don't know," Bettina bent to drop the calico to the ground beside her feet. "I think Peggy was just joking about that. Besides, it can't be done. It's against public policy or something. That's what they told me, anyway, when I was making the arrangements for Scott. Burials have to be in a real cemetery."

"We should let Mabel take care of it," Rory said, urging Bettina into the barn. "We've got our own work to do. Peggy trusted you to make the decisions, Mabel. I'm sure you'll do the right thing."

Mabel wasn't so sure, but Rory had disappeared into the barn with Bettina before Mabel could express her doubts.

* * * *

The funeral home was on the edge of the downtown historic district. Mabel had passed it earlier today on the way to the library without even noticing that it was anything other than a stately old Victorian residence. Only the large size of the paved parking lot suggested otherwise, and she would have driven past it again if not for her GPS. The elegantly discreet sign at the front door confirmed that she was, in fact, at the Stevens Funeral Home.

The door was answered by a young man who invited her into the lobby and then introduced himself as Wayne Stevens, the funeral director. He looked to be barely out of college. His expensively somber suit, while perfectly tailored to his height, was loose on him, as if it were designed for someone whose frame had filled out more than his had. He anticipated her reaction to his age, and immediately volunteered that he represented the fourth generation of his family to work in the undertaking business. He'd practically been raised in the funeral home, he explained with a fond smile. His mother had brought him to work with her when he was a toddler, just as she herself had grown up in the funeral home with her father.

"So," he said, sounding confident that he'd established his credentials beyond any doubt, "how can we help you today?"

"I'm Mabel Skinner."

"Of course. You're here for your aunt. We've been expecting you." He herded Mabel down a plushly carpeted hallway. "We're so sorry for your loss."

"Thank you."

He brought her to a cozy little room with a tufted sofa and two wingback chairs. Discreet brochures for caskets were scattered across a coffee table. "Do you have any specific requests that we should know about?"

"Actually, I do." Mabel sank into one of the wing chairs. "Aunt Peggy wanted to be buried on the farm. Can you arrange that?"

"A private burial?" He slowly lowered himself into the chair beside her. "It's not the sort of thing that's done every day."

"If you can't do it, perhaps someone else can."

"It's not that we can't do it," he said with a flash of irritation that was more consistent with his actual age than his facade of maturity. "It's that you'd have to petition for the board of health to approve the creation of a family cemetery. The board only meets once a month, and their last meeting was a few days ago. There's no guarantee you'd get approved, and it might take several meetings or even an appeal to get the permits. We wouldn't want you to have to wait that long for closure, only to possibly get turned down, especially since your aunt has been waiting almost two weeks already for her final resting place."

"But I could wait, if I wanted to?"

"You could, but it's not ideal," he said, with all the gravity of someone three times his age. "You need to heal and to move on after your loss. That process starts with the funeral services."

"Before I decide, I'll need to check with my attorney."

He didn't even flinch, unlike most people threatened with legal action. "That's a good idea. I'm sure he'll tell you just how impractical it would be to do a burial on private land. You might consider cremation instead, and then you can bury her ashes on the farm. Unless, of course, that's not an option for you. Did your aunt have any particular religious or philosophical objections to cremation?"

That sort of question was exactly why Mabel would have preferred that someone else had made these arrangements. She didn't have the first clue about whether Aunt Peggy had preferred burial to cremation, and things only got more complicated after that initial decision: where to bury the body or the ashes, what type of wake or service to hold, whether a particular church or other spiritual leader should preside.

She needed to check with Emily and Rory again for more parameters. It was Mabel's decision, and she would make it, but not until she had all the necessary input for the algorithm. She was reluctant to admit to the funeral director just how little she knew about her aunt, so she settled for saying, "I'll get back to you after I talk to my attorney."

"Very well," the young funeral director said, discreetly sliding a business card into her hand. "Call us when you're ready to make the final arrangements. We're here to make this as simple for you as we can."

"There is one thing you could help me with. I'd like to claim my aunt's personal belongings."

"Of course." He excused himself and came back five minutes later with a twelve inch square white box, which he placed on the table in front of her. "Here you go."

The box was sealed with tape printed with the funeral home's name, address and phone number. Mabel broke the seal and looked inside. All it contained was a pair of eyeglasses and two gold, pineapple shaped earrings.

"Where's the rest?"

"That's all there was," he said. "Her clothes were disposed of, before we were contacted."

"What about her cell phone?"

"If she had one with her at the time of her passing, it would be in there."

"It's not."

Wayne glanced inside the box and shrugged. "Then she didn't have one on her."

"Are you sure? Could someone have taken it, thinking it would never be missed, since it had been so long and no one had come to claim her things?"

Once again, his somber maturity broke enough to reveal a touch of irritation at the suggestion that he or his associates might have misplaced a valuable personal effect. "We have never, in fifty-eight years of operating, lost a single item belonging to a client. We keep the personal effects in a safe, and only our most trusted employees have access to it."

"I suppose Aunt Peggy could have dropped her phone when she fell, and no one noticed it at the scene."

The slight flush on his face faded. "Have you talked to whoever found her? Or you could check with the first responders. All I know is that it wasn't given to us. You're welcome to look at the inventory that we get from the hospital, detailing the personal effects."

"I'd like that."

"Anything to set your mind at ease." He disappeared and returned again in half the time he'd taken to get the box of Aunt Peggy's belongings. He had a file in his hand, its contents kept in order with a clasp that threaded through the two holes punched in the top of each sheet of paper. He flipped the pages up to reveal the inventory sheet at the bottom.

Mabel looked at the document with its official seal. Wayne's signature at the bottom was gothically elaborate, like calligraphy. There were only two entries in the typed inventory: one (1) pair of eyeglasses, bifocal, intact; two (2) gold earrings, pineapple. No phone, and nothing else that might explain what she'd been doing out by the creek in the middle of the night.

She let the top pages flip back into place. "Do you have an extra copy of the death certificate? I'm still trying to understand how it happened. Drowning in a few inches of water just seems so wrong."

He undid one of the clasps and freed a sheet of paper to hand to her. "Denial is part of the grieving process. It has been our experience that denial is particularly common in cases of unusual accidental death. You'll come to accept that accidents do happen. It just takes time."

It seemed a little odd for such a young person to be talking about his extensive experience with death, but she supposed he had a great deal more experience with it than she did. Her own loss of her parents and then her grandparents hadn't taught her anything other than that life was unpredictable.

Mabel glanced at the death certificate. The estimated time of death was between midnight and four a.m., and the cause of death was drowning, with concussion as a contributory cause. That much was consistent with what Emily had told her, but there was more in the medical section. "This says that Aunt Peggy likely had high blood pressure and high cholesterol, which might have induced a stroke or light-headedness that led to her falling. Don't they know for sure?"

"There didn't seem to be any real reason to perform an autopsy, and no one was pushing for one," Wayne said. "A stroke is a reasonable assumption, given her weight and her well-known disdain for doctors."

Aunt Peggy had always been a large woman, although she'd transformed much of her earlier fat into muscle when she'd left her work as an accountant to start the garlic farm. After several years of working her fields, she'd still been a bit overweight, but active and seemingly healthy. She'd had to be, given the demands of farming. It had been twelve years since Mabel last saw her, though, and there could have been more changes on the farm than just the house renovation and the additional field beyond the creek. Aunt Peggy had believed in the power of raw garlic and other natural remedies to keep her healthy, but if she wasn't getting routine medical checkups, she could have had health problems that she didn't know about. Doctors called high blood pressure the silent killer, after all, and Aunt Peggy might have assumed that her garlic regimen was doing more for her health than it really was.

"I'm sure you're right," Mabel said, picking up the box and standing. "I won't take up any more of your time."

"It's perfectly all right," he said. "It's natural to have questions when you've lost a beloved family member."

He was saying all the right words, doing much better than Mabel herself could have done in his shoes, but she left feeling worse than when she'd arrived. Wayne had meant well, but he'd managed to remind her just how little she knew about her aunt, and how relatively unaffected she'd been by the loss. She knew, on an intellectual level, that it was sad that her aunt had died, but her heart just wasn't feeling it. She and her aunt had had so few interactions in the last dozen years that there was very little for her to miss. The strongest feeling she'd had after hearing of her aunt's death had been the niggling thought that she should have done more while Aunt Peggy was alive. That was regret, though, not grief.

And regrets, unlike grief, generally became worse over time. Mabel had to make up for her past thoughtlessness by making sure Aunt Peggy at least got the burial she'd wanted.

* * * *

Everyone's favorite librarian was busy with a patron, so Mabel was able to slip past her without risking another hug. It didn't take long to send her boss the information he'd requested. As long as she had internet access, she decided to see if she could hack her aunt's account with her phone service carrier. The account might have been flagged if the phone had been reported lost or stolen. If not, she could remotely install an app that would notify her if the phone was used.

Mabel had added her aunt's cell number to her own smartphone directory when she keyed in the other contacts that Rory had given her, and she already had Aunt Peggy's email address in her phone. Between that information and what was on the death certificate, it only took a few minutes to request a reset of the password on Aunt Peggy's account with the phone company. Hacking the email account to get the activation code to reset the password was even easier; on the third try, Mabel used her own name as the email account's password and was rewarded with the home screen. She had to scroll down a good distance before she found the last email she'd sent her aunt a couple of months ago. It had been read, so Aunt Peggy had received the message and known that Mabel had remembered her. That was a relief, although it didn't completely erase the guilt she felt over not doing more for her aunt.

Mabel returned to the phone carrier's website to check the status of her aunt's phone. It was still active, as far as the phone company was concerned, and hadn't been cancelled or reported lost. The billing didn't itemize calls, but Aunt Peggy had a prepaid, bare-bones plan, so there was a separate charge for each of the three or four text messages she sent each month. In fact, she'd sent one the night she'd died, a little after midnight. Mabel would have loved a record of the message, but she'd have needed the phone itself to see the actual text. Or a court order.

More surprising than the existence of the text, was that it had been sent so late at night. Aunt Peggy had always been asleep by ten, and had been shocked by Mabel's much later hours. Anything after midnight, Aunt

Peggy had said, was an affront to a person's circadian rhythm, and likely to cause serious health effects.

Mabel scrolled through the list of other texts, none of which had been sent after five p.m. Just that one late text on the night she'd died. What on earth had Aunt Peggy been doing? She hadn't just been awake, but she'd been wandering around the farm, in an area she didn't even particularly like, with a cell phone that had since disappeared.

Mabel copied the destination number of the text message into her smartphone directory to check out later. Maybe one of Aunt Peggy's friends would recognize the number and it would help to explain what had happened that night. Wayne at the funeral home would tell her that she was just feeding her denial, looking for something other than a freak accident to explain her aunt's death, and maybe he was right, but she didn't think it was that simple. As she'd been forced to realize, she hadn't been that close to her aunt, so the loss wasn't as big a shock as it would have been if someone she'd known better had died suddenly. Plus, she wasn't imagining the serious aberrations in her aunt's behavior the night she'd died. Those were hard facts.

Too bad the authorities hadn't paid more attention to the aberrations before leaping to conclusions about her cause of death. Mabel had a hard time believing her aunt had been in poor health. She'd been such an advocate of the health benefits of farm life. Mabel vaguely recalled being shown medical studies that gave some legitimacy to the health claims for garlic.

She opened a new browser tab and did a search on "health benefits garlic." She didn't have time to read even a fraction of the more than eight million hits, but a quick glance confirmed that sources ranging from illiterate crackpots to highly respected medical researchers, all agreed that there were definite correlations between ingestion of raw, chopped garlic and the health benefits of lowered blood pressure and improved cholesterol levels.

It just didn't make sense that Aunt Peggy could have been in such bad health that she'd had a stroke. Sure, she was a little overweight, but she didn't drink or smoke, and she got plenty of daily exercise. Mabel found a site discussing the risk factors for a stroke, and concluded that, notwithstanding her weight, Aunt Peggy wouldn't have been in the high-risk category unless she'd had both high blood pressure and high cholesterol. It seemed improbable that Aunt Peggy had either condition, let alone both, considering how much garlic she ate.

Mabel needed to call her attorney about looking into the procedure for a burial on private land anyway, so she decided she might as well ask him about getting an autopsy too. It wouldn't change the fact of Aunt Peggy's death, but it might help her make sense of it. If there was scientific evidence that Aunt Peggy had, in fact, had a stroke, then Mabel could let go of the niggling suspicion that something less natural had happened to her aunt, something that Mabel might have prevented if she'd stayed in closer touch with her aunt. On the other hand, if the death was not due to a stroke, then Mabel owed it to her aunt to find out what—or who—had caused her death.

Her attorney would know how to arrange everything. Her cell phone was powered up, but the service was too glitchy, even here in town, to use it to call him. Maybe she could borrow a phone for a few minutes. It might be worth having to endure yet another hug if Josefina would let her use the library's phone to make a collect call to the lawyer.

Mabel closed out her internet session and headed for the lobby. Josefina wasn't at the checkout desk, but there might be another option. She'd assumed that the pay phone booths lining the lobby wall were remnants of a previous era, abandoned by the phone company and not worth the effort to remove, but they'd been remarkably well maintained. Maybe they still worked.

The current checkout librarian was a high school girl, still in her private school uniform. She glanced up from her Kindle. "Can I help you with something?"

Mabel pointed at the telephone booths. "Do they actually work?"

"Oh, yes," she said. "I know it's strange in this day and age, but we get a lot of tourists in the summer, and you know how most of the phone carriers don't work very well around here, so we were always getting people coming in, desperate to use our landline. The Friends of West Slocum Library purchased vintage phone booths and had them installed. They make a good profit during the summer. It helps to pay for the high-speed internet service we have."

"Brilliant." Mabel headed for the nearest booth.

"You can even use your credit card to pay for the call," the young librarian called out. "You don't need cash."

Even better. Cash was such an outdated concept.

"If you need a phone after hours," the librarian/salesperson said, "there's one outside too."

"Thanks." Mabel closed the booth's door behind her, and was immediately aware of the absence of all of the little sounds that hadn't consciously registered before. Too bad her bedroom at the farmhouse didn't have this level of soundproofing.

Mabel swiped her credit card and dialed Jeff Wright's number. It was his private number, that only she and his family members had, so he picked it up himself on the third ring. The distinctive static of a speakerphone crackled as he said hello.

"It's Mabel," she said. "I need you to look into the rules for burying bodies on private land."

There was a pause before he said, "How many bodies are you planning to bury?"

"Just one. Don't worry. I didn't kill anyone. It's my aunt. She wanted to be buried on her farm, and the local funeral home director said I can't do it without going through the local board of health. You can handle that, right?"

"I'd have to work through a local attorney, and I'd have to do some research first to see what the correct procedure is," he said. "The funeral homes usually know this sort of thing better than most lawyers, so at a guess, I'd say he's right. You'd need to get the approval of some local board or another."

"Look into it for me, would you?" Mabel said. "I also need to know how to get an autopsy done."

"Your aunt's, I presume?"

"Something just doesn't feel right about how she died," Mabel said. "The cause of death is pretty speculative. I'd like to know for sure."

"If the authorities didn't see any reason to do an autopsy before now, you'll have to hire someone yourself, and it's…not inexpensive."

"You don't have to be polite about it. I know I'm cheap." She couldn't help thinking of how her aunt had used her name as her email account password, and how she'd bragged about her to friends, both signs of just how much she'd cared about her niece, even if she'd never told Mabel herself. "Whatever the cost, it's worth it."

"Never thought I'd hear you say that." The faint sound of a pen writing on paper came through the speaker phone. "I'll look into it right away. I'll send you an email tomorrow, when I've got some options for you."

"It may be late before I respond," she said. "The farmhouse doesn't have internet, and my cell phone isn't working."

"Do you want me to call the carrier and get a replacement for you?"

"It's not the phone," she explained. "There's no service here."

"And you didn't just turn around and come back here?"

"I can manage without constant internet access for a few days. There's service at the library, and if I can find my aunt's phone, I can add internet service to the plan. Otherwise, I'll see about getting wired internet service at the house."

"I didn't think you'd be in West Slocum that long. It usually takes a few weeks to get the service installed. I'm sure your aunt's lawyer could handle matters there without you once you get the process started."

"I can't leave here until I get Aunt Peggy buried," she said. "As soon as I get that done, trust me, I won't even wait for the grave to be filled in before I'm on my way back to civilization."

CHAPTER SEVEN

Now that Mabel had handed the matter of Aunt Peggy's burial off to her attorney, she could forget about it and concentrate on more immediate problems, like finding her aunt's phone. She needed dinner first, so she stopped at a pizza parlor. That took care of planning for her dinner now and breakfast in the morning. Finding a grocery store could wait a little longer.

Back at the farm, Mabel tossed the pizza box on the kitchen table and filled a glass with water. She wolfed down the first slice, and then began a methodical search for the phone. Before, when she'd thought Emily might know where it was, she'd only checked the most likely spots. Now, she was determined to look everywhere. She started in the kitchen, carrying the second slice of pizza with her, and went around the room in a clockwise pattern, opening cabinets and drawers, not just looking on the surface, but even getting down on her knees to peer underneath the massive country table and the sideboard. She opened the door at the far end of the dining area, to find a small laundry and mechanicals room with the circuit breakers that Emily had forgotten to show her. All she found was some dust and a fork that had somehow ended up beneath the harvest gold refrigerator.

She used the same methodical approach in the rest of the rooms. It took a couple hours before she'd searched the entire house, including looking beneath the furniture cushions, which was where Mabel often lost her own gadgets.

Mabel finally had to face the fact that if she hadn't found the phone inside the house yet, she wasn't going to. If the phone hadn't been on Aunt Peggy when she died, and it wasn't in the farmhouse, then where could it be?

Mabel munched on a cold slice of pizza while she mulled over the possibilities. When it came time to put the remainder of the pizza in the refrigerator for breakfast, she declared an end to thinking about the phone. It was ten o'clock, and time to report to work. The moved-up deadline for the next app she'd been assigned meant that she needed to put in some overtime tonight and the next few nights, instead of wasting her energy on problems that couldn't be programmed away.

Four hours later, Mabel reached a stopping point. It was still fairly early for her, only two a.m., but she'd been up earlier than usual, and she could feel her concentration slipping. She stretched and went to the refrigerator for some of the orange juice Emily had brought over with breakfast, hoping the sugar would perk her up.

Mabel drank the rest of the orange juice directly from the bottle, and then tossed the empty container into the sink. She'd been making good progress with her coding, so assuming she didn't hit a major bug, she'd be able to meet the moved up deadline easily.

Mabel turned out the kitchen lights and climbed the stairs to her bedroom, carrying her laptop with her, planning to do a couple more hours of work. The bedroom was intensely dark, much like her own home in Maine on nights like this, when the sky was clear and the crescent moon was more decorative than illuminating.

All she needed was a small bit of artificial illumination, enough that her computer screen wouldn't be too jarring in contrast with the darkness that kept out the intrusions of the outside world. The tiny bedside lamp did that perfectly, giving her just enough light to avoid bumping into furniture in a room that was still new to her, without radiating far enough to rob her of the comforting sense of enveloping darkness.

The setup was perfect for her, but she had to wonder how Aunt Peggy had felt about the farmhouse at night. Not so much the darkness—her aunt had gone to bed shortly after the sun set—but the feeling of isolation. Mabel was used to not being able to see her neighbors, but her gregarious aunt might have preferred being able to at least see Emily's farm from here.

Mabel shook herself. She wasn't usually this maudlin about anything or anyone. Maybe the funeral home director had been more right than she'd realized at the time. If so, she must have felt more attachment to her aunt than either of them had ever imagined. Or at least more than Mabel had ever imagined. Her aunt might have felt differently. She had used Mabel's name—against the most basic advice on internet security—as her email account password, after all.

Her attorney, who was the closest she had to a best friend, would have been stunned to hear such sentimental thoughts. He would never say it, but she knew he thought she was a heartless misanthropist. Well, she was, she supposed, but not, as he believed, because she'd been irrevocably scarred by her parents' sudden death. She didn't understand people the way she understood algorithms and syllogisms and didacticisms, so she stuck with the things she did understand.

Amused by the thought of her attorney's reaction to her unexpected bout of sentimentality, Mabel let go of her regrets, at least for the moment, and prepared to get on with her work. She closed the curtains, wishing they were thick enough to block out the cacophony of too-early early birds. She'd have to see if there were sound deadening curtains in town tomorrow, although she supposed earplugs would be simpler. She'd forgotten to get the plugs today, but she'd make them her first priority tomorrow.

Mabel pulled off her bra and replaced her jeans with pajama bottoms before climbing onto the bed and hunching over her laptop.

She'd barely gotten back into the flow of her program when she heard something through the uninsulated walls and window. She wasn't sure exactly what it was, but it hadn't been the usual sounds of a house settling or the barn cats roaming the property. It had sounded vaguely metallic, like the squeak of a wheelbarrow or wagon axle. Cats sometimes made equally high-pitched sounds, but it hadn't sounded like something that might come from a living creature. At least not a mammal; she wasn't so sure about the local birds. The nocturnal birds she was familiar with had lower-pitched sounds, but maybe the birds here were different, or one of the diurnal species had gotten confused and stayed up past its bedtime.

Mabel set her computer aside and went over to the window to pull the curtains back and look outside. She didn't see anything moving, or anything that seemed out of place. Mostly what she saw was pure darkness. The farmhouse didn't have any exterior lights on, and the streetlight barely illuminated the first couple hundred feet of the driveway, without any chance of reaching past the marshy area, all the way to the house and barn.

She let the curtain fall back into place, belatedly realizing it probably hadn't been a good idea to stand there in the first place. Fortunately, the table-side lamp didn't throw off enough light to reach all the way to the window, so she wouldn't have been more than a vague shadow, rather than a clear silhouette, if anyone was watching the house.

She was just being silly, imagining someone skulking around the property. She wasn't usually this irrational or paranoid. Maybe everyone was right, and she was having a delayed reaction to the loss of her aunt. Mabel returned to the bed and picked up her laptop again, confident that its promise of logic and reason would settle her. She was perfectly safe here on the farm.

The part of her that kept dwelling on her regrets whispered: *Aunt Peggy thought she was safe here, and then she died in a freak accident in a place where she shouldn't have been at that time of night.*

What if someone had, in fact, killed Aunt Peggy? She could have been pushed, not simply fallen into the creek.

And what if whoever killed Aunt Peggy wanted something on the farm, something that Mabel now owned? What if Aunt Peggy's killer came back to finish the job, by killing Mabel?

Suddenly, being isolated in a dark place, without a phone or internet access, didn't seem like such a great thing.

Sure, there was a solid new lock on the front door that would stop anyone without heavy equipment or blasting powder, but opening the back door required nothing more than a little knowledge and just the right amount of a hip bump. How many people knew about that? Only Emily or pretty much everyone Peggy knew? Mabel had a feeling it was the latter. It should have been reassuring that only friends could enter the house, but if Aunt Peggy had been murdered, it was probably by someone who knew her, someone she considered a friend. Wasn't that usually the case, that the killer and victim knew each other? She'd read somewhere that stranger-murder was actually quite rare.

Mabel jumped up from the bed and closed and locked the window before dragging the heavy dresser over to barricade the bedroom door. She didn't care if she was being paranoid. It was better to be safe than dead like Aunt Peggy. And if she was just imagining the threat, there was no one here to see her foolishness.

She tried to get back into her work, but she'd lost the flow and couldn't find it again. The house was too silent. No wind, no sound of crickets or peepers, no annoyed meows from the barn cats. Nothing.

She couldn't work, and she really couldn't sleep, not with her body sending out fight-or-flight signals. She needed to figure out what was setting her nerves on edge. She liked the dark, she liked being alone in it, and yet something was making her wish there were bright lights and someone she trusted nearby, if not actually in the room with her. She wasn't a scaredy-cat, and yet she could feel the tension in her neck, as she strained to listen for any telltale sounds of an intruder.

If her adrenaline glands were working overtime, she ought to pay attention. Ignoring subtle warning signs was likely what got Aunt Peggy killed, whether it was a person or her own biochemistry that had killed her. Mabel wasn't going to make the same mistake.

She was just about to get dressed and drive into town to stay at a hotel when a wave of exhaustion hit her, and she realized she was finally feeling sleepy. She could hear normal night sounds again, not the unnatural silence from before.

Whatever threat she'd sensed before was gone now, and there was no need to risk falling asleep at the wheel of her Mini Cooper by driving into town. She turned off the light and slid under the sheets. With a little luck, she'd be able to get an early start on her errands tomorrow. First on her agenda was a new lock for the kitchen door. Then earplugs.

No, before that, there was something more important to do. She had to call her attorney and find out what he'd learned about getting an autopsy. She planned to tell him to go ahead with the autopsy, regardless of the cost.

Something was rotten here on Stinkin' Stuff Farm, and it wasn't just the compost heap.

* * * *

The stupid birds were having a frat party. Didn't they know that parties were supposed to happen at civilized hours? Like midnight? The birds back in Maine weren't this noisy. At least, not that she'd ever noticed. Most likely, it was because her five-year-old cottage had much better insulation against both weather and sound than this two-hundred-year-old farmhouse.

Mabel sandwiched her head between two pillows to muffle the sound. The stupid birds took it as a challenge and chirped louder.

She was finally drifting back to sleep, when she heard a new sound. The engine of a pickup truck. It came up the driveway, idled outside the barn, and then backfired before subsiding into silence. A moment later, the truck doors opened and slammed shut. Two women's voices, the words unintelligible, replaced the sound of the engine.

Rory and Bettina, here to feed the cats, Mabel assumed. No one would need to feed them if they'd just do what cats are supposed to do and go after the noisy feast flying above them.

It took a few more minutes, given how slowly Mabel's brain worked before noon, but eventually she remembered that she had a dresser barricading her bedroom door, and she needed to do something about it. Not just moving it, but figuring out what had scared her last night. Rory was just the person to ask.

Mabel dragged herself out of bed and made herself presentable, for a given value of presentable. This was a farm, after all. No need for makeup or pumps or even a business casual wardrobe. Yesterday's relatively clean jeans and a fresh t-shirt were more than adequate.

Rory and Bettina had finished feeding the cats and were moving plastic crates that were about twice the length of a standard milk crate, but only half the height. A massive tractor, twice the size of Mabel's car, had been backed into the barn. A wagon was attached to the tractor, and a couple dozen of the plastic crates had been loaded into it. Bettina was in the back of the barn, where there were tall stacks of crates.

Rory had just carried a load of crates over to the wagon, where several other stacks were already collected, and was about to go back for another batch when she caught sight of Mabel. "Good morning!"

"No such thing," Mabel said. "Mornings are evil."

Rory laughed. "I forgot. Peggy said you were a night owl. Don't worry. You'll get used to mornings on the farm, and today really is a glorious one. Not too hot, not too humid, and no rain in the forecast for at least a couple more days. Perfect garlic harvesting weather."

"If you say so."

"I do." Rory climbed into the wagon and pointed to the stacks of crates littering the floor of the barn near the tailgate. "Make yourself useful, and hand me some of those crates."

Mabel picked up the first stack and handed it to Rory.

"I stopped by the university yesterday afternoon," Rory said, "and posted a notice at the career development office, announcing that you'd be interviewing applicants at eleven o'clock today, and they should come prepared to stay and work if they're hired."

"I can write the checks," Mabel said, "but it would make more sense for you to interview them."

Rory shook her head. "It's got to be you. I wouldn't want to be accused of nepotism. My daughter's applying."

"I don't even know what's involved in the harvest."

"You just need willing workers, good attitude, no particular training. The harvest is simple enough. You pull as many garlic plants as you can hold, cut the stems about six inches from the bulb and lay both pieces in a crate. When the crate's full, it goes into the wagon to come back to the barn and get threaded into the openings of the drying racks." Rory pointed at what looked like a small table, about a foot tall, placed on sawhorses. Instead of a solid surface across the top, though, the racks had a wire mesh with openings about the size of a garlic plant's stem. "Once the racks are full of garlic, we'll move them into a shed for the next few weeks, depending on the weather, until they're dry enough for long-term storage."

That didn't sound too difficult. Still, interviews weren't her strong suit, regardless of which side of the table she was on. She'd gotten her current job by doing an app on spec and emailing it to the company she wanted to work for.

"Are you sure you couldn't do the interviews? I don't care if you hire your daughter."

"Nope. It's got to be you," Rory said. "My daughter doesn't actually want the job. She's just fifteen, and perfectly happy to be too young for most jobs. I'm tired of her sitting around the house, texting and eating and complaining about being bored, so I told her that if she wanted me to pay her phone bill, she's got to apply for this job. I haven't told her yet that she's still too young to be allowed to drive the tractor, so I'm counting on you to break the bad news to her."

Interviewing just one young girl who was guaranteed to be hired wouldn't be so bad. But there would probably be other applicants. "How many people do you think will show up for jobs?"

"Not enough," Rory said. "You need at least three or four people. Six would be better. I doubt you'll have more applicants than that, so you can hire pretty much anyone who has a Social Security card, is at least fourteen years old, and doesn't creep you out."

"I can do that." She might even find someone qualified to oversee the space at the farmers' market for her. "What about the paperwork?"

"Peggy should have applications and tax forms in her office," Rory said. "She was planning to hire some workers earlier in the summer, but she changed her mind."

"Any idea why?"

Rory glanced behind her to see if Bettina was in sight. "I thought she was going to hire Bettina as a sort of forewoman, but the next thing I knew, Peggy said she was going to do the harvest all by herself. No farmhands, so there was no need for anyone to oversee them. She didn't say why she changed her mind, and it wasn't really any of my business."

Rory's tone didn't quite match her words, probably because she considered everything to be her business. She was irritated, either because Aunt Peggy hadn't confided in her, or perhaps because she'd been looking forward to getting Bettina off her hands for a while, and was disappointed when that didn't happen.

"Aunt Peggy may have been struggling financially," Mabel said. "I reviewed her ledgers, and it looked like she couldn't afford any help."

"That's possible." Rory said as Bettina approached with another stack of crates. "Farming isn't exactly a lucrative business, even in the best of times."

Mabel knew Rory didn't mean it as a reproach, but the reminder still stung. She hadn't realized her aunt was struggling financially, but that was no excuse for her neglect. "I guess that rules out greed as the reason why someone might have killed Aunt Peggy."

Bettina gasped, shoved the crates onto the tailgate, and raced out of the barn.

"What was that about?" Mabel said.

Rory placed the crates on top of another stack. "We try not to mention death around Bettina. She still can't face it. Not her husband's death, not anyone else's."

"But she knows Aunt Peggy died. That's why she has to come here and feed the cats."

"She knows, but that's different from talking about it. And much different from thinking about suspicious circumstances. There were some silly rumors when her husband died. All completely without merit, and no one with half a brain believed them, but I'm sure Bettina heard them, and they must have been upsetting."

"I'm not crazy or stupid," Mabel said. "There's something suspicious about Aunt Peggy's death."

"You mean the drowning in just a couple inches of water?" Rory said. "I was shocked too, but it was a freak accident. They do happen. I did some research, and I couldn't find any statistics, but it's not without precedent that someone hits her head, falls into a pool of water, and then drowns while unconscious."

"It's not just the freak accident," Mabel said. "I've got too many unanswered questions. What was she doing out in the fields in the middle of the night? She wasn't a night owl like me. But she was out late at night. She even sent a text while she was out there, and she hardly ever texted anyone. And on top of that, the phone is missing."

Rory raised her arms, threatening a hug, and then dropped them again as she remembered that Mabel wasn't as touchy-feely as her aunt. "It's natural to look for reasons behind a loved one's death, even when there is no satisfactory answer. It's part of the grief process."

"I'm not grieving," Mabel insisted. "I didn't know Aunt Peggy that well. I loved her because she was my aunt, but I didn't really know her."

"That's denial talking," Rory said, jumping down from the wagon. "Come on, we need to get the rest of the crates. I'll show you where they're stored."

"I'll humor you if you'll humor me," Mabel said, as she headed for the back of the barn. "You've got to admit it was odd for Aunt Peggy to be awake and anywhere near the creek at midnight. And you haven't seen her phone since then."

"Farmers can work odd hours." Rory lifted a stack of crates to tower over her head. "The phone is probably with her personal effects at the funeral home."

"It's not. I checked." Mabel picked up her own smaller stack of crates. "Forget the details for a minute, and let's say I'm right, that someone wanted to hurt Aunt Peggy. Who would that someone be?"

"I can't think of anyone. She liked everyone, and everyone liked her." Rory placed her crates on the tailgate and climbed up to move them to the back of the wagon.

"There's got to be someone she liked less than everyone else. What about Larry Rose?"

Rory came back for Mabel's stack of crates. "How do you know about him?"

"I met him at Darryl Santangelo's office."

"That reminds me. You should talk to Darryl again, to see if he knows anyone who wants to pick up a day's field work." Rory jumped down from the wagon. "You think Larry might have killed Peggy? He's loud and obnoxious, but he wouldn't hurt anyone. Least of all, your aunt."

That was disappointing to hear. He would have made such a good suspect. "Are you sure there's no one else who might have been angry with Aunt Peggy?"

"I'm sure." Rory was on her way back to get more crates, and Mabel followed her. "Trust me. Everyone loved Peggy. Her customers adored her. You've met Emily, and I can vouch for Peggy's other close neighbors. An organic garlic farm doesn't produce any noxious fumes or loud noises or wandering livestock. No reason for anyone to get upset."

Mabel thought about compost heaps, noisy birds and wandering barn cats, but the neighbors couldn't really complain about them. They were facts of life in an agricultural community, and much smaller nuisances that most other types of farms. Emily's goats had much more potential for doing damage.

"What about the other way around?" Mabel said. "Did any of the neighbors ever do anything to damage Aunt Peggy's garlic? That could have started a feud between them."

Rory placed her latest stack of crates on the tailgate and nodded toward the barn doors. "The land on that side of the property, on the other side of the house, is mostly wetlands, where the creek widens a bit. Nothing could cross that. The back of the property abuts a residential subdivision. No wildlife there, other than a few chickens."

"What about the other side?" Mabel set her own stack of crates beside Rory's.

"Just Emily's farm, and they were the best of friends." Rory pushed the stacks toward the back without climbing up into the wagon.

"There has to be someone who didn't like her," Mabel said. "No one's universally loved."

"Peggy was," Rory said sadly. "Even the local town officials loved her. She's been a godsend for the barn cat program at the animal shelter. They could always count on her to take in the unadoptable cats, so they wouldn't have to live in cages all their lives."

An appreciation of cats was something Mabel shared with her aunt. She'd never owned one, but had always felt a kinship with them. They were night creatures, after all, and had the good sense to be quiet in the morning. "Maybe someone thought Peggy had stolen their cat, and came to take it back, and they got into an argument."

"The barn cats weren't anyone's pets," Rory said. "The ones that aren't out-and-out feral have other annoying traits. They may not be afraid of people, but most of them don't like humans much. A few will occasionally tolerate being patted or picked up, like the calico, but most of them tend to be aggressive. That's why the animal shelter gave up on finding homes for them. They definitely aren't confiscated pets."

"I still think there's something odd about Aunt Peggy's death."

"I know." Rory reached out and patted Mabel's upper arm before Mabel could avoid the contact. "We've had some time to get used to her being gone. It's still fresh for you. It will fade, and you'll be able to accept it."

Bettina could be heard talking to the cats outside the barn doors, and Mabel caught the name of Bettina's dead husband. Sometimes, as Mabel herself knew only too well from the loss of her parents and grandparents, the pain of loss stayed for a very long time before fading. What Mabel felt now was different. She wasn't grieving, she was confused by things that didn't fit any pattern. She needed answers, and she would get them with the autopsy.

CHAPTER EIGHT

Mabel found the employment paperwork in Aunt Peggy's office, in a file marked "hiring packets." It contained a brief application form, tax forms and a checklist for what had to be collected from the workers and even what had to be done with each item, from simply keeping it in a file to sending copies to various government agencies and the insurance agent. Aunt Peggy would have been a gifted app developer, with her sense of organization.

All Mabel had to do was make more copies of everything in the file. There was no copier or scanner in Aunt Peggy's office, but the library in town was sure to have one. Mabel needed to check in with her boss anyway. Considering that it was still only nine a.m., she had plenty of time to get into town, visit the library and even check in with the farmers' market manager to see if he knew of anyone looking for farm work, and still be back for the interviews at eleven.

Mabel ran upstairs to change into fresher jeans for her trip into town. She was on her way back downstairs when she heard the kitchen door open and a voice yell out, "Hello! Anyone home?"

She thought it was Emily, but wasn't entirely sure. After last night, and the suspicions she was harboring over Aunt Peggy's death, she wasn't taking any chances. She crept downstairs, prepared to run out the front door if it turned out to be someone other than Emily.

Mabel peered around the corner. It was Emily, all right. She had left an egg basket on the massive kitchen table, and was searching through the cabinets near the sink. It looked more methodical than someone simply trying to figure out where the glasses were kept, or looking for the coffee supplies. Emily opened the upper cabinet closest to the refrigerator, went through the contents as if she were taking an inventory, and then moved on to the adjoining cabinet, repeating the process systematically.

"Looking for something in particular?" Mabel said from the doorway.

Emily started and put her hand over her chest. "You almost gave me a heart attack. I thought you were out in the barn with Rory and Bettina."

Mabel waved the hiring file. "I was getting the paperwork for the farm workers. They'll be here later this morning."

Emily leaned against the counter, still a little breathless from being startled. "I brought you some eggs. My husband's gone for a couple weeks, and he eats more of them than I do. I'll have extras until he gets back, and I thought you might be able to use some of them."

"Shouldn't they be refrigerated?" Mabel said. "Not stored in a cabinet?"

"What?" Emily glanced behind her. "Oh. The cabinets. I was just checking to see what supplies you had on hand. You'll be expected to feed the farm workers. I thought Peggy might have had some supplies on hand, but the cupboard is pretty bare. If you want, I can make a list of what you'll need."

"I can call for pizza. I stumbled across a good place last night."

Emily shook her head, amused. "You want to fuel them, not weigh them down so they just want to take a nap. Sandwiches and fruit are the usual thing."

"I'm going into town now," Mabel said. "I'll stop by the grocery store deli on the way home."

"Take a look at their platter menu while you're there," Emily said. "Not for the workers, but for the memorial service. If you don't like the selection at the grocery store, I can give you the names of some local caterers."

"I'm not ready to deal with the memorial service yet." She suspected that mentioning the autopsy would upset Aunt Peggy's friends, who didn't think there was anything suspicious about her death, so Mabel settled for saying, "There are some complications with the arrangements."

"I understand." Emily emptied the contents of her egg basket into the refrigerator. "I brought you a crock of the garlic-flavored goat cheese that Peggy and I collaborated on. I hope you'll want to continue the partnership. It's been a really popular product."

There had been something in Aunt Peggy's journal about the collaboration. Mabel had only noticed because her aunt had begun preparing a spreadsheet on the costs and expenses of their partnership. All the other spreadsheets were complete, up to the time of her death, but the one for the partnership was spotty, missing chunks of data that Emily would have been responsible for. Mabel had wondered how the two of them could have worked together.

Aunt Peggy, despite her low-tech ways, was extremely organized, keeping detailed records. Emily seemed a great deal more random, and the blanks in their partnership spreadsheet seemed to confirm Mabel's impression.

"I'm not ready to make any major decisions yet," Mabel said. "Not until we get the crop harvested."

"There's no rush." Emily closed the refrigerator door. "I've got plenty of garlic for the next month or so. I just wanted you to keep it in mind for the future."

"I will. After things settle down a bit and I'm not too exhausted to think."

"Have you tried chamomile tea before you go to bed? I can bring you some the next time I visit. I grew more than enough for my own use."

Mabel didn't need herbal remedies. She just needed some peace and quiet. Instead, she had noisy birds and other uninvited visitors. Admittedly, some of them were trying to help, but they were still distracting. "You didn't happen to come over here late last night, did you? I thought I heard someone out in the fields."

"I go to bed with the chickens. Literally." She raised the egg basket and shook it for emphasis. "And then I sleep like a log. My husband is always telling me about thunderstorms that shook him out of our bed, and I never even realized it was raining until I got outside and there were puddles everywhere."

"Then you wouldn't have noticed if you had a late night visitor too."

Emily shook her head. "Sorry. It's probably just wildlife. Or things creaking. With all the outbuildings and equipment on a farm, there's always something settling or being jostled by the wind or the critters."

"It felt … I don't know. Intentional. Sentient. Something like that. It went quiet when I looked out the window, and started up again when I wasn't looking."

"It's just the isolation," Emily said. "I got anxious over every little sound when we first moved to the farm, and my husband was away. I don't know if Peggy told you, but he's a business consultant. Does on-site observation and implementation for at least a week at a time. His first contract after we moved here was for a full month, and he had to leave practically the moment the moving van was emptied. I still haven't let him forget the way he left me to do all the unpacking, but to be fair, it was my idea to buy the farm, and I knew he'd be gone a lot. That was the reason I wanted the farm, actually, so I'd have something I cared about when he was gone. Anyway, I got used to it, and so will you."

"You're probably right." About being nervous in strange surroundings, at least. She doubted it was the isolation that had set her nerves on edge last night. She was isolated in Maine too, even more so than here, considering how few people ever ventured onto her property back there, compared to the constant stream of visitors she had here. Still, she supposed she'd long since grown accustomed to the sounds of the home she'd spent most of her life in, and it was natural to be hyper-aware of the different sounds when staying in a new place.

"You don't sound completely convinced," Emily said. "If you need me to stay with you for a night or two while my husband's gone, I can."

"No, thanks." The only thing worse than noises outside, as far as Mabel was concerned, was noises inside the house, in her personal space. "There is one thing that would put my mind at ease. I checked with the funeral home, and they don't have her phone, but she must have had it with her when she died. She sent a text right around the estimated time of death. I can't help thinking that there was someone with her when she died, and that person killed her and then took the phone. Can you think of anyone who hated Peggy enough to do that? Someone who wasn't satisfied with killing her, and might come back to destroy the farm?"

"Peggy? Hated? No way. Everyone loved her."

"Still, there's got to be someone she didn't get along with. We've all got at least one irritant in our lives."

Emily leaned back against the refrigerator to think. "Well, there was the stock grower she was suing."

"Litigation can definitely take the edge off a friendship." Mabel hadn't personally known any of the owners of the company where her parents had been killed in an industrial accident, but it had been acrimonious. Even as a child, protected by her grandparents from most of the legal proceedings, she had felt the tension. She could only imagine how her grandparents had felt, having to face the people responsible for the deaths of their only child and his wife. There was no way they could have remained cordial after that ordeal.

"There was nothing personal about Peggy's lawsuit. Just business. She bought some seed stock for a new heirloom variety of garlic from a farmer in Rhode Island, Al Soares, and apparently it was infected with white rot, which ruined her new field. She wanted money from him, compensation for the one season's harvest, not blood. She wasn't even asking for long-term damages, because she found a way to put the field to good use with the lavender. Planting the field in lavender was a significant investment, but it paid off eventually. She's got one customer who buys at least half of it, in bulk, for making soap. That same customer buys some of the garlic too, and some of my rosemary, to make garlic-rosemary soap."

"Sounds like soup, not soap."

"It does, doesn't it?" Emily said. "But there's a demand for it, and every little bit helps keep small farms afloat."

Mabel sighed. "I'm trying to find some suspects for the police to investigate, and you're telling me Peggy even got along well with the guy who infected her field."

"They didn't get along, exactly, and the lawsuit is still active," Emily said. "He still owes her for that failed crop. It's just that, as far as lawsuits go, it was fairly amicable."

Mabel still thought someone ought to look into whether the grower felt differently. They should also be looking into any other suspects she might be able to round up. Like Larry Rose, the rival grower. And maybe, just maybe, Emily, who'd been snooping through Peggy's kitchen, after all.

* * * *

Josefina, dressed in a paler shade of pink today, was busy with a patron. Mabel waved at her on the way to the computer room.

There were only three emails from her boss today, asking for a status report and making a couple minor changes to the various projects she was working on. She'd never missed a deadline before, and she wouldn't now. It wouldn't be easy, though. Finishing the app for Friday was a full-time job in itself, and that was before she factored in the demands of the farm, and the effects of experiencing too-early mornings.

Mabel was about to log off when an email arrived from her lawyer. In a bullet-pointed list, he: 1) gave her the address of Peggy's attorney, who was expecting to see her at eleven tomorrow morning to sign the papers for appointment as the estate's personal representative; 2) advised against trying for a private burial permit, unless there was no other option, and 3) provided three estimates for autopsy services. She added the appointment to her phone's calendar before considering how to respond to the other two items in his email. She still needed to check with Aunt Peggy's friends to see if they knew whether she'd had any objections to cremation, so she replied with instructions to hold off on doing anything about the private burial. The cost of the autopsy was enough to make her hesitate, but it wasn't anything she couldn't afford, and, regardless of what Rory and Emily thought, Mabel was certain something was wrong. She hadn't imagined the noises on the farm last night. The cost of the autopsy was a small price to pay to get some peace of mind. Mabel finished her response with the authorization to go ahead with the autopsy, and then logged off.

She still needed to make some copies of the hiring packets, and that meant venturing into the lobby, where the copy machine and everyone's favorite librarian were both located. Initially, Josefina was too busy to notice her, but by the time Mabel had finished making a dozen copies of the documents, Josefina had finished with all her other patrons.

Mabel might have been able to pretend she didn't hear a whispered greeting, but the checkout area was sufficiently separated from the reading areas that even the librarians felt free to shout. There was no ignoring Josefina's demand that Mabel come over to the checkout desk.

Mabel made her way over cautiously, prepared to run if it looked like Josefina was about to launch herself into another hug.

Josefina stayed safely behind the checkout desk. "Is everything all set for this weekend at the farmers' market?"

"We're still working out the details," Mabel said, glancing longingly at the front door. She really needed to get her own internet access at home, so she wouldn't have to waste time on small talk. "I'm on my way to go see Darryl Santangelo again right now, in fact, and then I need to get back to the farm to hire some field hands."

"I'll spread the word that you're hiring." Josefina leaned forward anxiously. "You do think it will get done in time, don't you? This weekend will be the official garlic harvest weekend?"

"We're doing everything possible, but I can't say for sure."

"It's just that I need to ask for this Saturday off, if it's the garlic harvest weekend," Josefina said. "I haven't missed the celebration once since Peggy started it. This would have been the eleventh anniversary, you know."

It must have started the summer after Mabel's last visit here. "There's a lot about the farm that I don't know."

"You'll catch up soon enough," Josefina said. "If you have any questions, you can ask me. My favorite thing is the garlicky fried dough. Or maybe it's the garlic-scape rings. Or the bread with bits of roasted garlic in it. Oh, and the music. Have you talked to the band, to make sure they'll be there?"

"The band?"

"You know," Josefina said. "The Scattered Bulbils. At least, that's what they're called during the celebration before they go back to their regular name. Which isn't so regular, come to think of it. They like to change it from month to month."

"That must make it hard to figure out where they're playing."

"They send out text messages and Tweets." Josefina laughed. "Or if they really want the news to travel fast, they just tell me, and I get the word out."

"I'll look into it." There was probably a folder in her aunt's office labeled "harvest celebration," filled with everything she'd need to make the arrangements. If not, Rory and Emily could probably steer her in the right direction. Then maybe she could settle down to working on the app that was due on Friday. "Don't make any plans quite yet, though. I can't say for sure whether we'll be ready this weekend. It all depends on the harvest."

"Just let me know when you've got a firm date," Josefina said as she gestured to a waiting patron to come up to her station. "I'll spread the word."

"Thanks." Mabel escaped while Josefina was busy with her patron, and headed across the street.

* * * *

The receptionist told Mabel to go on into the conference room where Darryl was leaning against the windowsill, finishing up a phone call. He hung up, and then moved forward to greet her. She'd been prepared for his amazing good looks this time, so she wasn't distracted by them like before. Familiarity might not have bred contempt for his appearance, but it helped her to ignore it.

"Back already," he said with his perfect wide smile. "Have you made a decision about this weekend's market?"

"Not yet. We're just getting started on the harvest." Mabel stayed in the doorway to make it clear she didn't have time for a long discussion. "I'll have an answer for you on Thursday, as promised."

"I guess that will have to do," he said. "So, to what do I owe the pleasure of your company today?"

"I'm hiring field hands, and I thought you might know some people interested in jobs."

"If anyone does, I do," he said. "What are you offering?"

Oh, hell. In her relief at finding the hiring packets, she hadn't actually read them or looked for the past wages. She was horrible at finessing situations when she didn't have the necessary data, but she didn't have time to get the information.

"The usual. For three days." That would get the harvest in, but there was still the space at the market to staff. "Maybe a couple more, depending on how the work goes."

"I'll ask around," he said. "You could always reconsider Larry Rose's offer. He's got a crew already hired and trained. They could be at your place with just a couple hours' notice, and the work would be done in record time."

"I'd be glad to consider it," she said, watching Darryl's smile widen, only to falter again as she added, "as soon as he sends me a written proposal for my attorney to review."

"That's not how we work around here."

"It's how I work, and I'm here."

Darryl leaned back against the windowsill, and tried again. "You've got to understand, Larry's just an old-fashioned farmer, with dirt under his nails. He doesn't have much experience with lawyers and written proposals and the sort of fancy technology Peggy used."

Aunt Peggy was considered a techie? Since when?

Mabel didn't have time to find out. She needed to get back to the farm and do the hiring, so everyone could get to their respective jobs. "I'm just doing what Aunt Peggy would have done. As far as I can tell, she never worked with Mr. Rose before."

"You know how it is between rival growers."

"No, I don't," she said, tired of people expecting her to know all the details of her aunt's life and farm. "How is it?"

"Everyone thinks he's the only person who knows how to grow a particular crop, and that the competition is incompetent. Professional rivalry. That's all it ever is. Common in any industry, not just farming."

That wasn't the way Mabel herself viewed other app developers. She'd always been able to appreciate a particularly elegant solution to a coding challenge that had eluded her and someone else had found. The developers who did inferior work generally didn't even appear on her radar, and when they did, she tended to feel sorry for their clients, rather than feeling any animosity toward the incompetent developer. The only conflict she ever had with other developers was when they did something underhanded, like stealing her code or badmouthing her.

Mabel couldn't imagine Aunt Peggy feeling any differently toward her own competitors. She seemed to get along fine with other growers. She'd helped to organize the local farms into a CSA group, after all, despite some overlap in their crops. Sure, Aunt Peggy vigorously asserted her claim to the best garlic on the east coast, but she always said it with a smile, and she'd always been willing to help out a new farmer starting a garlic crop. If there had been friction between Aunt Peggy and Larry Rose, it wasn't because of professional rivalry.

"Are you sure there wasn't something more serious between them?"

"I never really thought about it before." He glanced behind him, out the picture window in the direction of the space where the market was held. When he turned back around, he said, "You know, there was an odd episode on the first day of this year's farmers' market. We always have an official grand opening each season, with barriers set in place to keep out the public until the appointed hour. The farmers try to get set up about half an hour early, and there's a little huddle, discussing any changes in the products being offered, and generally getting psyched to go out there and sell, sell, sell. Peggy was usually the life of the party. Not this year, though. She didn't get there until a few minutes after opening time. Larry was at the entrance with me, waiting in case there were any no-shows, and he could take the empty spot for overflow from his main space. I guess he'd started to count on getting Peggy's space, so when she did show up, he said something about her tardiness, and she lost her temper. I had to step in and calm things down before they scared away the buyers."

Aunt Peggy could have simply been irritated that once, if the other farmer said something stupid when she was running late and feeling stressed. Everyone had bad days, when they were unsociable, just like how Mabel had the occasional day when she felt sociable.

"I'm sure it was nothing serious," Darryl said with a reassuring smile. "Let me talk to Larry. I'm sure he can explain their little tiff, so you won't have to feel like you're doing something Peggy wouldn't have approved of."

Mabel could definitely see the advantages of accepting Larry's offer, assuming he reduced it to writing so her attorney could review it. Then she'd be free to do her real job instead of dealing with the harvest. Logically, it made the most sense, but even she couldn't resist making a decision based on pure emotion occasionally. She'd known that a Mini Cooper wasn't the ideal vehicle for driving on snow packed roads during Maine's long winters, but she'd fallen in love with it and bought it anyway. She'd never regretted the decision, no matter how foolish it had seemed while she was handing over the cash.

Just like then, she knew her response was irrational, but Larry Rose had triggered an instant antipathy as strong as her instant infatuation with the Mini Cooper. It didn't feel right to hand over her aunt's garlic to him. Mabel still had time to finish the app for Friday, even if she spent a few hours this morning hiring the field hands and then paying them at the end of each day.

"I'm not really interested in selling the crop to Mr. Rose," Mabel said. "If you really want to be helpful, find me some field hands."

CHAPTER NINE

Mabel had passed the grocery store before remembering that she needed to get lunch supplies for the workers she hoped were waiting for her at the farm. She backtracked, ordered a selection of lunch meats and cheeses at the deli, and then threw some bread, fresh fruit salad, paper plates, napkins, and assorted bottled drinks into her carriage. She had to fold down the rear seats to get everything into the trunk of her Mini Cooper.

Finally, she pulled into the farm's driveway at a quarter to eleven and, as she approached the barn's parking area, was disheartened by the total absence of any vehicles that might have brought job applicants.

The only vehicle parked outside the barn was a white van with the town's seal on the driver's side door and "Animal Control" written across the back. Checking on the barn cats, she assumed.

Mabel parked across from the van, on the grass next to the back patio, and lugged the perishable supplies into the kitchen. Once they were safely stowed in the refrigerator, she returned to the car for the nonperishable supplies, along with the hiring packets, which she planned to unload onto the patio's outdoor table. It was even larger than the one in the kitchen, and would be perfect for both interviewing and feeding her workers.

A man with red hair, and the height of a professional basketball player, but well past retirement age for the sport, unfolded himself from the Animal Control van. He left the vehicle idling and came over to the Mini Cooper. "You must be Mabel Skinner. You've got your aunt's chin."

"So I've heard," Mabel said, dragging a case of soda out of the trunk and balancing it on her hip. "Is there a problem with the barn cats?"

"Not that I know of." He reached into the trunk and grabbed two more cases and a sack of paper goods for her. "Rory told me that she and Bettina have been coming out to feed them since Peggy died. I'm sure they'd have said something if there was a problem."

Mabel led the way over to the patio table. "Are you a member of the CSA, then? Here to help with the harvest?"

"Not me. Don't take it personally, but I'm not much of a garlic eater. It's fine in its place, but I don't really get the enthusiasm that some people show for it." He set the supplies down on the table. "I need to talk to you."

"So talk."

"I can't leave the van unattended," he said. "Would you mind coming over there with me?"

He'd just saved her at least three more trips to empty her car's trunk, so if he wanted to talk over by his van for a couple minutes, she didn't mind. It wasn't like she had any field workers to hire. She slammed the Mini Cooper's trunk shut as she passed it.

He had already opened the two back doors of the van and dragged a cage toward him from where it had been wedged near the front seats. "I've got someone for you to meet. This is Pixie."

He moved out of Mabel's line of sight, revealing a beautiful orange tabby cat glaring out from the cage.

She glared back. "He doesn't look happy."

"It's a girl, actually," he said. "It was a good guess, since most orange cats are male, but Pixie isn't like most cats, orange or otherwise."

"Why are you showing her to me?"

He frowned. "Don't you like cats? Are you allergic?"

"I like them a lot," she said. "Although the ones here don't seem to be doing their job very well. There's an awful lot of troublesome wildlife that has eluded them."

"That's sort of why Pixie and I are here, actually," he said. "We've had her for about a year now, and she's been adopted six times, only to be returned within a few days. Apparently, she likes to yowl at inconvenient times. One couple kept her for a month, figuring it would stop after a while, but it never did. Any little thing moved outside the house, and she'd start yowling. They finally had to bring her back to the shelter, because the sleep deprivation was making them ill. Pixie is officially unadoptable. We're pretty much out of options, unless she can join your barn cats. I figured her yowling wouldn't be a problem if it happened out in the barn."

Mabel might need to work with the animal control officer later to find homes for the other barn cats when she returned to Maine, if the new owner of the farm didn't want the cats. She couldn't turn him down flat, but she also didn't need any more responsibilities right now. She already had more than she was used to, with Aunt Peggy's friends depending on her to carry on her aunt's legacy.

"I'll think about it."

"It's just that Pixie is starting to develop some signs of anxiety, from being kept in a cage for so long. The sooner she can get a little freedom, the better." He sounded more anxious than the cat looked. He opened the cage door and pulled the cat out. Instead of hissing and spitting the way her glare seemed to promise, she curled up on his chest. "See? She's really a sweet cat. It would be a shame to keep her locked in a cage all her life. Your Aunt Peggy would have taken her, if she was still with us."

Mabel sighed. That was the one appeal she couldn't refuse. As long as she was here, carrying out her aunt's wishes with respect to a funeral, the garlic harvest and even the farmers' market, she might as well do the same with the barn cat population. One more wouldn't make that big a difference. "Fine. You know where the barn is."

"Not just yet," he said. "Pixie is reasonably well socialized with other cats, but I'd still recommend that you keep her inside the farmhouse for a few days until she's used to the new location. She needs a small enclosed territory where she can feel safe. Once she's used to being here, then you can introduce her to the barn, and you'll have a better chance of getting her to fit in with the others."

"I thought she was too noisy to live in a house."

"It'd just be a few days." He didn't hesitate to use the magic words he'd stumbled on. "It's what Peggy would have wanted."

"All right," she said, holding out her arms to take the cat. Pixie accepted the transfer with total disinterest. It was hard to believe that this apathetic little lump could summon the energy to make so much as a squeak, let alone a disruptive yowl.

The Animal Control officer tossed a cat owner's starter kit containing some litter, a litter box and a bag of kibble, at Mabel's feet. Then he slammed the van doors and covered the distance back to the driver's side door in two rapid strides.

He moved so smoothly, she thought he must have made exactly the same moves hundreds of times before, escaping before a reluctant animal adopter could change her mind. His van was halfway down the driveway when it had to pull to one side to let another vehicle pass, coming from the other direction.

Pixie finally showed some interest in her surroundings. She glared over Mabel's shoulder and yowled at the approaching blue SUV.

It had better hold job applicants, Mabel thought. Otherwise, Pixie wasn't the only one who was going to do some yowling today.

* * * *

Mabel carried Pixie into the guest bathroom near the kitchen, and then quickly set up the litter box and a food and water station in there. Pixie had stopped yowling as soon as the occupants of the blue SUV had emerged to introduce themselves. There were two college-aged kids: a skinny blond male and a curvier dark skinned woman in dreadlocks.

Hidden behind the SUV until it reached the parking lot was a mid-sized white car. Inside it were Rory, Bettina and a teen who had to be Rory's daughter, judging by how much they looked alike. As soon as they emerged from the car, Mabel had handed authority over the applicants to Rory, with a promise to return in five minutes for the official interviews as soon as she got Pixie settled.

Now, her time was up, so Mabel backed out of the guest bathroom, preparing to close the door securely behind her. "Sorry, Pixie, but I've got to go hire some field hands. You can check out the rest of the farmhouse when I get back."

Mabel ran over to the barn, where Rory had apparently just given the three teens a brief tour.

"Come on over to the farmhouse," Mabel told them. "I've got the paperwork over there."

They all trooped over to the patio table, which was even larger than the massive one in the kitchen The two college kids sat on one side, and Rory's daughter on the other. As soon as they were seated, Rory excused herself to go check on Bettina in the barn.

No new vehicles had arrived, and it was already a quarter past eleven, so it wasn't likely there would be any more job seekers to choose from. Even assuming the three teens were acceptable workers, would they be enough to bring in the entire crop? Rory had said the ideal number was six workers, so, best case scenario, she'd be half staffed.

Feeling as frustrated as she did when developing an app for a client who withheld the critical information she needed to do the job, Mabel withdrew three of the dozen hiring packets and handed them out.

"Does anyone have a pen?" the young man asked in a British accent. "I thought we were going to be digging in the dirt, not doing paperwork."

Outside her comfort zone, Mabel was as unprepared as he was. She never carried any sort of purse, instead tucking her driver's license and a single credit card into a pocket. The college woman and Dawn had small backpacks, with phone-sized pockets on the side, along with a larger pocket on the front. They both immediately unzipped the larger pocket to simultaneously produce a handful of pens.

While the young man considered his options, Mabel wondered whether her aunt had carried her phone in a purse, like the teens, or if she'd gone more minimal like Mabel, carrying just the phone itself, at least while she was on the farm. Should she be looking for a purse, as well as the phone? Just one more thing she didn't know about her aunt, and would have to learn from Rory or Emily.

The young man said, "I'm always losing pens. Better go with something basic." He took a generic stick pen from the college girl, over Dawn's assortment of sparkly pens in a rainbow of ink colors.

"I'm Mabel Skinner," she announced. "We're going to do this as a group, rather than individually, if that's okay with you. Let's start with your names, what you're studying, and why you want this job."

The young man was Terry Earley, whose accent proclaimed him to be from the UK. He was studying marine sciences, but he was also interested in agriculture, especially in comparing the practices employed in the US with those in the UK. The other college student was Anna Johnson, majoring in art education, and looking for money to buy some art supplies.

Mabel turned to Rory's daughter last.

"I'm Dawn Hansen, and I'm studying an eclectic mixture of subjects. I want this job in order to …." She hesitated and then finished defiantly, "to broaden my horizons."

Mabel could hear Rory's influence in the last phrase, and guessed that Dawn had been planning to put a sarcastic spin on it until she'd seen Terry and heard his foreign accent.

"Let's get down to business then," Mabel said. "Did Mrs. Hansen tell you what the job entails and what the compensation is?"

All three of the prospective workers' heads nodded.

"Do you still want the job?"

The two college kids nodded again, and Dawn waited for their response before joining them.

"Good. You're all hired, subject to your providing all the information requested by the hiring packets. While you finish the paperwork, I'll go have a word with Mrs. Hansen about where you'll be starting."

Inside the barn, Bettina was seated between a drying rack and a stack of crates that someone had recently filled with the garlic and carried in from the fields. Bettina pushed individual garlic plants, stem end down and dirt crusted roots in the air, into the mesh of an almost full drying rack.

Rory stood beside an empty rack, prepared to swap it out for the first one when it was full. "A couple of the CSA members came by while you were gone, and put in an hour toward their commitment. It's a start, anyway. Bettina does such a nice job with the racking, so I thought we could use this one to demonstrate for the field hands. Assuming you've gone ahead and hired them."

"I did," Mabel said. "They're just filling out the paperwork. I was hoping we'd have more people. Will three be enough?"

"It depends on whether the other CSA members come through on their commitments," Rory said. "And how hard your new field hands work. I love my daughter, but you know that she's here against her will, so I'm not sure how much she's going to actually do."

"If the other two are diligent, I bet she will be too," Mabel said. "She seems to want to impress them. Unless things are a lot different here from where I grew up, it's not every day that a young teen gets to hang out with college kids."

"I'll stay out of sight, then," Rory said. "Goodness knows, she doesn't care about impressing me."

"I'm willing to give these three a go for today, at least," Mabel said. "If they don't work out, there are still a couple other options."

"Is there a garlic pulling cavalry somewhere that I don't know about?"

"Sort of," Mabel said. "Larry Rose offered to buy the crop from me and send in his crew to finish the harvest. Said he had enough people to get it done in forty-eight hours, guaranteed."

Bettina gasped, as startled as she'd been earlier when Mabel had mentioned her suspicions about Aunt Peggy's death. "You can't sell out. It wouldn't be right."

"You'd rather the garlic rotted in the field?"

"Well, no, but…." Bettina trailed off. "I don't know. It just wouldn't be right. It's Peggy's crop, or it was, and it's yours now. You can't just sell it."

Of course she could sell it. That was the whole point of farming. A good chunk of the crop was already under contract to bulk buyers and the CSA members. Mabel was about to say that Bettina was being ridiculous, when she caught Rory signaling that she should let it go, so as not to upset the fragile widow further. "Maybe you're right. I didn't particularly like the farmer who made the offer anyway."

"He's not that bad," Rory said. "His relationship with Peggy was complicated, though. I can't think of anyone else in town who ever rubbed her the wrong way, but he did. I wish I knew why, but she never said."

Bettina filled the last space in the garlic rack, and stood. "I need to take a break."

"Before you go," Mabel said, "I was wondering if either of you could tell me what kind of purse Aunt Peggy carried. I'm wondering if it's not just a phone that's missing, but a purse too."

"She didn't have much use for purses," Rory said. "Except for the farmers' market, she hardly ever left the farm. She had a cash drawer for the market, and she put the usual purse-type things in there, so there'd only be one thing to watch over instead of two."

"What about her phone? Did she carry it with her, or did she leave that behind too, except when she needed it?"

"She kept the phone with her in a pocket," Rory said. "It took a while for her to admit her friends were right, but we finally convinced her it was safer, especially when she was here all alone."

"That's what I thought. She should have had it with her the night she died, but it's missing."

Mabel had forgotten she wasn't supposed to talk about death around Bettina until Rory started shaking her head and pointing at Bettina from behind her back.

Bettina didn't seem particularly upset, although she did sigh. "Phones are so easy to misplace. I do it all the time, and Scott never understands. He gets so upset at the cost of replacing the phone, especially since his accident and having to live on disability compensation." She brightened suddenly. "Maybe Peggy got insurance on her phone, and you can file a claim. I wanted to get insurance on mine, but Scott said that was a waste of money too, and I should just be more careful with it, because he wasn't going to replace it the next time I lost it."

Okay, Mabel thought, so Bettina wasn't entirely unaffected by the mention of death. This time it hadn't startled her, but had sent her into some alternate universe where her dead and buried husband still controlled what she spent money on.

"I just saw your favorite calico go past the barn doors," Rory said. "Why don't you go find her and take a little break? Mabel and I will swap out the drying racks and then we can all go out to the field and get the harvest going."

Bettina lost her sad, distracted expression and hurried out of the barn.

"The cats are about the only thing that can snap her back to reality these days." Rory picked up one end of the filled rack and gestured for Mabel to grab the other end to carry it to a spot where it was out of the way, but still accessible as a model for anyone who needed instruction on racking garlic. "I'm hoping that eventually we'll be able to convince her to adopt the calico. I didn't think you'd mind."

"She can adopt them all, if she wants them," Mabel said. "There's even a new one in the farmhouse. Animal control dropped her off right before you got here with Dawn."

After the first rack had been moved, Rory said, "Are you really prepared to turn down Larry's offer to finish the harvest?"

"I don't really need the money," Mabel said. "We just need to bring in enough to honor Aunt Peggy's memory. As long as I can supply the CSA members and the local restaurants, and maybe one weekend at the farmers' market, I can handle the financial loss."

"There's still a chance we can get it all harvested. You talked to Darryl about spreading the word that you're hiring, right? Maybe he'll come through. Just one or two more full-time people would get it done. It would be such a shame to miss out on the last market season for Peggy's farm. It would definitely put a damper on the final garlic harvest celebration weekend."

"Are you sure we shouldn't cancel the event?" Mabel said. "Isn't it enough just to be at the market?"

Bettina wandered into the barn, carrying the calico cat. "You can't cancel the garlic festival. It's a tradition."

"Besides, it's a lot of fun," Rory said. "And we could all use some fun."

"I'm not much of a party person. I was hoping someone else could oversee the space at the market for me." Mabel tried to signal behind Bettina's back that Rory should encourage her friend to run the market space during the garlic festival. It would have been perfect for distracting Bettina from her grieving. When neither Rory nor Bettina took the hint, Mabel said, "The college kids I just hired might do it. Terry is interested in comparative agriculture, and working the market would give him a chance to study how we sell farm goods, not just how we grow and harvest them."

"You can have whatever help you want at the market," Rory said, "and we'll be there too, if you want, but not without you. When it's over, you'll be glad you didn't miss the celebration."

"There are lots of things that I'm glad to put behind me," Mabel said. "Like my annual mammogram, monthly period and daily exercise. If I could hire someone to take my place for any of them, I'd do it."

Rory laughed. "The garlic festival isn't that bad."

Rory had already done far more to keep the farm going than anyone could have expected of her, so Mabel decided to humor her. "Let's say we have enough of a harvest to justify a celebration. What do I need to do besides show up?"

"Most of it just sort of happens, as soon as word goes out that the harvest is in."

Finally, there was something that Mabel knew how to handle. "In other words, I just have to tell Josefina at the library, and she'll make sure everyone knows."

"See?" Rory said. "You'll be a full-fledged West Slocumber in no time."

"I'll be back in Maine before that happens."

"You're not staying?" Bettina set down the calico and brushed the fur off her denim jumper. "What's going to happen to the farm?"

"I don't know yet."

"Give her some time, Bettina," Rory said. "Mabel practically just got here. Soon there won't be any more talk about going back to Maine."

"Of course," Bettina said. "You'll change your mind once the hard work is over. Everyone in town comes to the festival. One of the local churches sets up a garlic braiding contest, and the results are auctioned off for charity. Another church makes and sells garlic dog biscuits. Jeanne's Country Diner makes garlic rings by dipping sliced scapes in onion ring batter and frying them. Peggy used to make and sell pickled garlic along with the fresh garlic."

"We even have a garlic king or queen," Rory said. "Peggy declared herself ineligible after winning three years in a row, but I bet they'll elect you to be the queen this year, no matter what, in her honor."

"I'd have to abdicate," Mabel said. "I don't look good in a tiara, and I'm pretty sure my lawyer would tell me I can't order anyone's head off. That's got to be illegal."

"There's more to being a queen than tiaras and decapitations," Rory said.

"If Mabel doesn't want it, I'd like to be queen," Bettina said. "Scott calls me his princess, but I think I'd rather be a queen."

"It's fine with me," Mabel said, earning a look of gratitude from Rory. "Of course, there won't be queens or anything else unless we get the harvest in. I'll go see if the field hands are ready. Would you two be able to show them what to do?"

"If Bettina will drive the tractor out to the field, I can manage the ten minutes it will take to show them what to do," Rory said, "but after that I'll need to leave. My daughter made me promise that if she came out for the job, I wouldn't embarrass her, and my mere presence is usually enough to do that. I can get them started, but that's about all she's likely to tolerate."

Mabel had hoped to put in an hour or two this afternoon on the app that was due Friday, and if she had to supervise the crew, her real job would have to wait until after the sun set. She looked at the petite Bettina, expecting her to have an objection to the plan, but she'd already started climbing up the side of the massive tractor as if it were an everyday occurrence for her. Maybe it was, judging by how efficiently she adjusted the seat and then started the engine.

As long as no one expected Mabel to drive the monster machine, she didn't mind postponing the work on her app until this evening. After all, she did her best work at night.

"I just need to get the employment paperwork sorted, and then I'll join you in the fields."

CHAPTER TEN

Mabel checked on Pixie, who was napping in the bathroom sink, before returning to the kitchen table, where she spread out the papers she'd collected from the three teens and compared it to the checklist her aunt had prepared. Everything seemed in order, so she was about to head out to the fields when Pixie began yowling. Even somewhat muffled by the solid bathroom door, the sound was earsplitting, louder than the joint effort of all the early birds on the farm. The crew could probably hear it out in the farthest field.

"It's okay, Pixie, I'm coming." Mabel peeked in the bathroom door, and the yowling stopped. In the sudden silence, Mabel could hear a vehicle parking outside the barn. The cat seemed perfectly fine now, with a full bowl of kibble and reasonably fresh water. The newly arrived vehicle might contain job applicants she couldn't afford to miss, so Mabel closed the bathroom door again, waiting a moment to see if the yowling would resume. When it didn't, she raced to grab the hiring packets and headed for the barn.

Standing beside a white convertible was a redheaded man in cargo shorts and a sweatshirt. Something about him seemed familiar, but the only males she knew in the area were Darryl Santangelo and Larry Rose. This man was shorter, older and whiter than Darryl, and taller, younger and whiter than Larry. He had the thick middle and pale skin of a middle-aged man who spent all of his time indoors, and wouldn't last more than fifteen minutes doing physical labor. But desperate garlic farmers, like beggars, couldn't be choosers when it came to hiring field hands. Even fifteen minutes of help was better than nothing.

"Hi. I'm Mabel Skinner. And you are…?"

"Kyle Sherman," he said, shaking her hand. "CSA member. I heard it's time for us to pitch in with the harvest, and I had a couple hours to spare, so here I am. Just tell me where to start."

"Have you ever done this before?"

"I've got farming in my blood," he said. "Just point me in the right direction, and I'll be good to go. You can keep doing whatever you were working on in the house, and I'll let you know when I'm done."

Mabel sidled over to the barn doors. "Let me just put these papers in the barn, and I'll walk out with you and introduce you to the crew. I was about to go out there anyway."

"The crew?" he said warily. "If you've got enough workers for now, I can come back later."

Mabel wasn't about to let go of a willing body, so she tossed the hiring packets into the barn, and said the words that would have shocked anyone who knew her well. "The more, the merrier. Having company makes the work go faster."

"I work better on my own."

So did Mabel, but she was afraid that if Kyle left, and had a chance to think about how hard the work was, he might not come back. "I can't have anyone working in the fields alone. Too much risk of liability. At least, that's what my lawyer tells me."

He glanced over his shoulder at the parking lot, and the three vehicles there. Seemingly reassured that his getaway vehicle wasn't going anywhere without him, he shrugged and said, "I guess you're right. As long as I'm here, I might as well stay."

Mabel set out for the farthest garlic field, where Bettina had parked the tractor. As they approached, Mabel was impressed by how much had already been done. The tractor had been turned around to face the barn, and the wagon was half full of crates overflowing with garlic. Bettina was sitting on the edge of the wagon, with her back to Mabel, and Rory was leaning over the bed of the wagon, stacking yet another filled crate inside.

Rory looked up, started to smile at Mabel and then noticed Kyle. Her head snapped back in Mabel's direction. "Tell me you didn't hire him."

"I didn't hire him," Mabel said. "He's one of yours. A volunteer from the CSA."

Bettina turned around to inspect the newcomer. "No, he isn't. That's Kyle Sherman. He was here yesterday morning, remember?"

Yesterday? There hadn't been any men on the property yesterday. And then Mabel recalled the luxury SUV driving golfer who'd been arguing with Rory and had stomped off before Mabel was close enough to see his face. His distinctive red hair might have given away his identity, but it had been covered by his golf cap yesterday.

"He's not a CSA member," Rory said. "And if he keeps this up, he never will be."

"Hey," Kyle said. "I just wanted to help. What's wrong with that? I'll be a member next year. Think of it as getting a head start on my work commitment."

"Oh, yeah?" Rory stomped over to stand in front of him, and suddenly punched him in the stomach. When she stepped back, the clingy fabric of the sweatshirt revealed that his beer belly had crumpled around her fist, like a beanbag. "Then what's the fake stomach for?"

"I don't suppose you'd believe it's part of some sensitivity training, and I was trying to see what it felt like to be pregnant?"

"Not on your life," Rory said. "And definitely not if you want the CSA to consider you a trustworthy enough person to join us in the future."

"All right, all right." He tugged the sweatshirt, which must have been cooking him in the full sun, over his head and tossed it aside, revealing a tank top underneath, and then the bandages wrapped around his torso and something that had been round until Rory had dented it. Beneath the bandages was a soccer ball that had been cut in half and lined with a canvas bag. He turned to Mabel. "I was just going to take enough to pay for the time I worked here. That's fair, isn't it? You'd get help with the harvest, and I'd get a couple pounds of the garlic I need."

"That bag would have held more than a couple pounds," Rory said. "Worth a lot more than your time."

"You should have just asked me, instead of going through all that," Mabel said, pointing at the discarded fake belly.

"I'm asking now."

Mabel could feel the irritation pouring off Rory and Bettina, and the confusion of the younger field hands as they paused in their work to see what was going on. Much as she wanted an extra worker, and even assuming she could trust Kyle not to steal an entire truckload of the crop, a couple hours of Kyle's time wasn't worth risking the morale of the other workers.

"I'm sorry," she said. "You'll have to wait until next year."

He sighed as he picked up his sweatshirt. "You can't blame a guy for trying."

"Some would say you can't blame a person for running over trespassers, either," Rory said as she climbed into the seat of the tractor and moved the seat back to compensate for her long legs. "Of course others might say I was to blame, but if you're not off the farm by the time the wagon is filled and I get back to the barn, just remember that I've never cared about what some people say."

* * * *

As soon as Kyle started trudging back to his car, Rory climbed down from the tractor. Bettina trailed Kyle back to the barn a few minutes later on foot, in part to get herself out of the direct sun, and in part to make sure he actually left.

With a glance at Dawn, who had resumed her harvesting, Rory said, "I need to leave soon too. Want me to run through the harvest process with you before I go?"

"What I want is for this to be all done, but I'll settle for learning what to do."

Rory handed her a stack from the collection of empty crates beside the tractor, and led her over to the first row past where the teens were working. "Pull the garlic like you did yesterday, and gather up a whole fistful of stalks."

Mabel bent and tugged half a dozen garlic plants out of the ground. "Now what?"

Rory handed her a pair of clippers. "Cut them about eight to ten inches from the head. If you need a measurement reference, the clippers themselves are about seven inches long."

Mabel squeezed the clippers around the bunch of stalks, which were considerably tougher than she'd imagined. They looked so much like onion tops that she'd expected them to be equally easy to cut. These stalks were more like really tough asparagus spears. She tried again, clipping fewer at a time.

"You can toss the scapes into the crates with the garlic for now. Later, we'll remove the bulbils from the top, and Emily will take the stems for her goats," Rory said, dropping a bunch of scapes into the crate at her feet and then carefully laying the garlic bulbs on top of them. "When the crate's reasonably full, carry it over to the wagon. Make sure the tractor goes back to the barn at least once every hour or so, even if the wagon isn't completely full. You don't want the garlic baking in the sun."

"That seems simple enough."

"It is."

Mabel looked around at the rows and rows of garlic in the fields. Simple as the process was, it would still take forever to harvest all those plants with her existing crew. Maybe she'd been hasty in turning down Kyle's help.

"Come on," Rory said. "I'll work with you until you get into the routine."

"Thanks." Mabel had already resigned herself to breaking her policy of always working alone, so she settled down to work, pulling the garlic from the four rows closest to her in the bed, while Rory pulled the four rows on the opposite side.

As Mabel worked, she wished she had the gumption to climb up on the massive tractor and threaten trespassers with it. She straightened to cut the tops off her latest handful of garlic, and noticed Rory was about to step on one of the flowering plants that grew in random patches between the rows of garlic. "Watch out!"

Rory's foot landed on the plant. "What?"

"Never mind," Mabel said. "I was just going to tell you to be careful where you stepped, or you'd squash one of the plants. It's too late now."

Rory looked down at the squashed flowers, and then shook her head. "You almost gave me a heart attack. I thought it was a wasp or something really serious." She prodded the ruined plant with the toe of her gardening clog. "That's just a marigold. They're pretty, and we sometimes pick the flowers to decorate the market booth, but they're mostly pest control. There's some evidence that marigolds can help keep the fields free of the nematodes that sometimes feed on garlic, and Peggy figured it was worth the minimal effort and expense to plant them. They grow like weeds from open pollinated seeds that can be saved from year to year. They get plowed back into the ground at the end of the season as organic matter. Once the harvest is in, it doesn't much matter what happens to them. Unless you want them for something, of course."

There had to be thousands of the pretty little plants on the farm. "I think my flower needs can be satisfied with however many you don't stomp on. But what about those things?" Mabel pointed to one of the weedy vines that filled a series of gaps in the garlic rows. There were patches of them at fairly regular intervals, around thirty feet apart, and the closest one was threatening to engulf the garlic on either side of it.

"They're butternut squash vines. It's a secondary crop. The plants have a complementary growing season with garlic. The squash is just taking off now, looking for room to expand as the garlic is harvested. Then the squash ripens in September, right before it's time to prepare the ground for the fall planting of the garlic."

By fall, Mabel thought as she went over to get a closer look at the squash plant, she would be back in Maine. She was perfectly willing to stay on her aunt's farm long enough to harvest the final garlic crop, but she hadn't counted on having to come back for yet another harvest in the fall. Aunt

Peggy had never said anything about having the best squash on the east coast, so it couldn't be that big a deal. Not like the garlic was.

Just in case, though, she decided not to mention that she was planning to leave before the next peak harvest time. She had enough to worry about right now, without having to hear about how everyone in town would be bereft if they didn't get their fair share of Aunt Peggy's butternut squash. There might even be a squash festival and a squash queen. Definitely not something she wanted to deal with right now.

Beyond the squash vine, the garlic plants resumed after a barren gap of several feet. "At the risk of demonstrating my cluelessness again, why would my aunt have popped in and harvested just a few garlic bulbs around the squash plants, without pulling the whole row?"

"What do you mean?" Rory came around the squash plant.

"Someone's already harvested a few feet in the middle of the row." Mabel looked down the row at the next squash vine. "And look, there's another bit missing down there too."

Rory knelt to examine the ground. "That's weird."

"Maybe one of the new field hands or the CSA volunteers did it earlier."

Rory shook her head. "The volunteers from this morning knew what they were doing, and I've been keeping a careful eye on the kids. They've been working well together. Chattering away, but not goofing off or running around where they don't belong."

"Could Aunt Peggy have been checking on the ripeness or something?"

"No need for that," Rory said. "There are easier ways to check without pulling them prematurely. Besides, it looks to me like the earth's been disturbed too recently for her to have done it. There aren't even any weeds germinating, and disturbed soil usually brings seeds to the surface. If these were pulled two weeks ago, there'd be weedlings by now."

"Is it critter damage?" Mabel said. "Maybe we need more barn cats patrolling the fields."

"Two-legged critters like Kyle Sherman, maybe," Rory said, "but there aren't any four-legged ones that eat garlic, as far as I know. It was one of the reasons why Peggy chose garlic when she started the farm. It meant she didn't need to build expensive fences to keep the critters out."

That sounded like Aunt Peggy. Open fields and unlocked doors. Mabel would have preferred a ten-foot stockade fence, possibly topped with barbed wire, all around the property. Then she would have known that the noise last night was either her imagination or some harmless wildlife, rather than anything potentially dangerous. Maybe not dangerous, exactly, but certainly criminal.

"Could the theft have happened as recently as last night?"

"I suppose, although it would have been an easier target while the farmhouse was unoccupied, with no one to notice an intruder." Rory stood with a sad sigh. "Peggy could have told you down to the minute how long it had been since the ground was disturbed, but the only thing I'm sure of is that it was sometime during the last week."

Mabel considered mentioning the noise she'd heard during the night, but she wasn't entirely sure it had been anything other than the normal sounds of the farm. Rory would probably think it was just Mabel's imagination, or another reflection of her grief over losing her aunt. Then Rory would organize a team of babysitters to stay with Mabel, so she wouldn't ever be alone again in her grief, much the way Rory was personally watching over Bettina. But Mabel wasn't Bettina, and she was neither grieving nor in need of any more companionship than she was already coping with. Better to keep her suspicions to herself until she had something more solid to go on.

Rory had returned to the harvest, and was filling up her crate, so Mabel followed her lead as best she could. If Mabel went back to Maine, she wouldn't just be dishonoring her aunt's memory, she'd be throwing away all the work that Rory and Emily had done to keep the farm going.

It wasn't just Rory and Emily who were counting on her now. The field hands were counting on their jobs, even if they were just temporary. Sad, fragile Bettina would miss out on being queen, which was the only thing she'd seemed even remotely enthusiastic about. Emily counted on the farm's garlic for the goat cheese she made. And then there was Josefina at the library; if Mabel cancelled the garlic festival, she'd probably find herself excluded from all libraries, worldwide.

"Hey!" Rory threw a clump of dirt at Mabel. "Less daydreaming, more working. Just because you're the boss doesn't mean you get a free ride."

Mabel reached for the closest scape, and tugged. For the moment, she didn't need to decide what to do about anything other than pulling the garlic in front of her. She had until tomorrow at eleven, when she met with Aunt Peggy's lawyer, to change her mind and decline the responsibilities of becoming the personal representative. Until then, she had work to do right here, pulling, topping and crating the best garlic on the east coast.

* * * *

When the wagon was full, Rory asked if Mabel wanted to learn how to drive the tractor.

That was one decision she didn't even have to think about. "Not in this lifetime. I prefer to pick on things that are my own size."

Rory shrugged. "It's not really about size or strength. You saw Bettina driving it, and you've got at least six inches and twenty pounds on her. I'm even bigger than you are, but she's better with it than I am. I tend to go faster, but she's more precise."

"I'm having enough culture shock without adding a monster machine to my world right now."

"Terry and Anna both said they'd driven tractors before," Rory said. "You can send them back to the barn for it when you've filled the remaining crates."

As it turned out, Mabel didn't need to test her workers' skills behind the wheel. Shortly before they ran out of crates, she heard the tractor returning. At the wheel was a stranger who seemed comfortable driving it. She assumed he was a CSA member reporting for his work commitment, or perhaps a job applicant referred by Darryl or Josefina.

As he came closer, she could see that he wasn't dressed for field work. His jeans and sport shirt were appropriate, but not the blazer he wore with them. The weather was mild for July, but definitely not cool enough to wear a jacket while working in the field.

Too bad. He looked like he could harvest an entire field single-handedly. As best she could tell while he was seated, he was tall, probably over six feet, and much more solid than the skinny Terry.

The man turned the tractor around so it was facing the direction of the barn before cutting the engine. Mabel set her latest bunch of topped garlic into her now full crate and carried it over to the tractor. The stranger was hefting stacks of filled crates into the wagon. She put hers on top of one of the loaded stacks.

"Hello. I'm Mabel Skinner."

"I'm Charlie Durbin." He continued loading the filled crates onto the wagon.

"Are you with the CSA? Or here for a job?"

"Neither." He placed the last crate on the tailgate and turned to lean against it. "I'm just here to pay my respects. I was a friend of your aunt's. I'm sorry for your loss."

"Thank you."

"Peggy always said you'd do the right thing if she ever needed your help," he said. "I wasn't so sure when you didn't show up right away, but it looks like she was right, as usual. Your aunt loved this farm. I'd hate to see it neglected."

"I haven't decided what to do with the farm, long-term," Mabel said. "Right now, we're just trying to get this year's crop in. If you know anyone looking for a few days' work, we're hiring."

"Any other time of the year, I'd send you a few guys from my crew, but it's peak season for us too." He took off his blazer and draped it over the side of the wagon. "I've got an hour or two to spare right now. It's not much, but I'd be glad to help out."

"What kind of farm do you have?"

"I don't," he said. "I'm a developer."

No wonder he knew how to drive the tractor. His admission also shed new light on his purported desire to pay his respects. He wasn't here out of any social obligation. He just wanted to be first in line to make an offer to buy the farm and let loose a fleet of backhoes on it.

"Forget it," she said, briefly wishing she'd taken Rory up on her offer of tractor driving instructions, so Mabel could have chased the developer off her property. "We don't need help that badly."

"What's wrong with me?"

"You're a developer," Mabel said.

"It's not contagious."

"Yes, it is," Mabel said. "First there's one backhoe and then there's six, and the next thing you know, every empty lot in town is infected with them. There was an outbreak back home near my house right before I came here. I'm not letting you take over this place too. Aunt Peggy rescued this place from someone like you. I'm not going to dishonor her wishes by letting you have it now."

"I'm just here to pull some garlic in Peggy's memory, nothing more," Charlie said. "I'm not interested in the land. I've got plenty of projects in the works already."

Terry and Anna came up to the wagon, both carrying a couple full crates. "Hey, boss," Terry said. "We're out of crates."

"I can take the tractor back to the barn, unload it and get you some empties," Charlie offered. "Unless you think that would somehow contaminate the farm."

"It would," Mabel said. "I don't want to be indebted to you for anything. Terry can take the tractor."

"Really?" Terry said. "I get to drive the tractor?"

"Unless Anna wants to do it."

Anna shook her head. "I'd rather not this time. I need a refresher lesson first."

"What about me?" Dawn had joined them with her own full crate. "I want a turn."

"Sorry, but you're not old enough," Mabel said. "I could get in trouble if I let you operate any machinery."

"My mother told you not to let me have any fun, didn't she?"

"That's exactly what she told me, in those very words," Mabel said before turning to Charlie, who didn't look like an evil, greedy bastard, which only went to show how bad a judge of character she was in real life. Give her an avatar and an online history, and she could profile the most anonymous of online posters in three minutes or less. It took her far longer in person. She couldn't wait to get back to her virtual world, where she wasn't as clueless as she was here on the farm.

She turned to the developer. "Dawn's mother also told me to watch out for two-legged varmints."

"All right, all right, I'll go." Charlie tugged his jacket off the side of the wagon. "On the way out, I'll leave my business card in the barn, in case you change your mind about needing some help."

"I don't need your help, and I'm not selling the farm to any developer. Not ever."

Mabel hadn't realized how strongly she felt about it until just then. That was one decision made, though. She was going to have to accept the role of personal representative for her aunt's estate tomorrow. It was the only way to make sure the farm wasn't sold to a two-faced developer who only wanted to unleash his army of backhoes on her aunt's defenseless fields.

CHAPTER ELEVEN

Dawn left with her mother at dinnertime, and the two college students worked until the mosquitos and incipient darkness made the field work impossible. After they left, Mabel spent another hour sorting the bulbs from the scapes and stuffing the garlic into the drying racks so they'd have some empty crates to fill in the morning.

When her back ached too much to ignore, Mabel went into the farmhouse and checked on Pixie, who was sleeping in the bathroom sink again. She freshened the water and kibble bowls, and then went to find some dinner for herself. She'd told the field crew to raid the refrigerator when they'd taken a lunch break, and now there was nothing left except the eggs and goat cheese Emily had brought over for breakfast.

Mabel decided to go into town, where she could get takeout and use the library's internet to remind her attorney she definitely wanted to arrange for the autopsy, regardless of cost. She'd also ask him to have a lawyer to lawyer chat with the local DA to see if there was any sort of investigation into Peggy's death that hadn't been made public. While she was out, she could get a cheap phone and activate it with the local cellular service.

Mabel got to the phone store with just enough time left to buy and activate a basic smartphone before the place closed. She picked up her take-out order and was back at the farmhouse shortly after nine. Normally, this time of night was when she got her best work done, but she was feeling the effects of getting up with the stupid birds. Unfortunately, she couldn't simply skip the night's computer work, not with the new Friday deadline looming.

First, she checked on Pixie, who woke up from her latest nap in the bathroom sink. Mabel patted her for a few minutes, and then refilled the kibble bowl. Pixie seemed content where she was, and she hadn't made a sound, as far as Mabel knew, since she'd complained about the arrival of Kyle Sherman earlier today. Maybe she just needed her own space, and she'd be fine.

Mabel left Pixie to her kibble, and settled at the kitchen table with her own dinner and her laptop. She opened her most critical work project, and reviewed the last few pieces she'd worked on, trying to get her head back into it, but she couldn't stop thinking about other projects. Like the pulled garlic that still needed to be sorted and racked, and the fields that still needed to be harvested, and the market celebration that she was going to have to attend.

Then she remembered she hadn't tried her new phone at the farm yet, so she checked its reception. It wasn't as good as it had been in the center of town, and she wouldn't want to try to transfer large files to her boss, in case it lost signal midtransfer, but it was enough for emergencies.

She texted her new number to Jeff, and then stared at the laptop for a while longer without making any real progress. She finally gave up and closed the laptop. Between her early rising the last two mornings, and the physical labor in the fields today, she was exhausted. Any coding she did tonight was likely to be buggy and clunky. It would take more time to fix it later than to simply write a cleaner, more elegant version when she was more alert and could concentrate. She still had a couple more days and nights to finish the project. By Thursday, the harvest would either be finished or abandoned as hopeless. After that, worst case scenario, she could simply work through that night and have the app ready by noon on Friday.

Even though she couldn't concentrate on work, she was too wired to sleep. She hadn't gone to bed by eleven o'clock since she was eleven. She wandered through the farmhouse, first checking Pixie again, who was asleep in the sink and not looking to play, and then ending up in her aunt's office. The leather bound book in the center of the desk reminded her that she'd meant to look through it some more. She still had to get contact information from it, so she could reassure the local restaurant owners that they would get the garlic they'd negotiated for.

Mabel opened the book and quickly found a chart that listed all of the current year's contracts, with the buyers' contact information, and the details of the contract: quantity, price and delivery date. Besides the CSA commitment, there were four major contracts, and a handful of smaller ones.

She couldn't help thinking it would have been so much easier for Aunt Peggy to keep this information in her own phone instead of on paper. There was probably an app on the market for farmers to use, and if there wasn't,

Mabel could have written one. In fact, the app she'd used to apply for her current job had been written for her aunt. It had just been a toy, really, designed to organize her aunt's friends' contact information, but Mabel had had fun doing it. She'd doubted her aunt would ever use it, but she'd sent it as an attachment to a holiday email. It was the one time Aunt Peggy had actually responded to an email, to say that she had successfully installed it on her phone. Mabel still doubted her aunt had ever actually used the app, but at least Aunt Peggy had known that her niece was thinking of her.

Mabel was growing sleepy, but doubted she'd fall asleep as early as midnight. She flipped through a few more pages of the ledger, this time paying more attention to the diary style entries between the charts. They weren't particularly intimate, just a little more personal and less like a scientific notebook. They would have made an engaging blog for customers of the farm, mixing observations and insights with enthusiasm for her work and her products.

There was one entry in particular that Mabel thought could have gone viral if it had been posted online. Aunt Peggy revealed the elusive "secret" to growing the best garlic on the east coast: hard work and lots of stinkin' stuff like manure and rotted vegetation. The hard work she had considered self-explanatory, but she went into greater detail about the manure. The stinkier, the better, Aunt Peggy had written. As far as she was concerned, "stinking" was a good thing, which was why she had celebrated it in the farm's name.

Mabel carried the ledger upstairs, where she changed into pajamas and continued reading in bed. She started with the most recent entries and worked backwards, looking for any indication that her aunt had noticed crop thefts in the past. There was one brief mention of crop damage about a week before Aunt Peggy died, but she hadn't been certain whether it had been from some sort of natural pest or a human one.

Mabel continued working backwards, through her aunt's reflections on various experiments Aunt Peggy had undertaken in what struck Mabel as a highly scientific manner. One such experiment involved growing parallel rows of garlic, and removing the scapes from one row, and leaving the scapes to mature in the other row, and then comparing the harvest. Aunt Peggy had repeated the experiment for five years in a row, concluding that there really wasn't any significant difference in the garlic bulb yield. After that, with the exception of a few scapes that were sold at the farmers' market due to local customers' demand for them, Aunt Peggy had opted to leave the scapes intact, since they produced a secondary crop of the garlic bulbils, which could be used to start new plants, to throw into stir-fry recipes or to sprout and toss on salads or sandwiches. Besides, as she'd written in the ledger, it meant one less chore that had to be done. Just because hard work was the major ingredient in her garlic's success didn't mean she had to do unnecessary work. The time she saved by not cutting the scapes, she could use on plenty of other projects that were more important to her, from weeding to helping out with the local community garden.

Mabel fell asleep midsentence, her aunt's ledger lying on her chest, and the bedside lamp still lit. She would have slept until the stupid birds started screeching, except Pixie beat them to it when it was still pitch black outside. Even with two doors, a hallway and a flight of stairs between them, the cat's yowling was louder than all the birds combined would have been.

Mabel automatically grabbed her new phone, which revealed that it was two a.m., and ran downstairs to check on the cat. Surely Pixie had to be in some sort of distress to be making that much noise.

As soon as Mabel cracked open the guest bathroom door, Pixie pushed her way through the narrow opening and raced from room to room in a frenzy, bouncing off the furniture, onto windowsills and back down to the floor before finally coming to rest on a windowsill in the kitchen. Pixie stared intently at the barn, no longer yowling, but still clearly on edge.

Mabel followed her line of sight and realized that one of the barn doors was open. She thought she'd closed it when she'd stopped working this evening, but maybe it hadn't latched properly and one of the barn cats had nudged it open. They had their own entrance, but they seemed to prefer using human doors whenever possible. She'd better go close it before Rory and Bettina arrived in the morning and saw the latest evidence of Mabel's incompetence as a farmer.

The finicky kitchen door refused to open at first, so Mabel set her phone down on the kitchen table to get a better grip. It finally flew open, wider than she'd intended. Pixie raced out into the darkness, where there was little chance of Mabel catching her. She ran after the cat, anyway, knowing it was what Aunt Peggy would have done.

Mabel was several yards behind when Pixie sailed through the open door of the barn and into the pitch-black interior. There might be a chance of catching her, after all, if she could corner the cat inside the barn.

Pixie stopped yowling suddenly. Mabel entered the barn and hit the light switch just inside the doors. Pixie was sitting a few feet away, her body oriented toward the back of the tractor, where the wagon was stacked with empty crates. Her face was turned so she could look over her shoulder at Mabel, as if asking what was taking her so long. Mabel went over to grab her, but wasn't fast enough. Pixie trotted off toward the back of the wagon.

Mabel didn't follow, but went around the other side of the tractor, hoping to catch the cat by surprise. As she passed the stack of filled garlic crates waiting to be racked, she realized it was shorter than when she'd stopped working, by at least two crates. She distinctly recalled planning to leave only ten crates for the morning, but she'd run out of energy when twelve were left. She doubted she'd miscounted. If there was one thing she could do well, unlike her poor performance as a cat owner, farmer, and niece, it was remember numbers. Even as exhausted as she'd been today, she wouldn't have made a counting mistake, and she didn't believe in fairies that materialized at night to finish people's work.

Two crates of garlic had disappeared.

No, that wasn't quite right, she realized, as she continued to the back of the wagon. The garlic was gone, but not the crates. The stack of empties on the wagon to go out in the fields tomorrow morning was higher than it had been. Whoever had taken the garlic had thoughtfully left the crates behind, right where they belonged.

Mabel considered calling the police, but, for one thing, she'd left the phone behind when she'd chased after Pixie, and she couldn't leave to get it until she'd caught the cat. For another, she didn't really have anything concrete to show the cops. She knew the garlic was missing, but there wasn't any physical evidence of the theft, like a broken lock or window, or even a haphazardly emptied crate, and the police wouldn't have any way of knowing how trustworthy her memory for numbers was. If she were back home in Maine, everyone would have known that numbers were her strength, but she didn't have that reputation here. The local people who knew her best, like Rory and Bettina and Emily, already thought she was a little unstable because of her grief, so even they couldn't vouch for her.

There was no point in calling the police, she decided. She'd just get on with her day.

Mabel continued around the wagon and saw that Pixie was sitting just inside the barn door, having apparently finished her inspection of the barn. As soon as Mabel stepped in her direction, Pixie stood and began walking toward the farmhouse. Mabel kept an eye on her while turning off the lights and securing the barn doors before following the cat back to the farmhouse, where Pixie was waiting at the back door to be let inside.

Apparently the Animal Control Officer had been wrong, and Pixie hadn't needed any time at all to become accustomed to her new home. That was at least one thing off Mabel's conscience. Too bad it wasn't that easy to finish the app for her boss, bring in the harvest for everyone who depended on the farm, and figure out what had happened the night Aunt Peggy had died.

* * * *

Even though Mabel had set her new phone's alarm for a ridiculously early hour, so she could greet the returning field hands, the stupid birds went off before the alarm did. Somehow, she'd forgotten to get earplugs yesterday.

Mabel dragged herself out of bed, trying not to do the math, but unable to avoid noticing that she'd gotten a grand total of three hours of sleep last night after the little escapade with Pixie and the open barn door. She wasn't likely to get much more sleep tonight, not if she wanted to get the app done for the Friday deadline.

After the jaunt to the barn and back last night, it hadn't seemed necessary to keep Pixie confined to the guest bathroom. The cat was sitting in the kitchen window, silently watching the barn as if it were prey that she might want to hunt.

Mabel scrambled the last of the eggs Emily had provided, and carried them over to the table. She might have fallen into her plate face-first from exhaustion if it weren't for Pixie's suddenly leaping from the windowsill to the table to investigate. Mabel put a few bits of egg on a napkin and bribed Pixie off the table and onto a chair.

Pixie poked at her snack while Mabel tried not to nod off between one forkful of egg and the next. After a few minutes, Pixie took off, yowling at top volume while racing all around the kitchen like a parkour athlete. She ricocheted off a base cabinet, hit the pineapple wallpaper beneath the avocado green phone, and then built up steam as she headed for the far wall, where she almost knocked the pineapple clock off its hanger. She landed on the windowsill that gave her a view into the back fields, and from there leaped past the back door, onto the top of the refrigerator and then down to the window above the sink, where she was finally satisfied with the view. She froze in place there, yowling in the direction of the barn.

Mabel abandoned the last of her eggs and peered outside to see what had set Pixie off. There was no one in sight, and the barn doors were securely closed. She was just about to chalk it up to the vagaries of feline nature, when Rory's white car pulled up in front of the barn.

"It's okay," she told Pixie. "It's Rory. You remember her. She's one of the good guys."

Pixie quieted but remained in the window. She watched Rory and Dawn get out of the car, and then looked at Mabel, as if seeking confirmation that the visitors were authorized.

"It's okay," Mabel told her. "I don't like company much, myself, but Rory and her daughter are okay, at least until the harvest is finished. Just one more day of visitors, and then we can have some peace and quiet."

Pixie yowled again, and Mabel watched to see if the cat had anticipated yet another arrival. Sure enough, a few seconds later Mabel finally heard the sound of an engine, and then the college kids' SUV parked beside Rory's car.

Another mystery solved, Mabel decided. Pixie wasn't yowling at random. She was sounding an alarm whenever she heard a vehicle enter the driveway. Mabel could see how that would be annoying for people who lived on a busy street or had a lot of friends visiting, but it shouldn't be a problem for her once the harvest was over, and the constant stream of visitors to the farm was cut off.

"They're okay, too, Pixie. Thanks for the warning, though."

Apparently satisfied, Pixie wandered off to find a good location for a nap, and Mabel went outside to oversee her crew. Inside the barn, Rory had already set her daughter to sorting and racking the garlic, Terry was loading the last of the empty crates onto the wagon, and Anna, who'd had a refresher course in operating farm equipment yesterday afternoon, was climbing into the tractor's seat.

"I can't stay this morning," Rory said. "My husband asked me to do some errands for him, but Bettina should be here any minute now. She called to let me know she was running late this morning, because of car troubles, but she'd be here as soon as she got the old clunker running again."

Rory was distracted briefly by the exodus of the field hands, with Anna clearly in charge of the trio. After they cleared the barn doors, Rory said, "I can't believe how receptive my daughter is to Anna's directions. If I'd told Dawn to hop on the back of the wagon to ride out to the field, she'd have walked, just to spite me."

"Hiring the three of them is about the only thing I've done right since I got here," Mabel said. "That, and listening to your advice. Could you tell me one more thing? I read Aunt Peggy's journal last night and got the names of the two local buyers. Ethan Baker and Jeanne Bettencourt. Do you know anything about them?"

"Everyone in town knows them," Rory said, as she headed for her car. "They own rival restaurants. One's a casual diner and one's fine dining, but they're both excellent at what they do. They're located in the touristy area in the center of West Slocum. Nice folks, but like all creative types, they need a good bit of hand-holding. The sooner you can reassure them that they'll be able to keep the best garlic on the east coast on their menus, the better."

"I'll look them up when I go into town later today," Mabel said. "Perhaps Bettina would be willing to keep an eye on the crew while I take care of some errands."

"I'm sure she'd be happy to help." Rory slid in to the driver's seat of her car and spoke through the open window. "She needs a distraction today, anyway. It's the fourth anniversary of when her husband was injured on the job. She believes he died of complications from his injuries, so it's a lot like an anniversary of his death too. I don't know if you've lost anyone you were close to before your aunt, but the first anniversaries after a death tend to trigger all sorts of emotions."

"I've been there before." Mabel didn't expect to be deeply affected by anniversaries of her aunt's death, but she remembered the aftermath of her parents' and grandparents' deaths. There had been days when even her app development work couldn't distract her from her grief. "If Bettina's not up to it today, I can probably deputize Anna. You saw how good a leader she is."

"She's good, but she's still young," Rory said. "I'm starting to think we've given Bettina a little too much time to get herself together. Sitting at home all alone only encourages her to dwell on her problems. She's becoming as dependent on me as she was on her husband, and it's not good for either of us. She needs to start taking on some more responsibilities. She can handle a couple hours supervising the field hands, for starters. If you're going to let her take your place as the garlic queen, she might as well earn the title. I already told her as much, so you can remind her of that if she doesn't want to help."

Rory left, and Mabel headed out to the fields, planning to work for a couple hours, until the library opened at ten and then Bettina could take over supervising the crew.

At nine thirty, when all of the available crates had been filled with garlic and it was time for Mabel to get ready to leave on her errands, she declared it was time for a break. Anna drove the tractor back to the barn, and then everyone unloaded the filled crates, replacing them with empties. Mabel sent the field hands into the farmhouse to raid the refrigerator for drinks while she stayed in the barn to rack garlic and waited for Bettina.

It was ten before a faint yowling from the farmhouse warned of Bettina's imminent arrival. Mabel went over to the barn doors to check, and sure enough, a few seconds later, a VW Beetle came racing up the driveway and screeched to a halt in Rory's usual parking spot. Bettina exploded out of the driver's side.

"I'm so sorry." Bettina's denim jumper was uncharacteristically wrinkled, and she wasn't wearing her usual tiny earrings. Her eyes were bloodshot and there were dark shadows beneath them. "I haven't been sleeping well recently, and I'm afraid I overslept this morning. I can stay late to make up for it."

"Don't push yourself too hard," Mabel said. "I need you to be in shape for the role of garlic queen."

"There won't be a garlic queen if we don't get the harvest in," Bettina said. "It would serve me right, missing out on the tiara, if the harvest is ruined because of me."

"You can atone for being late by keeping an eye on the crew while I go into town," Mabel said. "I should be back in a couple hours. Can you stay that long?"

"Of course," Bettina said. "Rory says I need to earn my tiara, and I will. I promise."

"The field hands are in the house getting drinks, and should be ready to go back out any minute now. The tractor's in the barn."

"I'll get right on it."

Mabel started across the dirt roadway to the farmhouse. Behind her, the tractor's engine roared, and a moment later Bettina drove the tractor out of the barn and toward the fields. Unlike Rory, who wrestled with the tractor, jerking it along a weaving path, barely staying within the boundaries of the dirt roadway, Bettina glided the tractor down the exact center of the roadway.

Mabel headed for the farmhouse to rout the teens from the kitchen and get herself ready to go into town. As she walked, she marveled over tiny Bettina's skill with the massive tractor. Kyle Sherman had been lucky that it wasn't Bettina who'd threatened to run him down. Rory could have maneuvered the tractor more or less in his direction, but the only way she'd have actually run him over was by accident. Bettina could have issued a more credible threat. She had enough control of the huge tractor to avoid running over the squash plants in the field where she'd turned it around, driving it in a sort of slalom pattern. She could probably have hit Kyle blindfolded.

Despite the impossible amount of work that had to be done in the next few days, Mabel was cheered by the knowledge that she now knew two people who could chase unwanted visitors away.

CHAPTER TWELVE

After a quick shower, Mabel dressed for the meeting with Aunt Peggy's lawyer. She was in the kitchen, putting on her shoes, when Pixie yowled briefly. Mabel glanced out the window to see who had set off the cat this time, and saw a little red sports car pull up next to Bettina's VW. A man got out, and Pixie yowled again.

"It's okay," Mabel said, although she didn't recognize him. He was average height and his dull brown hair was long enough to pull back into a loose ponytail. His face was almost completely covered, between the oversized sunglasses, and a bushy mustache and beard. He wore beaded leather sandals, skintight jeans and a black mesh tank top that revealed skin so pale it couldn't have been exposed to sunshine any time this year. He seemed to know where he was going, though, as he made a beeline for where the harvest was happening.

Mabel patted the cat's head to soothe both the animal and herself. "You'll get used to strangers showing up on the farm. He's probably a CSA member here to fulfill his work commitment. Bettina can handle him."

Pixie yowled again, briefly and without quite the usual earsplitting intensity.

"Really," Mabel said. "It's okay if people come here when it's light out. This guy certainly isn't a threat to anyone. I doubt he'll stick around for long. I give him about ten minutes before he's got one heck of a sunburn."

Pixie let out one last irritable yowl and then padded out of the kitchen, as if to say she'd done her job, and it wasn't her fault if no one listened to her warnings.

Mabel grabbed her keys and headed out the kitchen door, barely noticing that she'd finally gotten the knack of opening it. She could hear the tractor's engine running inside the barn, so she peeked inside to see who had driven it back. Bettina was unloading the wagon, surrounded by the filled crates she'd already removed. Mabel waved at her and then glanced toward the field. The newcomer was already out with the three teens. They weren't working, though. They looked like they were in a team huddle of some sort. As far as Mabel was concerned, the only thing worse than a hug was a huddle, but they didn't seem to mind.

Normally, she wouldn't have cared what they did to keep themselves motivated as long as they didn't try it on her, but it struck her that she hadn't seen them doing anything like that before. The three teens were friendly with each other, but not in any sort of touchy-feely way. The huddle could have been some new-agey sort of thing introduced by the newcomer, who did seem to have some hippie tendencies, judging by his appearance, but Mabel was aware that there could be less innocuous explanations for a man getting touchy-feely with teens.

She didn't know the man, and Bettina had been inside the barn when he arrived, so she hadn't checked him out either. Mabel considered asking Bettina about him, but she didn't have any time to waste, so she jogged straight out to the field where the crew was supposed to be working. As she approached, the man struggled to extract his wallet from the back pocket of his tight jeans and handed some money to each of the three workers. That definitely looked more suspicious than new-agey.

The huddle broke up, and the three teens and the ponytailed man all settled down to work.

After laying a handful of garlic in a crate, Anna straightened and waved at Mabel. "I thought you were going into town."

"In a minute," Mabel said. "After I meet the latest field hand."

"You've already met him," Anna said matter-of-factly. "It's Kyle Sherman in disguise."

Terry brought his crate over. "Hi, Mabel. You met Kyle Sherman yesterday."

At almost the exact same moment, Dawn called over from where she was still working, "Kyle Sherman is here."

"Hey," Kyle said, whipping off his fake beard and mustache. "I paid you guys to keep quiet. You can't rat me out."

"We just did," Anna said.

"I want my money back."

"You might be able to buy loyalty in the business world where you're from, but you can't buy it out here," Anna said, holding one hand out flat in Terry's direction while gesturing with the other for Dawn to join them. "We just held onto it as evidence. Mabel can decide whether you get it back."

Terry immediately dug the hundred dollar bill out of his pocket and handed it to Anna. Dawn wandered over and stuck her fist into her pocket, but didn't pull out the cash. "Do we have to give it up? I've never had a hundred dollars in cash all at once before."

"We have to," Anna said, and Terry nodded.

With the sort of impossibly drawn out sigh that only a teenager could manage, Dawn pulled out her crumpled bill and handed it over to Anna, who handed all three bills to Mabel.

Great, Mabel thought as she accepted the money. These kids all looked up to her, expecting her to know what to do, and they were probably all better at social interactions than she was. She didn't even understand the parameters of the problem or why anyone had made the choices they had. The amount of garlic that Kyle was likely to steal couldn't have been worth the three hundred dollars he'd paid as a bribe. The teens could have kept their silence and the cash they all could have used, and Mabel would never have even known she'd been cheated. Even if Kyle had been unmasked by Bettina, the teens could have claimed that they'd been taken in by his disguise. But they hadn't kept their silence. They'd been doing what was best for Mabel and the farm, instead of what was best for themselves.

What would the teens have thought if they'd known Mabel had been considering turning down the appointment as Aunt Peggy's personal representative? How betrayed would they have felt, knowing that even as they were choosing the farm's wellbeing over a tempting amount of cash, their boss had still been ambivalent about whether to finish the harvest?

Mabel heard Bettina returning with the tractor, a reminder that it was time to go see Aunt Peggy's attorney. First, she needed to figure out what to do about Kyle. He hadn't done anything criminal, but he was obviously desperate if he'd been willing to go to the trouble of assembling his horrible disguise. Even now, he was trying, with mixed success, to get the long haired wig off his head. It seemed to be stuck, thanks to a combination of bobby pins and some sort of adhesive. It had to be tremendously hot, like wearing a fur hat on this hot summer day.

"You'd better leave now, before Rory shows up," Mabel said. "You can have your money back this weekend, at the farmers' market, as long as you stay away from the farm until then."

There was a flash of fear in his eyes at the mention of Rory, but he stood his ground. "That's not fair. I'm just trying to help with the harvest."

"You didn't plan to also help yourself to a few pounds of the crop?"

"Absolutely not," he said, as the wig finally came free to reveal his own short red hair. "That's why I wore these clothes. There's no way I could hide so much as a single bulbil on me today. The jeans are too tight, and the shirt is both see-through and fall through." He raised one sandaled foot. "I'm not even wearing work boots that might hold a few bulbs."

Mabel wrinkled her nose. Commingling garlic with sweaty work boots would give new meaning to Stinkin' Stuff Farm.

"All I want," he continued earnestly, "is a couple pounds of garlic in return for a full day's work. That's reasonable, don't you think?"

Mabel didn't understand his desperation to acquire a bit of Aunt Peggy's garlic, but he wasn't faking the emotion. If she sent him away now, he'd find another way in. She didn't have time to keep unmasking him, and she couldn't afford to have him distracting her field hands by offering them bigger and bigger bribes.

On the other hand, it galled her to reward him for bad behavior. Someone should have knocked his sense of entitlement out of him before now, but she didn't have the time or inclination to do it herself. It might be more efficient simply to keep him where someone could keep an eye on him, and make him work for what he wanted, instead of demanding it as his right. Otherwise, he'd cook up some other crazy scheme to circumvent the rules that had originally prevented him from acquiring the garlic he coveted. He might even come back in the middle of the night and help himself to whatever he wanted. He'd probably convince himself that he was entitled to extra, as hazardous duty pay, for having to work in the dark.

For a moment, Mabel wondered if he'd already done just that. It would explain the patches of missing garlic, but if he'd already raided some patches of garlic, why would he go through all this trouble to get more? She didn't have time to get answers right now. She was going to be late for her appointment with Aunt Peggy's lawyer if she didn't leave right now.

"You can stay on one condition," Mabel said finally. "If you steal so much as one clove, I'll give your bribe money back to my loyal crew, and then I'll have you arrested for theft."

"I won't steal anything, I promise."

"There's more," Mabel said. "I'll also blackball you permanently from the CSA."

His eyes widened, but he nodded. "At least then I'd deserve it. But I'm not going to steal anything."

"Fine," Mabel said. "You're not a CSA member, so you need to fill out a job application. Then you'll work with a buddy at all times, and you'd better be good to the rest of the crew, because they're holding your garlic futures in their hands."

He scooped up his discarded wig and facial hair. "No problem."

"Good," Mabel said. "If you last the full day, with no complaints from the rest of the crew, you can buy a couple pounds of garlic from your wages."

They started back to the barn so he could fill out the paperwork, meeting up with Bettina after just a few yards.

Bettina pulled the tractor within a foot of Mabel before turning off the engine so she could be heard without straining her voice. "What's he doing here?"

"I just hired him for the day," Mabel said.

"It's against the CSA rules, having him here," Bettina said. "Scott always says that you can't trust people who break rules. Anyone who'd break one rule will break others, and all of society will fall apart."

Kyle was proving he had some survival instincts, remaining silent, with his head bent like a repentant sinner, and fidgeting with his wig as if it were a hat.

"Sometimes rules can be bent a little," Mabel said. "He's not here as a CSA member, but as an employee, and we're going to take precautions so he's not alone in the fields where there might be too much temptation."

"Peggy would never have let him set foot on this land," Bettina said.

"My aunt is dead," Mabel said, only belatedly realizing, by the shocked look on Bettina's face, that she'd been unduly blunt with someone who was having difficulty dealing with her own more devastating loss. "What I mean is that I'm doing the best I can to honor her wishes, but I can't know for sure what she would do, so I have to use my own judgment. We need help with the harvest, Kyle is willing to provide it, and I'm willing to take the risks involved with giving him one last chance to prove himself."

"It's hard to get used to the fact that it's your farm now." Bettina's stiff posture suggested that she was biting back the words she would have liked to say: *It's your farm now, for better or worse. Mostly worse*. Bettina didn't actually argue, though, perhaps for fear of losing her chance at a tiara this weekend. She started up the tractor and continued over to where the teens were working.

Mabel hurried back to the barn to grab the paperwork she'd left there earlier. She shoved a packet into Kyle's hands with instructions to fill everything out and then report to Bettina for work.

Bettina's words continued to echo in Mabel's head: *It's your farm now*. She was starting to feel like Stinkin' Stuff Farm really was hers. Not in the way Bettina had meant it, as a privilege that Mabel enjoyed, but in the opposite sense, as a burden that Mabel had to carry. She was responsible for the farm and everyone on it, from Pixie to the teens and even Kyle. As tempting as it was, she couldn't abandon any of them now.

CHAPTER THIRTEEN

Mabel barely made it to Aunt Peggy's attorney's office on time. He was surprisingly young, barely out of law school, running his own solo practice in a tiny office in a converted Victorian style house near the center of town. At first, Mabel was surprised that Aunt Peggy would have chosen him over someone more experienced, but then learned that the attorney hadn't been her aunt's choice. He'd inherited the file when he took over the practice of an elderly attorney who'd been forced into retirement by a debilitating stroke. Unfortunately, that meant that the young attorney hadn't met Aunt Peggy personally. All he knew about her was contained in the text of her will, which had been written a couple of years ago, shortly before he took over the practice.

The young attorney had apparently been expecting Mabel to know as much about Aunt Peggy's assets and final wishes as she'd been expecting him to know, leaving them both frustrated.

The will itself was pretty standard. All it said, translated from the legalese, was that Peggy wanted Mabel to inherit everything. There was nothing specific in the will or the file about funeral plans, nothing about the farm's future, and definitely nothing like those sentimental provisions in movies and television where the dead person professed eternal love or hatred for anyone.

The young attorney seemed knowledgeable about the probate process, and gave Mabel an overview of what to expect from the legal system, and what her responsibilities were. He couldn't help her with the things she really needed to know: how her aunt had died, where she'd wanted to be buried, and what she'd wanted Mabel to do with the farm in the long run.

The one thing Mabel was sure of, after the show of loyalty by her field hands, was that she needed to stay here until the harvest was completed and the estate, if not completely settled, which the attorney said would take at least a year, was at least in a holding pattern, where she didn't need to be involved on a daily basis.

Mabel signed everything the young lawyer put in front of her, committing herself to becoming the personal representative of Aunt Peggy's estate. Stinkin' Stuff Farm was truly Mabel's responsibility now, both legally and morally.

Next on her list of errands was another visit to the library. Her boss had sent her an email this morning with some revised specs on the app that was due on Friday, and she hadn't trusted her new phone's internet connection enough to try downloading the specs at the farm. The phone service was adequate for voice and text messages, but it had a tendency to cut out, which would have been extremely annoying in the middle of a download. Now that she'd committed to staying in West Slocum for the rest of the summer, she really needed to get hardwired internet service at the farm.

Josefina was too busy to engage in any hug assaults, so Mabel was able to go directly to the computer room. It only took a couple of minutes to download the file from her boss and send him a reassuring message that she'd have the app done by Friday, omitting her concerns about what it would take in the way of an all-nighter to get it done in time. She did warn him that it might be midday on Friday, instead of first thing in the morning, and if that was a problem, she wouldn't be upset if he wanted to reassign the project to one of her coworkers.

Next up was an email from her attorney. He'd spoken with the local DA, who didn't see anything suspicious about Aunt Peggy's death, but was willing to look again if Mabel could give him something solid to go on, either from the privately paid autopsy or any other reliable source of solid evidence.

Mabel doubted the DA would consider her uneasiness about the facts of her aunt's death to be a "reliable source of solid evidence." Even her questions about the missing phone, the timing of the death, and the location of the death weren't even remotely what anyone would consider to be solid evidence. Nevertheless, she typed up a quick summary of the things that had seemed odd about her aunt's death and sent it to Jeff with instructions to do whatever he thought best with the information.

Mabel still had a few minutes to spare before she would be expected back at the farm. She decided to take advantage of the reliable high-speed access to the internet to do some quick research to see what could be done about last night's theft.

She was stunned by the extent of the crop theft problem. Farmers in every part of the world were experiencing thefts of fruit, nuts, vegetables and even cattle. She'd always thought of it as something that kids did, like sneaking into an orchard and eating apples until they were sick. What she read about, though, was more like organized crime. One group had stolen a football field's worth of potatoes. Another crew, presumably with beekeeping expertise, stole 150 hives containing millions of bees. One of the most shared stories she found was about thieves in Austria who had stolen nearly nine tons of garlic. In fact, garlic seemed to be an extremely popular target of thieves. From Gilroy, the garlic capital of the world, came newspaper reports as far back as the 1980s about thieves swarming over fields where the garlic had been pulled from the ground but left in the fields to dry, and stealing forty or fifty pounds at a time.

Mabel sat back, appalled at the massive number of hits her search had generated, and the lack of any good answers to the problem. The random patches of stolen garlic that she'd observed on her farm weren't as catastrophic as some of the reported thefts. Her loss was closer in scale to her original concept of kids sneaking into a field, although she couldn't quite imagine kids eating garlic until they threw up. It seemed more likely that the garlic was being stolen for resale somewhere.

The sorts of protective measures that the major farmers took to deter theft would cost far more than the value of the garlic that had been stolen to date. On the other hand, some simple precautions might help. Aunt Peggy had practically invited thieves to steal her crop. Forget about security guards, Stinkin' Stuff Farm didn't even have so much as a gate on the driveway or a lock on the farmhouse doors. The surprising thing wasn't that some of the crop had been stolen from a farm that had been unoccupied for two weeks, but that there had been any crop left at all.

Mabel needed more information to extrapolate a pattern. The farm had been hit at least twice: once between her aunt's death and Mabel's arrival, and once last night. She didn't know if there had been any earlier thefts, or if Aunt Peggy had been aware of them. Mabel would have loved to have had some guidance directly from her aunt on how to handle the situation, but there hadn't been any mention of the thefts in any of the pages of the farm journal that Mabel had read so far. Would Aunt Peggy have just let it be, figuring it wasn't worth the expense to stop it? Or would she have hired guards? Gotten more feral cats to roam the fields and howl like Pixie? Trained the stupid birds to earn their keep by pecking the trespassers to death?

Mabel just didn't know, and she had no one to blame but herself. She should have done more than send Aunt Peggy the standard birthday and holiday emails over the last decade. Even a once a year visit would have given her a little more insight than she had now.

Mabel logged out of the internet. If the major commercial growers, with years or even decades of experience didn't have a good way to manage the crop thefts, a rank novice like herself wasn't likely to find a good solution.

On her way to sneak out the library's back door, Mabel realized that she had one resource that all those commercial farmers didn't have: everyone's favorite librarian and her store of gossip. Enduring a hug was a small price to pay to find out if there were any rumors of a local black market or other crop thefts.

Mabel turned around and headed for the lobby. Josefina didn't have any patrons waiting to check out materials, so Mabel braced herself for the hug that wasn't long in coming.

Josefina released her after just a few seconds and stepped back to ask, "So, how's the harvest coming along?"

"It's going to be a close call," Mabel said. "I need to get back to the farm, but I had a quick question for you first."

"That's what librarians are here for." Josefina straightened her bright pink cardigan on her way behind the desk. "What do you need to know?"

Mabel leaned over the checkout desk and considered her words. The librarian's eagerness to share what she knew was a two-way street. Anything Josefina heard was likely to be shared from one end of West Slocum to the other even before Mabel could drive back to the farm.

"Everyone seems so anxious to get some of Aunt Peggy's garlic that I'm wondering if I should do something to make the farm more secure," Mabel said. "I'd never really thought about crop theft, but I did some quick online research just now, and it seems like a widespread problem."

"None of my patrons would steal from you," Josefina said emphatically.

"Of course not," Mabel said. "But someone's been stealing from my aunt's farm, and it got me to thinking. What do the thieves do with the crop after they've stolen it? I read about a whole football field's worth of potatoes being stolen. Who needs that many potatoes?"

"Someone making moonshine," Josefina said promptly. "Otherwise, I suppose they were just planning to sell the potatoes to restaurants or distributors."

"What about selling them at a farmers' market?"

"Maybe elsewhere," Josefina said, "but it would be hard to do here. Darryl does random inspections of the vendors to make sure they have receipts for anything that they don't grow themselves, or anything they're selling in quantities greater than they could possibly grow. He's kicked out a few vendors in the last couple years for not being able to prove where they got their merchandise."

"Were any of them selling garlic?"

"No one would dare try that here," Josefina said. "No point, anyway. Everyone wants to buy Stinkin' Stuff garlic, not something inferior. Maybe a few tourists would buy from someone other than you, but I doubt it. If the thief is selling the garlic, he's not doing it here. Someone would have noticed, and I'd have heard about it."

That only confirmed what Mabel had feared: there was no way she could stop the thief herself, and there wasn't enough evidence for the police to do anything. She might as well forget about the thefts and concentrate on rescuing as much of the crop as she could before the even more significant threat arrived tomorrow in the form of Mother Nature's rain.

"I'd better get going," Mabel said. "We're making progress with the harvest, but there's still a lot to do by tomorrow."

Mabel had assumed that the prospect of delaying the harvest was her get out of library free card, the one thing that Josefina would accept as a good reason to end a conversation, but Josefina reached out one pink clad arm and took Mabel's hand to keep her from leaving.

"You know," Josefina said, "now that you've got me thinking about crop thefts, I wonder if that could be what Peggy was worried about in the week or two before she died. She looked tired whenever I saw her here, and she was almost reserved with the people she ran into, which wasn't like her at all. At the time, I thought she'd been working too hard, bringing in the harvest all by herself, but she might have been worried about the farm. If she was plagued by thefts, it would explain why she didn't hire any field hands this year. She might not have been able to afford them. It would also explain why she seemed so reserved the last few times I saw her. She could have been wondering if one of the people she considered friends was actually stealing from her."

"Do you think she suspected anyone in particular?"

"I don't even know for sure that she knew about thefts, but when you mentioned it, it seemed to fit," Josefina said. "Whatever was worrying her, she did her research online, and she didn't check out any materials, so there's no paper trail to show what she was interested in. That's the one annoying thing about the internet. I love the way information is so easily accessible, but sometimes a patron needs guidance or a different way of looking at a topic, and they just don't know it. If I could see what they were working on, I could make some suggestions, but unless they actually ask, I can't help. Peggy never asked. I wish she had."

"So do I," Mabel said. "I really need to leave now, though. Bettina's supervising the field crew, and I've already been gone longer than I'd planned. We wouldn't want to do anything to risk finishing the harvest, would we?"

"Definitely not," Josefina said, rising to the bait this time. "I'm counting on this weekend's celebration. I even put in for the day off on Saturday."

Mabel tugged her hand free of the surprisingly strong grip of Josefina's arthritic fingers. "I'll do my best."

"That reminds me," Josefina said. "I heard that you've abdicated the role of garlic queen in favor of Bettina. Are you sure that's a good idea? It's a lot of responsibility, and she hasn't been particularly stable since her husband died. Not that she was all that stable before, either. You should have seen the two of them together. She'd be hanging onto his arm so tight you'd think she'd fall flat on her face without his support. I guess, in a way, she did need him. She really fell apart when he was shot and ended up in a wheelchair. Then, just when it looked like she might have figured out that he needed her support now, instead of the other way around, he went and died on her. I was sure she'd latch onto some guy with a white knight syndrome within a couple months, but she didn't. Maybe there's more to her than I ever realized."

"Rory thinks Bettina can handle it," Mabel said, "and I trust Rory's judgment."

"Oh, well, in that case, I'm sure it's fine." Josefina glanced to the side, where a patron was arriving to check out a stack of books. "Rory knows what she's doing."

"I certainly hope so." Not just for helping with the choice of garlic queen, but for the bigger questions about Aunt Peggy's final wishes for her funeral and her farm.

* * * *

Mabel took the long route home by way of Main Road, so she could get a glimpse of the two restaurants in town that had contracts for a substantial amount of garlic. In the center of West Slocum, a three block long strip had been renovated into high-end boutiques, art galleries and antiques shops that attracted tourists from vacation homes on the ocean.

Jeanne's Country Diner was across the street from the Textile Museum at one end of the strip, and Maison Becker was on the same side of the street as the Textile Museum, but two blocks away, near the town green where the farmers' market was held. The diner had its own parking lot, which seemed to be completely full. Maison Becker relied on street parking, but that didn't seem to hamper its business, judging by the number of people eating there al fresco, and the equally substantial number of people in line at a discreet takeout window.

The sight reminded her that she needed to get lunch for her field crew. She continued on to the grocery store to visit the deli counter. While she was waiting for the platter to be made up, she automatically checked her email on her phone. Nothing there but a couple of messages from her boss, who was convinced she was sick or in some sort of trouble, since she'd never asked for so much as a single hour's extension on a project before. She didn't know whether he was more concerned about her or about his own reputation if she failed to complete the app on time, but she keyed in a brief reassurance that she was fine, and unless he decided to reassign the project, she'd make sure the app was ready no later than Friday afternoon.

She had just hit send on the reply message when she heard her name being called. At least, she assumed she was being addressed; Mabel wasn't a common name these days. She turned around to see Darryl Santangelo bearing down on her with his gorgeous face and his beaming smile. She didn't trust anyone who smiled that much.

"I was just thinking about you," he said. "Have you made a decision about your booth at the market yet?"

Mabel pocketed the phone. "I promised to let you know by Thursday, and I will."

"It's just that Larry's really anxious to take it over, and he's not the only one. It's not fair to keep them dangling." He gave her the full force of his smile. "It would make everyone's life much easier if I could let them know now, one way or another."

"It wouldn't make my life easier," Mabel said. "I'm not trying to cause you problems. The decision is largely out of my control too, depending on the weather. The other farmers should understand that, and considering how closely you work with farmers, you should know how we're at the mercy of the weather."

"I do." He waved at someone behind Mabel, sending his smile past her for a moment, before refocusing it on her. "I have lots of experience with the uncertainties of farming, but that doesn't make it any easier to deal with."

"It's your job to make my job easier, not the other way around," Mabel said. "In fact, there's something I could use some help with."

"Anything you want." He waved at someone else, before adding, "Anything except for actually working in the fields. I'm not that much of a hands-on guy."

She couldn't help glancing at his hands and comparing their large but immaculate appearance to what she knew hers looked like. She kept her nails cut short for ease of typing, but even so, she'd managed to tear bits off half of them yesterday, and the embedded dirt from this morning's work highlighted the ragged edges of the nails. She'd also gotten a little too enthusiastic a few times with the clippers, leaving cuts on her fingers. The backs of her hands also had a few shallow slashes from before she'd learned to keep clear of the sharp stems of the squash vines.

"You don't have to get your hands dirty. I just need some information." She glanced around to see if any of the people he'd waved to were close enough to overhear them. Fortunately the lunchtime rush hadn't begun yet. She and Darryl were the only customers in sight, and the clerk behind the counter was busy compiling Mabel's order. "What can you tell me about crop thefts in the area?"

He frowned for a moment before a voice shouted out, "Go, Sox," and Darryl's smile returned as he waved at the speaker. When he turned back to Mabel, he said, "You're new to farming, so let me give you some advice. You can't take it personally if some kids sneak into your fields. It's just what kids do in agricultural areas. Everyone plants enough to share a little with the young daredevils. It's not like a little crop theft is a gateway drug for more serious crimes. Besides, your garlic is relatively safe. Kids tend to be more interested in fruits and corn for eating, or tomatoes for throwing."

"I'm not worried about kids," Mabel said. "I've been reading about criminal gangs hitting farms. One group stole something like nine tons of garlic a few years ago."

"Not around here," Darryl said, waving at yet another person as if they were long-lost relatives. "Peggy's farm produces less than nine tons, and I'd have known if her entire harvest was ever stolen."

"What about smaller amounts? Did Aunt Peggy mention any small thefts from her farm this year? Or perhaps she had less on sale at the market this year than usual?"

"She didn't say anything to me." Darryl turned his smile on the deli clerk approaching with Mabel's platter.

Mabel took the platter and waited while Darryl placed his order before asking him, "What about other growers? Was anyone else selling garlic this year?"

Darryl shook his head. "Not at the market. Larry plants about an acre of garlic, but he sells it all in bulk to a distributor in Boston. Everyone else around here just grows enough for their own use, not for sale. No one in West Slocum wants to buy garlic from anyone except Peggy. She wasn't bragging when she said she grew the best garlic on the east coast."

"That's why I'm worried about the risk of theft," Mabel said. "Aunt Peggy's farm is such an easy target."

"Not really," Darryl said. "First, the thief would have to know where the farm is. Local folks would know, but it's far easier and safer for them just to join the CSA she participates in, and get the garlic legally. Or buy it at the farmers' market, of course. Most tourists wouldn't know where the farm is, and even if they did, they'd also need to know the right time to harvest the garlic, and how to process it for storage. No point in stealing it, only to have it rot afterwards. I just can't see it. Not for the relatively small amount of money they'd be saving by stealing even a full year's worth of garlic."

"Professional crop thieves would know the harvest cycle and the curing process," Mabel said, frustrated that Darryl didn't seem to care about something that potentially affected all of the farmers he worked with. "Plus, it's the best garlic on the east coast, and that makes it more valuable."

The deli clerk appeared with Darryl's order, which he took with yet another smile and a detailed inquiry into the wellbeing of what sounded like everyone in her entire extended family, naming each one of them. Mabel waited impatiently, anxious to get back to the farm to relieve Bettina, but equally determined that Darryl understand what was happening on the farm. The thefts were jeopardizing the farm's prospects, and that was going to have consequences for the farmers' market too.

Finally, Darryl was satisfied with his update on the clerk's family, and turned to leave with Mabel. As they walked toward the checkout, he said, "You're letting your imagination run away with you. Professional thieves couldn't advertise their haul as the best garlic on the east coast without admitting they'd stolen it from Peggy. And without that reputation, it's not worth as much. There are more lucrative crops around."

"I'm not imagining anything." Mabel hadn't wanted to make a big fuss, but Darryl's patronizing attitude pushed her over the edge. "I've seen the bare patches in the fields, and so has Rory. Someone is stealing my aunt's garlic. It's probably been going on for the last two weeks, and they're getting bolder. Last night, they didn't even bother to sneak into the fields. They stole it directly from the barn. Far more than a kid would take on a dare, and more than even a large family would be likely to use in a year. Someone's taking it for resale."

"Not at my market."

"Are you really that sure?" Mabel said. "Garlic is a pretty small crop, easy to hide from you, and to sell on the sly when you're not nearby. You can't be everywhere."

Darryl waved at a man in a Red Sox baseball cap. When he turned to Mabel again, his smile faltered. "Peggy never said anything about any thefts. I just can't imagine any of the regular vendors doing something like that to her."

"Someone's doing it," Mabel said. "There isn't much I can do to stop it myself, but you can spread the word among the local farmers to watch out for thieves. If they get away with stealing the garlic and selling it at a profit, what's to stop them from raiding other farms?"

"I'll ask around," he said. "Don't get your hopes up, though. Crop thefts are a fact of farming life."

And farming death, Mabel thought as she paid for the deli order. Enough thefts could send a farm into bankruptcy and ruin the farmer. Or worse. What if Aunt Peggy had surprised the thief, and been killed by him?

CHAPTER FOURTEEN

The trip back to the farm took Mabel past the Stevens Funeral Home. As far as she could tell, in West Slocum all roads led, not to Rome, but to its one funeral home. A depressing thought, and one that poor Bettina experienced every time she left her house. No wonder she'd wanted to barricade herself at home indefinitely. Rory and the rest of Bettina's friends had apparently been treating her with kid gloves the last six months, and today, in her first tentative foray into real life, Mabel had insisted that Bettina work with someone she distrusted.

Mabel pushed the accelerator pedal a little harder. What was everyone afraid what would happen if Bettina was stressed? The expected consequences couldn't have been too extreme, or Rory wouldn't have recommended giving Bettina some responsibility, especially when that responsibility involved Rory's daughter. Of course, Rory hadn't anticipated Mabel running late, or Bettina's having to supervise Kyle Sherman. Just how unstable was Bettina?

Mabel pulled into her parking space next to the farmhouse's back patio, spraying as much gravel as Kyle had when he left the farm in a huff. She raced out of the car and into the fields to find Bettina perched on the seat of the tractor, clearly anxious to leave, while the teens and Kyle went about their work.

"I'm so sorry I'm late." Mabel maintained a safe distance from the tractor's massive wheels, even though the engine was off. "I lost track of time while I was picking up lunch supplies."

"Scott's going to be upset," Bettina said without any particular emotion. "He hates it when I'm late, and I'm sure he has a lot to tell me today."

"You'd better get going, then. Don't wait for the rest of us. I'll check in with the crew and then walk back to the farmhouse to get lunch ready."

"You can't leave them out here alone." She nodded her head toward the teens, and then lowered her voice. "Not with *him* here."

"Was he that much of a problem while I was gone?"

"Well, no, but that's because I was keeping an eye on him. I never left him alone for one second. He didn't steal any garlic on my watch."

"I appreciate that," Mabel said, wondering how Kyle could have possibly stolen anything, given his current clothing, even if he'd been left in the fields completely alone. "I'll talk to Anna about keeping an eye on him for the few minutes left until lunch."

"If you insist." With one final glare at Kyle, Bettina reached for the key in the ignition, and then sat back again without turning it over. "I almost forgot. Rory called to say that her husband, Joe, will be picking Dawn up at dinner time. Rory's been delayed like you were. Must be the day for it."

"I'll watch for him."

"He'll be easy to spot in his uniform. He's a cop, almost as dedicated to his work as Scott was before...well, you know. Guys like them are always in uniform, even when they're not." Bettina started the tractor and sped off to the barn. She handled the tractor with such finesse that the garlic crates in the wagon didn't shift an inch, even as she encountered deep holes in the dirt roadway.

Mabel went over to where the four field hands were working. "Lunch in half an hour. Anna's in charge until then. Terry will be the foreman after lunch."

"Hey," Dawn said. "How come I never get to be in charge?"

"You can have a turn tomorrow," Mabel said. "As long as you don't try to drive the tractor."

* * * *

After lunch, Mabel asked Terry to drive the tractor back to the field, with the girls on the back of the wagon. Mabel stayed behind in the barn to sort and rack some of the harvested garlic that was piling up there, since they were likely to run out of empty crates otherwise. Bettina had already anticipated the problem and had spread out a row of tarps on the barn floor, where the crates could be gently dumped into a not too high pile that still allowed for air flow around the garlic. The tarp was only about a quarter covered with garlic, leaving space for tomorrow, in case they ran out of time to get everything done and had to settle for just getting the garlic under a roof before the rain came.

The tarps weren't an elegant solution, since it increased the total amount of work. Someone would have to pick up the garlic and refill crates to carry it over to the racking station. Plus, Mabel worried that they might run out of both crates and tarp space tomorrow if none of today's crop went straight into the racks. The teens and Kyle were good for an hour or so on their own, without her supervision, and meanwhile, she could empty a few crates straight into the racks.

Mabel lost track of time in the rhythm of the work, but it couldn't have been more than half an hour before she heard the tractor returning from the fields. More crates on the way, and she'd barely made a dent in the ones already stacked up beside the racking station.

A wagon she didn't recognize backed into the barn, stopping when it was fully inside the doors. The tractor engine stopped, and Emily came inside. "I'm here to collect the garlic waste."

Mabel's confusion must have been apparent, because Emily explained, "Peggy and I had a deal. She gave me the waste portions of the garlic plants, and I gave her the goats' manure to fertilize the fields."

"I thought the whole garlic plant was edible."

"It is," Emily said, "but the scapes are best for human consumption in the spring, when they're still tender. My goats don't care if they're tender, so Peggy always gave me the scapes after she'd removed the head from the bottom and the bulbils from the top."

"We haven't had time to cut the bulbils off yet. We've just been tossing the whole scapes into a bin to deal with later."

"I can help with that." Emily dragged a bin over beside her wagon. "I don't know whether the goats can smell the harvest, or if they just know it's the right time of year for it, but they've been looking longingly in this direction. If I don't feed them some scapes soon, I have a bad feeling they're going to find a way to escape the fencing and come over here."

"Does this mean I'm going to have to help pack up the goat manure?"

"Don't worry about that." Emily checked the many pockets of her white overalls, apparently coming up empty, and then went outside to the front of her tractor. She returned a moment later with a lethal looking knife. She grabbed a bunch of scapes, sliced the clumps of bulbils off the tops, letting the miniature garlic cloves fall back into the bin, and tossed the decapitated greens into her wagon. "The manure has to age before it goes on the fields, and the fields won't be ready for fertilizing and tilling until September or October. You'll have plenty of time to get used to the goats by then."

Why did everyone assume that Mabel would be here indefinitely? She'd only just decided today that she needed to stay longer than the few weeks she'd originally planned. Mabel knew she didn't really belong here, so why couldn't anyone else see it? All they had to do was look at how efficient and coordinated Emily was with her de-heading, wielding an obviously sharp knife without so much as a single scratch, and then compare that to Mabel's network of lacerations where she'd been unable to handle safer tools or even the scratchy bits on plants.

Mabel was much better off in her quiet little home, hunched over her computer, interacting only with the virtual world. The sooner she returned to that, the better. Assuming she still had a job after this week, and she didn't get fired for not completing the app on time.

She just needed to bring in her aunt's final crop, and find a use for the farm that she could feel confident her aunt would approve of. Then she could go home.

Actually, she thought, there was one more thing she had to do before she could leave: get her aunt buried properly. Emily might have some useful suggestions for that. "I spoke to Aunt Peggy's attorney this morning, and he doesn't know what she wanted for her final arrangements. Did she tell you anything more specific than that she wanted to be buried on the farm?"

Emily continued decapitating the garlic scapes while she spoke. "Not really. I doubt she ever thought about it much. She wasn't that old, and she seemed to be in good health."

"The death certificate said she had high blood pressure and high cholesterol, which led to cardiac arrest."

Emily tossed the latest handful of headless scapes into her wagon with more force than necessary. "They couldn't possibly know that without an autopsy. She might have had some health problems, I suppose, but they weren't documented anywhere. She hadn't been to a doctor in at least ten years, never had her blood pressure taken or her cholesterol levels tested in all that time. I wanted her to get a routine checkup, but she said she felt fine, and the garlic she ate did more for her health than any drugs the doctors could give her."

Mabel remembered her aunt once recommending that everyone eat five cloves of raw garlic a day. She didn't know if Aunt Peggy actually ate that much of it, or just preached it. Mabel felt she should have known. "I should have visited her more often."

"She would have loved that," Emily said. "But she wanted you to be happy, and she didn't think you were ready to make any changes in your life. Don't forget that Peggy wasn't always a farmer. She was a city dwelling accountant before she came here. It took her twenty years in her old job, plus the shock of your parents' death for her to realize it wasn't the right lifestyle for her. She thought you'd come around eventually too. I just wish she was still here to see it."

"I haven't come around to anything. I'm just here temporarily, until the harvest is in and the farm's future is arranged. Then I'll go back home to Maine."

"We'll see." Emily swapped out the bin she'd finished sorting for a new one. "I started out with just a single pair of goats and a couple chicks on a suburban plot. It wasn't long before I wanted to expand, and then when we came to West Slocum for a vacation, I fell in love with the place. You may find it's not so easy to quit, either the farming life or this town."

"I'm pretty resilient," Mabel said. "Besides, I think I'm like the cell phone carriers who manage to resist coming to West Slocum. Just like them, I get better reception in other territory, and I'm glitchy here, unable to make the connections I need."

"Perhaps." Emily shrugged and dove into the new bin to continue separating the bulbils from the rest of the scapes. "When do you think you'll have Peggy's funeral?"

"It depends on how and where she's buried. I talked to my attorney about arranging for a private cemetery on the farm, but he doesn't think it's feasible. Do you know if Aunt Peggy had any objections to cremation? We could bury her ashes here without any problems."

"I think she'd like that," Emily said. "Her ashes will nourish the farm, the way the farm nourished her all these years."

"Is there anywhere special on the farm that you think she'd like her ashes to be buried?"

Emily paused with the knife against a bunch of scapes. "She loved every inch of this place, so it would be hard to choose a single spot."

"We can rule out the creek where she died, and the lavender field too."

"Peggy definitely wouldn't want the smell following her into the afterlife. She'd come back and haunt both of us. You for putting her there, and me for letting you."

"Not the active fields either, I suppose," Mabel said. "It seems a little creepy to mix human remains in with a food product, even if it's just ashes."

Emily smiled. "I don't know. Some of Peggy's customers might think it was a bonus, knowing the garlic had been nourished by her one last time."

"It's going to be another week or two before I have to decide," Mabel said. "I'm open to suggestions until then."

"Why so long?" Emily said. "I thought the funeral home would be anxious to get her body moved to the next stage. Besides, waiting isn't good for the people who cared about Peggy, and there can be a lot of negative energy in the air when a person remains in limbo, without a final resting place."

"It takes time to get an autopsy."

"Didn't the authorities decide not to do one?"

"Yes, but something doesn't feel right about Aunt Peggy's death. You knew her and her work habits. You can't possibly think it was normal for her to be out in the middle of the night, in her least favorite corner of the property, during a season when that particular crop doesn't need any attention."

"Well, no, but accidents do happen." Emily's knife sliced cleanly through another tough bunch of scapes, underscoring her words. "Especially on farms. They're among the most hazardous of all possible workplaces, and have one of the highest fatality rates for work-related accidents. About half of them are related to tractor operation, but the other half happen in all sorts of settings."

"Maybe I'm just getting carried away with my ignorance of farm life, and Aunt Peggy died a natural farmers' death." Mabel glanced uneasily at where the tractor lurked outside the barn doors. How could everyone be so matter-of-fact about the risks of operating tractors? "I'd feel better if I know for sure that it was her heart and not something more sinister that killed her."

"We all grieve in our own way," Emily said. "If an autopsy will set your mind at ease, then you should have it done. I just don't want to see you get your hopes up and then have to go through the grief all over again when the autopsy doesn't answer all your questions. Peggy's the only one who could tell us what really happened that night."

"Unless there was someone else with her. That person could tell us what happened."

"You really think someone killed her?" Emily looked up from her work in surprise. "But everyone loved Peggy."

"Not everyone," Mabel said. "I can think of at least two people who didn't. Larry Rose and the guy she was suing over bad seed stock, Al Soares. And what about Kyle Sherman? He knew she'd been behind the decision to exclude him from the CSA this year."

"Kyle's got entitlement issues, but he's not a psychopath," Emily said. "Al Soares is a fraud and a coward. He'd never come here to confront Peggy. He lets his lawyer clean up after him. And Larry? I know he and Peggy were like oil and water, but I thought it was just natural rivalry among competitors."

"I'm just saying, Aunt Peggy definitely had some enemies. I don't know all that much about her daily life, and I can still come up with some examples. There could be plenty of other people she'd crossed paths with, who didn't particularly like her. Maybe they even disliked her intensely. She liked people, but she was also opinionated and she could be blunt when sharing her opinions."

Emily laughed. "I'd forgotten about that. You should have heard her when a bunch of kids drove their dirt bikes through her lavender field, killing everything in their path. She went straight to their parents, and let them have it."

"How upset were they?"

"Quite a bit, at first, when they thought she was going to have the kids dragged into juvenile court. They all relaxed when she told them she'd settle for the kids replanting every single one of the damaged plants by themselves, and then compensating her for the new stock by working on the farm one day a week for the rest of the season."

"Maybe one of them held a grudge," Mabel said.

"I suppose it's possible. If the autopsy suggests there was anything suspicious about Peggy's death, I'll get you a list of the families whose kids were involved." Emily wiped her hands on her white overalls, leaving behind a pair of green smudges. "Until then, try not to dwell on it. You don't want that kind of negative energy around you."

"See?" Mabel said. "That's just another example of how I don't fit in here. I thrive on negative energy."

* * * *

When Emily decided she'd collected enough scapes, she powered up the tractor and left to feed her garlic-craving goats. Mabel finished racking one more crate of garlic and then stepped outside the barn to check on the field workers. If they were already bringing another load of filled crates in, she could catch a ride back to the field.

She couldn't hear the tractor's engine, so she debated whether to walk out to the fields or rack yet another crate's worth of garlic. Either way, it was physically demanding work, but at least pulling the garlic would give her a break from leaning over the drying rack.

Before she had to decide, she heard a muffled yowl from inside the farmhouse. She turned to see if someone was coming up the driveway. Sure enough, a moment later, she heard a rough engine, and then a rusty beige truck rattled up the driveway, past Bettina's Beetle and the college kids' SUV to stop in the middle of the roadway, directly opposite the barn doors where Mabel was standing.

Larry Rose waved through the truck's open window. The engine was still knocking, and the sound of his ineffective tugging on the door handle was barely audible. Finally, he gave the door a shove with his shoulder, and practically fell out of the driver's seat. He pushed the door partway shut, taking care not to let it latch.

"You might as well get back in the truck," Mabel said without leaving the barn doorway. "I'm still not selling the crop."

"Not here for that," he shouted as he walked toward her. "We're both reasonable people. I know you know that Peggy and me didn't get along. Probably my fault, too. It's always the man's fault, isn't it?"

"Depends on the man," Mabel said. "And the woman."

"Peggy was a good woman." Either Larry had lowered his voice slightly, or she was growing accustomed to his loudness. "A better farmer than me, for sure. But the thing is, she had an unfair advantage. Peggy would never tell me what the secret to better garlic was, but I know she had one."

"I can tell you the secret."

"Really?" His voice had definitely dropped to a normal register, probably what he considered to be a whisper.

"Really," Mabel said. "I read it in her journal. She should have had a blog, and then everyone could have benefitted from her expertise."

"What is it?" This time, his voice had actually dropped to an expectant whisper.

"Hard work and stinky manure."

"And?"

"That's it," Mabel said. "The secret is that there is no secret. Just hard work and good farm management."

"You're just like her, never giving a guy a chance." Larry's voice had regained its loudness, and then some. "I know she had a special cultivar for her main crop. All I want is a shot at growing some of the same stuff."

Mabel recalled seeing one of her aunt's charts in the journal, listing all of the varieties planted on the farm, along with the source of the stock. Most of the fields were planted with a common Russian variety, and those plants were all the progeny of an original bulk purchase back when she'd started the farm. Much smaller beds were planted with five or six heirloom varieties, all of which had official names, and had been purchased from two major commercial farms. There hadn't been anything in the journals about developing a special cultivar, and Mabel was convinced there would have been a detailed spreadsheet on the subject if her aunt had been trying to create her own unique variety. "There is no special cultivar."

"What do you know? You're no farmer, just some sort of tech wizard, according to Darryl."

"I'm telling you what Peggy wrote in her journal. Her success was due to hard work. You can see it for yourself, if you want. She really wasn't holding anything back from you."

"I've got a better idea," he said. "Let me take some samples of the main crop. A few heads from each field. I'll grow them alongside my own varieties next year, and you'll see that they're different."

Samples from each field. Was that what the garlic thief had been doing? Not stealing large amounts, just collecting a random sample from each field? Except that wouldn't explain the crates full of garlic that had been stolen from the barn last night. That haul had been far more than the small sampling necessary for a scientific study.

Larry interrupted her thoughts with a grudging, "I'll even pay you the market rate for the samples."

He could have stolen the samples already, she thought, and now he was just trying to establish a paper trail, in case the stolen garlic was found at his farm. Had he sneaked onto the farm the night Aunt Peggy died, only to be caught in the act? Aunt Peggy was easily as tall as Larry and probably outweighed him by fifty pounds. But Larry was a farmer too, so he was probably stronger than he looked. If he'd stolen a "sampling" of garlic, and Aunt Peggy had tried to grab it away from him, he might have pushed her to her death without meaning to hurt her, not even realizing she was unconscious in the water before he ran away.

Before she accused Larry of theft and murder though, she needed more evidence. For now, Mabel just needed to avoid a confrontation. If Larry was more violent than anyone else knew, she didn't want to provoke him when they were too far away from the fields for the workers to notice a commotion here at the barn.

"I'll think about selling you some stock," Mabel said finally. "After the harvest is finished."

CHAPTER FIFTEEN

After Larry left, Mabel threw herself into the routine and camaraderie of harvesting the garlic with her field hands. The teens were hard workers, cheerfully teasing each other as they worked, and they didn't even seem to mind much the intrusion of an adult into their little clique. Kyle was surprisingly hardworking and amiable, now that he'd gotten at least part of what he'd wanted.

Around five thirty, a police officer wandered into the fields. As Mabel headed over to greet him, Kyle straightened from his work, and complained, "I haven't taken anything. I swear. Why'd you have to call him?"

"I didn't," Mabel said. "I think it's Dawn's father. He's here to give her a ride home."

She could see what Bettina meant about the man appearing to be inseparable from his uniform. There was something in the way Officer Hansen walked, and the way he kept an eye on his surroundings, that suggested he was a cop first, everything else second.

As he approached, he inspected the field hands, lingering longest on Kyle Sherman, either because he knew him and what his wife thought of him, or perhaps just because of the inappropriateness of Kyle's clothing for farm work.

Officer Hansen carried a large bag of cookies, which was apparently as much a part of his uniform as his badge and holstered gun, judging by the bulging waistline that threatened to take the shape of the fake stomach in Kyle's earlier disguise. He waved to his daughter and introduced himself to Mabel, telling her to call him Joe, before holding the bag of ginger snaps out to her. "I brought snacks to share."

She took the bag and peered inside. There were exactly five cookies left, out of what had to have been a couple dozen initially.

"Thanks." Mabel passed it on to her crew who fell on it ravenously, reminding her just how long it had been since she had last fed them. It was beyond time to let them go home for dinner. "I should have sent everyone back to the barn earlier, but I lost track of time."

He looked at her skeptically, probably because he always knew to the minute what time it was, without even checking his watch. She could imagine him in court, testifying that on Wednesday, at exactly 17:39 hours, he had entered onto the premises of one Mabel Skinner to escort a minor, to wit, Dawn Hansen, home, after the aforesaid Mabel Skinner failed to exercise proper supervision over her employees.

"You aren't in violation of labor laws or, worse, the curfew that Rory set," Joe said. "Dawn's got another hour or so before she needs to be home. I got here early to meet my daughter's new boss."

"Oh, Dad," Dawn complained, through a mouthful of cookie. "Don't scare her off. I like this job. Just don't tell Mom I said that."

"It's time for you to go home now," Mabel told her youngest worker.

"Can't I stay just a little longer?" Dawn pleaded. "Just until we finish the row, okay?"

Mabel remembered using the same stalling tactic when she was a child, asking her grandmother if she could stay up just until she finished a page of code. Somehow the coding for one page always required coding three or four additional related pages. "Sorry, but it's time for you to go, right now. Child labor laws. You don't want to see me get arrested by your father, do you?"

"I guess not," Dawn said morosely. She tossed her last handful of garlic into her half-filled bin and carried it over to Terry, who was closest to where she'd been working, to top it off.

"Anna and Terry and Kyle will be going home soon too," Mabel said. "Everything can go into the tractor for one last trip to the barn as soon as they've filled their current bins."

Anna turned around to inspect the remainder of the field, and Mabel followed her example. Over the course of two days, they'd harvested far more than she'd ever thought possible, but that was still only about half of the crop, leaving more than a full day's worth of harvest to be done tomorrow.

Anna said, "If we quit now, there's no way we'll get the rest of the harvest in before the rain arrives tomorrow. I can stay for a while longer tonight."

"Me too," Terry said. "Although I would like something more to eat first, if there are any leftovers from lunch."

"I may be able to stay too," Kyle said. "I'd need to make a couple calls to rearrange my schedule first."

"That's not fair. I want to stay too," Dawn said. "Please, Dad."

He shook his head. "The law's the law."

Dawn sighed, but apparently knew when she'd run into a brick wall. "Can I at least go back to the barn with everyone to unload the crates?"

Joe nodded. "It's fine with me. You just need to be off the clock by six, and we need to be home before your mother gets there at six thirty, or we're both in trouble."

The teens scrambled to fill the last bins and load them onto the wagon, before Anna jumped into the driver's seat and the rest of the crew hopped onto the back of the wagon.

Mabel called out, "Help yourself to whatever's in the fridge in the farmhouse. Just don't let the cat outside, no matter how loud she gets."

Terry waved an acknowledgment, and they took off. Mabel turned to Officer Hansen. "I'll walk back with you."

"I hope this isn't like a parent teacher conference, where you're going to tell me that while Dawn is a bright and creative young woman, she also has some less admirable traits." He ambled down the path, adjusting his stride to hers. "Because then I'd have to reconsider my initial impression of you, since you'd obviously be the devil incarnate for suggesting my daughter is anything less than perfect."

"Nothing like that," Mabel said. "Dawn has been wonderful. I've been terrified that she'd try to drive the tractor when I wasn't looking, but she seems to have accepted that it's off-limits."

"It probably helps that I threatened her with the loss of all of her electronic privileges if she so much as thought about driving the tractor."

"That would explain a lot," Mabel said. "There's something else you might be able to explain. We noticed some bare patches in the fields yesterday, where it looks like someone's been stealing five or ten pounds of garlic at a time. I think another couple crates' worth went missing just last night. Do you know if Aunt Peggy experienced any thefts before she died?"

Joe sighed and reached into his jacket pocket, only to realize he'd given away the last of his cookies. "Crop theft is a chronic problem in any agricultural area. There isn't much we can do about it. We just don't have the personnel to stake out all the acreage all season long. Not even during peak harvest time."

"I don't expect you to catch the thief," Mabel said. "I was just wondering how long it had been going on, and what Aunt Peggy was doing about it, so I can take the same precautions."

"She reported the first significant thefts two years ago, I think, but they started the year before that," he said. "Until then, she'd never lost anything more than a few plants to kids sneaking in and taking some on a dare, so they could see who could eat the most raw garlic. Then, all of a sudden, she started to notice bare patches. Just a couple dozen plants here and there, but more than kids could possibly want. She didn't report it the first year, thinking it was just some fluke, or perhaps some bad stock that had died, rather than thefts. The second year, the bare patches got bigger, so she reported it, and she must have scared the thief off somehow, because it stopped for the rest of the season. She thought whoever it was had lost interest, but apparently it started up again about a month ago with some of the heirloom varieties that ripen a little earlier than the main crop."

"Did she try to catch the person?"

"Not as far as I know," Joe said. "She might not have told me, though. She knew I would warn her not to do anything that foolish, but Peggy could be a stubborn woman."

"It's a family trait," Mabel said. "What about video cameras?"

"Peggy looked into them, but eventually decided they'd cost more than the stolen garlic was worth."

"I know what you mean," Mabel said. "In my line of work, we have to deal with pirates all the time. Some theft is unavoidable, without spending far more than the cost of the stolen product."

"It's still not right," Joe insisted. "We did send some extra patrols out this way after her last report, not that it did any good. I wish we could have done more, but I think I was more upset by our failure than she was. I wouldn't have been so accepting in her shoes, but she convinced herself that the thief probably needed the garlic, or the money from selling it, more than she did."

"That sounds like Aunt Peggy." It also explained why the farm was on such precarious financial legs. From what Mabel had read, small farms were always on the brink of bankruptcy these days, with little room built-in for the various disasters that Mother Nature could throw at them, and no room at all for the man-made disasters like theft. "I'm not that good a person. I want the thief caught and tossed into a dungeon."

"I don't like it either, but I can sort of understand where Peggy was coming from," Joe said. "The thefts began during a bad economic time for West Slocum, when a lot of people were hurting financially. It was before the center of downtown was revitalized and the boutiques and galleries and weekend markets began bringing in tourists from the coast. Back then, it wasn't uncommon for desperate people to resort to stealing from the local farms to feed their families. Everyone understood and we all sort of turned a blind eye to it." Judging by the pained look on his face, he'd hated having to ignore the crime, even as he'd known it was the compassionate thing to do in the circumstances.

"Garlic isn't exactly a food necessity," Mabel said. "No one steals garlic to stave off starvation."

"No, of course not. But your aunt didn't seem all that bothered by it." He went past where the tractor was parked to peer inside the barn for his daughter, but she wasn't there. She must have joined the others getting some food in the farmhouse. "Actually, that's not quite right. She wasn't bothered about it until maybe a week or so before she died. I ran into her at the farmers' market when I was on a detail. She looked … I don't know … not her usual self. Worried, maybe. Or depressed. Just not herself. Usually, she kinda' glowed when she was working the farmers' market. Like Rory did when she was pregnant. Peggy was usually so happy on market days, hanging out with friends, talking up her wares, converting new customers to the miracles of garlic."

"Did you ask her what was wrong?"

"I was on my way to her booth when I noticed a pickpocket team working the crowd. By the time I took care of them, Peggy was acting like herself again. I thought I'd imagined her being out of sorts, but now, I just don't know."

"What changed your mind?"

"She died," Joe said. "Made me wonder if she'd been ill, not just worried, when I saw her at the market. Maybe if I'd checked in with her that day, I could have convinced her to go see a doctor."

"Did you ever wonder if she'd been killed?" Mabel said. "Perhaps by the garlic thief?"

"Thieves don't generally kill anyone," Joe said. "Different sort of criminal, different sort of behavior."

"What about someone else who might have had a grudge against Aunt Peggy?"

"I did wonder a little, but I couldn't think of anyone who might want to hurt her," he said. "She had a run-in a couple years ago with some dirt bikers who damaged her lavender beds, but they settled everything out of court, and as far as I knew, no one had any hard feelings."

"What about the guy she was suing for selling her bad stock?"

"My wife told me about that, but I don't know any of the details. It was a civil matter, nothing I'd be involved with." Joe leaned forward solicitously. "Seriously. There's no reason to think anyone killed her. If I'd known anything at all that seemed relevant, I would have mentioned it to the investigators. It was just an accident. Sad, but not criminal."

"You might as well hear it from me, since I'm sure it will hit the grapevine before long," Mabel said. "I'm having a private autopsy done. I don't believe Aunt Peggy's death was from natural causes."

"Everyone goes through the denial phase. If the autopsy will help you to accept the loss, then you should do it."

"What if it reveals something suspicious, something that the official investigation missed? Is your department equipped to take the evidence and pursue it?"

"We're a small department, but we've got some good detectives. They'd want to know if they missed something." Joe paused outside the farmhouse's back door. "If the autopsy doesn't set your mind at rest, you can give me a call, and I'll do what I can. No one gets away with murder in my town."

* * * *

Joe had to practically drag Dawn out of the farmhouse at six. Kyle Sherman left at the same time, saying he had commitments he couldn't get out of that evening, but promising to come back tomorrow to put in a few more hours. He even offered to wait until then to collect his wages and purchase the garlic he so coveted.

Anna started to clear the kitchen table, taking Terry's plate out from under the sandwich he was still working on, but Mabel said, "Don't worry about the mess. I've got to make a few calls, and I'll take care of everything in here while I'm on the phone."

"We'll head back out to the field, then," Anna said. "I bet we can finish the last of the current field before it's dark. That will leave just one field for tomorrow."

Just one field. That sounded good. Except Mabel knew the fields weren't all the same size, and the remaining one was easily as big as the total area of both of the fields they'd spent two days harvesting. "If we do get it all in on time, there'll be a bonus for everyone."

The teens left, seemingly as full of energy as they'd been when they'd arrived this morning, and squabbling good-naturedly over which of them was going to drive the tractor out to the field. She didn't care who won the argument as long as she didn't have to drive it herself.

Before Mabel joined them in the fields, she called the two local restaurants who had large contracts for Aunt Peggy's garlic, and arranged to meet them at the library at eight thirty.

Anna turned out to have been right, and by the time Mabel had to leave for the library, they were on track to pull out the last of the plants in the current field before the bugs and the darkness overwhelmed them. They'd probably have to double-check the last few rows tomorrow to see what they'd missed in the poor light, but it was encouraging to think they only had one field left. Assuming Kyle pitched in tomorrow as promised, and so did Rory and Bettina and perhaps a couple of CSA members, they had a chance of getting at least most of the last field harvested before the rain. A remote chance, but still a chance. It might be interesting to develop an app to calculate the exact odds, but that would have to wait for another day and another harvest. Whatever time Mabel had for computer work between now and Friday afternoon was barely enough to develop the app that her boss was expecting, assuming there weren't any major bugs.

Mabel took a quick shower so she'd be presentable for the meeting with the restaurant owners at the library. While dressing, she realized just what a toll the work in the fields had taken on her, as muscles and joints refused to cooperate with the gyrations necessary to pull on jeans. Anna and Terry had seemed unaffected, even though they'd put in more hours of physical work than she had, but they were ten years younger than Mabel. How on earth had Aunt Peggy, at twice Mabel's age, managed to work the fields, not just one week out of the year, but day in and day out?

Maybe Aunt Peggy's death wasn't all that surprising, after all. She'd probably worked herself to death, bringing in at least one field's worth of the heirloom garlic varieties all by herself this year, without any temporary workers. That would certainly explain why no one around here thought her death was suspicious enough to investigate. They were all more aware than Mabel was, of both the farming lifestyle and Aunt Peggy's work ethic.

Mabel checked to be sure Pixie had water and kibble, before heading out to her Mini Cooper. On the drive into town, she couldn't help thinking that if she'd been more involved with her aunt's life, doing something more than simply remembering her a few times a year, she would have known just what a strain the farm had become, both financially and physically. If she'd known, she could have helped. Or at least tried to. She wasn't sure Aunt Peggy would have accepted any financial help, but Mabel could have at least visited, maybe taken a week or two off from her job during the summer to help with the harvest. Her aunt might still have died, but at least she wouldn't have been alone.

The library's parking lot was almost empty, except for the spaces reserved for employees. A pregnant twenty something was reading behind the checkout desk. Josefina was over in the video browsing section of the lobby with her back to Mabel, facing a man and a woman who'd apparently been ordered to stand in opposite corners of the space, like toddlers in time out. Except these "toddlers" were thirty some years old and wearing chef's jackets. The man's version was black, and on the upper left side of his chest was discreet white lettering that identified him as Chef Ethan Becker. The woman's jacket was white, and where Ethan had his name, she had the Jeanne's Country Diner logo embroidered in bright red and blue. Like their respective jackets, Ethan was elegant, subtle and aloof; and the woman—Jeanne Bettencourt, presumably—was relaxed, natural and outgoing.

Mabel went over to stand next to Josefina, who said, "Mabel, meet Ethan Becker and Jeanne Bettencourt. I've kept them from killing each other so far. It's your turn now. Better go on back to the conference room, so you don't bother the other patrons if there's any more foolishness. I'll unlock the door for you."

The two chefs took cautious steps out of their respective corners, as if half expecting to be told their time-out wasn't over yet.

Mabel tried to imagine what her aunt would have done when meeting new people. Aunt Peggy smiled a lot and expected the best from everyone. Mabel forced a smile onto her face and said, "I'm sure we'll all get along just fine."

Josefina snorted and zipped over to the corridor, blazing a trail to the conference room.

The smile didn't seem to be working on the two chefs either, so Mabel decided to go back to being herself. "Don't you two want an update on the garlic harvest? Everyone else in town does."

Ethan Becker was the first to reach out to shake Mabel's hand. Instead of the upper-class British or possibly French accent she'd been expecting, he spoke in the more earthy Boston dialect. "I want to know. I care about the ingredients I use."

"Ha!" Jeanne Bettencourt had the interesting French accent that her rival lacked. She rushed over to glare at her rival, for the perceived sin of holding Mabel's hand too long.

For a moment, Mabel was afraid she was going to be accosted with a European air-kissing, but Jeanne settled for a quick handshake before racing off in the direction Josefina had disappeared, as if getting to the conference room first would somehow get her a prize. Ethan was right on her heels, but Mabel followed more slowly, too tired from working in the fields to hurry.

She arrived just in time to see the two chefs trying to squeeze through the conference room door simultaneously. Neither of the chefs was fat, but the doors of the old building were somewhat narrow, definitely not designed for two people to enter a room shoulder to shoulder. Neither would give way until Mabel came up behind them and said, "Excuse me, but I've had a long day, and I really need to sit down for a bit. I can do that in the conference room or back in my car on the way home."

The two chefs jumped aside and let Mabel pass on her way to the head of the table. Jeanne slipped in behind Mabel, leaving an irritated Ethan to bring up the rear. He didn't say anything, just raced to take the seat at Mabel's right hand, where Jeanne had been planning to sit, as if it were the last chair in the entire building.

Jeanne dope-slapped the back of Ethan's head. "You are supposed to wait for the women to sit first."

"Since when did you ever expect special treatment?"

"I don't," she said. "I was talking about being polite to Mabel. She doesn't know how impossible you are. It wouldn't have hurt for you to try to make a good impression on her."

"You're not my mother," he said.

"Thank heaven for that," Jeanne said as she flopped into the chair on Mabel's other side. "Pay no attention to his childishness. I want to hear about this year's garlic crop. I heard there were problems."

"It's been a challenge filling Aunt Peggy's shoes."

Ethan took her hand. "Everyone in town misses Peggy, and we can only imagine how you feel."

"I feel tired right now," Mabel said, pulling her hand free. "We've been working to bring in the harvest, but we may not get it all before the rain gets here. I'll do my best, and you and the CSA will have first priority, but I can't make any promises yet."

"If there's not enough for both of us," Jeanne said, "you should fill my order first. I signed the contract before Ethan did."

"The garlic should go to the chef and the diners who can best appreciate fine ingredients," Ethan said.

"My customers are every bit as discriminating as yours," Jeanne said. "More so, since they know where the good food is. They don't need any fancy signs or faux-French menu items to impress them. Just good food, cooked well."

Ethan and Jeanne continued bickering while Josefina flashed an *I told you so* look, and then backed out of the room, closing Mabel in with the battling chefs.

Mabel leaned back and closed her eyes, too exhausted to break up the verbal scuffle. They both seemed to believe that Aunt Peggy's garlic was the secret to their respective successes so far, and that failing to get their fair share—defined as "some amount that's at least equal to, but preferably larger than, the amount purchased by anyone else"—would cause them to have to close their doors. Were they this passionate about all their ingredients, or did they really think their customers would desert them if they purchased, say, Larry Rose's garlic for die-hard locavores or generic garlic supplied by a wholesaler for non-locavores?

As the chefs' voices grew louder, Mabel was grateful for Josefina's insisting that they meet in this somewhat isolated private space, so they weren't upsetting the rest of the library patrons. Maybe it hadn't been the hard physical work that had killed Aunt Peggy, but the stress of dealing with fanatics like Kyle Sherman and these two chefs. Aunt Peggy's journals hadn't said anything to suggest that farming required anything more than a good work ethic and a never-ending source of manure, but apparently it also required the skills of an international treaty negotiator, when the various parties couldn't even agree on where to sit.

If she was this ineffective with just two people, what was she going to do with the crowds at the farmers' market this weekend? She'd have to convince Darryl and Rory that it really would be better if she delegated the market work to someone else. Perhaps Anna and Terry could do it. They'd proven themselves more than trustworthy and they'd probably appreciate a couple more days' wages.

"If you do," Jeanne was telling Ethan, "I'll go to court to get an injunction, and let the court decide who gets what."

Mabel knew from personal experience with her parents' estates that if they took her to court, it could take years to settle the matter, and in the meantime, the garlic they were fighting over would rot in the barn. It wouldn't do them any good, and it would cripple the farm, making it all but impossible to sell the property to another farmer who wanted to take over the operation.

Were the chefs really so passionate about garlic that they'd destroy the farm, and possibly their own restaurants, just to make sure they got what they considered their fair share of the harvest? They were working themselves up into a frenzy, fueled by their hatred of each other. Their antagonism hadn't happened overnight. They'd obviously been feeding it for weeks or months, maybe even years, until they'd reached their current irrational state.

Emotional decisions always got people into legal trouble. The two chefs were beyond reason right now. They pushed themselves to their feet and leaned across the table that was separating them, shouting at each other over Mabel's head.

She could really use a professional negotiator right now. Someone like Aunt Peggy's attorney. But he wasn't here, and Josefina had already washed her hands of the matter. That left Mabel to keep these two crazy people from destroying what Aunt Mabel had worked so hard for, and possibly had even died for.

"Stop," she said, channeling the quietly angry voice her grandmother had used on her when Mabel had pushed her independence a little too far. "There's enough garlic for both of you. One more word of squabbling, though, and neither one of you is getting so much as a single bulbil. Not even half a bulbil. Not even half of the very smallest, stalest, most squashed bulbil I can find."

In perfect synchronization, they both slowly inched down into their chairs, as if prepared to respond if the other jumped back up to gain some advantage from standing.

How far would they go to keep the other person from winning their little war? It seemed absurd to think that anyone would kill over garlic, but the two chefs were as obsessed with their food supply as most people were with more personal relationships. Was it possible that one of them, in the grips of jealousy over the division of garlic, had blamed Aunt Peggy for some perceived slight, and killed her?

Killing the farmer would also end the supply of garlic, so, logically speaking, their passion for garlic wasn't a logical motive. Still, Mabel couldn't rule out the possibility that one of them might have been carried away during an argument, since she'd observed, firsthand, just how irrational they could get. She didn't have enough evidence to get them arrested, so all she could do was to keep the two chefs from killing each other.

"It's just garlic, people. Sure, it's the best garlic on the east coast, but it's just garlic."

The two chefs looked at her with matching expressions of amazement. Apparently there was at least one thing they could agree on: Aunt Peggy's garlic couldn't be dismissed as *just* garlic.

CHAPTER SIXTEEN

Over the course of the next half hour, Mabel managed to persuade the two chefs that she hoped to fill their orders in full, but whatever happened with the harvest, she would treat them perfectly equally. They weren't appeased right away, but settled down and became fairly reasonable when she warned them that the only way she was going to get the harvest completed was if she didn't have to worry constantly about her customers' squabbling. She needed to be able to concentrate completely on the harvest and the drying process for the next few weeks. The chefs declared a truce, and Mabel set an appointment in a month's time, when the three of them could meet at the farm, and the chefs could oversee the packing of their respective orders. *Yeah, that was going to be fun.*

When Mabel got home, Pixie was waiting for her on the kitchen table. The purr was almost as loud as her yowling.

After making herself a sandwich from the lunch leftovers, Mabel sat at the kitchen table and used her slow and glitchy smartphone connection to check her email. She'd meant to do it before she left the library, but the meeting with the chefs had only ended when the library staff announced closing time.

Her boss had sent three more messages while she'd been focused on the farm work. In the first one, he declined to reassign Friday's app to any other developer, insisting she was the only person for the job and offering what was, for him, effusive praise for her work. She couldn't help thinking that his confidence in her was an indication that, in her own way, she was definitely her aunt's niece. Instead of excelling at farming, Mabel produced the best apps on the east coast.

The other two messages from her boss sounded more like his usual needy self. The first one sought reassurance that he hadn't made a mistake and she would have the app done by Friday afternoon, and the second one was a reminder that she had to complete not just the original assignment, but also the additional features in the revised specs by the deadline.

Mabel sent him a response that was somewhat more upbeat than she actually felt. She could finish the app on time, but it wasn't going to be easy after the long day she was anticipating in the fields tomorrow, from the moment the stupid birds woke her up to whichever came first: rain or pitch darkness. She was going to be in a race against the rain, and if she'd learned anything from Aunt Peggy's journal, besides the importance of hard work, it was that a farmer should never bet against Mother Nature.

Worrying about it didn't help. Right now, she needed to get some work done on the app, if she wanted to have any chance of finishing tomorrow night. Mabel forced herself to retrieve her laptop from upstairs and settle in at the kitchen table with her work, while Pixie kept an eye on both Mabel and the barn from the kitchen window.

Over the next couple of hours, Mabel managed to add two of the five changes into the work she'd already done, while absently nibbling on her sandwich. The remaining changes were part of the app that she hadn't coded yet, and would have to wait until tomorrow, when she'd had a nap and her eyes weren't scratchy and drooping from lack of sleep.

Mabel cleared away her dishes and refilled Pixie's food and water bowls. The pineapple-shaped clock on the far wall indicated it was just after midnight. Despite the physical exhaustion, her mind was still racing with thoughts of everything she had to accomplish in the next day and a half. She needed something to help her relax before she slept.

Mabel thought of Aunt Peggy's journal. From what Rory's husband and Josefina had said, her aunt may have known about the garlic thefts. Aunt Peggy wouldn't have left something that important out of her journal. Mabel had only skimmed the journal last night, looking for the equivalent of a bolded, large font headline, announcing all the details of the thefts. She might have missed something tucked away in smaller print.

She carried the journal up to her bedroom, and climbed into bed to lean against the headboard and read. Pixie followed a couple of minutes later to curl up at her feet.

Mabel found part of what she was looking for in a footnote to the spreadsheet that summarized the last five years of the harvests, month by month. It didn't identify the thief, but it confirmed that Aunt Peggy had to have known she was being robbed. The current year's June harvest of an early maturing heirloom garlic variety had been completed midmonth, and was down about ten percent from the previous year's. The two previous years' entries showed drops of five percent and three percent, respectively. The thefts were definitely increasing, and the loss had gone from something that might have been explained by the vagaries of weather, to something that could only be explained by theft. Aunt Peggy had even gone over her weather charts and other notes to prove to herself that nothing else could explain the drop in productivity.

At the very end of the footnote, in writing that was more cramped and cryptic than the rest, suggesting it might have been added later, Mabel read, "Saw thief at market on 6/20. Can't believe it. Why?"

That was what Mabel wanted to know too, along with "who?" More frustrated than ever, Mabel scrutinized the rest of the footnotes methodically, much the same way she looked for bugs in her coding. She no longer expected the bolded, large font headline that announced the name of the thief, but she'd hoped to find something that was suspicious or out of place, a starting point for the police to investigate. She found nothing useful in any other spreadsheet footnote, so she flipped to the dated journal entries, starting with the date when Aunt Peggy had seen the thief. The entry summarized the sales for the day, and concluded, "Observed possible black-market activity. Maybe. There could be, must be, another explanation. Need more evidence."

That entry was three weeks ago, the last farmers' market Aunt Peggy had ever attended.

She'd died the Tuesday after that. The timing couldn't possibly be a coincidence. The thefts and Aunt Peggy's death had to be connected.

Mabel kept going back to the idea that her aunt had been looking for more evidence on the night she'd died. Josefina had seen Aunt Peggy doing some online research shortly before she'd died. What else would Aunt Peggy have done? Would she have done what Officer Hansen had advised Mabel against, and set out to catch the thief garlic-handed?

The farm was Aunt Peggy's passion. She might well have considered a little risk was acceptable in order to keep the farm from bankruptcy. If she knew the thief, she might have thought she could reason with him. Aunt Peggy also knew the ins and outs of the farm, so she'd have known the best place to hide while staking out the fields. She might not have intended to confront the thief at all, just identify him and report it to both the police and the manager of the farmers' market to take the appropriate actions.

If that was the plan, there was a great deal that could have gone wrong. Aunt Peggy could have recognized the thief, and, thinking she could reason with him, she confronted him, with unexpected and fatal consequences.

Just then, Pixie began yowling. Mabel started, dropping the heavy journal before rolling out of bed and peering out the window. This time, she had enough sense to stay to one side, out of any direct line of sight. A few seconds passed, long enough for a legitimate visitor—if there was such a thing at one a.m.—to have driven into view, but the driveway remained deserted.

Pixie raced downstairs, yowling all the way as she made her rounds of the front of the house and then the kitchen, ending up in the window above the sink. Mabel stuck her phone into her pocket and followed. She couldn't see any signs of movement outside, but she trusted Pixie's early warning system. The thief had probably left his car on the road, or just out of sight on the driveway. If she could get the license plate number, that would be something solid for the police to investigate. Maybe even something for the DA to consider if the autopsy revealed anything even remotely suspicious.

Mabel checked her phone to be sure she had good enough service to call the cops when she got the license plate number. Only two bars, at most, winking down to one as she walked toward the back door, but it would do.

"Stay here, Pixie." Mabel went over to open the window where the still-yowling cat was peering outside. "You can be my alarm. If you get quiet, I'll know the thief is leaving, and I'll skedaddle out of sight."

Whether the cat understood or not, Pixie stayed on the windowsill, maintaining her nonstop yowling. As Mabel slipped out the back door, the caterwauling turned into surround sound, with additional feline voices joining in from the barn.

The moonlight was almost nonexistent, and Mabel hoped the thief was stumbling around as blindly as she was, trying to find out where the daytime harvest had left off and his illicit harvest could begin. Mabel continued away from the fields and toward the road, only to wander off the side of the driveway and fall into a prickly clump of weeds. At this rate, she could walk right past the thief's car and not even realize it. She needed some light, and her smartphone could provide it, but she didn't want to make herself a target for the thief. The plan wasn't to confront him, just get a look at his car.

Mabel glanced back at the barn, where a security light above the doors created a small pool of illumination, and a landmark for orienting herself. The fields were mostly hidden from her view by the farmhouse, and the small slice of the unharvested field that she could see was completely dark. There was no way a thief could be working without light, so he had to be somewhere out of her line of sight. That meant that she was out of his line of sight too. A little judicious use of her smartphone's light would be safe enough.

Mabel picked herself up and continued down the driveway, all the way to the end, without seeing a car. At the farm's entrance, she looked in both directions. She could see about a thousand feet in each direction, before the road curved. There was no vehicle in sight. That didn't make any sense. The thief would have had to park right on the edge of the road, in clear view. A vehicle parked any deeper into Stinkin' Stuff Farm's property would sink into the wetlands all along the frontage, unable to leave again without the assistance of a tow truck.

So where was the vehicle that Pixie had heard?

Maybe there wasn't a vehicle. Maybe Pixie had heard something else that set her off. Or else Mabel had been completely wrong about why Pixie yowled, and the earlier predictions of incoming visitors had been coincidences.

Feeling a bit foolish, Mabel trudged back up the driveway, not even trying to hide the light of her phone. Pixie was still yowling, so something was upsetting her, but it wasn't a vehicle in the driveway.

At least the cats in the barn had gone silent. Mabel frowned at the thought. She couldn't remember if she'd heard the cats making noise in the barn before she left the house. What if they had started it, and their noise had provoked Pixie, rather than the other way around? Maybe one of them was hurt, or some sort of dangerous critter, like a coyote or a fisher cat, had invaded the barn.

Back home, if she'd been worried about a wild animal, she'd have called the animal control officer. Here, though, in an agricultural area, she'd be laughed out of town if she couldn't protect her own barn from wildlife. Mabel turned off the phone and stuffed it into a pocket, so her hands would be free to grab the pitchfork leaning against the wall just inside the door.

She crept cautiously toward the pool of light outside the barn doors, hoping that she was, once again, foolishly reading too much into Pixie's yowling. Right now, she'd be just as happy to believe that the cat just liked to yowl at random, as her previous owners had apparently thought, and there was no real meaning to her cries.

Mabel had just reached the edge of the lighted area outside the barn, when the sound of the tractor starting broke the silence inside the barn, and provoked Pixie into renewed heights of furious yowling. Mabel froze.

She should have trusted the cat and called the cops from the safety of the farmhouse, but it was too late for that now. She fumbled in her pocket for the phone and dialed 911, only to realize she was apparently in one of the many voids in the cell signal on the farm, and she had no bars at all.

She had to get back to the farmhouse, where she would have both cell service and a door between her and the thief. As she turned and ran, she couldn't help wondering just how much protection the old farmhouse would offer against a commercial tractor.

Mabel glanced over her shoulder to see the tractor emerge from the barn. Behind the wheel was a figure with a hoodie raised over his head. He aimed the tractor straight at Mabel. In the daytime, Mabel could have outmaneuvered the ungainly tractor, disappearing into the wooded areas where it couldn't follow, but in the dark, there was too much risk that she'd trip and fall before she reached the trees.

She abandoned any attempt at evasive movements and sprinted straight for the back of the farmhouse. As Mabel approached the edge of the patio, she felt the heat of the tractor at her back and the vibrations of the engine through her feet. She veered to the left, toward the stairs onto the farm's wraparound porch, but the tractor cut her off, sending her running back toward her original destination: the patio and the kitchen door.

Please, please, please let it not stick this once.

Mabel touched the doorknob and, as if she'd touched the "home free" spot in a child's game of tag, the tractor stopped and idled in place. Mabel jerked the door open, slipped inside and threw the door shut again, although she was only too aware that the lock wouldn't keep anyone out. First thing tomorrow, she was getting a deadbolt installed.

She leaned against the door for a moment to catch her breath and then headed for the window at the sink to see what the tractor was doing. Surely it hadn't been as close as she'd thought. It had probably stopped at the edge of the driveway, rather than following her all the way onto the pea stone surface of the patio.

But no, the tractor, minus the wagon, was smack-dab in the middle of the patio that ran the length of the farmhouse, taking up a good chunk of the open area and threatening the massive picnic table at the far end of the space.

Getting the tractor out of there wasn't going to be easy, Mabel thought. It had barely fit between the shrubs lining the driveway at the entrance to the patio, and the other three sides were blocked by the house, a built-in outdoor kitchen with a massive fireplace and more shrubbery with much smaller gaps. With a little luck, the driver would abandon the tractor and run away, and Mabel might be able to get a better look at him. Possibly even get a picture of him.

She pulled out her phone, automatically checking for the nonexistent bars to call 911 before switching to the camera app. When she looked outside again, the tractor was making a neat three-point turn within the confines of the patio, carefully avoiding contact with the picnic table and landscaping.

The tractor left the patio, barely brushing the shrubs on its way out, and headed for the path leading to Emily's farm. It passed through the pool of light near the barn, but instead of making the driver more visible, the light merely silhouetted the figure, leaving the face and other details completely unrecognizable. All Mabel could see was that the body was fat and lumpy, with what looked like a misshapen and hunchbacked spine. It took a moment for her to realize that some part of that silhouette was actually a bag filled with what had to be fifty or more pounds of garlic and tossed over the thief's shoulder.

How dare he steal her aunt's garlic? How dare he so easily make off with the fruit of her field hands' hard work?

Rage propelled her toward the back door, which stuck and forced her to stop and think about what she was doing. Chasing after the thief might have gotten her aunt killed. Mabel didn't need to repeat that mistake. Despite being younger than her aunt, Mabel doubted she was any stronger or more capable of defending herself than her aunt had been. Besides, the thief had an unfair advantage behind the wheel of the massive tractor, which definitely qualified as a dangerous weapon.

Mabel continued watching the thief's retreat, just in case he did something that might help her identify him, or turned around for a kamikaze run at the farmhouse. Once he was out of sight, lost in the trees between the two farms, Pixie continued yowling for another minute. Her sudden silence confirmed that the thief had completed his escape.

Only then did Mabel leave the window, staring at her treacherous phone as she wandered around the farmhouse until it finally taunted her with three bars eager to offer her service. She dialed 9, and then stopped. What was she supposed to tell the police? That her cat, with a widely known reputation for being noisy, had warned her of an intruder, and she'd seen someone take a joy ride on her tractor? Mabel hadn't found the vehicle he'd used to get here, and, given how dark the night was, she couldn't even swear to the fact that the intruder had stolen anything, just that it looked like he'd had a sack of garlic slung over his shoulder.

With an irritated click, she erased the 9 and stuffed the phone back into her pocket. There was nothing the police could do. She'd mention it to Joe

Hansen the next time she saw him, just so he'd know about it, but it was a waste of time she didn't have to drag the police out here.

There was one thing she could do, though. She could go back home to Maine. Getting her aunt buried properly, and carrying out her responsibilities as the estate's personal representative didn't require Mabel to live on the farm. She could do both of those things from Maine. Bringing in the crop couldn't be done from there, but it wasn't safe for Mabel to live here. Not now. The thief was getting too bold. Surely, ensuring the safety of her aunt's favorite niece was at least as important to her aunt as the final garlic harvest.

One Skinner had died on this farm already. Mabel had no intentions of being the second one.

CHAPTER SEVENTEEN

Mabel should have been too wired to sleep after her confrontation with the tractor driving thief, but reading about the minutiae of garlic farming in her aunt's journal helped to calm her adrenaline levels, and she fell asleep midsentence.

She woke a couple of hours later when it was only half-light out, just long enough to shout at the stupid noisy birds, move the journal from where it lay on her chest and roll over onto her side while dragging a spare pillow over her head to drown out the cacophony. She couldn't wait to get back to Maine and good insulation against morning noise.

What felt like mere minutes later, Pixie started yowling, loud enough that even if Mabel had remembered to get earplugs yesterday, she still wouldn't have been able to sleep through the noise. The room was little brighter than when the birds first woke her, but it still felt far too early to be awake. She peered at her phone to see it was a few minutes after six. Dinnertime. No, wait, the other six. When sane people were asleep.

Apparently, though, there were an awful lot of crazy people in the world, and they were all drawn to Stinkin' Stuff Farm. If Pixie was yowling, that meant someone was coming up the driveway. It was too early for the field hands to arrive, but they'd be here soon and she did want to be up and waiting for them, so she could send them home with a day's wages and her apologies for not being able to run the farm any longer.

Pixie's yowl dwindled while Mabel finished dressing and went downstairs, by which time Pixie started up again. Mabel looked out the kitchen window to see not just one, but three vehicles parked outside the barn. Rory's, Bettina's and Anna's.

She ran to get her checkbook. It wouldn't be fair to let her loyal crew do any more work when she'd already decided to abandon the harvest.

Rory was standing by her car, talking on the phone. The sound of young voices coming from inside the barn explained where everyone else was. It was a relief not to have to face the whole crowd all at once. Mabel could explain her decision to Rory first. She would understand, and would know how to explain it to everyone else. Rory was good at that sort of thing. Then Mabel could go back to sleep and be fully refreshed in time to finish the app for tomorrow. Shutting down the harvest really was the best decision for everyone, from the field hands, who'd be getting paid without having to exhaust themselves in the field, to the garlic thief who could take whatever he wanted, and even the tech client who would get his app completed on time.

Rory disconnected her phone call and smiled. "I see we're making a farmer out of you, after all, with you getting up at the crack of dawn."

"Is that what this is?" Mabel said. "I thought it was the apocalypse."

"It can't happen today. We've got too much work to do," Rory said. "Bettina and the kids are in the barn feeding the cats before we go out to the fields."

"The garlic thief came back last night."

Rory frowned. "Joe didn't say anything about it this morning."

"He doesn't know. No one knows. Except me and the thief, and now you."

"I thought you had a working phone. Why didn't you call 911?"

"There's nothing the police can do without catching the thief red-handed. I wasn't about to chase after him last night, and he'd have been long gone before the police could get here. I did try to find his getaway vehicle, but it wasn't in the driveway or anywhere in sight on the road."

Rory jabbed her phone's screen and then held it up to her ear. "You still should have reported it. I'm calling Joe right now."

Dawn came running out of the barn. "Morning, Mabel. I'm supposed to find out where you put the tractor. We can't start work without it."

Rory said, "call me" into her phone and disconnected it. "He must be in a meeting. It went to voicemail. I'll make sure he comes out here sometime today, though, so you can make a report."

"I'm not sure—"

"I am," she said, stuffing her phone into her pocket and turning to Dawn. "What's this about you and the tractor?"

"I wasn't going to drive it, Mom. I'm just supposed to find it. It's not parked where it usually is. We've got the wagon loaded with empty crates, but there's no tractor to hitch it to."

"It's probably on the path to Emily's farm," Mabel said. "At least, that's where I last saw it."

"Mo-o-o-o-m," Dawn said. "It's not fair that even Mabel got to drive it, and I'm not allowed. If she can do it, so can I."

"I wasn't driving it," Mabel said.

That got through Dawn's teenaged self-absorption. She stopped giving her mother pleading looks, and said, "Then who was?"

Mabel was tempted to tell her it was the headless tractor man, but it was too early in the morning for jokes. "The person who's been stealing garlic from the farm. He made off with another fifty pounds last night."

"Someone stole the garlic we harvested?" Dawn's young voice rose with each word, rivaling Pixie's yowl by the end.

Bettina and the two young field hands came out of the barn to see what the commotion was all about.

Dawn's face was younger, smaller and less worldly than her father's, but the outrage on it was every bit as intense as anything he could manage. "That's not right. We've got to get the garlic back. I know looking for it has to wait until we finish the last field, but we *will* get it back for you. My dad will know where to look."

Rory explained to the others, "The thief struck again last night. He took more than Mabel could afford to lose."

Rory had jumped to the wrong conclusion about the consequences of the theft. While Aunt Peggy had struggled financially, Mabel could afford to lose the entire garlic crop. What she couldn't afford to lose was her life.

She was about to explain the real problem, and how she was planning to fix it, when Anna spoke up. "What are we doing standing around talking? We need to be out finishing the last field, making up for what was stolen."

"Right," Bettina said, sounding like the strong-willed teacher she'd been before her husband's death. "If we can wring every last bit of garlic out of the ground, Mabel should be able to meet her basic obligations and still have a little bit for the garlic festival. I'm not giving up without at least trying to earn my tiara." Her voice turned wistful. "I'm sure Scott will understand my being late to visit him, especially when I tell him that I was working to be crowned the garlic queen. He'll be so proud of me."

Mabel forced herself to look from face to face, trying desperately to understand them. Even she could read their enthusiasm and determination, barely held in check while they waited for Mabel to give them the signal to get to work.

Didn't they understand? There was no way they could finish the final field before the rain hit this evening. Even if they did, the harvest had already been reduced so badly by the thefts that Mabel would be lucky to make good on the contracts with the restaurant owners and the CSA. There wouldn't be much, if anything, left for the farmers' market, and there certainly wouldn't be anything worth celebrating.

Everyone was frozen in place, leaning forward, waiting for Mabel to say something. She didn't want to be here. She should be in her home in Maine, hunched over a laptop, looking at code that didn't have any expectations of her and couldn't be disappointed. Actually, at this hour of the morning, she should be at home, sound asleep, not trying to make any decisions at all.

She had to decide: finish the harvest or cancel it. Stay here or go home. Force herself to do work she wasn't suited for, or break the hearts of Rory, Bettina, the three teens and all the fanatic alliumphiles in town.

Mabel didn't care about the harvest for herself, but it obviously mattered to the people waiting for her decision. They all had good reasons for taking on an impossible task, and needing to believe that they could beat Mother Nature. Bettina needed the challenge to distract herself from her excessive mourning. The college kids needed it for the money and the experience. Dawn needed it to hold onto her faith in happy endings. Rory needed it to reinforce her belief that she could make anything right—even the death of a friend—if she tried hard enough.

It wasn't safe for Mabel to keep investigating the thefts, but there was no real risk in simply finishing the harvest and then locking herself inside the farmhouse overnight. All they needed to do today was bring in the last field of garlic. Once they proved to themselves that they could do it, and they had their little weekend celebration, everyone would be happy, and Mabel could go back to Maine where she belonged.

"Let's do it," Mabel said, with less conviction than she'd been striving for, but no one seemed to notice in their excitement to get to work.

"Go on," Bettina said, clapping her hands at Anna and Terry, as if they were her elementary school students. "Go find the tractor. It can't have gone far. All the paths end in gates or other obstructions."

"I bet I can find it before anyone else can," Dawn said. "And then you'll have to let me drive it."

Mabel ignored the last bit, since Dawn was already running in the wrong direction, toward the gazebo, and Anna and Terry had split up, with Anna heading for the path to Emily's farm and Terry jogging over behind the farmhouse along the path that went in the other direction to wrap around the fields that had been harvested before Mabel arrived. They'd figure out soon enough that Anna had correctly guessed where Emily's farm and the tractor were.

"I'll make some more calls," Rory said. "I've got four CSA members lined up for at least an hour apiece today, but I bet I could get a couple more."

"I'll go feed Pixie and get some water bottles for everyone," Mabel said, not that anyone was listening, now that they'd guilted her into endorsing their unreasonable expectations. Maybe that was the trick to dealing with people: just tell them what they wanted to hear, since they weren't going to hear anything else anyway.

No wonder Mabel always found it easier to work with lines of code on her screen. They never behaved irrationally and they never tried to make her believe in the impossible. They certainly wouldn't have had her thinking that maybe, just maybe, if they could do the impossible and bring in the entire harvest of garlic, then maybe, just maybe, she could do the impossible and figure out what had happened the night her aunt had died, all without getting herself killed.

* * * *

Pixie was sleeping in the guest bathroom sink again, apparently exhausted from having announced this morning's visitors. Mabel left her some kibble and fresh water, and headed out to see where she was needed.

Rory was in the barn, gently emptying the crates filled yesterday by tipping them over onto tarps that didn't have much room left on them, considering the amount of garlic they were hoping to bring in today. Someone needed to do some fast racking or else they'd have to risk piling the garlic deeper than a single layer. Mabel recalled reading in the journal last night that one of the reasons Aunt Peggy could claim to have the best garlic on the east coast was that she was very careful never to let the bulbs get bruised, which meant that the garlic could be stored safely for longer periods without the risk of rot.

She settled at the racking table, confident that the field hands didn't need her supervision. She could empty a few more crates into racks, and then Rory's CSA volunteers could do some racking when they arrived. *If* they arrived. The weather today was not as conducive to outdoor work as the last couple days had been. The weather front that would deliver rain later today had already pushed higher temperatures and humidity into the area. Any sane person who wasn't either completely dedicated to the CSA or terrified of Rory's wrath was likely to look for any excuse to avoid showing up today. It was only seven a.m. and the temperature was already in the 80s.

Rory turned around and carried the crate she'd just emptied over to a pile near the barn door. "I talked to my husband, and he'll stop by later this morning, whenever he can get away for a few minutes."

"Okay." Mabel still didn't see any reason to make an official report, but it wouldn't hurt to have a quiet, unofficial chat with Joe. She was going to be safely out of harm's way in a few days, back in Maine, but he might have some suggestions for someone she could hire to watch over the barn while the harvest was drying. Mabel would have liked to catch the thief and question him about the night her aunt had died, but after being chased by the tractor last night, she'd accepted that catching the thief wasn't going to happen. She'd have to settle for posting a guard to act like a scarecrow did with feathered thieves.

Mabel settled into her work, picking up the garlic heads and slotting them into the mesh. The movements had already become so automatic, it was hard to remember that just a couple of days ago, she hadn't even known that garlic needed to be dried. She was already feeling the strain in her lower back, the sort of ache she usually got when she lost track of time while hunching over her laptop with a particularly challenging bit of code. At this rate, if they brought in anywhere near what they were aiming for, her back was going to make her wish she'd never heard of racking garlic. "Do you really think we can get the entire last field harvested today?"

Rory shrugged before picking up the next crate. "Probably not, but if the rain holds off and everyone shows up as promised, we should be close."

Mabel found she could continue racking without watching what she was doing, relying instead on touch. She watched Rory empty yet another crate and carry it over to the barn doors. She stayed there for a moment, stretching and rubbing her lower back. Rory was human, after all, and not the superwoman she'd appeared to be until now.

Mabel asked, "Why are you doing this?"

"We need empty crates." Rory grabbed another full crate and carried it over to the tarps.

"No, I mean, why are you helping with the harvest? I don't know much about farming or CSA's, but I'm pretty sure you're going way beyond any responsibilities you have as the coordinator of the CSA. It's not like Darryl does any hands-on work with the crops, just because he's in charge of the farmers' market. He hasn't even been willing to do anything about the thefts, like warning the other farmers. So why are you helping so much?"

Rory carefully spread out the garlic she'd just dumped on the tarp. "Someone had to do it."

Rory obviously didn't want to talk about her reasons for working so hard on a farm she had no financial interest in. Mabel knew she was getting into areas she wasn't equipped to deal with, and she should let it go. But the answer might help her figure out what had happened to her aunt. "I'm serious. Why are you working so hard for the harvest? Why do you care about it more than I do?"

Rory sighed and paused with a half emptied crate on her hip. "I hate being self-analytical, but you're right. I don't have to be here, and I'm not doing it just so I can keep Bettina occupied and Dawn away from the keys to the tractor. I guess in my own way I'm as stuck in the denial phase of grief as Bettina is. As long as the farm keeps going, I don't have to face the fact that Peggy's gone. I'm doing this so I don't have to let her go."

Rory brushed away the tears that had fallen while she spoke.

"I'm sorry." Mabel had bought into the image of Rory always being in control and hadn't realized how much grief she was carrying, since she didn't display it the way Bettina did. "I shouldn't have pushed. I'm not very good with people, if you hadn't noticed."

"I love people who aren't good with people." Rory resumed emptying the bin onto the tarp. "They're so easy to manipulate for my dastardly plans. Just ask Dawn. She'll tell you how much of an evil overlord I am."

Relieved that she hadn't done any serious damage to Rory or their budding friendship, Mabel said, "Speaking of evil plans, your husband said thieves don't usually get violent, but I almost got run over by the tractor last night."

"Seriously?" Rory looked over her shoulder. "And you didn't call 911? I'm going to kill you if the thief doesn't beat me to it."

Mabel waved her hand, and the bouquet of garlic bulbs in it, dismissively. "He missed me by at least three inches. But it made me really wonder about whether he might have been involved in Aunt Peggy's death. Did the police look for tractor prints near where she drowned?"

"That tractor's been on just about every inch of this farm, so it would only be surprising if there weren't tracks out by the creek. Besides, the weather had been pretty dry around here before she died, so the ground wouldn't have been soft enough for fresh impressions."

"I can't help thinking that if the thief was desperate enough last night to chase me with the tractor, then he might have done the same thing with Aunt Peggy."

"I suppose it's possible," Rory said. "It's hard to believe that a killer would come back to the scene of the crime a couple weeks later, though. He got away clean, so why risk being caught for a minor crime like crop theft, when it would make him a suspect in murder?"

Mabel reached for another handful of garlic, only to find that the bin was empty. She swapped it for a full one. "Maybe the thief can't stop himself. He could be connected with the farm somehow, someone who knows just how special this garlic is, and it's become an obsession with him. Ever since I got here, people have been demonstrating just how crazy they can be about their garlic."

"You mean someone like Kyle Sherman?" Rory shook her head. "He's a self-important jerk with entitlement issues, but he's not violent. He might steal, but he wouldn't run you down with the tractor. I'm not sure he even knows how to operate farm equipment. All the locals are used to tractors, but he's a city boy, just moved here recently."

"Kyle isn't the only one who's obsessed with Aunt Peggy's garlic," Mabel said, thinking of the restaurant owners, Ethan and Jeanne.

"I can't believe anyone I know could have killed Peggy. And it's not just my denial talking. Everyone loved her."

And yet, Aunt Peggy was dead in what Mabel was convinced were suspicious circumstances. "What about someone who didn't know her well enough to love her? Or someone who isn't from around here?"

"Then what would they have been doing on the property?" Rory said. "The only people who came here were her friends and the CSA members. We all wanted her and her farm to keep on thriving forever."

"Potential employees visited here too," Mabel said. "She brought in farm workers."

"Not this year," Rory said. "She did the early harvest in June herself, and she hardly ever hires for the spring squash planting in May, so no one would have come looking for a job then."

"Maybe someone was angry that she wasn't hiring?"

"And killed her for it?" Rory shook her head. "Now you're the one in denial, trying to make her death into something that makes more sense than a freak accident. No one would have been looking for work here in the spring. Garlic grows on a different schedule from most crops around here, with the bulk of the work now in July, and then again in October for planting, not in the spring and late summer when most other crops require the most attention. There's plenty of work on other farms in May and June, more jobs than there are people willing to do it. Besides, only a dedicated psychopath would kill over a job that didn't exist. Maybe someone like Kyle Sherman would kill over a prestigious CEO job, but I can't imagine anyone around here killing for the chance to sweat in the fields for minimum wage."

"I don't want to believe there's a psychopath on the loose either," Mabel said, "but being chased by a tractor makes a person consider all the possibilities."

"At least you can rest easy that it's not one of us," Rory said. "Dawn and I were so tired last night that we barely managed to eat dinner before we collapsed into bed. Terry and Anna probably did the same thing, although you never know with college kids. They wouldn't have had any reason to hurt Peggy, though, or to steal the garlic last night. On the way here this morning, Dawn regaled me with stories about her new BFFs, in the context of trying to decide whether she wants to be an artist or a marine biologist. According to Dawn, Anna didn't even know there were farms around here until Terry told her about the job listing. He's familiar with the local farms, of course, but he was busy with his classes and exams until late May. After that, he picked up full-time work on other farms that do have a busy spring schedule. Dawn had to ask me what marrow was, since he kept talking about how much of it he'd planted."

"I can't imagine Anna or Terry hurting anyone," Mabel agreed. "I was thinking more along the lines of Larry Rose or the guy Peggy was suing over the bad seed stock."

"Al Soares?" Rory said. "His farm is in Pennsylvania, I think. From what Peggy told me, all their dealings were through the internet when she ordered the stock, and then through their attorneys after she discovered the rot. As far as I know, he never came anywhere near here."

"What about Larry?"

"He's no psychopath," Rory said. "In fact, he and Peggy were pretty good friends until two or three years ago, and after that, they just avoided each other. Mostly, his bark is worse than his bite. I've had to deal with him for the CSA, since he supplies most of the tomatoes and peppers and a few other things. The wide variety of crops on his farm is part of why he isn't more successful, according to Peggy: he doesn't fully commit to anything. Well, except for shouting at his employees to work harder. He's very committed to shouting."

"I noticed that."

"Peggy always said the reason she grew the best garlic on the east coast was because she was totally committed to just the one crop. That way, she could put all her effort into it, without being sidetracked by other things."

That was how Mabel worked best too, focusing on one app at a time and perfecting it before moving on to a new project. "What about the squash? And the lavender?"

"Those were just side projects, nothing that really mattered to her. If it ever came down to choosing between them and the garlic, she didn't even have to think about it. She always chose what was best for the garlic. Mostly, she didn't have to make the choice, though. The other crops contributed to the garlic harvest, instead of taking away from it. The squash and the beans—" Rory looked up from her work. "You haven't seen the beans yet, have you?"

Mabel shook her head. "I really don't need any more crops to worry about right now."

Rory went back to work. "You don't need to do anything with the beans yet. They're over in the fallow field. They improve the soil when the plants are tilled under, and the lavender is just making use of land that can't grow garlic because of the rot infection. That's different from the way Larry grows a dozen or more crops, all intended to produce a major profit."

"He seems reasonably successful," Mabel said. "I got the impression that he had several full-time employees. Aunt Peggy couldn't afford any regular employees."

"He does okay. His crops aren't bad, they're just not outstanding the way Peggy's are. People buy his tomatoes and peppers because they're local and grown during their preferred season, which pretty much guarantees that they're better than the varieties grown off-season or transported across long distances."

"Still, he's got to be doing better than Aunt Peggy was, in financial terms."

"It's not about the money," Rory said. "For Larry, it's more about bragging rights. His family have farmed here in West Slocum far enough back that his ancestors knew the town's namesake, Joshua Slocum, personally. Larry saw Peggy as a hobbyist, with her relatively small acreage, and a one person operation. It had to rankle when her reputation grew to surpass his."

"So she really did grow the best garlic on the east coast?"

Rory smiled sadly. "She did. But she was also a good businesswoman, and Larry isn't. He's pretty old-school, growing the same crops that his father and grandfather planted, and marketing them the same old ways, without taking advantage of new technologies and opportunities. It took me a couple years to strong-arm him into participating in the CSA, because he considered it too newfangled. Peggy took to modern niche marketing before anyone else in West Slocum did."

"Was Aunt Peggy jeopardizing Larry's farm with her success? The prospect of losing a family farm could motivate a person to do something drastic to prevent it from happening."

"Larry isn't at risk of losing his farm," Rory said. "At least not any more than other farmers. He doesn't need to steal Peggy's garlic, and he didn't have any reason to kill her. Getting rid of her wouldn't change the fact that he's a mediocre farmer."

"I'd trade all the work you've ever done on the farm for just one lead on who's been stealing the garlic." Mabel stuck the last garlic bulb in the rack and stood to place the empty crate in the pile next to the door. "I hate to think the thief will never be caught, and the police will never get the chance to question him about the night Aunt Peggy died. If it was just the thefts, I wouldn't mind so much, but I hate the idea that he might have gotten away with her murder."

"If I had a lead, you'd be the first to know about it." Rory put her most recently emptied crate on top of Mabel's and then wrapped her in a hug before she could get away. "Okay, maybe not the first. That would be Joe, because he could do something about it, and he is my husband, after all. But you'd be the first after that."

"Thanks." Mabel didn't struggle against the hug this one time. Rory needed it, and Mabel owed it to her for making her cry earlier. Mabel could endure this one hug. She'd be gone soon enough, back to where no one would think of invading her personal space.

CHAPTER EIGHTEEN

Mabel wasn't sure how long the hug would have gone on, if it hadn't been for Pixie's yowl. Even somewhat muffled by the farmhouse walls, the sound couldn't be ignored.

Rory returned to emptying crates, and Mabel went outside to see whose arrival the cat was announcing.

Kyle Sherman's convertible pulled in beside Bettina's Beetle. As he walked to the barn, he slathered sunscreen in a solid, quarter-inch-thick layer over his arms and neck, which were already so red it was painful just to look at them. He'd traded in yesterday's "nowhere to hide the garlic" costume for more appropriate harvesting clothes: military green cargo shorts, a matching tank top and a floppy beige hat that covered his red hair.

"Don't look so surprised," he said. "I told you I'd be back. I've been monitoring the weather, and they're saying the rain will be here earlier than expected. I didn't want to miss out on all the fun."

"Or the heirloom garlic you've been salivating over."

"That too."

Rory joined them. "Bettina told me you'd hired him." She made it sound like Mabel had hired a cockroach.

"We need every possible worker if we want to bring in the harvest."

Rory sniffed. "Just don't turn your back on him. Never forget where he came from. Corporate ladder climbers like him will do anything to get what they want."

Kyle shrugged. "Good thing, then, that what I want and what Mabel wants are the same thing today. I just want the garlic she promised me. I'm willing to work for it."

Rory peered at the oversized pockets on his cargo shorts, and then at his hat, as if calculating exactly how much garlic he could hide there. "We'll be watching you. If Mabel takes the first shift, I'll go round up some CSA members. Sometimes phone calls and texts aren't enough motivation, and a personal visit is required. I'll be back in an hour or so."

Kyle stepped aside, so Rory wouldn't be tempted to steamroll her way right through him on her way to her car. He waited until Rory was out of earshot before he said, "That is one tough woman. She'd be running a Fortune 500 company if she'd ever gone into the business world."

"I like her."

"Oh, sure," Kyle said cheerfully. "Everyone likes her. That's because she's so good at what she does that no one notices how they're being manipulated into doing what she wants. But if you cross her, you'd better watch out. She takes no prisoners. I heard she had a guy run out of town when he pissed her off. He had to sell his house and everything."

"No one seems to hold it against her," Mabel said. "She must have had a good reason for convincing him to leave."

"Perhaps. But the thing is, it's always her way or the highway, and she never gives anyone a second chance. I'd really like to try to make up for our little disagreement over the CSA."

Mabel gestured for him to follow her inside the barn. Sunscreen notwithstanding, he might be best off staying in the shade as much as possible today. It wasn't entirely a kindness. Racking the garlic was hard, monotonous work. It needed to be done, though, with more attention and speed than they'd managed so far, or they were going to run out of crates and storage space before they ran out of rows to harvest.

"Peggy was famous for giving people second chances," he said as he settled at the racking table and began working. "Look at how she named you as her heir, when you never even came and visited her."

Mabel had to laugh. That sounded like the sort of rude comment she herself would have made if their circumstances were reversed and only belatedly realized was insensitive. But Kyle was right; she should have visited more often, and she hadn't deserved her aunt's generosity. "Aunt Peggy didn't have much choice but to forgive me. I'm her only remaining relative."

"There's always an excuse." He was filling the garlic rack quickly and efficiently. He might not have spent much time outdoors before yesterday, judging by the state of his sunburn, but he was in good physical shape.

Mabel dragged a stool and a pile of crates over to the opposite side of the table and settled in to work with him. “Who else got a second chance from Aunt Peggy?”

“Emily Colter got a huge one.” He tossed the first empty crate onto the floor and started in on the second one. “I heard that the first spring she was here the goats escaped into Peggy’s fields. They ate a good chunk of the plants. That had to have reduced the size and quality of the entire harvest that year.”

Emily hadn’t mentioned that when she’d talked about how much her goats loved garlic. “What did Aunt Peggy do?”

“Most people would have sued Emily for everything she had. But not Peggy. She didn’t just give Emily a second chance to keep her goats out of the fields, but she actually went into partnership with Emily to make garlic-flavored cheese. That would be like a phone company landing a crippling blow on a competitor and then deciding to work together on a new phone service. Who would do something like that?”

“My aunt would.” After all, she’d forgiven Mabel for her shortcomings as a niece. On the other hand, Aunt Peggy had never forgiven the owners of the company where her brother and his wife—Mabel’s parents—had died. That was a far cry from some crop damage, but it confirmed that Aunt Peggy was capable of holding a grudge if she wanted to. The way she’d given Larry Rose the cold shoulder suggested he’d done something she couldn’t forgive too. So, had she really forgiven Emily completely? Maybe there was a mention of the kerfuffle in the journal. She’d have to look when she had some time.

“It’s just not fair.” Kyle scraped his stool over a couple of feet to where there was open space in the rack. “Peggy gave everyone second chances. Except for me.”

“I’m sure she would have eventually. She just ran out of time.”

“Yeah.” He racked the garlic silently for a couple of minutes, seemingly lost in thought. When he spoke again, there was sadness in his voice. “I really wish I’d had the chance to prove to her that I’m not as big a jerk as she thought I was.”

Intimate confessions fell into the category of tricky interpersonal moments that Mabel never got right. She wasn’t about to hug anyone, so she settled for saying, “I’m giving you a second chance. Does that help?”

“Yeah, I think it does.” He grinned. “Although, the fact that you’re babysitting me to make sure I’m not tempted to stuff garlic into my cargo pants kind of undermines your supposed faith in me. As if I’d even bother to steal the standard variety. I’m holding out for the heirloom crops.”

Mabel really would have liked to be out in the field instead of watching over him. She wanted to make sure they had enough water to drink, and there ought to be some sort of rotation plan so they'd each get some time in the shade of the barn every so often. She could take Kyle out to the fields with her, but it might be better to keep him here in the barn, where his sunburn couldn't get bad enough to send him to the hospital, and where he'd be out of sight of Bettina and Rory.

She was inclined to give him that second chance he wanted, by trusting him not to steal any of the main garlic crop if she left him here alone. Even if he did, the few pounds he could slip into his pockets wasn't going to make a difference at this point.

Mabel was done with babysitting him. She got up from the racking table. "I need to go out to the fields for a bit. I'll send someone back in a while to help with the racking. Would you be able to drive the tractor out to the fields then?"

"Whatever you want. I meant it when I said I'd earn my garlic supply."

"You've definitely worked hard." Mabel couldn't help thinking that, because of that hard work, Kyle would have been in a good position to make the brief, efficient raid on the barn last night. He'd have known exactly how much garlic they'd brought into the barn yesterday and where it had all been stored. He would have known where the tractor was parked and the key was left. The only thing she wasn't sure about was whether he'd ever driven a tractor. It wasn't exactly the sort of skill he would have perfected in his corporate career. "They can be dangerous if you're not familiar with them."

"Oh, everyone around here has driven a tractor or two. It's practically a prerequisite to living here."

"Even someone who comes from a corporate background like yours?"

"Depends on the person," he said. "The guy next door, at Capricornucopia, is definitely corporate, and I've never seen him drive a tractor. His wife does all the farm work. He flies his own plane, though, so you've got to figure he could handle farm equipment if he wanted to. For the rest of us who don't own our own jets, we have to make do with anything that's got a reasonably powerful and noisy engine. Tractor events are among the most popular of all the things that farmers do to attract tourists to West Slocum. I mean, really, who doesn't want to drive a tractor?"

"Me."

He shook his head disbelievingly. "You must be the only one within a hundred miles. Everyone else is looking forward to the tractor competitions in October."

"That sounds dangerous."

"Not really," he said. "They don't have jumps or pulls or anything like that, except for some demonstrations by professionals. For the amateurs, it's easy stuff, and there are rules about speeding. It's mostly about handling and teamwork. You know, maneuvering around bales, and there are some team events that involve loading and unloading the tractor wagon to see who can move the most product. I just watched the action last fall, but I've been practicing so I can compete this year."

He'd probably hired a coach, which meant he would definitely have the skills to drive a tractor. It also meant he could have been behind the wheel of the tractor last night. It had been too dark to get a good look at the driver, and his exact size had been obscured by the sack of garlic draped over his shoulder. She could only rule out anyone who was big and beefy or basketball-player tall, and Kyle was none of those things.

On the other hand, why would Kyle have bothered to work so hard at sneaking onto the farm and then putting in long hours in the field if he'd already stolen more garlic than he could possibly use between now and next year's crop, when he'd be eligible to join the CSA? Could it have been his corporate training that made him greedy, inspiring him to see just how much of the crop he could lay claim to, just so he could have a bigger hoard of garlic than anyone else?

Maybe she was just feeling particularly softhearted because she could see how red his shoulders were, and how he was working hard enough to send torrents of sweat dripping down his biceps, but she was having a hard time picturing Kyle as the thief.

"You ought to know what I told the rest of the crew," Mabel said. "There's going to be a shortage of Aunt Peggy's garlic this year. You'll get what you worked for, but don't expect too much. A thief has been targeting the farm."

"A thief?" Kyle looked surprised and then outraged. "I bet it was an inside job. Employees always steal more than outsiders. They know how to really hurt a business."

"Maybe if they're disgruntled, but as far as I can tell, everyone who ever met Peggy loved her, even her workers."

"What's love got to do with it?" Kyle carried a tall stack of filled bins over to the racking table to replace the ones he'd emptied. "People have to eat. How much garlic has been stolen, anyway?"

"I'm not sure what was taken before I got here. At least a couple crates' worth was stolen the night before last, and a huge sack last night."

Kyle whistled. "That's a pretty decent haul for a few hours' work. More than the thief would get for an honest part-time job in the same amount of time."

"But not as much as it's going to cost me to hire a security guard."

"Welcome to the world of executive decision-making," Kyle said. "If you want the short version of most business textbooks, it's that there usually isn't a right or wrong answer. Just make a decision and move on."

"I'm way ahead of you." Mabel had made her decision, and she'd be moving all the way back to Maine next week.

* * * *

Before Mabel could leave for the fields, she heard the tractor returning to the barn. Bettina backed the wagon inside and hopped down. "I've got to make some calls. I'll be right back."

Kyle stretched before heading over to unload the wagon. He set a stack of crates down next to Mabel and returned to get another stack for his own place at the racking table.

Mabel could hear Bettina's voice, but not the individual words. Rory hadn't had any trouble getting service when she made calls this morning either. Last night's lack of service when Mabel had needed it to call 911 had apparently been an anomaly. If she were superstitious, she'd consider it an omen, one more sign that it was time for her to leave West Slocum.

Kyle and Mabel finished emptying the wagon and filling it with empty crates while Bettina was still on the phone. She seemed to have recovered from yesterday's anniversary, but Mabel wanted to make sure Bettina wasn't pushing herself too hard, before either of them went back out to the field. "Would you mind taking the empty crates out to the field hands for me?"

"I'd love to." Kyle climbed on board. "I could use some more practice behind the wheel before October."

"Don't let Dawn convince you that she's got permission to drive the tractor."

Kyle left, and Bettina came inside to take Kyle's place at the racking table. Mabel grabbed a water bottle from where they were stashed beneath the racking table and handed it to Bettina.

"Thanks." Bettina took a long drink before adding, "It's getting hot out there. I don't know if the CSA volunteers will show up in this weather, no matter what Rory threatens them with."

Mabel nodded at the stack of crates that had just been unloaded. "Still, it looks like everyone's been working at top speed."

"We have, but I'm not sure how long we can keep going." Bettina set her bottle down beside her and grabbed a handful of garlic bulbs to stuff into the drying rack. "I guess this is when we find out who Peggy's real friends are. Like Emily. I wonder where she is."

"With her goats, I assume."

"Probably just as well," Bettina said. "I've never had any animals of my own, because of Scott's allergies, but a lot of my students raise livestock. It takes a lot of work and skill to be successful at it. I'm sure Emily tries her best, but I've heard that her farm's on the verge of bankruptcy, and it's affecting her marriage."

Mabel wasn't any more comfortable hearing about Emily's marital troubles than she'd been hearing Kyle's regrets over losing Aunt Peggy's goodwill. Normally, Mabel would have done her best to change the subject, but she'd started to think that if she'd been more open to listening to personal matters, her aunt might have confided her financial worries, and Mabel could have helped her. Becoming a better listener now wouldn't bring Aunt Peggy back, but perhaps there was something Mabel could do to help Emily, in her aunt's memory.

"I'm sorry she's having trouble."

"Well, you know that her husband is a lot older than she is, right?"

"I haven't met him yet. Emily said he travels a lot for business."

"It could be for business," Bettina said without looking up from her work. "But when a husband is gone that much, you have to start wondering. It's probably a relief for him to be away, so he doesn't have to constantly look at the evidence of all the money he's spending on his trophy wife's dream of being a goat farmer, or listen to the other farmers laughing at all her crazy ideas about the role of moon cycles and astrology in farming."

"Her farm looks quite prosperous."

"Of course it does," Bettina said. "Her husband's got the sort of job that Kyle would kill for. He can afford to cover all of the farm's losses. I just don't know how long he'll be willing to do it. From what I hear, it won't be much longer."

"Emily must have been doing something right if Peggy was willing to partner up with her to produce the garlic-flavored cheese."

"Oh, you know Peggy. The biggest heart on the east coast, to go along with the best garlic, but she wasn't much of a business person. Just look at how much time she spent volunteering at the community garden, helping people grow their own garlic, so they wouldn't have to buy hers. Some women just aren't good with money. I always let Scott deal with our finances, since he's so much better at it. Peggy probably didn't even know how much money the partnership was losing."

"I doubt it." Apparently Bettina didn't know that Aunt Peggy had been an accountant before starting the farm, and hadn't seen the journal where everything about the farm had been methodically charted. She wouldn't have been any less diligent with her partnership finances. "If Aunt Peggy lost money on the partnership, she did it knowingly, to help a friend."

"Peggy did like to help people out. She's just like Rory. They both do so much for their friends. You don't know Rory as well as I do, so it must seem too good to be true, the way she's been helping out here." Bettina laughed. "She even got me to work in the fields. I much prefer being here inside the barn, but when Rory wants something, she gets it. Of course, she didn't need to push me too hard. I want my tiara."

"You'll get it." Mabel wished she had an equally simple way to thank Rory for all her help. She really had gone beyond the call of duty to a friend. Rory had said she just wanted to pretend for a little while longer that her good friend wasn't gone, but she was doing far more than Mabel had ever seen anyone do for someone who wasn't a close relative. After Mabel's parents died, no one except her grandparents had done anything more than attend the funeral, drop off some casseroles and offer condolences. Why was Rory really putting so much time and energy into keeping Aunt Peggy's memory alive? Could she be feeling guilty about angry words that had never been taken back, or something even worse?

Mabel hated suspecting everyone she'd met here, but the simple fact was that someone had stolen a lot of garlic, and she thought Kyle was onto something about its being an inside job. The thief must have been someone familiar with the farm, given that the emptied crates were put away neatly the first night, and he—or she—had known where the keys to the tractor were last night. Could Rory have been using her role as CSA coordinator to gain Aunt Peggy's confidence and then betraying her by stealing from the farm? If so, she might even be doing the same thing with the other farms that were part of the CSA. If the thefts had been small enough, the farmers might not have reported them to the police or to Darryl. They might have mentioned it to other farmers, though, or to their friends.

"I don't suppose you've heard whether any of your students' farms were hit by thieves this year, have you?"

Bettina paused in her racking to take another drink before she answered. "Not that I can think of. I haven't really seen my students much this summer. Mostly, I've been here or at home with Scott. It's too bad Scott isn't here. He's a cop, you know."

"Never mind," Mabel said. "It was just a thought."

"I'll talk to Scott about it," Bettina said. "I already told him about the tiara, and he's looking forward to the festival."

Too bad Bettina wasn't actually talking to Scott in the afterlife. She could have asked him to talk to Aunt Peggy and find out what happened the night she died.

CHAPTER NINETEEN

Bettina might not have been entirely in touch with reality, but she seemed reasonably cheerful and energized, so Mabel left her to the racking, and headed out to join the workers in the field. She'd just stepped out of the barn when she heard Pixie yowl. She turned to see who would come up the driveway.

After a few seconds, she had her answer: a police cruiser. Joe Hansen pulled up in front of the barn, left the engine running and climbed out.

He handed Mabel two six-packs of sports drinks and an opened bag of oatmeal-raisin cookies. "Rory asked me to make sure everyone was staying well hydrated."

"Thanks."

"She also insisted that I bring some paperwork for you to report last night's theft."

"It's a waste of time," Mabel said. "I didn't get a good look at him, and we both know there's nothing you can really do about it without more to go on."

"That doesn't mean we won't try."

"You know what would be more helpful?" Mabel said. "I'd like to hire a guard to watch over the barn while the harvest is drying. Can you recommend someone?"

"Give me a couple hours, and I'm sure I can line up some candidates." He helped himself to another cookie from the bag he'd brought. "Are you sure you don't want to file a report? We could send a cruiser out this way occasionally, but only if there's something official on record."

Mabel shook her head. "Your department has more important things to deal with." Like her aunt's murder.

"At least tell me what happened last night," Joe said. "Off the record, if you prefer."

"I need to get out to the field, but if you come with me, you can check on your daughter while you're here. I'll tell you about last night while we walk."

He fell in beside her. "So talk."

"It happened around two a.m. My cat heard something outside, and I went to see if I could find the getaway vehicle."

Joe moved in front of her, blocking her progress. "Are you insane? Rory didn't tell me you went out to confront the thief."

"I didn't confront him. Just tried to find his car."

"Don't do that again."

"Trust me, I won't. I thought he was out in the fields, but he was in the barn and came barreling out of there on the tractor." Mabel could still picture it, although in the light of day, she had to wonder if he'd actually been chasing her, or if she'd just panicked and imagined how close he'd come to hitting her. He might not even have seen her in the dark. She skipped over the chase, and said, "He left by way of the path to the farm next door, carrying a sack of garlic. That's all there was to it. I would have called 911, but my phone service was out."

Joe took back one of the sports drinks she was carrying, and then moved aside so they could continue walking out to the last field. "Next time, stay indoors."

"I will."

They had just passed the path to Emily's farm, and Joe said, "Is that where the tractor went?"

Mabel nodded.

"Hunh."

She wanted to ask what he was thinking, but she was afraid she knew, and she didn't want to hear it said out loud. There was nowhere for the thief to go in that direction, except for Emily's farm. Why would he go there? Unless the person driving the tractor had been Emily. Could she have been so desperate to prove to her husband that she could get her farm operating in the black that she'd steal her business partner's garlic?

If Emily was the thief, it would certainly explain why Aunt Peggy might have been in denial when she'd had her first suspicions about the thief's identity. Mabel didn't know Emily anywhere near as well as Aunt Peggy had, and she still didn't want to believe it was possible.

"The thief might have parked on the road in front of Emily's farm, so his car would be less conspicuous if the police were responding to a call from me." Mabel desperately wanted Joe to agree that the explanation made sense. "Or he might even have been planning to steal from Emily too, after he was done here."

"I'll have a word with Mrs. Colter, see if she's noticed anything missing," Joe said, but he didn't sound optimistic. "And I'll talk to the detectives. Just do me a favor and don't try to do our job for us. Next time you hear something outside, call 911 right away."

"I will," Mabel said. "The way that tractor came speeding out of the barn, I thought I was going to end up like poor Aunt Peggy, except squashed instead of drowned."

He shook his head. "Everyone thinks he can drive a tractor like a pro, but they're never as good as they think they are. If you ever watch a beginner trying to drive in a straight line, you'll think he was drunk, but he'll tell you he was in complete control of the machine."

"At least you don't have to worry about me getting behind the wheel of a tractor, drunk or sober," Mabel said. "I know what my limits are, for both alcohol and farm equipment."

* * * *

Joe stayed just long enough to wave to his daughter at the far end of the field, explaining to Mabel that he knew from experience that any closer contact with a parent, especially one in a police uniform, would only embarrass her. He stole another cookie before hopping on the back of the wagon to ride back to the barn with Kyle. Half an hour later, the tractor returned with Rory behind the wheel.

Mabel went over to swap out her filled crate for one of the empties in the wagon. "Where's Kyle?"

"He stayed behind with Bettina to rack the garlic." Rory climbed down from the seat and began unloading the empty crates. "Much as I hate to admit it, he's really pulling his own weight."

Mabel glanced over her shoulder at the wilted but still determined teens silently sweating their way down their respective rows of garlic. She thought they were too far away to hear her at a normal pitch, but she still lowered her voice to say, "Even with Kyle's help, there's no way the existing crew can get the whole field harvested today. Any luck finding more workers?"

"Everyone's hiding from me," Rory said irritably as she grabbed an empty crate and headed down the path between the nearest garlic beds. "I finally decided I was just wasting time out there, when I could be pulling garlic here. I'm just one person, not the two or three that I was hoping to enlist, but it's better than nothing."

Mabel took that as her cue to get back to work herself. Rory took up a position across from her. They worked in silence until Mabel had to stop to stretch. She brushed back the leaves of the nearest squash plant to see if there were any little butternuts on it. There were three, along with a stake topped with a copper disk engraved with a stylized vine inside a circle of foreign words printed along the outer edge.

"I've got another stupid question for you," Mabel said, pointing at the disk. "What's that?"

Rory straightened and looked where Mabel was pointing. She laughed. "Oh, that's one of Emily's garden talismans. She had hundreds of them made, and sticks them wherever she thinks there's negative energy."

"I never realized Aunt Peggy was into that sort of thing."

"She wasn't. Emily probably slipped it into place when Peggy wasn't looking." Rory continued pulling garlic while she explained. "The talismans are one of Emily's more far-out ideas. Most of her other practices come from long-standing traditions. Her favorite topic is moon cycles, and how crops should be planted according to the phase of the moon. From what I've read, the moon's gravitational pull is different during the various phases, and its light is different too. The basic theory is that the gravitational pull affects soil moisture, and the light affects growth. There might be some truth to that, but I don't know that there's any scientific evidence to support it."

"I can picture Aunt Peggy doing some experiments. She'd want to figure out which crops need which phase of light and gravitational pull at which stage of the plant's life cycle."

"Mostly she just deflected Emily's suggestions without completely rejecting them." Rory clipped the bunch of garlic she'd pulled and laid it in her crate. "About the only use Peggy had for moon cycles was when she developed insomnia. Farmers tend to be instinctively attuned to nature and light, which is probably why Peggy had difficulty sleeping during the full moon. When it was bad, she would do what farmers sometimes did before the advent of electricity: sleep from sunset to midnight or so, and then get up for a couple hours to work in the moonlight, and then go back to bed until it was time for morning chores."

"I should have come to visit her during a full moon. I'm always wide awake at midnight."

"She would have loved that," Rory said. "But she understood that you had other things to do. She was always telling everyone about your work.

She kept one of your apps handy on her phone so she could show anyone who didn't know what an app was."

"Did it look like a stylized pineapple?"

"I hadn't thought of it that way before, but it did look like what a cubist might do with a pineapple. Four pineapples, with the pointy ends meeting in the middle."

"That was one of my very first apps after I finished school," Mabel said. "I needed a sample to apply for the job I have now. The assignment was to combine mobile tech with something traditional. I doubled up on the traditional by using an old quilt block design and the pineapple as a symbol of hospitality for an app that would help hosts cater to the needs of their houseguests. It helps to manage information about their schedules and their preferences for foods and activities. The company liked my work and hired me, but that was the end of the road for the app, since we didn't have a customer for it at the time. Aunt Peggy got the only download, although she didn't really need help remembering what her visitors liked. It came naturally to her."

"She didn't care what the app did," Rory said. "She was just pleased you remembered her."

"I should have done more."

"We could all do more with the people we love," Rory said. "You're doing the right thing now."

"It doesn't feel that way." Mabel surveyed the vast expanse of the field that was left to be harvested, and then the approaching dark sky near the horizon. At least the gathering clouds were cutting down a bit on the intensity of the sun, even if the rising humidity made the dropping temperatures feel like they were actually rising. "Some of her garlic is going to rot in the field because I didn't get here sooner. Worse, she might still be alive if I'd been more involved in her life. At the very least, I might have a better idea of how she died. If it was natural causes, I might have been able to get her to see a doctor before it was too late, and if it was murder, I might have had a better idea of who should be questioned about it."

"That's just part of the grieving process," Rory said. "You're still in denial, dwelling on unanswered questions so you don't have to think about your loss."

"Someone needs to dwell on them, and no one else is doing it."

Rory sighed. "It was an accident. No one had a reason to kill Peggy."

"The thief did, if she caught him red-handed," Mabel said. "I may be in some sort of denial, but you are too. Not just denying your loss, but denying that the circumstances were suspicious. You were one of Aunt

Peggy's best friends. You must have noticed that she was anxious the last couple weeks before she died. She knew who committed the thefts, and she was looking for proof."

"She knew?" Rory said, obviously startled. "She named the thief?"

"Not in the journal. She wanted more proof. I think it was someone she was close to, and she was hoping she was wrong. I don't know. Did she seem out of sorts with anyone those last couple weeks?"

"Not particularly." Rory stopped working and looked at the dark horizon. "She seemed a little tired the last few days before she died. I thought it was because she'd been working out in the fields for twelve hours straight for several days, all by herself. Then when she died, I couldn't help thinking she'd worked herself to death."

"I probably would have thought the same thing if I hadn't read about the thief in her journal."

"She did tell me about one thing that was bothering her, but it wasn't crop thefts." Rory abandoned her study of the sky to look at Mabel. "About a week or two before she died, she went to see Darryl and came back furious that he was planning to expand the farmers' market to out-of-town vendors. She was afraid it would lose its unique character, which would make tourists less likely to come to it. That would hurt everyone who participated in the market, both the local farmers and the newcomers. She warned Darryl that she'd fight his proposal, and he had to have known that she'd win."

"Had he already contacted any out-of-town farmers about joining the market?" Mabel said. "Could they have blamed Aunt Peggy for keeping them out, after Darryl had gotten their hopes up?"

"I don't think anyone except Darryl and I knew about the disagreement. Eventually he and Peggy worked out a compromise, opening up a few extra slots, giving local farmers first dibs, but allowing out-of-towners to apply for any unclaimed spaces. Peggy even let Darryl take credit for the final plan, and supported it wholeheartedly."

"Still, Darryl could have been irritated with Aunt Peggy for meddling with his plan."

"I suppose," Rory said, getting back to work. "But it's hardly worth killing over."

Mabel followed her example. Pull, clip, crate and repeat, ad infinitum, or at least until the rain came. She wasn't entirely convinced that she could cross Darryl off the list of people annoyed with Aunt Peggy. Sure, it was unlikely that such a small disagreement would escalate to murder, but most feuds started with something small. She'd seen massive flame wars online that had been started by a typo. Emotions ran even higher in person. Darryl might have been insulted by Aunt Peggy's interference in his plans. He obviously thought he was a big man on the farmers' market campus, and Peggy had proven that she was even bigger. That sort of an ego blow could fester. Maybe not into an intentional murder, but possibly a confrontation that got out of hand.

Still, Rory was probably right. There wasn't anything Mabel could do with what was nothing more than wild speculation. For now, she had to concentrate on the things she could do, like pulling garlic, developing apps and handing her tiara off to Bettina. Investigating a murder that might have been an accident really wasn't part of her skill set.

Too bad there wasn't an app for finding killers.

CHAPTER TWENTY

Mabel had thought the weather couldn't get any more oppressive, but the humidity kept rising, and the skies kept darkening, promising relief from the heat while threatening an end to the harvest. Her crew was still working their way through the fields, although they'd all stopped their previous chattering, saving their energy for their work. Three of the CSA members had made good on their commitments, and Rory had somehow convinced them to stay longer than they'd planned by moving them into the only slightly more comfortable barn when they'd reached their limit in the field.

While everyone was taking a hydration break on the patio, gulping down sports drinks and using the hose to cool themselves down, Mabel went inside the farmhouse to order an extravagant lunch for her dedicated crew. She also wanted to check on Pixie, since the house wasn't air-conditioned. Opening the door to the kitchen, Mabel was pleasantly surprised by how cool the air was, courtesy of the strategically planted trees shading the old farmhouse.

She pulled out her phone, intending to call the two local restaurants with garlic contracts, but noticed that she'd gotten an email from her attorney. Apparently the DA was resisting the idea of even a private autopsy because he'd been getting some calls from local residents, suggesting that it was a waste of taxpayers' money to open an investigation into a death that had obviously been an accident. Jeff recommended stepping back from the whole situation and coming back to her safe home in Maine.

It was tempting. Ironically, though, knowing she'd hit a nerve actually made her more determined to get answers. She was fairly certain it meant that she was on the right track, and her aunt really had been killed. She'd been prepared to abandon the farm a few hours ago, but now she couldn't disappoint all the people who were depending on her.

She was making her aunt's killer nervous, and nervous people made mistakes. She'd seen it happen often enough with colleagues who'd crumbled under the pressure of client deadlines and unreasonable demands. They'd taken shortcuts to produce the app on time, only to find that it was glitchy and had to be coded again from scratch.

Given the unanimous belief that everyone loved Aunt Peggy, it seemed logical that the killer hadn't planned to hurt her aunt, so he wasn't a professional with nerves of steel, immune to making mistakes. All Mabel had to do was keep asking questions and keep the killer off-guard until the autopsy results came in, and the DA could be convinced to do a proper investigation.

Mabel owed her aunt that much. Besides, she didn't like the idea that there was a killer here in West Slocum. If he got away with one murder, what was to keep him from killing someone else? If the killer was also the thief, then all the other farmers were at risk. Starting with Emily, who might have been his target last night until Mabel scared him off. No, she couldn't leave now. She had to stay here until the investigation was complete and the killer was put away.

Mabel responded to say she wasn't in any rush to go home, and she still wanted to go forward with the autopsy. As long as she was paying to get some answers, she decided she might as well give her attorney some additional work to do. She added a request to investigate Charlie Durbin, explaining that he was a local developer, and she wondered if he'd been cozying up to her aunt so she'd sell him the land. And she also wanted to know about Al Soares, Pennsylvania garlic grower and the defendant in a lawsuit that Aunt Peggy had filed.

She hit *send* and then found the phone numbers she'd been looking for originally. A woman answered at Jeanne's Country Diner. Mabel couldn't pinpoint where in New England the woman came from, but she definitely didn't have the slight French accent of the owner.

"I'd like to order six of the lunch specials for pick-up in an hour, if that's possible."

"Sure." The sound of a pencil scratching on a pad came through the phone. "What's the name?"

Mabel hesitated. The whole plan was to remain incognito, to avoid giving Jeanne and Ethan another thing to compete over. She needed a pseudonym, fast.

Pixie wandered into the kitchen.

"My name is Pixie," Mabel told the woman on the phone.

"Last name?"

Mabel scanned the kitchen for more inspiration. Pineapple just didn't work as a last name. Table, sink, walls. No good. Everything else was either avocado green like the phone, or .... "Gold. Pixie Gold."

"All right, Ms. Gold. We'll have six of the luncheon specials ready for you in an hour."

After placing the same order, under the same name, at Maison Becker, Mabel patted Pixie and headed into town. Darryl Santangelo's office was her first destination. He was on the phone when she arrived, talking about some team that Mabel had heard of, but couldn't match to a particular sport. He gestured for her to come into his office and have a seat. She wasn't planning to stay that long, so she wandered over to look out the window at the library.

A couple of minutes later, she heard him end his call, and she turned away from the window.

Darryl was smiling at her as if she were his best friend, and he hadn't seen her in six months. She started to smile herself, until she remembered she wasn't anyone's best friend, and they'd seen each other just yesterday. She couldn't trust his pretty face.

"Ready to cry uncle?" he said. "I hear you're behind schedule on the harvest, and it looks like the weather isn't cooperating."

"It's not the weather's job to help," Mabel said. "Or anyone else's except mine and my loyal crew. If it's humanly possible, we'll get the harvest done. That's what I'm here to tell you, actually. I'm not abandoning Aunt Peggy's space at the farmers' market. We'll be there this weekend, and we'll be celebrating the completion of the harvest."

Darryl's smile faltered slightly. "I'm sure you're doing your best, but you're running out of time. You really ought to consider Larry's offer. He'll be here in a few minutes if you want to talk to him about it."

"No, thanks. We'll manage."

"What have you got against Larry, anyway?"

"Nothing in particular," Mabel said. "I just don't think Aunt Peggy would have accepted his help, and I'm trying to carry out her wishes."

"Peggy knew when to ask for help." Darryl leaned back and fidgeted with his chunky ring. "It sounds like you've been talking to someone who doesn't like Larry. Rory Hansen, maybe."

"Rory's been very helpful, but I make the final decisions."

His smile changed, a more natural indication of amusement. "That's what everyone thinks when they've been steamrolled by Rory. She's got a knack, not just for convincing people to do what she wants, but also for making them believe it was their idea in the first place."

Kyle had told her something similar, but Mabel still couldn't believe there was anything malicious about Rory's actions. "It's not like she's some sort of grifter, conning me into giving her my life's savings. She's out sweating in the fields right now, harvesting my crop."

"You've still got to ask yourself what she's getting out of it. Who would do that kind of work without expecting anything in return?" For once, his smile completely disappeared, and the earnestness of his expression seemed honest. "Don't get me wrong. Rory always has the best intentions, but she's also got some sort of angle for herself. Sometimes it just takes a while before you find out what it is, and then it's too late."

"What did she get you to do that you came to regret?"

"Me? Nothing," he said too quickly. "I suppose you could say that she got me to take this job as the market's manager. I don't regret it, exactly, but I sure hadn't planned on it when we first met. It's not an easy job, the pay isn't great, and everyone thinks she can do a better job than I can."

"Like Aunt Peggy?" Mabel said. "I heard about your disagreement over expanding of the market to admit out-of-towners."

He shrugged. "That was nothing. I'd just tossed an idea out there, and we talked about it, and the final rules worked out great. I've been getting compliments on the expansion from the local farmers and even other market managers who want to copy my rules."

"No hard feelings?"

"The only people I hold grudges against," he said, "are the thieves and black-marketeers. Them, I'm willing to get angry with and stay angry."

"Is it that big a problem?"

"Big enough. I heard you got hit by a thief again last night. That's why I thought you might be willing to reconsider Larry's offer." Darryl turned his head to listen to the new voice in the reception area, and then jumped to his feet. "Here he is now. I'll just step outside and send him in here so you two can talk privately."

Darryl shoved Larry inside the room and closed the door behind him, leaving Mabel and Larry alone.

"My crew is on standby whenever you're ready to call it quits," Larry shouted.

Mabel took a step back to protect her ears. "I've got my own crew."

"You've got three kids and a couple of old women." He snorted. "That's not a crew. That's a tea party."

"Thanks for reminding me," Mabel said, moving toward the door. "I need to pick up some iced tea on the way back to the farm so we can continue our partying."

"Hey." Larry moved to block her exit and shouted from much too close. "You're not giving me a chance. Let me explain how I can help."

"I don't have time for this." She stepped to the side to go around him, but he moved too.

"You're just like your aunt," he shouted, and this time there was real anger behind his voice.

Mabel couldn't tell just how angry he was, or whether he was likely to do anything more than shout. He was between her and the door, with no escape other than through him. He was only a couple inches taller and twenty or thirty pounds heavier than she was, but he had the advantage of being a farmer, doing physical chores, in addition to yelling at his crew. The only exercise she usually got was typing on her laptop, and strong, fast fingers weren't going to do her much good in a fistfight.

Darryl was just outside the door, and if she screamed, she was reasonably sure he'd come rushing in. Larry had to know that too, so there was no reason for her to panic. "I really need to leave now."

He didn't move out of her way, but he didn't raise a fist either. "You Skinner women never give a guy a chance. What do you have against men, anyway? It's like you've got some sort of feminist commune. No boys allowed."

"That's just silly," Mabel said, although it struck her that there were far more women at the farm than men. Even Pixie was female. It was quite a change from the male-dominated world of computer science that she was used to. "You'd be welcome on the farm if you had anything useful to do there."

He huffed in annoyance, and then took a step backwards, making room for her to pass him. "I'm just trying to help." He managed to infuse a plaintive note in the shouted words.

Mabel raised her voice to match his, so she would be absolutely sure he heard every word. "I don't believe you." He didn't care about the harvest or the farm or even the garlic. He was just feeling sorry for himself. Exactly why, she wasn't sure. Was it just his usual irritation over being an inferior farmer? Or was there a new reason for him to dwell on his failures? How frustrating would it be to know he'd killed for the chance to get his hands on Aunt Peggy's garlic and still hadn't managed to lay claim to it?

"You're not trying to help. You're trying to steal my aunt's reputation. I can't do anything about the thief who's stealing her garlic, but I *can* protect her reputation. If you really want to help, you'll stop wasting my time. I've got a crew to feed and a harvest to finish before the storm hits."

Mabel brushed by him, jerked the door open and rushed into the lobby. Darryl looked up from where he was chatting with the uninterested receptionist. Mabel held her hand up to block both his advice and the shine of his smile. "I don't want to hear it. I don't need you to broker a deal with Larry. I need you to do your job, protecting the market. If anyone can find out who's selling stolen garlic at the market, it's you. You should be looking into what the other farmers might know about it, and they should be cooperating with you to find the culprit. It won't be good for any farmer when word gets out that West Slocum farms are easy targets. If you and Larry really want to help, you'll figure out how to catch the garlic thief before he empties my barn completely."

CHAPTER TWENTY-ONE

Mabel was so irritated as she left Darryl's office and stomped down the stairs to her car that she almost forgot she needed to send her boss a reassuring note and the updated draft of her app. She ran into the library, mouthed, "sorry, can't talk," at Josefina on her way past the front desk, and claimed a computer station. She skimmed the three anxious emails from her boss and sent him a quick but reassuring response, along with the updated draft of her app. Nothing else in her in-box looked important, except for a message from her attorney.

He'd managed to get copies of the court filings on the lawsuit against Al Soares. A full status report on the litigation would follow later, but for now, he could share his impression that there was nothing to suggest that Al Soares might have gone to West Slocum to confront her aunt. Apparently, they'd come close to a settlement recently, and only Peggy's death had prevented the deal from being finalized.

Jeff also confirmed that Charlie Durbin had a number of projects under construction, which would keep him and his crew of loyal, long-term employees busy for at least the next five years. The developer was also reputed to have a considerable amount of land in reserve, waiting to be built on; he had a reputation for doing environmentally friendly work; and he was well liked by the local planning/zoning boards and building department.

Mabel still wasn't entirely ready to trust him. She'd had a run-in with a developer back in Maine, and he'd been well enough liked by the various boards to get his permits too, although in his case, it had been because he'd paid them off. For all she knew, that could have been how Charlie Durbin had gotten his reputation too. A greedy man wouldn't care how many projects he had lined up or how much land he already owned, if there was a chance he could get a deal on more, more, more.

Mabel continued reading the email. There was one other interesting fact, Jeff reported. Charlie Durbin had done so well with his previous projects that he was able to finance all of his projects with very little in the way of mortgages, sometimes even providing low-rate financing for the buyers of his properties.

Mabel sighed. Okay, so Charlie Durbin wasn't greedy like the developer who'd threatened to develop all around her quiet little home in Maine. One more perfectly good suspect down the drain.

As Mabel was closing the email, her phone pinged with a text from her aunt. At first she thought it was just a spammer spoofing her aunt's number, and she started to delete it without even reading it. Curiosity got the better of her, so she paused to read the message, which had apparently gone out to everyone in her aunt's contact list. It was just random letters, not a sales pitch or phishing scheme. A spammer wouldn't send gibberish. The text looked more like a mistake, with the sender pocket dialing or otherwise hitting random keys without noticing it.

Someone was using her aunt's phone.

Mabel logged into her aunt's account, but the website didn't provide the numbers of the recent phone calls, or any indication of the phone's physical location. She would have liked to install an app designed to recover lost phones, but she needed the phone itself to do that. She might not be able to track down the phone, but the police could get the call logs and locations, once she convinced them her aunt's death was worth investigating.

If the thief and possible murderer had been foolish enough to use the stolen phone, he might be easy to catch, after all. After making sure her own caller ID was blocked, Mabel dialed Aunt Peggy's cell phone number, only to get her aunt's old voicemail message. Mabel waited until the entire message played, wallowing in the bittersweetness of hearing her aunt's voice, before hanging up. As a result, she was distracted on her way out of the building and forgot to avoid the front lobby.

Josefina called her over to the checkout desk. "Is the harvest done yet?"

"Not even close."

"Then what are you doing here?"

"I'm picking up lunch for the crew. Just stopped in here for a quick email check on the way."

"I won't keep you then," Josefina said. "I know you're running out of time, with the rain coming, but everyone's looking forward to celebrating the new crop of garlic this weekend. They're going to be disappointed if it's delayed. Not just locals, either. I've been talking to people who are planning to come from Rhode Island, Connecticut and New Hampshire. Bringing in all those tourists will be good for the other farmers too."

Great. Now Mabel wasn't just responsible for the wellbeing of her field hands, Rory, Bettina, Kyle, Darryl, Josefina and Pixie, but for the whole town and a good chunk of New England.

"I never realized how crazy people could get about garlic," Mabel said. "I still don't get it. It's just garlic."

"Peggy would be turning over in her grave, if she had one," Josefina said severely. "It's not *just* garlic, any more than my work is *just* distributing books, or your job is *just* a job. If you don't feel passion for your work, then you should find something else to do."

"I'm sorry," Mabel said. "I'm tired, and garlic isn't my passion, it's my aunt's. I'm doing my best, but I don't understand the obsession everyone around here has with garlic. I might understand it with food professionals, like Jeanne and Ethan, but not with everyone else."

"Jeanne and Ethan are different, all right, but not because they're professional chefs," Josefina said. "Food isn't the only passion they're struggling with. They've also got a passion for each other, and they're acting like the ten-year-olds who come here for storytime, and spend every spare minute teasing the objects of their crushes. Ethan and Jeanne are old enough to have better social skills, but I think they've convinced themselves that their professional rivalry makes a personal relationship impossible. Instead of admitting they're attracted to each other, they're trying to provoke a reaction that will prove that the relationship is impossible. Sometimes, I want to treat them like the children they're being, and put them in time out until they promise to kiss and make up."

Mabel never would have guessed they were anything other than lifelong archenemies. "Are you sure they don't really hate each other?"

"Absolutely," Josefina said. "I just wish they'd hurry up and figure it out before one of them does something really stupid."

"It's reassuring to know they won't really kill each other if one of them happens to get an extra clove of garlic from me."

"They might almost be grateful to have a reason to argue about it," Josefina said. "They don't have that many excuses for seeing each other. It's not like either of them can ask the other one out to dinner, and they're both working such long hours that they don't have time for other kinds of dates. I was hoping they might realize their mutual attraction when they were both at the local food sourcing conference at UMass Amherst a couple weeks ago, but they'd only been there for a day or so when your aunt was killed, and they got into a huge argument over who was Peggy's favorite."

The conference might have been a disaster romantically, but at least it gave them an alibi for the time of her aunt's death. That just left all the other thousands of garlic obsessed residents of West Slocum as suspects.

* * * *

Mabel set the box containing the order from Maison Becker in the Mini Cooper's trunk, next to the box from Jeanne's Country Diner. As she went around to the driver's seat, her phone rang. Probably a telemarketer, she thought, since the only person who had the new number was her attorney, and he knew she preferred to interact by text or email. Nevertheless, she checked her phone. There was an incoming call from Stevens Funeral.

She answered, and Wayne Stevens identified himself. "Your lawyer gave us your number. It seems there has been a slight glitch in the handling of Peggy's personal possessions."

"I told you her phone was missing."

"Her phone?" The sound of papers being rifled came through the line. "Oh, no, it's not a phone. And we didn't lose the item. It was misplaced before her possessions were packed up for us."

"What is it?"

"Binoculars."

"How could you lose binoculars?"

"We didn't misplace them, and we don't know who did," he said. "We spoke to the first responders, and they told us that the strap was wrapped around her wrist when they found her. No one quite knows what happened to them after that until they showed up during an inventory of the ambulance, and they were sent on to us. We even have the receipt. We weren't the ones who misplaced them."

"When can I claim them?"

"Whenever it's convenient for you to stop by," he said. "Or, given the circumstances, we can deliver them to the farm if you'd like."

"I'll be driving right past your building in a few minutes," Mabel said. "I can pick them up then."

"We'll be waiting for you."

Ten minutes later, Mabel added the box containing the binoculars to the other contents of her car's trunk. Before leaving the funeral home, she'd unsealed the box to confirm that there was, indeed a pair of binoculars inside, and nothing else. Mabel had never owned binoculars herself, but it didn't take an expert to know that they had definitely belonged to her aunt. The standard-issue strap had been replaced by one with pineapples printed on the leather. A closer inspection revealed that her initials had been engraved on the body of the binoculars.

As Mabel climbed into her car, she couldn't help wondering how the binoculars had gotten themselves tangled up around her aunt's wrist the night she'd died. Nighttime wasn't exactly ideal for bird-watching. The birds were quiet until shortly before sunrise, presumably asleep and difficult to spot.

A more likely explanation was that Aunt Peggy had been staking out the garlic thief the night she'd died. She'd thought she knew the culprit, and recognizing someone she knew was a lot easier than trying to get a clear enough look at a stranger to describe him to the police or identify him in a lineup. The binoculars were definitely consistent with Mabel's theory that her aunt had been killed by the garlic thief, but unfortunately she doubted they qualified as the solid evidence needed to convince the local DA to order an official investigation.

Mabel turned onto the street leading to the farm, frustrated that the binoculars hadn't given her any new insights. There were too many possibilities for what had happened the night her aunt died. She'd only been able to rule out a few possibilities, like Al Soares, Charlie Durbin and the local chefs, all of whom had alibis for the night Aunt Peggy had died. The likelihood that Aunt Peggy had known the thief, and the thief had been a friend of hers, ought to have narrowed down the possibilities, but she'd known too many people. If the circumstances were reversed, and Mabel had been killed by someone she'd known well, it would have been easy to identify the culprit since there were only one or two people who fit that description.

Unfortunately, given Aunt Peggy's gregariousness, limiting the suspects to her friends wasn't much of a limitation at all. Just about everyone in West Slocum had to be considered suspects. Plus, according to Josefina, there were all the people coming to this weekend's celebration from Rhode Island, Connecticut and New Hampshire. Why stop at New Hampshire? Mabel might as well consider every single resident in New England as a suspect. Maybe the whole east coast, given Aunt Peggy's tendency to treat all her customers as if they were her best friends. After all, she hadn't claimed to grow the best garlic in New England, but on the entire east coast.

It was starting to look like the odds of ever identifying Aunt Peggy's killer were even worse than the odds of finishing the garlic harvest before the rain arrived.

CHAPTER TWENTY-TWO

Mabel parked next to the patio and then went into the barn to get a volunteer to collect the field hands for lunch. Kyle and Bettina were racking garlic, and Kyle explained that the CSA members had sneaked out of the barn and gone home when Rory wasn't looking. Mabel sent Kyle out with the tractor to bring back the rest of the crew and any filled bins.

Bettina helped carry the lunch orders from Mabel's car to the picnic table on the patio. Once liberated from their generic cardboard boxes, the individual take-out containers clearly identified where they'd come from. The ones from Jeanne's Country Diner were bright yellow containers with stylized blue flowers, more French Provincial than American country. Ethan's containers were severely elegant, in black with white lettering.

Bettina placed the two dessert boxes, one from each restaurant, at one end of the table, and then formed a long row down the middle of the table with the twelve individual meals. She found a stack of napkins, a stack of paper plates and a basket of plastic cutlery, which she placed at the opposite end of the table from the large boxes. Satisfied with the layout, she headed indoors to collect drinks. Mabel followed to make sure Pixie didn't escape. The cat was seated on the windowsill, her back to the barn, watching Bettina warily, but remaining silent.

Rory was the first to come through the kitchen door. "The rest of the crew is washing up in the barn. They'll be here in a minute. I'm not staying, just grabbing something to eat. I'll take my lunch out to the barn so Dawn won't feel like I'm watching over her while she eats."

"You can sit inside the kitchen if you'd prefer," Mabel said. "You'd be out of Dawn's sight, and Pixie seems resigned to having visitors in the house, so she won't bother you."

"The barn is fine," Rory said. "I can do some racking while I eat, or make some more phone calls to the CSA members who were avoiding me earlier today. The phone service is better out there than in here."

"That's not saying much," Mabel said as she walked out to the picnic table with Rory. "At least the food should be good. Lunch specials from Jeanne's Country Diner and Maison Becker."

"You're spoiling us," Rory said, opening one yellow and blue container and one black and white one. The contents were startlingly similar. The diner had produced a simple turkey club sandwich on what looked like a fresh baguette, with a side order of potato salad. The more upscale restaurant had produced a deconstructed version of the sandwich: a fresh salad that included baby red potatoes, topped with turkey slices and pancetta and herbed croutons.

Rory closed the yellow and blue container and picked up the black and white one. "If that oversized box from Jeanne's Country Diner is what I think it is, we're lucky that Joe isn't here, or no one else would get a bite. Jeanne makes a mean apple pie, and Joe has a bit of a sweet tooth."

"I noticed he doesn't seem to share your enthusiasm for locally grown foods."

"Not unless they've had a bunch of sugar added to them," Rory said. "He's a big fan of your aunt's butternut squash, but only after she added a ton of brown sugar and cooked it into jam."

"Does it bother him? The amount of time you spend on the local farms?"

"Joe?" Rory laughed. "There are a lot of things he cares about, including me, but as long as I'm not doing anything illegal and I'm happy, that's all that matters to him."

"I can't picture you doing anything illegal." Assuming Aunt Peggy's killer was also the garlic thief, then Rory had a sort of alibi. There was simply no way Rory would have stolen a few hundred or even a few thousand dollars' worth of garlic. The risks of getting caught were worse for her than just about anyone else. Even if she only got a slap on the wrist from the legal system, she was jeopardizing her marriage and potentially her husband's career in law enforcement. "You wouldn't really have run Kyle over with the tractor."

Rory grabbed one of the sports drinks that Bettina had delivered to the table and left for the barn, with a reminder to save her a piece of Jeanne's pie.

The field crew were coming in the opposite direction, and at Rory's mention of dessert, Terry, who was holding down the rear with Kyle, suddenly perked up and passed his friends on the way to the table. "Pie? There's pie? What kind? Where is it?"

Mabel pointed at the large yellow and blue box at the far end of the table, and Terry flopped onto the bench in front of it. If he harvested garlic as quickly and efficiently as he grabbed a paper plate and dug out the first slice of what was, in fact, apple pie, the last field might actually be finished today before the rains came.

Bettina returned with more drinks. "You'll make yourself sick, eating all that sugar on an empty stomach. You need to have something nutritious first."

Terry swallowed, and wrapped his forearms protectively around his plate. "My grandmother always said that life was uncertain, so you should eat dessert first."

Mabel took one of the yellow and blue containers and sat across from Terry. "If we finish the harvest today, I'll get you another whole pie, just for yourself."

"What are we waiting for?" Terry jumped up, dessert plate in hand.

"We're waiting for everyone to eat, so you won't pass out from hunger," Mabel said, encouraging him to sit down again.

Dawn sat between Anna and Terry, and Kyle dragged himself over to sit at the end of the bench, apparently unable to move any farther. He looked dreadful, even though he'd been spared the direct sun for most of the day. Mabel couldn't believe anyone would go to all this much trouble to con her out of a few pounds of garlic.

Fifteen minutes later, the take-out containers had all been emptied and only Rory's slice of pie remained. If the lunch had been a referendum on the quality of the two restaurants, the vote would have been tied. The two chefs had every reason to be proud of their respective restaurants.

Terry left, vowing to earn himself a whole pie by finishing the harvest, and Bettina and the rest of the crew joined him. Mabel quickly stuffed the few leftovers into the refrigerator.

Pixie remained perched on the kitchen windowsill, still quiet, and seemingly unfazed by all the activity out on the patio. Maybe the animal control officer had been right, and the cat had only needed a little time to get used to her new surroundings, and with familiarity would come an end to her yowling.

Mabel refreshed Pixie's food and water bowls before heading outside to see where she could be the biggest help. Just as she stepped outside, Pixie began yowling. So much for the theory that she was settling down.

From the patio, Mabel could hear the tractor's engine idling in the final field, indicating where the crew had left off before lunch. Based on the location of the tractor, they'd managed to get about half of the field harvested. It would have been an amazing accomplishment even in cooler, dryer weather, and was something of a miracle in this heat and humidity.

Unfortunately, it still wasn't going to be enough. The crew was exhausted, no matter how much they tried to deny it, and there was less than half a workday left before the rain arrived. Mabel glanced at the overcast sky where darker clouds were visible near the western horizon. Depending on how fast the storm was moving, there could be less than two hours left to finish the harvest.

The vehicle that Pixie had forecast arrived, and Mabel went over to introduce herself to the thin, redheaded woman who got out of the car and identified herself as a CSA member. Over the next few minutes, three more cars arrived, each one announced in advance by Pixie, and two of them containing more CSA members. The very last one was the developer, Charlie Durbin. He parked and turned off the truck's engine, but stayed inside it, talking on the phone. He could stay there permanently, as far as she was concerned. She had to accept that Charlie Durbin wasn't outright evil, but she still wasn't inclined to trust any developer.

Mabel sent everyone else into the barn to check in with Rory, and went over to see what Charlie Durbin wanted.

She knocked on the window and he held up one finger, while he told the person on the other end of the phone, "I'll call you back tomorrow. If you don't hear from me by then, tell the cops to look for my body over at Stinkin' Stuff Farm. The new owner doesn't like me much."

He hung up and rolled down the window. "I ran into Darryl a few minutes ago, and he said you could use some help."

"Not from a developer who wants to turn my farm into a subdivision," Mabel said. "Don't you have other people's lives to ruin? Backhoes to set loose on defenseless tracts of forest and wildlife?"

"I try to do one good deed every week to make up for the bad karma I've got from all that pillaging," he said. "Darryl really seemed desperate. He was probably talking to the wrong crowd, though. Unlike me, they all had jobs to go back to, where they were on the clock and would lose their pay or their entire job if they skipped an afternoon without a better excuse than volunteer work. That's the nice thing about being the boss. No one can fire me."

"I can, if you're working for me," Mabel said. "We don't even have to wait for you to finish applying for the job. You're fired. Go home."

"Look. You need the help. I want to pay a debt I owe your aunt." He pointed past her, at the sky where she already knew the storm clouds were approaching much too fast. "You don't have time to argue with me, and you can't afford to turn down help that I promise comes with no strings. How about a truce? Just for today. Not even the whole day. Just until the rain starts. You can get a restraining order against me after that, and I won't even contest it."

It was tempting to accept his help. Charlie was one of the few local residents who had a confirmed alibi and no real motive to kill her aunt, at least not for another few years, when he ran out of the buildable land he'd stockpiled.

Rory's voice came from behind Mabel, near the barn doors. "Charlie! It's so good of you to volunteer. I didn't even bother to call you, not with the grand opening of your seniors-only subdivision in just two weeks. You must be going crazy, getting everything ready so you don't have to postpone the move in date."

"Hi, Rory. I just stopped in for a minute to check on things here." He glanced at Mabel. "Not sure I can stay, though."

Rory's face fell. "Oh. I understand. I'd just hoped...You know it's Peggy's last harvest, and she deserves to have every last bit of her work honored. We've got maybe four more hours before the storm hits, and we could get a lot done in that time."

Mabel glanced at the storm clouds. Rory was in denial again. They'd be lucky if they had two hours before the rain started.

"Well?" Charlie said, keeping his voice too low for Rory to hear from where she stood in front of the barn. "Are you going to let me out of the truck to help, or are you going to break Rory's heart?"

Mabel stepped back. "You can help, but I'll be keeping a close eye on you."

As he got out of the truck, she couldn't help thinking that keeping an eye on him was something that many women would consider quite pleasant, rather than a chore. Fortunately, she wasn't that easily impressed. She'd never trusted first impressions, or anyone with obviously good people skills.

It took less than half an hour for Mabel to conclude somewhat begrudgingly that if Charlie was intent on sabotaging the farm, he wasn't planning to do it today. While they'd been arguing, Kyle had driven the tractor into the barn with the wagon stacked high with filled crates. Charlie had thrown himself into emptying the wagon, and then, taking in Kyle's drooping posture and red, sweat-drenched skin, had offered to swap places with him in the field, so Kyle could stay in the shade of the barn.

Mabel hopped onto the back of the wagon to escort him out to the fields. Once there, Charlie set a brutal pace, filling his crate, and then carrying both his crate and hers back to the tractor.

Terry, Anna and Dawn chattered intermittently as they worked in the next row. Their voices were cheerful, although Mabel couldn't make out the individual words. She didn't know how they kept going. The heat, humidity and monotony of the work was weighing her down, and she'd had more breaks from the field than they had.

Charlie caught her eyeing the field hands, and said, "The resilience of youth, huh?"

"I was never that young," Mabel said. "Were you ever not a greedy developer?"

"Depends on who you ask. My mother says I was an angel. That's probably not enough of a character witness for you, and I can't blame you for not taking her word for it. I'm pretty sure I could have been a serial killer by the age of four, and she'd still have thought I was an angel. Just like I could have been a canonized saint by the age of four, and you'd have thought I was a creep."

She had been hard on him, but she had good reason to distrust developers. "What would Aunt Peggy have said you were?"

He straightened, cutting the scapes from the bulbs in his hand, and then looked at the oncoming storm clouds. "She would have said that I was a friend."

"She thought everyone was her friend," Mabel said. "But someone was stealing her garlic, and I'm pretty sure it was someone she thought was a friend."

"Wasn't me," he said. "I never told her, and I'd be drummed out of the CSA if anyone knew, but I can't really tell the difference between her garlic and anyone else's, or between fresh garlic in a recipe and the powdered stuff."

"That doesn't completely let you off the hook," Mabel said, although she knew he wasn't much of a real suspect. "You could have sold the stolen garlic and used the proceeds to pay your crew to work extra hours so your senior housing would be ready on time."

"No offense intended," Charlie said, "but the farm's entire harvest wouldn't earn enough on the black market for my overtime expenses in the next two weeks."

"Sounds like you know an awful lot about the going rate for black-market garlic."

"Just guessing." He tugged the next several plants out of the ground. "Peggy and I never really talked about her finances."

"What did you talk about?"

"Nothing in particular," he said. "Life in general."

"Did you ever wonder about how Aunt Peggy died?"

"I haven't thought of much else since I heard about it." He hacked at the scapes, leaving uneven edges.

"I can't help thinking her death wasn't an accident, but everyone says I'm just going through the first stage of grief, and I'll come to accept it eventually," Mabel said. "It's only been a couple days since I got here, but I'm not getting any closer to acceptance. In fact, I'm getting closer to being convinced it was murder."

"By the same person who was stealing the garlic?"

Finally. Someone didn't think she was crazy. Or was he simply humoring her? Even if he was, it would be nice to be able to bounce her ideas off someone who didn't automatically reject them.

"The garlic thief is the most likely suspect," Mabel said. "Aunt Peggy died late at night, when she would normally have been asleep, so something serious must have caused her to be outside. She suspected that someone she knew was the thief. Just today, I learned that she was carrying a pair of binoculars when she died. I think she was staking out the farm that night, waiting for the thief to come back so she could identify him. She confronted him, they fought, and she died. That's murder."

"It's all circumstantial," he said.

"The binoculars are pretty convincing, though," Mabel said. "She certainly wasn't birdwatching after midnight. What else could she have had them for?"

"I gave her the binoculars. To watch for critters. The four legged kind. A couple years ago, she had some trouble with woodchucks nibbling on her squash plants. The woodchucks won't touch the garlic or lavender, and the smell of the garlic often disguises the squash, but that year something had found the vines. Peggy needed to figure out where the critters were coming from, so she could set traps. If they came back this year, she would have been up above where she was killed, using the height and perhaps the coverage of the gazebo to view all the fields without being spotted by the woodchucks."

That didn't completely rule out the possibility that her aunt had been staking out a human instead of woodchucks, but it did mean that Mabel had less compelling evidence than she'd thought she had. The DA would likely be as unimpressed with her theory as Charlie was.

Mabel glanced at the nearest clump of vines. "I haven't seen any critter damage to the squash plants, and Rory hasn't mentioned any."

"I wish I'd been home, and not at some stupid conference." Charlie stomped over to his bin, becoming more gentle only as he placed the garlic and scapes into it. "If she was trying to ID the thief, she might have called me to help. I've had my own experiences with thefts at job sites, and I could have sent over some backup for her. Or been here on the stakeout myself. In fact, I should give you some names to call to get someone out here to keep an eye on the barn while the garlic is drying. Unless, of course, you'd refuse to hire them, just because I recommend them."

"I wouldn't hold it against them." She hoped she wasn't proving, once again, how bad she was at reading people, but Charlie did seem to have her and her aunt's best interests at heart. "I don't need any names, though. Joe Hansen is getting some names for me."

"I should have done more," Charlie said. "I knew she was upset. I didn't know she suspected a friend of betraying her, though."

"Did she tell you about any other thefts and when they happened?" Mabel said. "Maybe it would help if the police knew the timing of the raids."

"Just one, and I didn't get any real details," he said. "Someone stole some of the scapes that had been cut for the opening day of the farmers' market the beginning of June. A whole crate was taken, which is too much for even the largest, most garlic loving family to use, so she was pretty sure it was someone who planned to sell it."

Or someone who fed the scapes to livestock, Mabel thought. "Wouldn't someone have noticed if anyone other than Aunt Peggy was selling scapes at the farmers' market?"

"Not necessarily. Larry Rose and a couple other local farmers bring a few scapes to the market, and even the experts wouldn't have been able to tell where they'd been grown."

"I've had a couple run-ins with Larry Rose," Mabel said. "I wouldn't put it past him to sneak on over here and steal some of Aunt Peggy's crop."

"I would," Charlie said. "Larry's not so bad, once you get to know him. Peggy rather liked him, in fact, until he pushed her too far. They were a regular couple until about three years ago."

"They were *dating*?" Mabel would never have guessed they'd ever been anything other than rivals. "Seriously?"

"Seriously." Charlie smiled at Mabel's astonishment, a more natural seeming smile than Darryl's professional version. "Larry asked her to move in with him, and I'm pretty sure he'd have put a ring on it if she'd wanted one."

"What happened?"

"I don't know all the details. Maybe Rory or Emily would. It had something to do with the strings Larry placed on his offer. He wanted to combine the two farms under his banner and his control."

Even with as little contact as Mabel had had with her aunt over the years, she knew Aunt Peggy would never have agreed to that deal. In fact, back when Aunt Peggy had moved to West Slocum, she'd had to choose between her new farming lifestyle and the lover she'd lived with for years. There weren't any farming opportunities in downtown Boston, at least not back then, when no one had considered rooftop gardens, and the lover's job was one that couldn't easily be done outside a major city. Peggy and Larry wouldn't have had any of the complications of a long-distance relationship. All they'd needed to do was run their farms separately. Mabel wasn't exactly sure where Larry's farm was, but if it was within the boundaries of West Slocum, it couldn't have been more than a ten minute drive from here. There would have been room for compromise, but not if Larry had insisted on being in charge. "It sounds like Larry didn't know my aunt as well as a husband should."

"Or Peggy didn't care about Larry as much as he cared about her," Charlie said. "She might have convinced him to operate separate businesses if she'd thought it was worth the effort."

"I guess she didn't," Mabel said. "Or Larry could have realized she wasn't right for him."

Charlie shook his head. "He's still pining for her."

Mabel's eyebrows shot up. "Larry? Pining?"

"It's what guys do when they're dumped."

"But you said it's been three years."

"He's a little stubborn. Much like Peggy," Charlie said. "Up to the day she died, he was convinced they'd get back together eventually. He was smart enough to stay on good terms with her after they broke up, and he didn't burn any bridges."

"Unless he was passive-aggressively burning them in the middle of the night, when she couldn't prove it was him," Mabel said. "He could have been stealing from her, either to cause the farm to fail so she'd need to turn to him for help, or just to lash out and hurt her for hurting him."

"Now you're giving him too much credit as an evil bastard," Charlie said. "He's not big on advance planning. I think he stayed friends with her just because he honestly liked her, even though he was hurt. I'm not sure he'd be as good at faking a friendship if he hated her."

Mabel sighed. "I'm running out of suspects here, and he was such a prime one."

"Who else is in the lineup?" He smiled again, but this time it was rueful. "I guess I should say, who else is standing in the lineup next to me?"

Right or wrong, she was starting to trust him, and didn't see any point in making him suffer any longer. "You got excused from the lineup, along with Ethan, Jeanne and Al Soares. You've all got alibis."

He straightened and looked at her. "You've been busy, investigating the locals."

"I had help. I may not have as many friends as Aunt Peggy did, but the ones I do have are top-notch."

"I'm starting to see what Peggy liked about you," Charlie said. "I wasn't sure you'd do the right thing by her, but so far, you're doing okay. Have you made any arrangements for a funeral service? I'd like to be there."

"I'm still working out the details. It will be next week before the autopsy is completed, and the harvest seemed more important than making funeral arrangements. The basic idea, though, is to have her cremated and then spread her ashes somewhere on the farm. I just haven't figured out exactly when. Or where."

He nodded in the direction of the farmhouse. "She spent a lot of time out on that patio with her friends. If you were planning to erect some sort of memorial, it should be something that you can see from there."

"You're the builder. What kind of memorial would you recommend?"

He grinned. "If I were the greedy developer you think I am, I'd tell you she'd love a series of McMansions crammed next to each other on postage stamp lots carved out of her fields. But what I really think she'd have liked is a small fountain. She told me about one she'd seen in Newport a few years ago. She kept a picture of it somewhere in her office and showed it to me once. It looked like a birdbath, but with a larger than life sized pineapple in the middle. Water dripped down from the pineapple leaves at the top, into the basin."

"I'll look into it." With a little luck, the stupid noisy birds might be so busy bathing in the basin that they'd be quiet until a civilized hour, and Mabel could sleep beyond dawn. Pixie could sit in the kitchen window and watch the birds playing in the water, and she might not be as interested in announcing all of the farm's visitors. Mabel just wished she could have gotten the fountain before now, when her aunt could have enjoyed it too.

"I could help with that," he said. "If you can find the picture for me, I've got a concrete subcontractor who's an artist. He can make the fountain itself, and I've got plumbers and electricians on call too if you need a referral for installing the water and electric lines."

He was moving too fast, and she had too many other decisions to make right now. "I'll think about it."

“Look,” he said in a frustrated tone. “I’m not going to blackmail you into selling the farm, just because you accepted a couple referrals from me.”

“I’m not doubting you.” She was doubting herself. She was confident that Charlie hadn’t had anything to do with her aunt’s death, but he might still want to get his hands on the property someday, and she couldn’t trust herself to resist his charm. Next thing she knew, she’d be signing over the deed to him.

How could she be sure what Charlie was suggesting for the memorial was a good idea? She hadn’t known her aunt well enough to know if she really would have liked the fountain or if, perhaps, Aunt Peggy had hated the stupid, noisy birds as much as Mabel did, and would have hated giving them a treat. For all she knew, the barn cats were the evidence of a failed attempt to eradicate the local birds.

Mabel needed to check with other people to see if there was something about the fountain that wasn’t right. After all, her initial plan to spread the ashes in the lavender bed had seemed reasonable until she’d learned how much her aunt disliked the smell of lavender. There could be something wrong with the fountain idea too.

“I just have too much to do right now, getting the harvest completed and the market celebration organized for this weekend,” Mabel said. “I’ll figure out the memorial arrangements later. Whatever I decide, I’ll at least let you know when the service will be held.”

“Thanks.”

She owed him that much, at least. His help with the harvest was getting them closer to the end of the field. Not close enough, but it wasn’t his fault. No one person could possibly be as fast or as unstoppable as the approaching storm clouds.

CHAPTER TWENTY-THREE

The next time the tractor was ready to return to the barn with filled crates, Mabel decided to go help with the racking. She convinced Anna, who hadn't taken a break from the direct sun yet, to drive the tractor and then stay with her for a while. After the filled crates were swapped for empty ones, Bettina took the tractor back into the field. Rory was seated on the back of the wagon, along with the empty crates and a couple of cases of water and sports drinks. She kept an eye—solicitous now, rather than suspicious—on the drooping but determined Kyle beside her. It looked like Kyle wasn't going to have any opposition to joining the CSA next year. Of course, if membership was easy, he might not want it so much.

The other CSA members had already left, and even the experienced Bettina and Rory hadn't been able to rack the garlic as fast as the field hands had been pulling it up. The filled bins were stacked a good six feet high. Getting through them to the table was like traveling through a maze.

Anna approached the racking table from one direction to take the seat that Bettina had just vacated, and Mabel made her way to the opposite side. They were both too tired to chat while they worked, but it was a relief to be out of the sun.

Sometime later, the sound of the engine signaled the return of the tractor to the barn. It was too soon for the crates to have been filled, so Mabel retraced her steps through the bins to see if there was a problem. She got to the door just in time to see Emily turning her tractor around to back her wagon inside.

Emily parked and hopped down, looking fresh and cool in her white overalls and pale pink tank top. "I'm sorry I couldn't get here earlier. One of the goats was limping, and I had to make sure it wasn't anything worse than a sprain. And then my husband called to let me know he's extending the contract with his current client for a couple days, and he needed me to send him some stuff so he could go straight to the next job without coming home first. At this rate, it'll be Christmas before we see each other again."

Mabel looked out at the field where Bettina had taken the tractor. Had she been right about a rift between Emily and her husband, who was coming up with excuses to stay away from his wife? Emily didn't seem upset and she didn't wait for any sympathy before striding over to the barrels of scapes.

Mabel followed and helped her drag the first overflowing barrel over to the wagon.

Emily pulled out her knife and set to work. "As soon as I get the scapes loaded up, I'll park the wagon in the shade, and then I can help out in the field. You need all the free space you can get inside the barn, and it won't matter if the scapes get wet. I could go pull garlic first, though, if you prefer."

Mabel checked the approaching dark clouds. There was probably less than an hour left before they arrived, and about four hours' worth of harvesting. There was absolutely no chance of getting the entire crop in now. They'd need at least six people—fresh people, not her tuckered out crew—to have any chance of finishing. There was no point in exhausting anyone else.

"No, I think you're right," Mabel said. "We're running out of space faster than we can clear it already. One more person bringing in garlic would only complicate the situation."

"How bad is it?"

Mabel glanced at where Anna was hidden behind the stacks of bins. The teen was exhausted but not deaf. "If anyone can bring in the harvest today, it's my crew."

"Peggy would have been proud of everyone. Especially you."

Mabel went to get another barrel of scapes. She wasn't so sure her aunt would have been pleased with Mabel's progress so far. She was doing the best she could with the harvest, but it wasn't going to be enough. Even if she brought in all of the garlic, she still didn't have any real insight into who was stealing the garlic or how she could prove he had also killed her aunt. Given how exhausted she was, she had to face the possibility that she'd also fail at the one thing she was usually good at, meeting her app development deadlines.

Mabel rolled the barrel into place next to the one that Emily was emptying. "I was talking to Charlie Durbin about maybe installing a fountain with a pineapple design near the patio. Aunt Peggy's ashes could be spread at its base."

"That's a great idea. I've got some spare herb plants we could put around the base. Creeping thyme and garlic chives would work nicely."

"Whatever you recommend." Mabel didn't know any more about herbs than about the birds that would likely play in the fountain, and she had no real interest in learning about them, not even now that she had her aunt's bird and critter watching binoculars. "That reminds me. I got a call from the funeral home. They found Aunt Peggy's binoculars. She had them with her the night she died. Did she say anything to you about critters getting into the squash this summer?"

Emily shook her head. "As far as I know, the worst critters who've ever been in her fields were my goats. It was the first year after my husband and I moved here, and I didn't know enough about securing the goats or their obsession with garlic. They got through my fences and into Peggy's fields. They ate garlic scapes until they were full, and it takes a whole lot to fill up a goat."

"Didn't that kill the entire crop?"

"We were lucky. I only had a tiny herd at the time, not enough to eat their way through all of the fields. They wiped out one of her heirloom varieties, but didn't touch the main crop. I compensated her for the lost profit, of course, but she was pretty upset. They ate a variety she couldn't replace easily, and she only managed to rescue a few bulbs. It took a few years to get her stock back up to a reasonable quantity."

That meant Aunt Peggy had a reason to be angry with her neighbor, not the other way around. Mabel tried to imagine her aunt arguing with Emily in the middle of the night, until heated words became a physical altercation, with Emily knocking Peggy into the creek.

No, the whole scenario was just too implausible. Mabel had never seen her aunt lose her temper, and if her death had truly been an accident, or self-defense, there would have been no reason for Emily to lie about it. She could have simply called the police and explained what had happened.

"How did you two get past the bad feelings?"

"It took a while," Emily said. "I felt awful about the crop damage, but there's a reason for everything, even when things look bad at first. I discovered that after eating all those scapes, the goats were producing sweetly garlic-flavored milk, which made the most amazing garlic-flavored cheese you can imagine. It was a big hit at the farmers' market, and the Capricornucopia brand took off after that. It's not easy to stand out from the crowd of small-dairy cheesemakers these days, but the garlic did it for me. I owed the success to Peggy and her garlic, so we worked out a partnership. I get the scapes at harvest time, in return for paying Peggy a percentage of the profit from the garlic-flavored cheeses."

"So the goats get garlic take-out, rather than dining in my aunt's farm, and everyone's happy."

Emily laughed. "Exactly. Even Peggy would have had a hard time forgiving a second invasion. Definitely no goat damage in the garlic fields this year, and not even much in the way of other critter damage that I've seen, here or at my place. We had a hard winter, and the wildlife has been a little less abundant overall this year. There's been a little nibbling around the edges of my kitchen garden, probably from rabbits, but nothing worth getting out the binoculars and traps for."

"If she wasn't looking for critters, then she had to have been staking out the thief the night she died."

"I suppose it's possible. The moon was full on the night Peggy died, so there would have been good visibility."

Mabel still didn't have solid evidence, but the circumstantial evidence was piling up. "Are you sure it was full?"

"Definitely." Emily paused in her work, and this time it was obvious how upset she was. "I remember thinking, when I found her, that she'd finally decided to experiment with harvesting during the full moon. I knew she didn't believe in my theories, so if she was trying one of them out, it was only to humor me. Which made her death my fault."

Tears started to flow, and even Mabel couldn't miss that sign of Emily's grief. "It wasn't your fault."

"I want to believe that," Emily said. "Nothing about that night made any sense to me. If she was actually harvesting by the full moon, why didn't she invite me to be there with her? Or at least tell me she was going to do it?"

"Because she wasn't experimenting with harvesting by the moon," Mabel said firmly. "She was staking out the thief."

"That does sound more like something she would do," Emily said, smiling through her sniffles. "I think it was a full moon back when she staked out the lavender field and caught the ATVers."

"See? It's not your fault," Mabel said.

"Peggy's actions the night she died still don't make sense. She told me about the stakeout of the lavender bed before she did it, but she didn't say anything about watching for the garlic thief. If she was doing something that risky, she should have mentioned it to me."

Unless Aunt Peggy had suspected Emily. "I think she knew, or at least suspected, who the thief was, and she didn't want to cast aspersions on the person by naming him, in case she was wrong."

Emily swiped irritably at the tears on her face. "If Peggy weren't already dead, I'd have to kill her for being more concerned about hurting someone's feelings than about her own safety."

* * * *

Emily finished loading up the scapes and headed out to the fields. Mabel remained in the barn, trying to keep up with Anna's efficiency. They'd managed to lower the stacked bins enough to be able to see over them by the time Terry brought the tractor back from the fields with more bins than they'd emptied.

When they were done emptying the wagon, Terry said, "Rory wanted me to tell you we've only got eight rows left, but it's all hands on deck, because the storm is almost here."

Mabel estimated that each row would take two people at least an hour to harvest, even at top speed. With the eight people she had, including herself, that meant they needed a couple of hours to finish the field. Realistically speaking, they had, at most, only half an hour left to work. Still, the more they could do, the less of her aunt's beloved garlic would be damaged by the rain.

"Let's go." She joined Anna, who'd already hopped onto the back of the wagon, and Terry drove them back to the field at top speed.

Mabel took a bin to the far end of a row and began working. The young field hands were too tired to chatter, but they kept doggedly pulling the garlic and laying it carefully into a bin. They'd abandoned the step of removing the bulb from the scape, to save time, and they were moving through the row slightly faster than they had been earlier, despite their exhaustion.

Mabel caught Rory grimly observing the approaching storm clouds. They shared a desperate glance before returning to work. A moment later, she heard, ever so faintly, Pixie's distinctive yowl from the farmhouse.

Mabel looked toward the driveway, and a moment later two trucks appeared. She turned to Rory. "Are you expecting any more volunteers?"

Rory remained focused on her work. "No. Why?"

"We've got visitors."

Rory straightened and looked toward the barn. "The trucks look familiar, but it's hard to tell at this distance. There are a lot of trucks in West Slocum."

Mabel didn't have time to worry about identifying them. If they were here to help, they could figure out where the work was happening, and if they were a gang of garlic thieves, they'd be gone with their loot before she or her crew could get back there. Besides, after her close call with the tractor last night, she wasn't about to confront anyone herself. If the people in the trucks did anything suspicious, she was going to follow Joe Hansen's advice and call 911.

While she dug her phone out of her pocket and prayed that she wasn't in yet another of the farm's dead zones, the two drivers and six passengers climbed out of the trucks.

Rory said, "That's Larry and some of his crew. And Darryl."

"What are they doing here?" Mabel squinted at them, and immediately picked out the tall, dark-skinned Darryl. She wasn't entirely sure from this distance which one was Larry, since he and his crew were all dressed alike in t-shirts, jeans, work boots and hats that cast shadows on their faces. "I told Larry I wasn't willing to sell him the garlic. Does he really think I'm going to change my mind now?"

Rory nodded at the approaching visitors. "I guess we'll find out in a minute."

Mabel held onto her phone and headed over to where the tractor was parked, with Rory right behind her.

Darryl was in the lead, and as he came within talking distance, he held up his hand in front of him. For once, he restrained his smile to the bare minimum. "I know what you're going to say. You don't want to make a deal with Larry."

"I don't want to, and I'm not going to," Mabel said. "The rest of the garlic can rot in the ground, if necessary."

"It's not necessary, though," he said. "Larry isn't here to make a deal. He's here because he wants to help. You were right when you said I hadn't been doing my job. I should have done more to make it clear that the community won't tolerate any crop thefts. Letting the criminals put one farmer out of business is bad for all farmers, and we all need to stick together. That's why I'm here."

"You can stay, then," Mabel said, handing him an empty crate. "But Larry and his crew have to go."

From behind Darryl, Larry spoke so quietly that Mabel almost couldn't make out the words. "I need to do something to help. It's my fault she died."

Mabel froze. Had he just confessed to causing her aunt's death? She'd thought she was prepared to confront the person responsible for her aunt's death, but nothing could have prepared her for the sudden dizziness and blinding anger that claimed her. "What did you do?"

"I couldn't let her go," Larry said, still speaking softly. "She was such an amazing person, and if I'd treated her better, she would have been with me that night, not out working herself to death. I should have found a way to protect her."

Mabel let out the breath she'd been holding. Larry hadn't killed Aunt Peggy. He was just hurting as much as all of her aunt's other friends. She didn't know how to comfort him, though.

Fortunately, Rory did. "It wasn't your fault, Larry. Peggy was doing what she wanted to do, and there was nothing that any of us could have done to prevent what happened. Not you, not me, not Mabel." Rory turned to Mabel. "I think you should let Larry and his crew pitch in."

Apparently, Rory's words had helped, because Larry returned to shouting. "I just want to help. I owe it to Peggy."

Mabel was aware of her own crew and volunteers behind her, all of them sweat-soaked and exhausted, watching her expectantly. They would go back to work alone if she asked them to, and they'd convince themselves that they could do the impossible.

She didn't want Larry's help. She didn't like him, didn't like the way he'd tried to make her aunt into someone she wasn't, and didn't like the way he'd tried to take advantage of Aunt Peggy's death to get what he thought was the secret to her success.

But the decision wasn't just about Mabel and what she wanted and who she liked. It was about Aunt Peggy and her friends. Mabel didn't like Larry, but her aunt had. Quite a lot at some point, apparently. Plus, all of Aunt Peggy's friends would be hurt if the final harvest was less than it could have been.

Bettina picked up an empty crate and said, "All this standing around and talking isn't getting the garlic harvested. I, for one, want as much help as possible so the celebration will be fantastic."

"Me too." Mabel took the crate from Bettina and held it out to Larry. "We wouldn't want Bettina to lose out on her chance at a tiara. Larry, you don't owe my aunt anything, but I'm sure she'd appreciate your willingness to help save her final harvest. You're welcome to stay, if you still want to."

Larry took the crate and shouted for his crew to follow him. They collected their own crates and spread out to the farthest ends of the remaining rows. Mabel's loyal crew set to work at the opposite ends of the rows, setting up a race to the middle, although the real competition was the impending storm.

The final wagonload had just made it into the barn, along with all of the workers, when a misty rain began to fall. It wasn't the overwhelming drenching they'd been expecting, but according to Rory, and confirmed by Larry, it was more than enough to have reduced the quality of any garlic that had remained in the field. The damp bulbs wouldn't have been horrible initially, but they would have stored poorly, which would have been enough to ruin Aunt Peggy's reputation as the best garlic grower on the east coast.

Mabel's exhaustion gave way to the sort of euphoria she'd experienced in the past when completing a particularly elegant app that everyone said couldn't be done, after a series of all-nighters. She was going to crash soon, but right now, she felt invincible.

"We're going to have one heck of a harvest celebration this weekend," she announced.

"Glad to hear it," Darryl said. "I'd better get back into town and start spreading the word that it's definitely on for this weekend."

"Me too," Larry shouted, and urged his crew over to his truck.

"I've got to check in with my construction crew," Charlie said as he followed the other men. "I'll see you at market this weekend."

"Are you sure you don't want the tiara?" Bettina said, as she helped with unloading the overflowing wagon.

"You more than earned it," Mabel said. "Besides, I'm not sure I'll even be at the celebration."

"You have to be there," Rory said. "It's your farm now. Not just because of the inheritance. You made it really yours these last few days."

"Think of me as the Howard Hughes of garlic farming. I can own and manage the farm without going out in public." Mabel turned to the teens who were slumped against the back of the wagon. "I thought my three loyal field hands might be interested in a few more hours' work, managing the space at the farmers' market."

Terry perked up enough to ask, "Will you feed us like you've been doing?" and Anna shook her head at him, while saying, "I could use a few more hours' work. I've been coveting some new brushes for a while."

Dawn looked at her mother, "Can I, Mom? Please?"

Rory hesitated, obviously torn between her own desire to see Mabel at the celebration and her daughter's desire to make it easy for Mabel to skip the celebration. Finally, Rory said, "You can work the market, but only if Mabel is there to supervise."

"I could do it long-distance," Mabel said. "I could set up a laptop at the booth, and we could Skype."

"No Skype. Mabel will supervise in person. She's got to be there, in the flesh, not virtually, or no one else will be there. Right?" Rory stared first at her daughter until she got a reluctant nod, and then repeated the process with the two college students. She turned her attention back to Mabel. "Deal?"

Even Mabel could read Rory's expression well enough to know that there was no chance of changing her mind. She could either supervise from the dark recesses of the booth or she could do it all by herself. She didn't need an app to figure out which was the better option. "Deal."

Bettina and the field hands returned to unloading the wagon while Mabel escorted Kyle to the storage room in the back of the barn, where the previously harvested heirloom garlic had been locked up. She handed him a bag and let him take whatever he wanted. True to his original word, he only chose a few of each heirloom variety, before declaring himself satisfied. After they arranged for him to pick up his paycheck at the market, she sent him home to get some much deserved rest.

Mabel's euphoria was starting to dissipate, making her aware of just how sore she was, how hot her skin felt where she'd missed with the sunscreen, and just how long it had been since she'd had more than a very few hours of sleep. She needed a nap, until midnight or so, before she settled down to what she estimated was about eight hours of her real job. The sooner she got to bed, the better her chances of finishing the app before tomorrow's deadline.

She returned to where the last half dozen crates were being unloaded inside the barn. "We might as well leave that until tomorrow, after we've had some rest. It's safe from the elements in here, and if you're as tired as I am, you're more likely to drop the crates than to get them safely put away."

"Good idea," Rory said. "Just let me unhitch the wagon first. We need to move the tractor out of the doorway and close the barn doors in case the rain gets hard enough to splash inside."

Dawn walked out with her new friends, making plans for tomorrow and the weekend celebration.

Bettina climbed behind the wheel of the tractor. She took out her smartphone to check for messages and called back to Rory, "Tell me when you're done."

Joe Hansen slipped into the barn, between the tractor and the edge of the doors and waved at his wife. "I knew you'd still be here."

Either Pixie had finally quit announcing visitors or Mabel had been too tired to notice the warning yowl.

"We'll just be a couple minutes." Rory tugged at the uncooperative hitch, but didn't ask Joe for help, and he apparently knew better than to offer. "Did you find some people to guard the barn overnight?"

"That's why I'm here." He dug three Skittles wrappers and a scrap of paper out of his jacket pocket. "Here you go. Any one of them would do a fine job."

"Thanks." Mabel took the list and made sure she could read the handwriting before slipping it into her pocket for later.

She wasn't sure Joe heard her, since he was focused on his wife. Mabel looked at Rory, wondering what he saw. The woman was dressed in worn jeans and a t-shirt that, like her hair, was stuck to her skin with a layer of sweat. Her face was covered with a layer of dust, and her nose was pink with the promise of darker red later. She was thumping the hitch awkwardly, and swearing under her breath at it.

Mabel glanced back at Joe, and she was pretty sure that the look on his face meant that he didn't see the messy reality of his wife's current appearance.

"Does it bother you?" Mabel asked.

"Everything bothers me." Joe pulled his attention away from Rory. "Could you be more specific?"

"I mean the amount of time Rory spends on her volunteer work, helping out people like me, instead of being at home with you and Dawn. Does that bother you?"

"It did a little, in the beginning, when we were first married. I'd come home from a long shift, and there'd be no one home, and nothing in the fridge, and the house was a mess. Eventually, I realized the volunteering is just the way she deals with being a cop's wife. It's her way of trying to make my job safer. I think she believes that if she can do good things in the community, she can make the place better and happier and most especially less violent. Once I realized her volunteering was largely about keeping me safe, in addition to doing things she enjoys, it was hard to care about the empty fridge and messy house. Besides, she's really good at what she does in the community. She probably contributes as much to the quality of life here in West Slocum as I do. That part kinda' bothers me, because I'd like to think that what I do matters, but the volunteering itself is kind of sweet." He laughed. "And you probably know how much I like sweets."

"As much as Aunt Peggy's customers like garlic."

"Exactly." He stuck his hand in his jacket pocket to pull out another bag of Skittles. It seemed to remind him of the paper he'd handed her. "The people on the list are expecting to hear from you. It's not too late to call them for tonight. A couple said their schedules were clear, and they could be here with an hour's notice."

Mabel was going to be asleep within the hour. Within fifteen minutes, if at all possible. She was so tired, she didn't even care if the thief came and stole the entire harvest. "It can wait until tomorrow. I'll be fine for just one night."

"That's what most victims say, when I interview them at the hospital. They thought they'd be fine for just one night."

"I'll barricade myself in the farmhouse, and I'll call 911 if I hear anything outside. I've got a cat with hearing that's impossibly good, and she yowls as soon as anyone turns into the driveway. If she so much as utters a sigh, I'll start dialing."

"All right," Joe said with obvious reluctance. "You've got Rory's number too, don't you? We'll be home, so you can call us if you don't feel safe, but don't have enough cause to make an official emergency call."

"I'll be fine."

The tractor engine started, and Bettina shouted for Mabel and Joe to stand clear, so she could take the tractor out to the parking lot, where it wouldn't be blocking the barn doors. As she passed, Mabel thought she heard Bettina say something that sounded like her husband's name. She seemed to be carrying on a conversation with an invisible person sitting beside her on the massive seat that could, in fact, have held a second person, at least if he was as petite as Bettina. Or as immaterial as her dead husband.

A pang of guilt managed to work its way through Mabel's exhaustion. She'd pushed Bettina too hard today, and the fragile woman had retreated to her fantasy world where her husband was still alive.

Rory stumbled over to her husband, letting him hold her up, and asked Mabel, "Do you mind if I leave my car here tonight? I'm too tired to drive legally, and Joe hates having to arrest family members. I'll catch a ride with Bettina tomorrow morning."

"Is Bettina okay to go home alone?"

Rory turned to watch Bettina park the tractor and climb down with more bounce to her step than even the teens had displayed as they left. "I don't see why not."

"I'll see you tomorrow then." Mabel watched them leave. Rory had a word with Bettina, presumably arranging for the morning ride and confirming that Bettina was capable of driving. Joe's car and then Bettina's headed down the driveway.

Mabel dragged herself across the driveway and patio. Just one last responsibility—checking on Pixie and her kibble and water—and then she could collapse on her bed for a few hours.

CHAPTER TWENTY-FOUR

Pixie swished her tail in irritation over the empty kibble bowl and wove between Mabel's already unsteady feet. At least Pixie only yowled at visitors, not at things that annoyed her.

Mabel refilled the bowl and headed upstairs. She set the alarm app on her phone to wake her for midnight, and then the alarm on her laptop. As exhausted as she was, she might sleep through the two electronic alarms. She needed a fail-safe, just in case. After a little searching, Mabel retrieved a clock radio from her aunt's bedside table. It was so old, it had an analog display, but it still had clear radio reception.

She didn't bother to undress, just kicked off her shoes and flopped onto the bed on top of the covers. There was a slight breeze from the open window, just enough to keep the room from sweltering, not enough to make her reach for a blanket.

Mabel had just closed her eyes when Pixie yowled.

The garlic thief was back. She jumped up again, as wide-awake now as if she'd downed a dozen energy drinks. She scrabbled for the phone on the bedside table and keyed in 911 while she crossed the room to look out the window. She held off connecting the call so she could confirm that the visitor coming up the driveway wasn't someone she knew, perhaps one of the crew who'd left something behind.

When she saw Bettina's Beetle turning into the parking lot, Mabel was glad she'd waited. She disconnected the call, and watched Bettina get out of her car and go into the barn.

If it had been anyone else, Mabel would have flopped back onto the bed, but Bettina was fragile and had pushed herself too hard today in pursuit of the right to wear the garlic queen's tiara. She should be at home, resting, not returning to work.

Mabel struggled to get her hot and swollen feet into her shoes. She found Bettina standing in the middle of the barn, staring into space. "Are you okay, Bettina?"

Bettina started, and then focused on Mabel. "I'm fine. I just can't find my phone. I must have left it here somewhere. I'm trying to figure out where I might have put it down. Scott said the next time I lost one, he wouldn't buy me another."

Mabel didn't bother to explain that it no longer mattered what Scott wanted, and Bettina could buy her own replacement phone. It would be quicker and more effective to search every inch of the barn.

Not just the barn, but the tractor too. She'd seen Bettina scrolling through messages on the phone when she was in the cab a little while ago, waiting for Rory to unhitch the wagon. "I've got an idea," Mabel said. "I'll be right back."

The phone was on the floor of the tractor's cab, within her reach, so she didn't even have to climb the steps to retrieve it. As she carried it back to the barn, her professional curiosity got the better of her, and she turned it on to see what apps were on the home screen. It was still booting when she arrived at the barn doors, so she waved it at Bettina. "Is this it?"

Relief spread across Bettina's face. "Oh, thank goodness. I really didn't want to have to explain this to Scott. He'd be so angry."

Mabel glanced down at the screen that had finished booting, and saw just two icons. One was the standard symbol for a telephone, which she ignored to focus on the second one: a traditional pineapple quilt block in avocado green and harvest gold, and the word "hospitality" underneath it.

Mabel knew that app. She'd designed that app. Only one copy had ever been distributed. To her aunt. And yet, here it was, all by itself, in a place of honor in the center of the screen.

This was her aunt's missing phone.

How had Bettina ended up with Aunt Peggy's phone?

"Oh, thank you," Bettina said, reaching for the phone.

Mabel backed out of the barn, clutching the phone to her chest, aware that her exhaustion was making it difficult to think logically. If her aunt had fallen while she'd been alone on her farm, shortly after making her last, late-night call, then the phone would have been near the body. The most likely candidates for picking it up were Emily, who'd found the body, and the emergency responders. None of them would have given it to Bettina. She had to have found it herself.

"This is my aunt's phone," Mabel said, stopping finally at the edge of the driveway. "Where'd you get it? I've been looking everywhere for it."

Bettina's face reddened. "I'm sorry. I should have given it to you when you first arrived, but I forgot, and then when I lost mine, I didn't think anyone would mind if I used Peggy's."

"Where'd you find it?" The location it had been dropped might be exactly the sort of solid evidence that would convince the DA to look into Aunt Peggy's death. "I need to know."

"I don't remember exactly." Bettina waved in the direction of the creek. "Somewhere out there."

That didn't make any sense, and not just because Mabel was so tired. Bettina wouldn't have had any reason to go beyond the barn or patio, to the far end of the fields near where the body had been found. In fact, she would have had every reason to stay away from the tragic scene, given how even the mention of death traumatized her. Rory and Bettina had been inseparable for months, and Rory never would have exposed Bettina to anything that would have reminded her of her husband's death.

Mabel couldn't think of any reason why Bettina would lie about where she found the phone, though. If she'd really found it out by the creek, she must have been here sometime without Rory babysitting her. Mabel could easily imagine Bettina coming out to visit the barn cats, but she couldn't imagine any reason why she might have gone out into the fields alone.

Unless Bettina was the garlic thief.

Mabel took another step backwards, into the dirt driveway, clutching her aunt's phone as if her life depended on it. If Bettina was the garlic thief, she could have been here, looting the fields, when she stumbled across the phone. That would also explain why she hadn't confessed earlier to having the phone, since it would have led to awkward questions about what she'd been doing in the fields in the middle of the night. The only question in Mabel's mind now was whether Bettina had been a witness to Aunt Peggy's death, or had found the phone sometime later.

"I need to know what happened to Aunt Peggy," Mabel said. "You can have the phone, and I won't press charges against you for the crop thefts, if you'll just tell me what happened that night."

"I don't know what you're talking about." Bettina closed the distance between them faster than her short legs should have been able to carry her.

"Yes, you do." Mabel stumbled backwards across the ruts in the driveway. "You're the garlic thief. I don't understand why you stole from your friend, but I know you did. Aunt Peggy knew too. She just didn't want to believe it. That's why she staked out the fields the night she fell. It's your fault that she died."

"I didn't kill anyone," Bettina said. "It's just that people who love me tend to die. First, my husband, and then Peggy."

It suddenly struck Mabel that no one had ever said exactly how Scott had died, just that it had been an indirect complication of a service-related injury. "How did your husband die?"

"Poor Scott," Bettina said. "He never wanted to ask for help. He saw it as a weakness. If he'd asked me for help, he wouldn't have fallen down the stairs."

"Scott died in a fall?"

Bettina nodded. "Just like Peggy. It was terrible. Both of them, dying on me like that."

Mabel's heart stopped. She couldn't explain how she knew, but the clarity she usually only experienced when reviewing lines of code, she was feeling right now. Bettina had killed Aunt Peggy. Possibly Scott, as well.

Mabel vaguely recalled Rory saying something about rumors that had circulated at the time of Scott's death, but they'd been quashed pretty quickly, leaving intact Bettina's image as a sad, weak creature, never truly suspected of killing her husband. If Bettina hadn't been the long-suffering spouse of an officer who'd been injured in the line of duty, she would have been scrutinized more carefully. Her connections would also explain why the DA had complained about people bothering him about Mabel's investigation of Aunt Peggy's death. Bettina could have visited her husband's colleagues at the station, and sadly dropped some hints about how her heroic husband would have dealt with misguided amateurs meddling in police work, and the DA's phones would have been ringing off the hook before she'd even left the building.

If Bettina had convinced the authorities of her innocence in her husband's death, a situation where she should have been an obvious and prime suspect, how much more evidence would the authorities need to even consider that Bettina had killed someone over a few pounds of garlic?

"I still don't understand why you stole the garlic," Mabel said.

"Scott made me do it," Bettina said. "When he was first injured, three years ago, he was on temporary disability, and it wasn't enough to pay our bills. We only needed a few extra dollars, here and there, and he said Peggy would never even notice the missing garlic. Besides, he said I'd earned it, with all the volunteer work I do for the CSA. Everyone in town owed us. They owed him for risking his life, and me for all the extra, unpaid hours I put into teaching their kids."

"If you really believed that, you should have simply asked Aunt Peggy for a donation."

"I wanted to," Bettina said. "But Scott said it was better this way. And then after the first time, he said that if I told anyone, he'd turn me in for theft, claim it was all my idea. His friends would have believed him. There was nothing I could do, except keep on taking the garlic. I tried to take the smallest bulbs, but it's hard to tell for sure until the bulb's been pulled up, and then it's too late to put it back."

"Your husband died before this year's crop was raided," Mabel said. "He didn't make you do it this year."

"He had to die," Bettina said. "I couldn't take it any longer. I couldn't do anything right, according to him. Well, I showed him. I stole twice as much garlic this year as any previous year. He would have been amazed at what I can do."

"I doubt it. You aren't a very good thief. Peggy identified you." Mabel glanced down at the phone she was holding, and remembered that it included a camera. "I bet she even took a picture of you, stealing from her."

"The picture's gone." Bettina grabbed for the phone, but Mabel raised it up, out of reach. "I erased it before I checked to make sure Peggy was dead. I was going to toss the phone into the creek after I wiped the prints off it, but it was the same model as my own phone, so I kept it as a backup. It's a good thing I did. I didn't have to tell Scott when I lost my phone yesterday. I just dug this one out of my sock drawer."

Bettina didn't seem to understand that, even without the incriminating photograph, the mere fact that she'd had a dead woman's phone in her possession was suspicious. If she was that unaware of the consequences of her actions, Mabel might be able to use Bettina's disconnect with reality to elicit a detailed confession. That had to be enough to convince the authorities to investigate.

"You didn't have to kill Aunt Peggy. Just erase the picture, and it would have been her word against yours."

"I didn't want to kill her," Bettina said. "She made me do it."

Mabel nodded encouragingly. "Just like Scott did."

"Exactly. She told me about the picture on her phone, so what did she expect me to do? I couldn't let anyone else see it. My arrest would have destroyed Scott. He would have been humiliated when it came out that his wife was a thief. If Peggy had just given me the phone, she wouldn't have had to die." Bettina advanced on Mabel. "Now give me the phone."

"No." Mabel was *not* letting Bettina get her hands on the only tangible evidence that could connect Bettina to her aunt's death.

In other circumstances, Bettina's belief that she could overpower a woman who was six inches taller and thirty pounds heavier, might have been amusing. Aunt Peggy had probably underestimated Bettina, like Scott and the local authorities had done. Forewarned by what had happened to her aunt, though, Mabel was taking Bettina very seriously. It was time to dial 911.

Keeping Aunt Peggy's phone high out of Bettina's reach, Mabel fumbled for her own phone. She couldn't dial it one thumbed, while also avoiding Bettina's flailing attempts to grab the phone. She needed to get some distance between them. The farmhouse wasn't a safe refuge, thanks to the broken lock on the kitchen door, which Bettina undoubtedly knew how to open, and Mabel didn't have her car keys to let herself into the Mini Cooper.

The only other option was to put some distance between her and Bettina, just enough to have the time to dial three digits. She turned and jogged past the Mini Cooper in the direction of the main road, with Bettina in hot pursuit. Bettina was keeping pace easily, and Mabel's legs were already dragging.

Bettina suddenly darted to her left, and Mabel realized she was aiming for the tractor. If Bettina got behind the wheel of the tractor, Mabel was dead. This time, Bettina wouldn't just be trying to scare her off.

Mabel needed to get the key out of the tractor's ignition. She chased after Bettina, passing her in time to climb up the steps of the monster machine and throw herself into the driver's seat, with her feet poised to defend her position. She even managed to dial 911 on her phone before Bettina's head appeared at the top of the steps.

"Give me the phone," Bettina said.

Mabel ignored her to concentrate on the person answering the phone.

"Do you need police, fire or ambulance?"

"Police."

"Please hold."

"No." Too late. She was already on hold. Her frustration lent her a moment of strength, and she jabbed at Bettina's shoulder, trying to push her down the steps.

A moment later, a male voice said, "West Slocum police, what is the emergency?"

"This is Mabel Skinner, and I'm at Stinkin' Stuff Farm, and Bettina Parker killed my aunt, and now she's trying to kill me."

"Would you repeat that?"

"No. Just send a cruiser, please. Fast. I don't know how long I can keep her out of the tractor."

"You do know it's a criminal offense to lie to a dispatcher, right?"

"I do now," Mabel said. "So, come arrest me. While you're at it, you can arrest my aunt's killer."

"Very well." The dispatcher's sigh came through the line. "Please stay on the line until the cruiser arrives."

Bettina had gone around to the other side of the cab while Mabel was on the phone, and was reaching for the railing to climb the three steps up to the cab.

"I can't." Mabel tossed her recently purchased phone over Bettina's head. "You want a phone? Go get it."

She had to get away from Bettina before the woman realized she had the wrong phone. Mabel was too exhausted to go back to running away from Bettina, whose break with reality seemed to have given her superhuman strength and endurance. Mabel was at a disadvantage physically, and needed to find something that would even the odds, at least long enough for the police to arrive. Assuming the dispatcher hadn't marked the call as low priority.

Mabel was out of time. Bettina's frustrated shrieking was louder than Pixie's yowling. She was on her way back, and this time, it would take the power of the tractor itself to stop her. If only Mabel knew how to drive the tractor, she could take it down to the road and meet the police on the way here.

The key was in the ignition. The temptation to use it warred with her conviction that she was as likely to have a fatal accident with the tractor as she was to use it to escape.

Bettina had reached the bottom of the steps to the cab. Mabel had to do something now, or it would be too late. Perhaps just starting the engine would be enough to convince Bettina to keep her distance. Surely, there were some self-preservation instincts too strong to be overridden.

Bettina was at the top of the steps again, and Mabel twisted in the seat to kick her feet, creating a virtual barrier. Bettina kept coming, seemingly oblivious of the danger, until her head thunked into Mabel's foot.

Bettina slipped back down to the ground, dazed, and Mabel took advantage of the reprieve to use her aunt's phone to log onto the internet and do a search on "how drive tractor." She didn't have time to watch the YouTube video, so she opted for the five-step written lesson. She skipped over the safety precautions since she wasn't planning to actually drive the behemoth, just start the engine.

It looked simple enough. Step on the clutch pedal, push the throttle, make sure the gear was in neutral and then turn the ignition. She could do that. If she absolutely had to.

Bettina's head popping up over the floor of the tractor forced Mabel to act. Clutch, gear in neutral, throttle. Done, done, done. Mabel took a deep breath, and turned the ignition switch. The engine roared to life, startling her so badly that her foot slid off the clutch, and the tractor began to roll forward, toward the driveway. She stomped on the middle pedal, and the tractor stopped.

She glanced to her right and was gratified to see that either the noise or the movement had slowed Bettina down, although she kept a solid grip on the railing that ran along the steps.

Bettina shouted over the engine. "Turn it off. You don't know how to drive."

Feeling invincible, Mabel waved her aunt's phone at Bettina. "I can learn anything, with a connection to the internet."

Bettina's eyes narrowed in rage, and she resumed climbing the steps to the cab.

Mabel barely had time to acknowledge that waving this particular phone at Bettina hadn't been a good idea, before Bettina reached inside the cab, trying to swipe the key from the ignition. Mabel had to take her feet off the brake to kick Bettina's hand away. The tractor began rolling again, heading straight for her beloved Mini Cooper.

She couldn't just turn off the engine, or she was done for. Bettina would become even more aggressive, and Mabel might as well just hand over the incriminating phone and go drown herself in the creek.

The only way to save the Mini Cooper was to actually drive the tractor. First, she had to get a little room to maneuver within the cab. She slid her aunt's phone beneath her left thigh, safely out of Bettina's reach. Mabel braced her hands on the seat and planted both feet on Bettina's shoulders to push her away from the ignition.

With Bettina out of her way temporarily, Mabel turned to face the steering wheel. She gripped the wheel with both hands and turned it to her left, hoping the tractor would go the same direction, away from the Mini Cooper and down the driveway.

The tractor turned, continuing to roll slowly down the driveway. The Mini Cooper was safe, but Bettina wasn't giving up. She was climbing back up the steps, having found her tractor legs, unfazed by the slow, bumpy ride. It was going to take something more extreme to stop her.

Something like putting the tractor in gear. There wasn't time to go back and read the safety instructions, and in any event, "avoid getting killed by a madwoman" trumped "wear your seatbelt."

Mabel pulled her aunt's phone out from under her thigh for just long enough to review the diagram for the gears, and then shouted at Bettina. "Get down now. I don't want to run you over."

Bettina kept climbing, calling Mabel's bluff.

Mabel was really going to have to drive the tractor. Kyle said everyone in town did it, so how hard could it be? Sure, there were thousands of fatal tractor accidents every year, but Mabel wasn't going to be doing anything extreme. The only person likely to get hurt was Bettina, and at this point, that was an acceptable risk.

Mabel gingerly pushed the stick shift toward where she thought first gear was, but it wouldn't stay. She shoved it harder, and when it didn't move, she eased up on the clutch and down on the gas pedal. The tractor lurched forward, causing Bettina, who was once again reaching for the ignition, to fall back and grab the railing.

Mabel kept going down the driveway, and the only difference was the increased noise of the engine as she drove barely faster than when the tractor had been rolling in neutral. After a moment, Bettina got her bearings and renewed her efforts to steal the key.

Enough was enough, Mabel thought. If she was going to crash the tractor and die, that was still better than letting Bettina get away with murdering Aunt Peggy. Mabel accelerated, and Bettina gripped the railing with both hands. As long as the tractor was moving reasonably fast, Mabel thought she was safe. She could just keep driving toward town, all the way to the police station if the dispatcher hadn't actually sent a cruiser out to the farm.

Meanwhile, she needed to make sure someone else, someone who wasn't an incredulous dispatcher, knew about Bettina. Mabel slid her aunt's phone out from under her leg and dialed Rory's number.

Joe answered.

"It's Mabel."

"What?" he said. "Can't hear. Too much background noise."

Stupid noisy engines. Getting away from them was the reason she'd come to West Slocum in the first place, and now they were going to be the death of her.

To reduce the noise, she needed to either turn off the engine, which wasn't going to happen, or shift into a higher gear. Hoping she remembered the diagram correctly, she stomped on the clutch and moved the gear stick. The engine quieted, and she could hear Joe saying, "Mabel? What's wrong?" but the tractor was slowing while she hesitated, and Bettina was experimenting with releasing one hand from the railing. In order to get the tractor moving faster again, Mabel had to risk stalling the engine by letting out the clutch.

Bettina's hand was inching closer to the key. Mabel swatted at her hand, and then released the clutch. There was a heart-stopping moment when the tractor sputtered, but then it jumped forward, faster than before, and Bettina was back to clinging onto the railing, a reasonable distance from the ignition.

"Can you hear me now?" Mabel asked Joe.

"What's wrong?"

She checked on Bettina, who looked as scared as Mabel had felt when she'd shifted into second gear. Bettina hadn't given up, but she also couldn't do anything as long as the tractor was moving at a good clip.

"No time to explain. Bettina killed my aunt, and she's trying to kill me. Not sure if the dispatcher believed me when I called a couple minutes ago. If anything happens to me, get Aunt Peggy's phone logs from this week, when Bettina was using it."

"Tell me where you are, and I'll be right there."

"You can't miss me," Mabel said, giddy with both relief and the triumph of controlling the monster tractor. As long as there wasn't any traffic on the road when she got there everything was going to be fine. "I'm almost at the end of the farm's driveway, heading into town. I'll be in the tractor with Bettina hanging off the side."

CHAPTER TWENTY-FIVE

The only West Slocum resident who didn't attend Aunt Peggy's memorial service at Stinkin' Stuff Farm a week later was Bettina. She'd been charged with murder, and was being held for psychiatric observation after bemoaning the unreasonableness of the rules that wouldn't let her wear a tiara in jail.

So many cars had turned into the farm's driveway this afternoon that even Pixie couldn't be bothered to pay attention to them any longer. She'd retreated to the upstairs bathroom to nap in the sink. Mabel wished there was room in there for her too, but she had to go out and deal with the crowd, rather than lurking just inside the kitchen door where she could pretend she was watching an online video.

Despite the huge size of the patio, it couldn't hold everyone who wanted to say goodbye to Aunt Peggy. Apparently offering condolences at the garlic festival hadn't been enough. Mabel had only agreed to accept the role of the garlic queen in the hope of avoiding any additional social obligations. It hadn't worked, though, as evidenced by the people outside, spilling onto the driveway and the grass between the patio and the fields. Rory was organizing the crowd, while her husband oversaw the traffic and parking.

Terry was over at the outdoor kitchen area, sneaking bites of everything while he helped Anna and Dawn set up the various food donations, including several containers instantly recognizable as coming from Jeanne's Country Diner and Maison Becker. Emily and an older man in a business suit, presumably her husband, were greeting newcomers, trying to keep them from hunting down Mabel and overwhelming her with their condolences. Darryl Santangelo was mingling, offering everyone some degree of his gorgeous smile. Larry Rose was chatting with someone a few feet from the farmhouse, quietly enough that Mabel couldn't hear him through the closed kitchen door.

She couldn't hide in the kitchen any longer. It was time for the service and the burial of the ashes. The kitchen door was as reluctant as she was, though, and Mabel had to tuck the simple gray urn containing her aunt's ashes into the crook of her left arm, while she threw the weight of the right side of her body against the door. As soon as it flew open, Rory started herding everyone over to where the fountain was covered with a tarp, waiting for the official unveiling.

Panic at the prospect of mingling with so many people kept her from moving beyond the landing just outside the door. Catching Aunt Peggy's killer had almost made up for all the neglect Mabel had shown her aunt over the years, but it didn't excuse her from participating in this memorial service, no matter how tempted she was to go hide with Pixie until everyone left. Mabel glanced back at the safety of the kitchen and noticed that Pixie had left her sanctuary and was seated in the kitchen window, as if she too felt an obligation to participate in the memorial service.

There was no going back. Mabel swallowed and forced herself forward, braced for the inevitable hugs. Someone must have spread the word, though, and only Josefina insisted on anything more than a handshake or a pat on the arm.

When Mabel reached the covered fountain, Emily stepped up beside her to start the service with a minute of respectful silence.

Then Emily began speaking. "If it were up to me, I'd talk for days and days about how wonderful Peggy was. That isn't what she would have wanted, though. Mostly, she would have wanted to be here with all of you, because you know how much she enjoyed parties. Beyond that, she would have wanted her guests to be happy and enjoy themselves. She also preferred action to speech, so let's do what we came here to do."

Emily looked at Charlie Durbin, who was standing across from Mabel, on the other side of the fountain, and he whisked away the covering. The fountain was perfect, even better than the one in the picture from Newport. The installation crew had disturbed the grass as little as possible, and the only visible reminder of their digging was a little trench less than a foot wide around the base of the fountain, where the ashes would be buried. Later, Emily would plant creeping thyme and garlic chives there.

Mabel crouched and managed to tip the ashes into the center of the trench without her nervous hands making a mess of it. When she stood up, Emily cued someone to turn on the water, and a soothing bubbling sound emanated from the fountain. Water dripped down the leaves of the pineapple into the basin at its base.

Emily took the empty urn and Rory came over to run interference for Mabel on the way to the buffet line. Before they reached it, though, Pixie's yowl pierced the chattering of the mourners.

"I'll go see who it is," Rory said, leaving Mabel alone in the crowd.

Mabel continued over to the table, even though she wasn't hungry. She wanted to talk to Terry, who could be counted on to be near the food, about possibly taking on the role of part-time agricultural adviser while he was finishing his education. She didn't need the farm to make a profit, but she'd decided to maintain its current operation until she could find something more permanent to do with it. Meanwhile, she could live here, help in the fields occasionally, during planting and harvest season, and still be able to do her night owl work. She'd managed to finish the app in time for last Friday's deadline, after all, and that was despite enduring both a condensed harvest schedule and an attempt on her life.

Pixie stopped yowling, and Mabel glanced behind her to see who had reawakened the cat's instincts to protect her territory. A van with the local high-speed internet carrier's logo on the side was parked in the middle of the driveway, directly in front of the entrance to the patio. A sumo wrestler sized man in a generic worker's uniform was carrying a tool box and heading straight for Mabel.

As the crowd noticed him, heads turned to watch his progress, and all conversation stopped. In the silence, he sounded as loud as Larry Rose. "I'm here to install your internet service. They said it was an emergency job."

"It was," Mabel said. "Last Friday, when you were supposed to be here."

He shrugged. "I'm here now."

"And I'm busy now. This is a memorial service for my aunt."

"Whatever." He shifted the toolbox to his other hand. "Where do you want the service installed?"

"It's not a matter of where, but when," Mabel said. "You'll have to come back later."

"Can't," he said, in a bored tone. "I've got other jobs to do."

"I'll reschedule, then."

"There's no refund of the rush fee," he said, clearly expecting her to change her mind. "And it'll be two to four weeks for regular service."

A month without internet service. Just a couple weeks ago, that would have been unthinkable. Today, she didn't care. She could use her phone for basic access and visit the library if she needed the high-speed access. Josefina's hugs no longer fazed her.

"No problem." Her attorney was going to think she'd finally snapped and needed to be locked up for her own safety, but she'd deal with him and the rescheduling later. She was going to need the internet eventually, but it could wait a few more weeks. "Now go away. I've got a party to enjoy and a farm to run."

Mabel turned her back on him and proceeded to the buffet table, aware that she was surrounded by people, but not feeling the urge to escape to her computer. Instead, she felt satisfaction at a job done well. Her solution of the murder hadn't been elegant, and it hadn't been as organized and efficient as she expected of the apps she developed, but it had gotten the job done. And, really, she decided, that was all that mattered, both online and in person.

ACKNOWLEDGMENTS

Many, many years ago, before I decided to write a novel, I thought that books sort of just happened effortlessly, first with the author spilling the story onto the page, fully formed, no revisions needed, and then with the publisher simply transferring the words straight to magically formatted pages inside a compelling cover that came from a mind meld between the author and the artist who simply drew the image in the author's head.

Ha!

In reality, my books start out messy, with the first draft incomprehensible to anyone but me, and peppered with placeholders for virtually all of the characters' names and descriptions, with notes like "What time did I say the victim died?" and "Go back and plant this clue earlier." And I never have any idea of what the cover should look like.

Fortunately, no one but me sees the early versions or all the work that goes into taking the raw manuscript, making it the best it can be and then getting it into readers' hands. I'm so grateful to everyone who helped to spare you the earlier versions and turn my manuscript into a much better book. In particular, I'd like to acknowledge:

My agent, Rachel Brooks, who has exquisite taste in clients, pets, and beverages.

Editor Martin Biro, who immediately recognized that the world needs a cozy mystery series set on a garlic farm.

Editor Norma Perez-Hernandez, who adopted the series and raised it like her own after it was orphaned.

My beta readers, Kathleen Koch, Cally Perry, and Elaine Hansen, who pointed out some of the errors I missed in my drafts.

Trixie and Zoey, who jointly inspired the feline character, Pixie.

Everyone at Kensington Publishing who worked behind the scenes to make the book so much more than a raw manuscript, from the copy editors and the art department to publicity and marketing.

The Argh Ink community, who surround me with wisdom and happiness.

Sisters in Crime, which offers education, advocacy, and sisterhood.

RECIPES

Roasted Garlic Bread

The garlic is baked into the dough, not drizzled on the finished bread. You can, of course, make double-garlic bread by then slicing the cooled loaf, drizzling a mix of melted butter and minced garlic inside and reheating.

2 or 3 heads of garlic
olive oil
1 cup milk, scalded
2 T. sugar
1 t. salt
3 T. butter
1 cup warm water
1 package dry yeast
5 1/2 cups bread flour

Roast garlic by wrapping heads in aluminum foil and baking at 400 degrees for about half an hour or until soft. Cool to room temperature. Separate cloves and squeeze them to remove the skins, saving only the mushy garlic. Set aside.

In a bowl, combine milk, sugar, salt, butter and stir until butter melts. Set aside to cool to room temperature. Dissolve yeast in warm water and let sit five minutes. Add to cooled milk mixture. Add flour gradually and then once it's all been mixed in, turn out onto a floured surface. Knead until smooth. Let rise until double (about an hour). Punch it down and mix in the roasted garlic by kneading again just enough to distribute the garlic throughout the dough. Form into two loaves and place in greased loaf pans. Let rise until double again (about an hour).

Preheat oven to 400 degrees and bake for 25 minutes. Cool slightly before slicing. Makes 2 loaves.

Garlicky Chicken and Rice

This is an easy, all-in-one-pot meal, halfway between chicken soup and chicken with rice. This recipe is more of a guideline, and you can use whatever vegetables you have on hand or even substitute pork for the chicken (and in that case, add a pinch of dried rosemary).

Olive oil
1 onion
1 green pepper
1 pound of skinless chicken breast, cut into bite-sized pieces
4 cloves of garlic, minced
1 1/3 cups rice
3 cups water
2 carrots, peeled and sliced into rounds about ¼" thick
1 t. dried thyme
1 t. dried sage
2 chicken bouillon cubes
1 cup fresh or frozen peas
1 cup fresh or frozen corn

Sauté the onion and pepper in olive oil, just until soft, using a Dutch oven or other large pot with a cover. Add the chicken and sear it. Add the garlic and cook until fragrant (not long!). Add the rice, water, carrots, thyme, sage and bouillon. Bring to a boil, cover and reduce temperature to low and simmer for 20 minutes or until rice is done. Turn off heat, uncover to stir in peas and corn, and replace the lid. Wait a few minutes before serving for the peas and corn to heat through. Serves 4.

Pickled Garlic

I've seen this on menus as a condiment or for serving on crackers with cream cheese, but I mostly use it to preserve my usual over-abundance of garlic so it will last longer than it does on the shelf. Depending on variety, garlic can be kept at room temperature for about six months, but if you're growing your own, there are a few months' gap before the next year's harvest begins.

1 cup whole garlic cloves, separated and peeled
1/2 cup white vinegar
1/2 t. sugar
1/2 t. pickling salt

Place the cloves in a pint-sized glass jar. (The jar needs to be glass and have a lid, but it doesn't need to be a heat-proof canning jar.)

Combine the remaining ingredients until the sugar and salt dissolve, and then pour the liquid over the garlic. Screw lid onto jar. (If it's a metal lid, put a sheet of plastic wrap between the jar and the lid, so it doesn't react to the vinegar.)

Store in the refrigerator at least a month before using. Then the cloves can be rinsed off and used in place of fresh garlic when there is no more fresh garlic, or when you don't have time or energy to peel fresh cloves. Keep refrigerated and use within one year.

When the cloves have all been used, the left-over vinegar can be used to make vinaigrette with a garlicky flavor.

Meet the author

Gin Jones became a *USA Today* bestselling author after too many years of being a lawyer who specialized in ghostwriting for other lawyers. She much prefers writing fiction, since she isn't bound by boring facts and she can indulge her sense of humor without any risk of getting thrown into jail for contempt of court. In her spare time, Gin makes quilts, grows garlic, and advocates for rare disease patients. Visit her at www.ginjones.com.

Printed in the United States
by Baker & Taylor Publisher Services